FOLIO

ALSO BY BOBBIE CALHOUN

Fiction

Model Daughter Model Spy (Coming Fall 2026)

Poetry

Mise-en-Scène

FOLIO

BOBBIE CALHOUN

This is a work of fiction. Names, characters, businesses, places, events, and incidents are either the product of the author's imagination or used in a fictitious manner. Any resemblance to actual persons, living or dead, or actual events is purely coincidental

For more information, visit www.bobbiecalhoun.com

Cover design by Tabitha Lahr
Interior text design by Backstory Design
Back cover postcard art copyright © Mystique Photos

PB ISBN: 979-8-9927373-0-1
EBOOK ISBN: 979-8-9927373-1-8

10 9 8 7 6 5 4 3 2 1

For D and D, Always

FOLIO

PART ONE

The Cause

"My esteemed colleagues, in accepting this marvelous award, it is my duty to tell you this today: your portfolio of work is all that remains."

—Cameron Plumb

ONE

New York City

DECEMBER 1983

Terry

What bothers me most is that I never know which slide is going to be first.

In a moment, the Kodak Ektagraphic III projector will spring to life, its single eye blindingly bright, shining its tiny lightbulb on my various wounds, the random shrapnel, the poorly-set broken bones. All of them in the name of art. The sore spot in my gut calms down, exactly two inches of surgical scar tissue born in the Mekong Delta.

"People, eyes forward!" Professor McMickle is chipper, bouncing on the balls of his feet by my side at the front of the lecture hall.

The students look bored. Hungover. The boys with sketchy beards and skinny ties slouch in their seats. The girls whisper to each other in the back. The only change I can see—over the past ten years of doing this—is what the students wear to class.

The professor is undeterred. "Everyone, this is the final lecture of the term. You'll be happy to know you don't have to listen to *me* drone on. We have a guest."

No response from the students. Professor McMickle gestures in my general direction. Like he always does. Like I'm the opening act of a circus.

"Mr. Terrance Tusley, vaunted *Life* photographer, is here to discuss some of his most famous photographs. You may recognize some of these from the galleries where his work is displayed across New York. Mr. Tusley, thank you for joining our class today."

"Delighted, Professor. Damn delighted." I rub my freshly shaven chin and scan their faces for a hint of recognition of my name. Not too much to expect from a college classroom full of photography students in the middle of New York City, the center of the universe.

As usual, there is none. Not yet.

I make a great show of pulling off the old Zephyr coat, Cameron's gift to me from so many years ago. A consolation prize. From another time. The cuffs are frayed but it keeps out the December chill. I lay it gently across the back of an empty chair, straighten up, clasp my hands behind my back, and face the students. They regard me with mild interest now, their smooth faces reflecting the indirect sunlight from the ivy-covered windows of this storied lecture hall. They are trained enough at this point to notice the coat, unusual in its dove-gray color, in the glossy sheen picked up from years of wear. They drag their eyes from the coat back to me, and I meet them.

They are all around twenty years old.

They are beautiful.

I am beautiful, too, in my own way. Damaged to a lovely burnish, and here to tell the tale. My bright-white Ralph Lauren shirt, its soft folds starched to nonchalant perfection by my laundress Harriet, reflects off the fluorescent lights overhead, and I practically glow.

"Good morning," I say. "Call me Terry. Thank you for inviting me to your class."

They begin to lean forward, elbows on their little flip-desks. Pens appear. Notebooks are fished out of backpacks.

McMickle clears his throat. "Yolanda, please, can you draw the shades?"

The student called Yolanda uncrosses her long legs and heads for the windows amid a ripple of low laughter from her bevy of friends.

I come here twice per year, at the end of each semester, and there's always a Yolanda to walk around the perimeter of the lecture hall, young and vivacious as my Francine once was. The boys follow her every move until she sits back down, the room now as shadowy as a jungle cave.

I am sixty years older than any one of them, and I feel the weight of my years as I anticipate the next fifty-five minutes, entombed in here together. The space between life and death. Then they will leave for their next class.

But I never really leave, do I?

Professor McMickle scans the lecture hall in the semi-darkness, waiting until each and every student sits up straight. Then he turns to me.

"Let's start at the top, shall we?" McMickle says. "Mr. Tusley, where is home?"

I force a smile. He asks me this every time.

"Home," I say. "A nice idea, in theory."

The students get quiet. The professor melts away, out of my peripheral vision, and I alone have the stage.

"I've never really had a home," I continue. "The smell of breakfast in the morning, wafting up the stairs. The lawn mowed, the dog fed. You know, if that's the theory, I'm all in."

The students chuckle, amused. They are not aware of all that will come next.

"However, my experience was different," I say. "My only real home is the camera. Lens like a doorway. Shutter like a key. And I will be forever grateful to George Eastman—my first boss—for introducing this wayward high school science nut to the wonders of his invention."

I begin to walk in a slow circle around the slide projector, still dormant on its little table, just an arm's length away.

"In the years that followed that fateful day, I became an intern at George Eastman's Kodak laboratories, and then a full member of his corps. There was much to celebrate. I rubbed shoulders with men from all over the world, learning about the chemistry of film, as well as optics, lenses, all sorts of things. It was the perfect preparation for my true calling. I handled the earliest cameras and eventually became a small part of the work that went into perfecting Kodak film. Europe was restless, and many of our best scientists had arrived on an escape route from a growing stew of Bolshevism in Russia, fascism in Italy, and a new order that was beginning to take hold in an unhappy, humiliated post-armistice Germany. I didn't understand much of this back then, a high school kid among giants.

"But there was one thing I did know. When I held a camera, I forgot about everyone. In Eastman's lab, I had found a home when I peered into the viewfinder of the camera. And there was one other thing I began to understand."

The room is completely silent. Waiting.

"Light. But, not just light," I say. "Light plus time. There was a moment of truth when the shot meant something, captured something you couldn't see with the naked eye. Students, we know that photographers take pictures of all sorts of subjects. Most of them are worthless."

A gasp from my young friends. I ignore it and go on.

"I collect images of the truth. Others may fill their photographs with props and illusion. But those things don't matter to me."

A few hands go up, and the professor steps forward from the shadows, saving me from them. From myself.

"And now," McMickle's voice is loud, like a game show announcer. "For your sheer entertainment, I bring you... the portfolio of photographs taken by the controversial and famously disruptive war photographer, Terrance Tusley."

I touch a button on the slide projector and the motor whirrs awake. The lamp comes on, dim at first, then stronger. Heat radiates out from the contraption like warmth from a lone soldier's campfire.

And the whole damn thing begins again.

TWO

Occupied France

JULY 1943

Terry

A beacon of light cut across the dark outline of Paris, the city laid out like a lover below me.

The street was quiet, the café deserted. It was nearly two in the morning. Just me and the latest issue of *Life* magazine, my precious 1939 Zeiss Ikon hanging from my neck, my empty beer glass resting on the lower left side of the cover. Some beautiful girl, close up, her eyes the focal point of the photo. Beneath her perfect chin, the caption: Vivienne, Last Name Unknown. The Women of Occupied Paris.

So this was what passed for news photography now, I thought bitterly, fingering the strap of my camera.

A raucous gang of German soldiers turned the corner, deep into late-night reveries in Montmartre's catacombs of saloons and brothels. One of them walked right up to me, his bulk casting a shadow across my table.

"Fotograf, machen Sie mein Bild!" His pistol, half-hidden in his holster, gleamed in the moonlight.

Without a word, I crouched down on one knee like he expected me to. It was a throwaway shot, another bully looking for fame. His vanity satisfied, he moved off, just as an old Renault truck skidded up beside me and a pale hand waved me in. I jumped into the back compartment while the truck was still rolling, my camera bouncing against my chest, destination unclear.

That was Francine's technique, always.

"Eh bien, Monsieur Tusley? You okay?" the driver said, twisting his head to look at me.

"Keep your eye on the road, son," I growled.

He was grinding the gears unmercifully.

The road was uneven, the driver yanking the wheel back and forth like a madman. I held onto the bench as we swung around potholes like we were on the Tilt-A-Whirl at Coney Island on a late July night. Except it wasn't nearly as safe, traveling around Occupied France, many miles out of the city now, alone but for a camera, with a secret mission in my pocket.

That was what I'd wanted, right?

With an enormous thud, the truck hit something hard, throwing me into an uncontrolled slide.

"Whoa, *pardonnez-moi…*" the driver exclaimed.

I scrambled back up to the bench and Francine's voice, smooth as maple syrup, crept into that part of my memory where she'd taken up residence. I was hers as long as I could hear that seductive voice in my head, and all the images it conjured. My sorceress. My vain and powerful princess. Descended from *Les Filles du Roi*, as if anyone knew what that meant anymore.

I went over her instructions in my head. I was to meet with

someone British, someplace south of Paris, and deliver the sealed message resting in my jacket pocket. His name resembled fruit. Apple? Pear? I couldn't remember right now. It would come to me. It always did. Then I'd be free to get back to Paris.

A sickening crack filled the air. My young driver cried out, and then was quiet.

The engine sputtered into silence, and the driver was still, his body slumped, lifeless, across his seat.

"Jesus..." Hugging the camera tight to my chest, I rolled out the back of the truck and landed on my feet in a squat. Tinny pistons rattled to life from somewhere in the darkness. I could make out two Germans in helmets, some thirty, forty yards away, perched on shiny black motorcycles.

Demonic outlines against the indigo night, heavy boots straddling glinting metal machines.

A wonderful photo, by any measure.

Welcome to the 1944 Pulitzer Prize ceremony, here on the beautiful Columbia University campus, New York City. And for photography, in recognition of his tireless work...

I pulled up my camera and peered through the viewfinder. At that moment, a siren wailed in the far distance, and the Germans sped away. From the corner of my eye, I saw a figure in white shirtsleeves emerge from the shadows. His overalls were covered with dark mud.

"Get up," he barked, his French accent thick in the air. He stepped back, regarding me with a look of disdain, his eyes lingering on the Zeiss hanging from my neck. He pointed a large, very heavy-looking shovel at me. "Verify your name."

He couldn't have appeared by accident. I duly complied.

"Tusley. Terrance Tusley."

His tired face lit up in a flash of recognition I'd seen too many times before.

"Follow me." He turned and started walking. "Did you get the driver's name before he was shot?"

"No," I said. "The less I know the better, right?"

"*Tant pis*," he muttered.

"Yes, too bad," I said trudging behind him, any hope of a good shot gone.

My contact revealed to me that he made cheese in Chartres. We walked out to a sweeping meadow. He told me he traveled to various farms to demonstrate his craft. This was his cover, and he'd worked for ten years to perfect it, an admirable tenure that was far longer than he'd signed up for. He wasn't about to give me much more information than that. He was sent to meet me. I wasn't sure where we were going, but at least the network was functioning.

"How is *Madame* Tusley?" the Cheese Man asked, his rough hand resting heavily on my arm.

Ah, one of Francine's *protégés*. Had she placed him here, before she was exposed and banished to Quebec? Another one of her chessboard pieces? Maybe, back then, he was a good model of a man, his girth not quite so wide, his face bright with expectation at her attention.

"*La belle femme*. She is well. I'll let her know you asked about her," I said, keeping my voice even.

"*On n'aime que ce qu'on ne possède pas entièrement*," he said, almost to himself. "We love only what we do not wholly possess."

Perhaps it was true, I thought, walking beside him, but in my mind, Francine and I were equally possessed with each other, from the minute she'd sunk her red manicured nails into me in that smoky Paris cabaret. I was on assignment for Mr. Eastman, full of Kodak confidence, young and stupid, ready to set the world on fire. It was between the wars, a time that shimmered in my mind like the dress she wore that night. I was eighteen. I would find out later she was five years older than me. At that moment, it wouldn't have mattered. And it still doesn't.

I'd never seen anyone even remotely like her before, and she knew it. Paris was a long way from upstate New York. She wore a dress made of tiny mirrors, metallic in the flickering light. She strode directly to my little table.

"*C'est votre appareil photo*?" Her voice was sultry and low. I looked up. She was impossibly beautiful. I glanced at the perfect curve of her neck, where her smooth skin met the fine mirrored edge of her gown.

She reached for the camera Mr. Eastman had given to me, an experimental Kodak No. 1A Junior folding baby with bellows. Her eyes flashed in the cabaret lights as she clasped her fingers around it.

Dazzled as I was, I locked my hand around her slender wrist. She tried to wriggle free, but kept her grip on the camera.

She switched to English, frantic. "Give to me, please, *monsieur*!"

That distinctive accent, not Parisian at all. French-Canadian. I'd grown up a stone's throw from the Canadian border, after all. I stood up to her, our eyes meeting level. This was my camera we were talking about.

The cabaret crowd roared with drunken laughter around us, and her face betrayed fear. Of what? Behind her, a thug came through the open cabaret door, eyes searching the room. With one deft motion, I'd pulled her against me, encircling her in an embrace before brazenly kissing her lush mouth. We'd melted into the shadows of the room, just another couple in the depths of a Paris night.

I didn't expect her to change the trajectory of my life, goddammit.

"*Faites attention*!" the Cheese Man said suddenly. "You are to go to the abbey on the far side of the barn."

"Abbey?" I said, but he'd already turned away, muttering something under his breath, and headed back to the truck. I felt a flicker of pity for him, and for the boy driver, and for all that was happening here, but I also knew, in the deepest part of my heart, that this was exactly where I wanted to be. Here, and the next war-torn place I would go.

Frame after frame, as long as my film would last.

And where, oh where, was my lovely wife Francine right now? Not caring for our children in Rochester, that's for sure. Most likely sipping wine in Quebec City with her latest lover. Just like her mother, the great Dominique D'Or. Every hair swept into place, their crystal glasses filled to the brim.

Les Filles du Roi. Descendants of the Daughters of the King, selected for their beauty hundreds of years ago to wed and prosper in the new French Canada.

I was three thousand miles away, across the mighty Atlantic Ocean, yet I could picture them both with complete clarity, as if I were viewing them through a pinhole.

THREE

Rochester

NOVEMBER 1983

Katie

The cold morning air ruffles the folds of my nightgown, too thin for November in upstate New York. I stand halfway in, halfway out the doorway of my new Rochester house.

"See you Friday night, Katie," Manny says, blowing me a kiss on his way out.

He never seems to mind taking those Monday-morning flights back to DC. White shirt, black tie, crewcut. The All-American.

"I'll have dinner on the table when you get back," I say, even though I know I won't.

I feel my pulse quicken with the lie.

Manny's voice floats up to me from the sidewalk. "You just take care of yourself, okay? The week will go fast."

He is freshly shaved, ready to go. The yellow taxi glides up the driveway.

"You have to travel so much because of me," I say, pouting the way I know he likes.

He climbs back up the steps and, despite myself, I can feel his concern, his love, and I'm grateful for it. He caresses my arm, sending prickles across my skin. It's amazing to think he can still do that to me after so many years.

"Living near work is not as important as making sure you live in a home, a real house, in a nice, peaceful place," he says softly.

I smile the best I can as he turns to go. I wave goodbye and he waves back through the window as the taxi crunches down the driveway, kicking up gravel dust. Thirty minutes from now he'll be just another middle-aged guy running through Rochester Airport to catch the People's Express morning flight to Dulles. He'll wolf down a bagel and black coffee on the plane. He'll be at his desk by 9:30 on the dot, the Pentagon casting its long shadow just outside his office window.

And all is quiet once again in this fresh new house in my old hometown of Rochester, just like every other Monday since we moved up here in July. But now I have a mission. The dusty cardboard box can come out of its hiding place behind the broom in the hall closet. When I drop it onto the gleaming Formica table, it makes a light thud in the silence.

I pour a cup of coffee. It's just the house and me now. Bright new kitchen, bright new start. Same old urge for the needle. I take a few deep breaths to calm myself, the way Dr. Pine taught me.

I look around the bare kitchen at the too-cheery dinette set, the yellow-and-white checkerboard linoleum floor. The kitchen's big enough to hold a crowd—a far cry from our brownstone in Georgetown, with its maze of pantries that hid a million secrets, its worn wood floor that I sank to on my knees, my veins punctured with holes.

Here, I have blank walls. No pictures, no stories, no mistakes.

The plastic clock radio makes its hourly click, resonating like a pistol cock. It's full-on morning, and my heart starts to race. Time is getting away from me, goddammit. I have six weeks, max, before the grand Francine and Terrance Tusley 60th Anniversary Party. Whether my parents want it or not. If I can stay off the pills, I can get it done. I *have* to get it done. I just need to get focused.

Daylight barely makes its way into the fortress of the house. I'd forgotten about the gray gloom that surrounds upstate New York when winter starts to set in. In those glowing days in DC, before our golden-haired boy went away, before we moved here to Rochester and depression came to sit in the corner like an old aunt, the sunlight from the cathedral windows of the DC townhouse played across dozens of framed photographs on the piano and antique whitewall shelves. Nearly everywhere, my father—Terry to his buddies—smiled out at me from his black-and-white world, leaning against a tank or squatting next to a military helicopter, a camera always dangling from his neck.

Picture after picture, all over my walls.

My treasure trove, back then, captured in black metal frames so chic. I'd been smart to mount them professionally. Images in the moment, on the front lines. A few from Korea. So many more from Vietnam. Just the right amount of grit under the gloss. Photographers standing around, aviator sunglasses hiding their eyes, the mountain range behind them like the stunning backdrop of a movie set. Hats cocked a bit backward off their foreheads. Tan skin and short haircuts.

Our son must have pondered the images above his sweet blond head, cast in that soft yellow sunlight, and imagined himself there, with an obscured ferocity burning in his little body. I wish I'd hidden them, but no, they defined me. Framed magazine covers from *Look* and *Life* marching down every hallway silently cajoled him.

Go, Troy, go.

We weren't here a week before Troy found the pile of Dad's things, those goddamn framed magazine covers I'd finally, finally pulled off the screaming white walls of our Georgetown brownstone.

Troy spent too much time alone in his room once we got to Rochester, never getting to know the other kids around here.

Not alone. With the photographs.

They just don't shut up.

Go, Troy, go.

And so, therefore, he went, in the early fall, and we are waiting for him to return. I know a lot about waiting. It's the hole you fall into on your way to the laundry room. It's the darkness of the hallway near the kitchen, where the stash was, and it's the nightmares you can't escape from, in the bedroom at night, the trees looking in on you like hired guns from outside the big window.

I hear a rustle from the corner of the kitchen. I glance over the top of the cardboard box, only half-afraid.

I can see her clearly. She is one of a parade of visitors I've had over the years.

"What do you want, old lady?" I ask. My voice is loud in the empty kitchen. She snickers and reaches for the tattered umbrella leaning by her side, which I can see so clearly that I can make out its paisley pattern.

And, dear God, she begins to talk back.

"Gonna rain today, Kate," she says flatly, and I think I detect a smirk.

"Just stop it," I say, and she yawns. Bony yellow fingers the exact color of sunlight rise to cover her mouth, then fall to rest on her heavily embroidered skirt. I can see the wall behind her because I can see through her. She draws a deep and rattled breath.

"You're late, you know, Katie-did," she continues. "You have a party to prepare. Oh, and I was wrong. It's going to snow."

This is more than I can take, and the old anger rises in me. I throw the coffee mug at her with all my strength. It shatters against the smooth, clean wall above her head.

"Missed me," she says.

Another waste of time. I have to ignore her. With a deep breath, I sit back down at the kitchen table, reach into the box, and pick up the letter on the top of the pile. My youthful handwriting scrawls across the yellowed envelope. Just like now, I never had any idea exactly where my father was, so each letter is simply addressed to *Mr. Terrance Tusley, Photographer*. A young girl's handwriting, in fountain pen. On the address line, it just says *France*. There is no postmark. It came as something of a shock to be handed this box when I went to the Rochester post office to set up my new address, to return to my hometown only to find the letters I'd sent my father lying like spent shells in this stupid box, never even sent.

Of *course* they were never sent, I chide myself silently. You didn't have an address for the old man, did you?

He got the ones in Vietnam. I was better at tracking him down by then.

I pull the letter from its onionskin envelope, taking care not to rip it. Across the top, very proper like I'd learned in school, I'd written the date: *July 7, 1943.*

Forty years ago.

Dear Father,

Hello from beautiful Rochester! We miss you as always. My birthday was last week. Eighteen! Your little girl is all grown up. Mother says you're in Paris. Golly! She also says you're too busy to write back anymore. That's okay. We love you anyway.

I remember writing this letter.

I was in my parents' house, only blocks from here. My brothers had been arguing upstairs, and then I'd heard Joe and Harry laugh and the sound of stomping feet.

"Cut it out up there!" I'd shouted up to them.

"Ladies do not shout, Katherine," my mother had chided.

Mother had sat beside me at the French pine table, one of the few times she was home. Her delicate hands with their pointed, white-and-pink manicured nails lay idle in her lap, the dishes piled in the sink behind her. I'd looked at her face, so composed, her hair so perfect, coiled atop her lovely head. She wasn't going to bother herself to do those dishes, was she?

Across the middle of the page, I'd glued a strip of printed words, my scissor marks jagged and uneven around the edges, yellowed now. I run my finger across it.

THEIR PHOTOGRAPHS OF THE WAR WEAVE RIBBONS OF GLAMOUR INTO OUR LIVES.

Do you like that, Dad? I found it in Harper's Bazaar *and pasted it here just for YOU. Don't worry, we still get* Life *magazine. And, of course, the* Rochester Observer-Herald! *Harry gets so excited when we find a picture with your photo credit—Terrance W. Tusley, United Press Service! He said to me: I am going to go there and help Daddy take pictures to save the people.*

Send me something beautiful from Paris for my birthday!

Love,
Katie-did

I try to calculate. Harry would have been nine years old. I don't know where my little brother got the idea that Dad was away for any reason related to actual *people*. Knowing my father as I do, I suspect that the famous Terrance Tusley's fascination with film, light, and shadow far outweighed his interest in any of the terrible things that happen to real people in wars, especially the people closest to him.

Paris, London, Seoul. People do not figure in most of Dad's photographs. They are incidental, necessary only for scale and composition. Cities. Horizon lines. Buildings. These, to him, are either already bombed or not yet bombed. The sunrise could play with both, and tell a tale without words either way.

FOUR

Occupied France

JULY 1943

Terry

I searched the area for an hour or more, looking for the Cheese Man's so-called abbey. I expected to see some sort of soaring French spire with stained glass windows. Finally, I stumbled across a dirt road. Beyond it, a bombed-out abbey rose before me against the unsettled dawn sky, complete with a massive cross sticking out of its shattered roof. I could make out a crumbling doorway in shadow. A slender woman suddenly appeared at the entrance, looking out as if expecting a visitor. She wore a flowered dress, cinched at the waist. A cardigan was draped around her shoulders. I registered a heart-shaped face. She scanned the road and disappeared inside.

Whoever she was, she looked harmless. Any further hesitation could be deadly.

I darted into the abbey, pulling my camera forward to my

chest, ready for just about anything that would be waiting within.

I ducked against an inside wall, slightly out of breath. The wall was cool. The smell of cigarette smoke lingered in the air. My eyes started to adjust. I could see a blown-out vestibule at the far end of the vestry. I pulled the camera into position and slid my index finger onto the shutter button. A quick inventory showed there was no real roof left overhead, only pure sky. A dark spray of something—dried blood?—was splattered across the gray stone floor at my feet.

I had an eerie feeling that someone was watching me. I crouched closer to the wall on my left, and, in a moment, she appeared from the shadows, luminous and lovely, followed by a tall, lean man in a hat and long trench coat, a cigarette dangling from his lips. He was obviously not a soldier. A ray of morning sunlight peeked into the interior, briefly illuminating them both. We sized each other up. I got the shot before they could react. Captured by me forever. If, of course, I could get the film back to the bureau. Possibly underexposed, but it would have to do.

"*Pas de photo*!" The girl all but lunged at my camera.

"It's all right, darling, he's all right." The man soothed her in a British accent, the cigarette now pitched to the side of his mouth. My contact?

I patted my jacket pockets, checking for the message from Francine.

"*Qui êtes vous*?" The girl was polite now.

"*Photojournaliste*," I said, slipping into French, not sure what role she played here.

"*Regardez—le ciel est argenté*," she said, a sweetness in her voice, one perfectly red manicured finger pointing toward the entryway behind me.

Instinct took over. I turned to look back at the silver sky and a loud knock thumped the back of my head. The pain was sharp and immediate.

"Lights out," I heard myself say, before I hit the cold stone floor.

FIVE

Rochester

NOVEMBER 1983

Katie

I dig out a stack of letters from the box on the kitchen table and carry them into the living room, gently laying them down on the new white couch. I lean over them and brush my fingertips across them before I shake a few letters free from their envelopes, like a nurse attempting to cut loose the patient's clothing to find the source of the bleeding. I unfold one or two and spread them out across the cushions. A torrent of memories tumbles from the letters, threatening to drown me. I stagger back against the living room wall. The bottle of pills is so close. So easy to get to. I tiptoe up the stairs to the hall bathroom, to a mirrored medicine cabinet all too willing to show me who I have become.

Before Old Aunt figures out what I'm doing, I gulp down a few yellows and drag myself back to the living room. The familiar weariness overtakes me, and I let myself fall across the couch, the letters scattering to the floor.

I thought I'd left it all behind, all those years ago, when I married Manny and moved to DC, the letters forgotten, part of something that is simply no more.

The desire for sleep is undeniable. This is the sleep I need, thick with the dreams of a loyal daughter, the daughter who did everything, who learned to make meals, to clean, to provide some kind of discipline over her brothers.

My own hand, a teenager's hand, pushes open the screen door to the back porch of my parents' house.

She is me, and I am there again. The memory floats before my weary eyes like a movie.

I stepped through the door. I held beneath my arm a sheaf of writing paper and an envelope. My father's fountain pen was tucked behind my ear. I took a seat in the little wooden chair. The scent of sweet pine trees filled our cozy patch of yard. Dad's photography shed, windowless and vacant, was partly hidden behind a grove of big maples and oaks. I heard my brothers out front playing tag in the gravel driveway, yelling back and forth.

Most of my chores were done for the day. But this chore was the most important one of all. I took a deep breath, ready to begin.

I examined the pen. The tip was still good. The light was still good. I felt like I had a lot to say. My words began to fly across the page.

July 31, 1943

Dear Father,

How are you? Mother set her blue suitcase (the biggest one) in the hallway last Wednesday, all dusted off. On Saturday, Joe and I noticed a ONE-WAY rail ticket to Quebec City sitting on the kitchen table for an entire day. No one dared move it. We ate around it at dinner, a strange little centerpiece.

I can't understand why Mother didn't take all of us with her. Grandma Dominique's house is enormous—it could fit us all and more. School doesn't start for a few weeks, so both Joe and Harry could go. She left without even saying goodbye. Gee whiz.

When are you coming home?

Love,
Katie-did

I try to sit up, but the couch is so warm. When did I take those pills? I float back to the porch, to the old wooden chair.

Surrendering. The movie resumes, clicking into my memory… frame by frame.

A noise came from the shed. It was Dad, rattling his collection of brown bottles, shaking them to see how much photo processing fluid was left inside. He shuffled through a stack of glossy paper. I was next to him, small, and I pulled on his sleeve. He lifted me up, standing me on a stool so that I was at eye level with him. We'd been here all day, missing out on the beautiful summer weather, but I didn't care. We were together. Shelves full of chemicals and acids surrounded us, a happy pair.

I shake loose from the memory, try to sit up. I have to ask myself, in the here and now: where did it all begin for my father?

But I know the answer.

Kodak Park.

A sheet of copper washed with silver, an even flow of liquid mercury, a glass plate. Iron sheeting, then paper, then rolls of film. Arguing for hours about this lens or that exposure, with people who shared the same affliction, the same compulsion to see where this technology—or, rather, this new art form—would take them. And then, later, jockeying for the best position to record history. He started out as a chemist and became an artist, chasing the god of light. He thought of himself as the next Matthew Brady, photographer of Lincoln and the Civil War. But even Brady's photos had a dark side, didn't they? His photographs of those poor boys lying dead in the grassy fields of battle would forever be Brady's legacy.

Boys like my brother Harry.

I cannot ponder this, or I will truly go insane. I am surrounded by Kodak, here in the company's hometown. The original, antique Kodak signs still dangle on nearly every street corner, covered for six months of the year with a topping of snow. Joe, Harry, and I survived when Dad went away and mother escaped to Quebec. We were left behind in our house—all alone, no parents at all—the three of us like those faded Kodak signs. Too hard to take down, too easy to ignore.

It wasn't that bad. We were like a little gang. We had our fun. No one noticed when I graduated from old Proctor High School. It's okay. I didn't like a fuss. We had everything we needed. Dad's checks kept coming. But sometimes I wondered: was this what a girl of eighteen was supposed to be doing?

Joe tried to act like he didn't need me. We both knew better. He would go out with friends, free and easy, but he was worried he'd be called up; the war wasn't ending anytime soon. His seventeenth birthday was right around the corner. We didn't know it would work out differently, had no idea that it would be Harry, not Joe, who would, years later, go to war. But back then, blissfully ignorant, all I could think about was how I was stuck there, watching Joe have a life while I was taking care of Harry. Not stuck, exactly, but doing everything a *parent* should be doing.

I liked Harry—no, I loved Harry. I just don't think Harry loved me. I remember making up a rhyme when Harry was asleep in bed.

"He loves us, he loves us not. Harry's love runs cold and hot." I sang to Joe, up to my elbows in dishwater.

"Mother's train ticket sat on that table for a week before she left, Katie," Joe said, irritated.

"And so, dear Joe, I guess we know . . . our own mother loves us not."

I drag myself off the couch. It takes only a few minutes to find the notification letter about Harry. It's rested for nearly thirty years in my old sewing basket, tucked behind the satin fabric inside the lid, never far from my side when we lived in DC, hovering like an angel above the needles I used for good, honest mending.

The other needles came later.

I carry Harry's letter over to the musty box and bury it at the bottom. Let it lie there, entombed beneath the letters that never reached my father.

SIX

Occupied France

JULY 1943

Terry

Vivienne's pale face hovered over me, blurry and indistinct. I blinked until she came into focus. Velvet-blue eyes, brunette hair curled into a knot on one side. A polished abalone clasp above the right ear.

I tried to sit up, feeling dizzy, but she gently pushed me back down.

"*Comment vous sentez-vous*?" she said, her voice charming, lightweight. "I see you understand me. I am so sorry. *Pardonnez-moi*… your actions led me to believe you were a German spy." She laughed a little, showing perfect teeth behind rosebud lips. She held out a metal cup and I took a sip. Burgundy wine. I gulped the rest of it down. She stared at me. Those eyes.

"*Je m'appelle* Vivienne."

Looming behind her was the man in the coat, the cigarette still dangling from his lips, smoke obscuring his face. He looked to be about six-one. But the coat was too big—it nearly swallowed his slim frame.

A few drops of warm rain hit my face. Full daylight streamed through the rafters of the shattered ceiling of the abbey now, the sky a mix of gray and white. I sat up and the throbbing in my head got worse.

"I have to give—" I started to say, but the man stepped in front of the woman. He bent over me, his hands in his coat pockets.

"Quiet now, chap. Sorry for the Punch and Judy show there!" He smiled. "You gave Vivienne a moderate scare in that costume, you know, the Zeiss and all."

"What do you mean, *costume*?"

"Calm down, now," he said, like he was talking to a child. "You sounded a bit confused when you wandered in."

"I'm just here to take pictures," I said, unsure of who exactly he was.

"Of course you are!" His tone was condescending. "Aren't we all?"

Now I was starting to dislike him.

The girl leaned around him, her petite body nearly obscured by his outsized coat. They formed the perfect photo, these two, and I instinctively reached for my Zeiss.

But it wasn't around my neck.

"Where the hell's my camera?" I shouted, the headache giving way to anger.

"It's right there, old man," he said, his voice calm. He nodded to the end of the pew, where my camera sat alone on its side, the leather strap neatly wound around its body.

I jumped up and threw it on.

"You're lucky no one else has stopped you," he sneered. "With that perfect German Zeiss on you. Not the best cover to have in France."

"It's not a cover, dammit. I have a—"

"Smoke, old chap?"

As if in slow motion, he produced a mirrored cigarette case from the pocket of his enormous coat. The girl delicately took one. She smiled at me until I took one too. He handed her a silver lighter that came out of nowhere. She flipped it open and shared the flame with me before lighting her own, then she slid the lighter back into his coat pocket.

Smooth. These two must go way back. I wasn't sure what I'd walked into, but my job here would be done once I could confirm he was my contact, give him the packet from Francine, and get the hell back to Paris.

Otherwise, why would the Cheese Man have directed me here?

The cigarette pitched to one side of his mouth, he scanned the broken ceiling and the stone walls, his eyes alert, the reflected light bouncing off his finely chiseled features. His narrow chin with its scant growth of beard was reddish in the morning light. Some women would call him handsome.

I could see he was just self-absorbed.

The cigarette smoke curled away from his face in a tendril, as if orchestrated by his will. He gave me an artificial smile and stretched out his hand.

"Cameron Plumb. A pleasure to meet you, Mr. Tusley."

Ah. Not apple, not pear. Maybe I should have paid better attention when Francine gave me instructions. He obviously knew who *I* was.

"You might have seen my work," he continued, placing a hand on my shoulder.

"And what work is that, exactly?" I retorted, but the girl interrupted us.

"*Ecoutez*," she said. "Listen."

A low rumble filled the abbey. The sound was coming from the road outside, far away but distinct.

"What is that?" I asked, but she started to laugh, her eyes on the doorway.

"You can be one of the actors, old boy," he said, regarding me like I was a small dog he might buy for a pet. Then he turned his back to me and took a few steps toward the vestibule. "The stage will go over there, Vivienne. Hurry, they'll be here soon!"

"*Oui*," she said, her voice bright. "I knew you would have me stand *pour un chant de débauche* in the holy vestibule!" With a delicate motion, she snuffed out the cigarette and tucked it behind her ear. She lifted a shawl off one of the pews, tossed it across her arm, and glided over to the vestibule.

I couldn't take my eyes off her.

"If you want a longer look at her," Plumb snapped, "go find *Life*'s last issue. My photo is on the cover." He turned and followed her.

A wave of recognition swept over me.

"Vivienne," I said, remembering the photo of her on the cover back in Paris.

This bastard took *that* picture?

So, my connection was another photographer. No, worse: an insolent *Life* news photographer who had at least one cover.

Something else was going on here.

"Did he say *actors* were coming?" I asked. The rumbling sound was getting louder.

"Oh yes, *c'est très dangereux,*" the girl said from the vestibule, her tone serious. "Cameron's latest assignment for the British News Corp." Then she turned away from me, hands on hips, surveying the vestibule like an artist might consider a canvas.

The rumbling turned into a roar. Tires screeched outside the abbey's entry, then someone killed the engine. I moved to the stone doorway and ducked behind a half wall near the entrance. A battered bread truck, open at the back, had pulled up in front of the abbey. People started spilling out the back, carrying a mishmash of weapons, in broad daylight.

There were women among them.

I pulled my camera forward. Through the viewfinder, I saw more. As they streamed into the abbey, it dawned on me that these were *les Francaises de l'Intérieur*—the French Resistance, the country's shadow army. They were so hidden in Paris that I'd never knowingly had a glimpse of them, and certainly not armed in any way.

I cocked the tension lever on the Zeiss. Something seemed different about it. I pulled the camera away from my face to see if the knob was loose or damaged.

"Perfect timing." Plumb ambled up beside me. "They could use your help." He motioned to the men standing near the truck, and then he sauntered back through the abbey's crumbling doorway.

"*My* help. What about *your* help?" I called out to him, but he ignored me.

Well, Cameron Plumb be damned. Curious, I slung my camera across my back and walked over to the men. They promptly started handing me boxes and crates from the back of the truck. One, curiously, was a box of flashbulbs. As they unloaded a heavy generator and a mass of black electrical cables that took three men to carry inside, I started to wonder what the hell was going on. No one was talking at the moment—they seemed intent on getting the truck unloaded. Questions peppered my brain: why would they risk detection, out here in the open? And when was I supposed to deliver Francine's packet to Cameron Plumb, who was deep inside the abbey now, shouting at everyone like a general giving orders to the troops?

The men filled my arms with more boxes, and I had no choice but to pass them along to the next man, forming a human chain that stretched into the abbey's interior.

Cameron Plumb finally stepped out of the abbey, and before I could speak, he swept his hands out in a grand gesture.

"Welcome, Mr. Tusley, to our little production!"

SEVEN

Rochester

NOVEMBER 1983

Katie

August 2, 1943

Dear Father,

I hope you get this letter. Something's wrong with Harry. He's taken to guarding the front door of the house, his toy rifle across his lap, staring straight ahead at the road. He told us no one's safe, and something about President Roosevelt's legs...? It was all Joe or I could get out of him.

That was three days ago, and he won't talk at all now!

We telephoned Mother and convinced her to come back from Quebec. She'll get here tomorrow. Joe will meet her at the train station downtown. Not sure how long she plans to stay.

Word is getting around town that Harry is acting strangely. Inky Matthews agreed to come by to talk to him. Harry's known Inky forever so I thought it would be a good idea to get him over here, and for Inky to let Sam and everyone else at the paper know that we're all okay.

None of us is sure what happened.

Maybe you could come home?

Yours,
Katie-did

EIGHT

Occupied France

JULY 1943

Terry

Vivienne rushed outside the abbey and a cheer came up from the men. They gathered around her in a tight circle. I saw a spot near the doorway and crouched into it, hitting the shutter as they all strode into the abbey together, the men delighted to see Vivienne, who, in return, seemed happy to be seen. Again, my camera felt funny, but I didn't have time to think about it as I followed behind them, taking any shot I could get.

Cameron Plumb stood off in a corner, one well-shod foot propped up on a crumbled stone pile. His back was to me. I quietly got closer.

The coat he wore truly caught my attention. It was enormous, made of a shiny woolen weave, very unusual, possibly some Zephyr-wool that Australians wear, distinctive in texture and drape. It didn't look like something a person would wear on the street. It was too showy. Luxurious and rich. I knew for sure now that I was dealing with a type I'd always hated: the peacock. Wandering around Europe, pretending to care.

He sensed me and lifted his head. I waited for the peacock feathers to flare.

"Do you have an extra focusing knob? Mine seems to have broken off." He turned to me, a Speed Graphic cradled in his arms. It was outsized, to fit his ego, a heavy camera to haul around, especially here.

"You already tried harvesting one from me, apparently," I replied, scanning his camera for any mismatched parts.

"In our world, we are like brothers, Mr. Tusley," he said. "Either one of us could be dead in a minute. I hope to get this done before midnight."

"Get *what* done, Plumb?" I asked, jerking away from him.

"Ready, *Metteur en Scène* Plumb?" a soldier called out. "*Regardez*, we have all the equipment you ordered."

"All good, François. All good," Plumb said with a smile, his eyes on something behind me.

I followed Plumb's gaze. The abbey interior was transformed. Several little tables covered in white tablecloths were lined up against the abbey walls alongside twenty-some café chairs with curved backs. A few tiny lamps with fringed shades sat on the stone floor. I gawked, astounded, as Vivienne strode past me. She didn't pause. The neck of her dress was unbuttoned now, down to her cleavage, and the cardigan had been replaced with a flowered shawl that looked a bit threadbare, even from this distance. The men continued to hustle around us, dragging large items into the nave. I got a closer look. Movie lights. My jaw dropped in astonishment.

They were setting up lights on stands all around the shattered altar.

To my further surprise, generators suddenly kicked on, their engines echoing across the stone floors and what was left of the abbey's walls.

As if on cue, the sun settled, and the abbey darkened. Cameron Plumb, taller than the men hurrying around him, rose above the crowd. He waved his hand, and the movie lamps flashed on, illuminating Vivienne, her hair glowing around her face. She stood at a microphone that nearly dwarfed her, pretending to sing, her arms held out from her body, her fingertips turned into the light, her mouth open in a perfect O, the dress cinched tight at her waist.

"Jolly good, Vivienne. Fantastic!" Plumb yelled out to her.

"Is the light good for me?" she asked, shielding her eyes from the glare.

"*Oui*," several of the men across the room replied together, breaking into laughter.

Then Plumb turned to me.

"I suggest you and your Zeiss park yourselves at that table back there," he said, pointing me toward a table about midway across the abbey where three women were waving. I stepped over the jumble of electrical cables that crisscrossed the abbey floor, torn between anger and curiosity.

A dozen tables now filled the cavernous abbey. At each table were men and women, wine glasses in hand, faces lit by glowing lamps. Cameron Plumb sauntered around like the father of the bride, crouching here, standing there, taking photo after photo of the scene with his Speed Graphic, a flash unit now affixed to it. He held up the camera's bulk, nearly dancing across the abbey floor, the flash reflecting off the walls and floors. Plumb, Plumb everywhere. Changing flashbulbs, swapping film cartridges like a goddamn acrobat. He even got one of me, the bastard, just when I thought he'd passed my table by. Vivienne was right. *Très dangereux*. Only… not for Plumb. A setup. A goddamn setup.

Or was it? Wine—real wine—was flowing at every table. Vivienne was really singing now, leading the crowd from the altar. No one seemed to be worried about the enemy, who could be right outside the abbey door. Everyone sang with her, raising their glasses, the generators behind them rumbling in unison. First, *La Marseillaise*. Then the new song, the Resistance song I'd heard snippets of in Paris, *Le Chant des Partisans*. I felt French pride well up. It was not mine to feel, I realized. It was for Francine.

"Courier!" Plumb shouted, pulling together his pile of film cartridges. "I'm done."

A young man ran up to him, and Cameron Plumb gave him a smile.

"Caption!" Plumb shouted, commanding the attention of the entire room. "Free France Sings While Nazis Sleep in Paris! *Comment c'est, mes amis*? How's that sound?"

The crowd cheered, the boy nodded, and then he took all of Plumb's film.

Plumb pointed to me. "Mr. Tusley over there also has some film to deliver. *Life*'s deadline is at 22:00 hours. Scoot!"

The boy scanned the crowd. I stood up, eyes still burning from Plumb's flash. I'll take it, goddammit, and get my film to *Life* too.

The boy made a beeline for me and waited for me to unload my Zeiss and mark the film with my name. I did a quick mental inventory. I'd photographed the hidden side streets of Paris, crawling with unsavory German soldiers. Plus, there was the one I'd nabbed of Cameron Plumb and Vivienne, and the shot of her laughing with the Resistance soldiers. The boxes being unloaded. Somebody's grand hoax.

But who had ordered it? And goddamn it, Francine! Why didn't I know about it?

"*Fini, monsieur*?" the boy asked anxiously.

"*Oui, c'est tout...*" I told him, the hesitation clear in my voice.

I felt the physical pull of the film leave my presence, wondering what would happen to it. I sat back down and reloaded the Zeiss immediately, pulling a ready roll of film from my jacket pocket.

The boy sprinted out the front of the abbey.

I decided to follow him.

The boy-courier stood just outside the abbey doorway, silhouetted against the blue night. A perfectly appointed, shiny black Citroën trundled up from out of nowhere. Its headlamps were not extinguished for safety. The boy bent down and spoke through the open passenger window, gesturing to the film cartridges under his arm, nodded, then jumped into the car.

The Citroën's tires ground into the gravel and off it went, racing down the country road that seemed to isolate the abbey from the rest of the war, carrying my film who knows where. Hopefully, the car was headed to one of the active *Life* outpost bureaus.

The men and women inside the abbey sang with gusto behind me as I lingered, watching the Citroën cut through the darkness as it raced away into the Occupied night. I pulled another roll of film from my pocket and reloaded, thinking I may as well go back inside. Yes, this was Cameron Plumb's party, not mine. But some of the women looked half decent.

And a party's a party, after all. That's what my Francine would say, wouldn't she?

NINE

Occupied France

JULY 1943

Terry

It was past midnight by the time everyone left, the bread truck repacked and gone, when Vivienne offered me a ride with her and Cameron Plumb. She told me they planned to stay overnight at an inn about ten kilometers away on the other side of the lake, in *La Zone Libre*. I was welcome to join them, she said, then blew me a kiss and spun away to get her things together.

I remembered hearing that Matthew Brady did setups in the Civil War. I'd dismissed these as rumors, besmirching the man I'd admired my whole life, a man whose footsteps I'd followed in unblinkingly. He was a giant to me, as was Mr. Eastman, the mighty founder of Kodak, the man who'd trusted me enough to call me a chemist, allowing me to experiment with his newest cameras, even come to Paris.

And then I'd met Francine.

"Maybe that part wasn't so lucky," I said to myself, remembering how my wife had lured me into her web. As the years went by, she made clear she didn't want me to leave Kodak, but she'd been called back into service, and I'd had enough of toiling in Kodak's basement lab after Mr. Eastman's death. By then, I was desperate to be a photographer out in the field.

Not just any photographer, either: I wanted my name in lights. As much as Francine loved to work from the shadows, I had the urge to be known. I got a gig at the *Rochester Observer-Herald* on the side, and became a photographer of news.

But, my true wish was to become a photographer of war.

And Francine owed me, for saving her that night in the cabaret, for being her consort home when she was called back to Quebec. From nearly our first meeting, I knew what Francine was: a highly trained and experienced spy, and we were able to reach a compromise. I'd travel as her courier, hiding in plain sight as a photojournalist, and the children would live their lives unknowing.

It worked for a long time. But Francine broke our agreement by leaving the children home alone, our teenage daughter Katie playing mother to her younger brothers. I couldn't go back now. I wasn't done yet. Far from it, considering what Cameron Plumb had just pulled off.

Vivienne crept up beside me. "*Attendez, mon chéri…*" She hesitated, coquettish. "*Votre moment arrive bientôt.*"

"Bullshit, Vivienne. This isn't my moment. It's Cameron Plumb's."

She looked surprised and a little hurt, and I instantly regretted my words. But who was she, anyway? *Life* would have done a background check before putting her on the cover, though that can be very difficult in wartime.

Cameron Plumb walked over to us, grinning broadly. "All done here! If you're looking for something to do, Tusley, we need a bloke to change a tire on the car out front. It went flat. The driver's waiting for help."

How could this man have the nerve to ask me to do his bidding, I thought indignantly, and how on earth did he think he could leave without me, when he knew he was my contact?

"Plumb," I began, through clenched teeth, but a bright light filled the abbey entrance, bathing us in a splash of heat. A blast of artillery followed.

"*Ah, non.*" Vivienne's voice splintered the air.

We staggered against the abbey wall as bits of stone blew past us. Vivienne dropped to the floor, and I spun to face the doorway to shield her from whatever would come next, a wave of hot wind charging past me.

"*Eh bien*! I am okay, I am okay!" She jumped up, covered with dust. A look of sheer determination shone from her eyes.

"Get to the back of the abbey, Vivienne! There may be another blast!" I pushed her toward the vestibule, and she ran off.

"Plumb, you and I will check it out," I said, thinking he was right behind me.

The air in the abbey cleared in the dead quiet.

"Plumb?" My voice echoed across the stone walls.

No response. I scanned the floor for his body, bracing myself. In the far corner of the abbey, near the vestibule, I thought I saw something move. Rubbing the soot from my eyes, I could just make out the flap of his big Zephyr coat, his arm around Vivienne's waist. They swung open a vestry door at the back of the abbey and dove through it together.

Wait a minute.

News photographers run *to* the news.

Don't they?

TEN

Rochester

NOVEMBER 1983

Katie

August 3, 1943

Dear Father,

I wanted you to know that Mother came home to help Harry...

I remember waiting out on the swing set while Mother talked to Harry on the back porch. I knew my Mother would want to feel like she was playing her role. I can hear her voice even now, rising and falling in that melodic way as evening settled around us, explaining something at great length to my little brother.

"Katherine, come tell... *ton petit frère* that the president does have legs," she'd said, surprising me so much I almost fell off the swing.

"Mama says the pictures don't mean anything. How can she say that, Katie?" Harry sniffled, wiping his nose with the back of his hand.

"What I said was that you should not be reading magazines full of war stories," Mother replied in her lilting French-Canadian accent, glaring at me in the darkness. "Or being allowed to watch *zee* newsreels that frighten you."

"But why is President Roosevelt always sitting down?" Harry asked. "I think he's being held prisoner!" He gripped the toy rifle even tighter in his little hands.

Mother smiled, her red lipstick dark against her perfect skin. "I will call the authorities immediately..."

"Will you? Tonight?" He sounded like this would be *almost* good enough.

I took the opening and dove in. "If we let you go to bed with the rifle, will that make you feel better?" I asked, resting my hand on his small shoulder.

"I guess so," Harry said.

He didn't ask for ammunition, but—as I rightly suspected, even way back then—that would come.

Afterward, Mother and I sat alone together in the kitchen, an event so rare that neither of us could choose a chair to settle in, and we tried to figure out how to undraw the conclusions, and the deep fear, which were now a part of Harry.

"Why don't we just tell Harry that the president had polio? That's the truth of it, even if people don't talk about it," I said to Mother.

"*Inapproprié*," she replied, disdain in her smooth voice. "We must be careful what we say about a president."

"Why?" I'd asked, surprised.

Her eyes shining in the dim light of our little kitchen, my mother sat up straight in her kitchen chair, sparkling like a queen on a throne.

"Because one never knows who is listening," she'd said, with a look that told me we were quite done with this topic.

I feel eyes on me. Old Aunt clears her throat in the corner. "Sixty years. That's the diamond one. A diamond anniversary is nothing to sneeze at."

"They weren't together for sixty years. It would add up to, maybe, sixty days at most, or sixty minutes! Their lives were fake."

The Old Aunt sucks in her breath, rattled and raw. "How would you, Katie Tusley, of all people, know what is fake?"

I ponder the question. Coming as it does from a hallucination, I shouldn't give it more than a few seconds' thought. And yet, I feel that it's necessary to respond somehow, especially since I've never had the guts to respond to my mother.

But no words come to my lips. Nothing at all.

ELEVEN

Occupied France

JULY 1943

Terry

Waving away the smoke and dust, I headed outside the abbey alone. The wreck of a car sat right at the entrance, half-hidden in the shadows. This was a different car from the one that ferried our film earlier, I thought with some relief.

I got closer. No Cameron Plumb. No Speed Graphic. No popping flashbulb, and no carefully orchestrated setup.

Just me and the war.

I assessed the light. My mind percolated with possibilities.

A low moan came from somewhere in the wreckage. Someone in there was still alive. I dropped to all fours. The mix of burning leather and petrol reached my nose. I tucked the camera under my arm and crawled toward the back of the car.

Another moan.

I reached the gaping hole where the driver's side door had been. I pulled the camera into position, keeping my eyes locked on the shadow of him, what I could make out in the gathering darkness. He was slumped to one side.

"*Prends ça*," he panted. Take this. With a gasp, he swung his arm out of what remained of the shattered driver's window. In his bloodied hand, a white square. I squinted at it in the darkness. Scalloped edges, something written across the back.

A photograph. Suddenly, the driver sucked in his last breath, and his whole body shuddered then went limp. He was gone.

All around me were well-funded setups with actors and props. This was reality. Even more important, it was the truth, and my role was clear. The Pulitzer again lifted its head, and I looked it right in the eye.

I plucked the mangled photo from his dead hand. In the unnatural quiet I smoothed out the photo. It revealed a smiling young blonde woman, hair swept up, standing in a striped dress. An older woman stood behind her, all in black, her girth wide enough to fill the frame. A smaller girl with long curls stood beside them— a miniature replica of the blonde, dressed in a matching striped frock. I turned the photo over. "*Prends soin de toi*!" was written across the back in fountain pen script.

Take care of yourself.

I realized that I'd disturbed the scene, something I never thought I would do. I'd changed it, essentially, from what it was, by removing the photograph from the dead man's hand.

But then… Reconsider, Tusley. How different was this manipulation from Cameron Plumb's fake abbey café?

Time was running out to take the award-winning photo. April 1944—the Pulitzer deadline—was only nine months away. That included everything: seeing and seizing the photo opportunity, developing, reviewing, editing—if that were even possible—then submission, all amid the achingly slow pace of a courier network in wartime.

I put the photograph back into the dead man's stiffened hand.

Nothing fake here.

I stood up and got to work.

I took three steps back, checked the light again, pulled the camera up, focused on his face and shot two more that included his hand holding the photo.

Scattered gunfire peppered the air. The roar of an engine kicked up from somewhere behind the abbey. I turned around and broke into a flat-out run, expecting to see the two Nazis from last night, barreling down the road to kill me. Instead, on a gigantic motorcycle sporting a sidecar, Cameron Plumb blasted toward me, his big coat flapping in the wind. Beside him, in the battered sidecar, Vivienne's white hands gripped the flowered shawl around her body. They nearly ran me over as they screeched to a stop.

"Get on, Tusley!" Plumb yelled over the engine.

I jumped onto the seat behind him, and, in a spray of mud, we set off. We chewed up the grass and hit the dirt road fast. Soon, we were miles away from the abbey and I could see little white dots in the darkness ahead. A small row of tents, behind a grove of dark trees. A tiny, tattered French flag was nailed to a pole, low yet proud, fluttering in the breeze.

We turned hard and raced toward it.

"I have a message for you, Cameron Plumb!" I shouted in the wind.

"I know!" he shouted back, turning his head just enough so I could see his wide grin.

God, I hated Brits—always so smug. Actually, it wasn't the Brits I hated. Most of them were good guys. Hanging onto the motorcycle as we flew across the fragrant French fields soaked in midnight blue, it dawned on me.

I hated anyone else with a camera.

TWELVE

Occupied France

JULY 1943

Terry

At the entrance of the camp, a figure approached in the relative darkness, tall and commanding. His officer's uniform was in rags, but he struck me as supremely photogenic: dark eyes in a white sneering face, a regal black mustache. He looked down his nose at Cameron Plumb and me, but his expression softened when he recognized Vivienne. In soothing French tones, she convinced him to let us sleep here, assuring him quickly that we'd be taking no pictures.

"*Pour toi*," he muttered to her in a low voice, glaring at Plumb and me like the interlopers we were. "Only for you."

I followed them to a tent at the far edge of the encampment, feeling elated. I was back in the action. Vivienne waved to us as the officer led her away, presumably to better quarters. I stretched out across a rickety plank that served as a bunk and fell asleep, the Zeiss secure in my grip, assured I had a prizeworthy photo of the driver in my camera. My thoughts drifted to Francine, and then Vivienne, and as sleep crept over me, I imagined Vivienne next to me, lighting a cigarette for me from a silver lighter, then one for herself, before she…

I heard something click. I bolted upright, alarmed, only to find Cameron Plumb sitting on the ground a few feet away, cross-legged, facing me, his camera in pieces spread across a tattered blanket.

"*There* we go…" His voice jolted the dream away.

I squinted bleary-eyed in the early morning sunlight that filtered through the canvas, then I laid back down, desperately wanting to get back to that dream, but it was too late. I watched him through half-closed eyes. Plumb was examining the lens he'd disconnected from the bellows of his Speed Graphic. A tongue of cigarette smoke hovered over his head, licking the low canvas ceiling. With a swiftness that startled me, he assembled the various parts of the big camera in a series of quick cohesive motions, snapped the bellows shut, and stuffed it into an enormous duffle bag.

He stood and held out his hand to me.

"Message, please, Mr. Tusley."

Okay, now I was fully awake. I sat up and reached into my jacket pocket to pull out the small packet I'd carried from New York to London, from London to Paris, from Paris to the abbey.

Plumb ripped it open immediately, a move I didn't expect. Usually I'm dismissed, sent on my way, the message never opened in my presence. And back to photography I would go, until the next coded dispatch reached me, orchestrated from Quebec by my lovely wife.

He paused to read the message then glanced at me, suspicion in his eyes, the cigarette still dangling from his lips.

"Do you ever read these?" he asked, his voice low.

"Never."

"You are a strangely uncurious person, Tusley. Chasing pictures instead of news..."

"You call what you did in the abbey *news*?"

"Don't scoff. I've made the cover more than once. Never seen anything *you've* done. But then, it seems this is only a part-time gig for you."

I stared at him in disbelief. Even the Cheese Man showed more respect.

"You shot the pretty girl on the cover," I said. "My work is inside the pages of the magazine, where the *real* war is covered."

"Oh, how petty! So, you think your photographs are more important than mine, is that it?"

"We're done here, Plumb. I'm leaving you now," I said, picking up my Zeiss.

He looked at me over the top of his smoldering cigarette and proceeded to extract a smaller bit of paper from the packet.

"Hold on, Tusley. Looks like you've been given a job."

"Not possible." This was out of bounds. My instructions to Francine were clear, and they never changed. I would be an asset, nothing more. I worked in plain sight. I went by my own name. If it got too hot, I was out.

"Someone wants you to take my film to London, then..." Plumb hesitated. "And then go to me mum's house in Solihull to pick up another package." He tucked the message back into his shirt pocket, eyeing me expectantly.

"That makes no sense. Didn't you give all your film to that courier in the abbey?"

"I have other film," he said quietly. "I have some very important pictures from my time in Paris."

"*You* wouldn't get two yards in Paris without getting arrested, or shot on sight!" I snorted.

He took a long drag from his cigarette, dropped it, crushed it out, and pulled the blanket off the ground, the one he'd dismantled his camera on. He draped it across his head and around his shoulders, like a shawl or a scarf, his face lost in the folds of matted wool.

The sound of soft crying emanated from somewhere inside the blanket, low at first, then louder. "*Mon fils! Mon fils unique! Pris par la guerre! Perdu, perdu…*"

The voice was Cameron Plumb's, yet transformed. A woman's cry.

I couldn't move. Part of me knew he was acting beneath the blanket, but—almost involuntarily—I heard and saw an old French woman. Hunched shoulders, stooped over. Then a sob, and a full translation.

"Me son, me only son," he cried, in a clear, high-pitched Scottish brogue. "Taken by war! Lost! Lost!"

With a chill I thought of my older son Joe, sixteen and at risk of enlisting if this went on much longer.

Plumb yanked away the blanket, squashing it into a ball in his hands.

"That—that was quite a performance, Mr. Plumb," I said.

He actually bowed. "Thank you. I learned all I know from me mum. Greatest actress there is! And here is the film." From the balled-up blanket, he produced a small courier bag and three film cartridges, then tossed the blanket aside. "Take these to a man named Tom Young in London. And then, on to Solihull!" Without waiting for a reply, he pushed the film and bag into my arms and flapped his hands around my head like he was sending me off to Oz.

"Solihull. Your little hometown, way up North," I said, throwing his goddamn film into the courier bag. Francine and another one of her wild goose chases. There was nothing to photograph in Solihull. Probably just a bunch of miserable, bombed-out buildings. Small villages all across England were easy fodder for the Luftwaffe.

"Now, get it *straight*, Tusley," Cameron snapped. "London first. *Then* Solihull. Via Birmingham." Smiling at me, he extracted the message from his pocket, held it in the air, pulled out that goddamn silver lighter, and touched the flame to the paper. It disappeared in a ripple, then he dropped it and ground it to bits with his boot.

He picked up the Zephyr coat and slid his lean frame into it. "Where are *you* from, old man? Where in the vastness of America, I mean." He coughed out a laugh.

"Rochester, New York," I said, gazing at the sooty remains of the message I had couriered for so many miles, never thinking to rip it open. It had arrived, sealed, from Francine, at our home. Via regular post, to avoid suspicion. That said, I'd needed to evade Katie a bit, making sure she wouldn't see it. It was the only way to manage things at home. That was always the rule.

Rules were starting to make little sense.

"I'll drop your film off in London to this Tom Young person," I said, brushing past him to leave the tent. "But beyond that, I'm not promising anything."

He reached out and grabbed my sleeve before I could get clear of him. "Obviously, you think you can land in the right part of London without any more instruction. Although they are in a lull, they are preparing for the next onslaught, and it is still dangerous. You also need me mum's address."

He deftly pulled out yet another slip of folded paper and stuffed it into my jacket pocket. Then he paused.

"You are the type who wants to win," Cameron Plumb said, looking me up and down. "An American prizefighter, a man who fights to win."

"And aren't you, Cameron Plumb, a man who wants to win? A prize for your bit of theater, back there in the abbey? The Academy Award, maybe?"

Plumb smiled again, unperturbed.

"I have no equal, of course," he said, to which I started to laugh, but he continued. "However, if you insist, Tusley, we could engage in a bit of … well, it's almost like a *duel* you're challenging me to, isn't it? With our cameras! There is the new Pulitzer, you know."

I wiped the smile off my face and, deep in my chest, I felt the zing. I'd hoped he didn't consider himself experienced enough to go that high. It was definitely time to end this discussion. I took a step toward the tent flap before he caught me again by the sleeve.

"This is only a friendly rivalry, Tusley. Are we aligned?"

"It couldn't be anything else!" I said, feeling my blood run hot. I would look forward to meeting any challenge from this English asshole.

"Excellent!" He finally released my arm. "Because we have a bit more to discuss. I think you need to know that our Vivienne is in danger. I told her to get to the States somehow, with things going from bad to worse here. But she was relentless. She sneaked out of camp last night, tagging along with her Resistance *amis*." He sighed. "In my view, she doesn't have a chance if she stays in France."

He waited to see how I'd register this news.

"Why would I care?" I heard myself say. He'd captured my attention, though. Vivienne was someone you couldn't shake off. It didn't matter how married you were.

Cameron Plumb paused, his face now grave, and I had the odd feeling that he was readying some sort of speech and timing his delivery to my involuntary reflexes. "Well, it might interest you to know that Vivienne is a Jew, Mr. Tusley. She's on the move, looking for her missing brother. Hoping against hope he escaped Paris just ahead of the Nazis, heading to Lyon, a safe haven. Think of the drama! She's desperate."

"I don't see why that should matter—"

"I'm going after her," he interrupted. "She's in danger. Plus, it's a story, a good one. That's what we do, isn't it? Find all the little stories, amplify them, make them bigger than *Life* magazine?"

He chortled at his own joke, waiting for me to catch up.

"So…" I said, puzzled. "We would *both* go after this story?"

"—And see who gets the best photos," he finished.

"You just sent me to far-off Solihull," I sneered. "Some duel."

"Well, we all have our parts to play. Yours includes carrying my film to London, then a slight detour to me mum's, then the duel begins. Agree?"

This had to be the most asinine plan I'd ever heard. I did see him open the message packet I'd delivered, though. Unless someone had tampered with it between Francine creating it and me receiving it, it was legit.

But Cameron Plumb was done oversharing with me. He turned and swung his heavy duffle across his back. "I can get you to Marseille. I have friends who can guide you out of France from the port, as long as it's at night."

"I don't want or need—"

"Decide, old boy. In or out."

We stood as far apart as the tent allowed.

"All right. Fine."

"All right, then!" He extended his hand, as if to shake on it, friendly-like. Just then, a French *camarade d'armes* in a battered beret poked his head inside the tent.

"*Monsieur* Tusley? Zee truck is almost here."

I glanced at Plumb.

"Ah." He smiled. "Looks like someone's beat me to it. Your journey out of France has already been arranged. Let me know if you need me when you're in London. I have friends there, too. They can help you more than I can at that point," he said airily.

An ancient truck squealed to a stop in front of the tent.

Climbing in next to the driver, I had a singular thought: What kind of help, exactly, did this moron think I'd need?

THIRTEEN

Rochester

NOVEMBER 1983

Katie

Coming back here to face my ghosts was brave, and Manny ought to know that. But he doesn't know about the boxes of letters thrust at me by the good people at the Rochester post office the minute I'd arrived. He doesn't know I've been counting the years in quantities of film. Mountains and mountains of it, under which my life is buried.

Syringes and spent needles on the floor. Acid blotters. Reggie and, before him, Trombone. Finally, Manny. And now I will make sure we hold a grand and explosive 60th anniversary celebration to honor my parents, Francine and Terrance Tusley. This is the diamond one, sharp and clear. Ironically co-hosted by their only daughter, the permanently damaged Katie Tusley-Price, and their only living son, the accomplished and urbane Kodak PhD engineer, Joe.

One voice will be silent at this party.

Harry's.

It's what he would have wanted: to stay in the background. But this is the least we can do to repay him for all we owe him.

Fifty years of their marriage, that was the marker I was originally going for, ten years ago. But I couldn't find Dad. I'd been smoking a lot of pot that year. I would drop off Troy at George Washington Elementary School, then wind my way back home to our DC townhouse. I'd perfected the ability to extract a single sheet of rolling paper from the packet and fill it from the bag of weed while driving, steadying the entire operation against the steering wheel of my brand-new '74 Plymouth Valiant, a gift from Manny. He was doing well. The Pentagon was still crazy with work for defense contractors, even though the Vietnam war was over, at least publicly.

Snaking down Pennsylvania Avenue behind a trail of stinking city buses, I'd lick the joint to seal it, avoiding the eyes of other drivers. Soon, my head would be enshrined in a cloud of pot smoke, windows all rolled up to make sure none of the sweet smell could escape the car compartment, and I'd concoct all the ways I could possibly get my parents together and celebrate—if that's what you'd call it—fifty years of marriage.

But it was impossible. Even my muddled brain knew that I couldn't track down my father. He was just back from Vietnam. There'd been sightings of him in Manhattan, roaming the art galleries in Soho. He was famous, and everyone in our area of DC seemed to know I was his daughter.

But I didn't need to hear about him. I could imagine, with the clarity of a photograph, his ever-present camera hanging from his shoulder, his army jacket unbuttoned in the early autumn. The wind whipping all around him. He was out there, somewhere. It took me ten more years to pin down exactly where.

I'd settle for the diamond anniversary now. I'll pull my parents into Rochester, where it all began, and ask them why—why they saw only the *other*, reflected in each other's eyes.

Why have children? Why at all?

FOURTEEN

Occupied France

AUGUST 1943

Terry

Francine's instructions—the second note, the one Plumb had shoved into my jacket pocket—did a good job of detailing how I was to get out of France, indicating I'd find a transport ship departing Marseille to London Docks, and, once there, I would be directed to my contact. All I had to do was get from where I was to Marseille.

So much for Paris.

After the truck dumped me in Orléans, about an hour south of the encampment, two ancient French policemen in Vichy uniforms walked up to me from out of nowhere. I flinched, then realized the uniforms were disguises. The men stood on either side of me and escorted me down the street, whispering in French that they were the *maquis*, a band of rural operatives who spanned from Lyon down to Marseille.

Following a path of labyrinthian alleyways, they handed me

off to other men as the day and the next night wore on, some asking to see my instructions, some not seeming to care. I was tossed in and out of every kind of vehicle along the way, even walked through empty houses. A ruddy-faced man dropped me at the port of Marseille, in front of a ship tied to the dock and ready to depart.

I didn't know how I could've gotten out of France without my wife's help—the expanse of her network could be quite surprising, even after all these years—or the many *maquis* who steered me in the dark of night. Although I wanted more than anything to photograph each step along the way, I kept my camera hidden, respectful of their desire to remain undercover, unlike Cameron Plumb, who had photographed whomever he pleased in the abbey.

I, too, was guilty of photographing the *maquis*, thinking ruefully of the dead driver outside the abbey. I put the thought aside, confident my role was a necessary one.

Several hours later, the sun just starting to rise, I stepped onto the London docks, finally free to pull out my Zeiss. I threw the strap around my neck as seagulls screamed overhead and uniformed men hurried here and there across the rotted wooden boards. A heavy fellow approached, breathless, and hustled me along the pier to a row of buildings.

"Callin' this the Lull, we are," he shouted, his face a swarm of boils half-hidden by the brim of his woolen cap.

"Yes, I heard," I said, grimacing, muscled forward by his great weight.

When we reached a rounded, metal hut with a sign on the door that said MESS, he finally loosened his grip. "'Ere ya go, mate, yer on yer own now."

I grabbed the handle and swung the door open.

There, at the table closest to the coffee, a whole goddamn team of photographers sat eating breakfast, press badges and cameras hung haphazardly across their chests. A lone writer among them stared straight ahead, a small blue portable typewriter on the table before him, a piece of paper extending from its spindle. His hands hovered above the keys.

A motley crew, to be sure.

"Terrance Tusley, UP," I said.

One of them jumped to his feet.

"Welcome to the Docks! I'm Tom Young." He reached out to shake my hand. Good-looking bloke. Photogenic. Blond, wavy hair, close-cropped around his ears. Blue eyes and straight white teeth.

He motioned to me to step outside, and I dutifully followed him out. As the mess door banged shut behind us, he looked at me like a teacher assessing a student's intelligence ahead of an exam.

"I've been wondering when you would get here," he said in a low voice.

"Well, I had a lot of help, or I never would have made it out of France."

"You are in possession of photographic intelligence," he said.

"You think this crap is any good?" I pulled Plumb's bag forward. "The fellow who gave it to me wasn't exactly… normal."

Tom stopped me with a stare, physically pulling the bag off me and securing it around his body.

"It's important for the war effort. How long have you been at this game, Tusley? A few weeks? This isn't like some… science experiment. It's real."

"Actually, I spent some time in—"

"What is it you're after, actually? I mean, what do you think you're doing here?"

I returned his stare with conviction. "I'm here to win the new Pulitzer for photography."

"Ah, so that's your expectation. Very interesting. Any idea how to do that?"

"Be in the right place at the right time and be damn ready for anything," I said, thinking of Cameron's challenge. For a flicker of a moment, I thought about how far I was from Vivienne.

Idiot. She's not the story.

"Brilliant! I've heard enough," he scoffed. Just then, a buzzing sound reached us; it was coming from upriver. He raised his hand to shield his eyes from the hazy glare that ricocheted off the gray water.

"Ah, here he is," he said, a disgusted tone in his voice. "That Romanian stray who stole a Messerschmitt. Right on time."

Baffled, I followed his gaze. Out across the bend in the Thames, about a thousand yards upstream, a single German light bomber was flying haphazardly toward us, looking like it was trying to find a place to land.

I reached down for my Zeiss and dropped to one knee.

Tom tried to drag me up by my arm, but I wouldn't budge.

"We don't have time for this!" he shouted before sirens started blaring all around us.

Amid the din, men running all around, he tried to yank me up again as the plane approached in slow motion, bright flashes of fire spitting out its wing-mounted guns.

No. This is what I came here for.

The gunfire hit a small fuel tank less than a hundred yards

away. I checked the camera settings in a practiced motion, experience taking over. One hundred ASA. Film speed 160. Aperture F8. Partly cloudy. 1/250th shutter speed. A warm glow rose around me. The first set of docks was hit. I caught the Messerschmitt in my viewfinder, hit the shutter button and advanced the film for the next shot.

Tom threw himself over me just before something exploded behind us. He blew clear off me—*oh my God!* —and my ears started ringing. The peal of alarms reached us from far away. Water, cold and green, lapped at my shoes. I held my breath, hoisted the Zeiss high above my head, and jumped to the lower docks that protruded into the river. The water was waist high. I willed the Zeiss to stay dry, but I sensed that the camera had caught some flak.

And in a moment, the incident was over.

Beside me in the water, Tom lay moaning across a large wooden plank. He was intact, his clothes and Cameron's camera bag barely blackened, but I could tell he was going into shock. He reached out to me and latched onto my arm. I was still holding the damaged Zeiss aloft. The mournful, two-note wail of an ambulance reached us, winding its way through the chaos that led to the shattered docks, heading directly for us.

That was fast. A little *too* fast.

"Maybe you are that man you think you are, Tusley!" Tom Young gasped, the wind knocked out of him, struggling to talk. "Taking photos—under fire! Go to—Pall Mall… the Carlton Club… across from St. James Park… get out of here, now!"

He cringed a bit, his handsome face like the tragedy mask in a play. Before he passed out cold, he released me as the screaming ambulance pulled up above us on what was left of the dock.

Two men with Red Cross armbands jumped into the water, landing with a splash in perfect unison next to him.

Amid the carnage, I noticed that Tom Young was the only person they picked up.

Impressive, I thought. Fastest rescue I'd ever seen. Film bag and all. It was like they knew exactly where he was when the enemy plane came in. I scrambled out of their way, realizing Plumb's film bag was more important than me.

And I wondered what was next for me at Pall Mall.

FIFTEEN

Rochester

NOVEMBER 1983

Katie

Mother is insisting that everyone she knows be invited to the anniversary party. Dad just goes along with anything she says. It's a three-way conversation: me to Mother, me to Father, me to myself.

I've paced between these rooms for weeks now, the phone glued to my ear, the cord stretched taut. Names taken, long-distance, from my mother in Quebec. Garbled names from my father, shouted into the pay phone from a bar somewhere in the Big Apple. Beneath his words, I hear the strains of background music from the tavern jukebox—The Police and Bowie and Billy Joel. The soulful music comes through the receiver cleanly and fills the long spaces between his words while he constructs his list from memory, each person like a photo in an album in his head.

"Did you invite Cameron Plumb?"

"Dad, do you have an address?"

"Dammit Katie-did! Who knows! He's world-famous, look in the newspapers, goddammit! Now, don't forget Roy, he pulled my ass out of trouble many a time..."

"The pilot? I have his last name somewhere, Trombone knew him."

At the mention of Trombone's name, my father falls silent. I can practically hear the ice in his glass as he downs the rest of his highball.

I look over my list. Cameron Plumb's name is at the top. Off to the Rochester City Library I will go, searching through phone books for him. Should be an exciting dude, for an old guy. And there was a beautiful lady my father talked about. Mother knows about her, some girl they still argue about, according to Mother's latest vitriol. She's still jealous, even though, you know, who is she to talk? And she says my father and his friends are all just *des vieillards*—old men. She's right. Dad turned seventy-eight this year. I have to stop and think about the woman's name because Dad did mention it, and I remember it was just one name, like Cher or Madonna. But it was French.

Vivienne. That's it.

I put my pen down and peek around the kitchen corner. No hallucination lurking. It's been six hours since my last pill. I only have a few days to get this thing pulled together. Otherwise, the invitations won't be received, and I won't be able to find a caterer anywhere in Rochester.

There isn't time for old aunties swinging umbrellas.

Right on cue, her voice reaches me from the living room.

"Grenada is a resort in the Caribbean, 2,343 miles from Rochester."

Or, more correctly, from Fort Drum, my son Troy's last known departure point.

"And, as can happen," she continues. "A military coup—"

"I know, Old Aunt. I know."

As can happen, a military coup in this remote, tropical place results in an all-out multinational invasion, in a place no one is sure how to pronounce.

Our boy Troy left three weeks ago. "Don't worry," he'd said. He was shipped to the action, only days after finishing basic training, one of my father's photographs stuffed in his knapsack. The recruiter from his high school took him to Corgie's downtown for a foamy-cold congratulatory Genesee before he left. I can still see the two of them laughing and smacking each other on the back as they saunter from the house to the recruiter's big green Pontiac parked out front, with the US Army bumper sticker and the faded Reagan '80 decal in the back window.

Troy is now one of about 7,500 troops stationed at Grenada Airport. His high school diploma is still in its envelope on the hallway table.

Manny is down in Washington finishing up a proposal for a multi-million-dollar bid. The Pentagon is flush with money again—he'd hurried down there yesterday morning. Call me immediately if you hear from Troy, he'd said, assuring me he'd be back home by the end of the week. The slam of the taxi door is still ringing in my ears when I go upstairs to the bathroom, gulp down three different colored pills, and slide one of the pill bottles into my bathrobe pocket, vowing to call Dr. Pine at eight o'clock when his office opens.

But that call can wait.

A low-pitched thrumming, like the throb of a helicopter's rotors, reaches me in the bathroom from down the hallway. It's coming from the attic, I think. I pull down the attic steps and climb up the fresh wooden staircase, wondering if Troy left the attic window open. My father's photographs are scattered across the new floorboards. Troy had already picked out the best ones to hang on the walls of his room. Morning sunlight streaks in from the tiny attic window.

I am my father's daughter. I notice how the beautiful light filters across the dead air of the attic. The photographs whisper to each other: Remember Paris, my lovely? Remember London, my friend? And then Inchon and Seoul, how beautiful, and Saigon, and Bien Hoa—remember them all?

SIXTEEN

London

AUGUST 1943

Terry

I followed Tom Young's sketchy directions to Pall Mall and the Carlton Club. I looked up at a freshly painted white door, at the top of a three-step rubble-strewn stairway. A bronze plaque that had survived the blitz was hanging at a lopsided angle, held to the doorframe by a single bolt. Apparently, this was all that remained of the glorious entryway to the Carlton Club. The door opened before I could figure out how to clamber up to knock.

"Take a step there, and then there," the man indicated, his index finger encircled with a heavy gold-and-black insignia ring. He had to be over six feet tall, fat and with a serious face. He sighed impatiently as I picked my way over the mess, and then he backed up reluctantly to just barely let me squeeze past him through the narrow doorway.

"Terrance T—" I began, but he held a finger to his mouth.

"Yes, I'm aware." He frowned. "Name's Frankel. You don't

need to get acquainted with me. I'm only here because I insisted on keeping up the club until this whole bloody thing is over." He coughed loudly in the dusty entryway. "They've been expecting you and were wondering what took you so bloody long."

As he swept down the hallway, if a man that size can be said to move fast at all, I noticed a gray-haired woman, in silhouette, standing at the far end of a cavernous, wood-paneled room. She turned at the sound of the door slamming shut. But my eyes went to the beautiful new Zeiss Rangefinder sitting on a bureau in the corner. She followed my gaze to the camera. She walked over to me, her brown dress swishing in the deep quiet of the room.

"This is for you." She picked up the new Zeiss from the cabinet, slid it into a polished black leather case, and placed it near enough to touch.

"But, first..." She smiled faintly. "You must give me your damaged one."

"You can trust your film with us. Hand it over, Yank," Frankel said, leaving no doubt he would stand there forever until I did so. "That new Rangefinder isn't free, you know!"

I hesitated, wondering how these Brits obtained a new German camera. It was wartime. Some German slob must have been in the wrong place with it hanging from his neck. I pushed the thought away.

Was it worth it to hand over my film of the dead driver from the abbey? I had to admit, if only to myself, that the shots I'd taken were my way of injecting some drama into the scene.

Artificial drama.

With a jolt I could feel down to the soles of my shoes, I knew that wasn't what I wanted to be known for. Cameron Plumb might stoop to that, but I wouldn't.

Not ever again.

I pulled my '39 Zeiss over my head and handed it over in exchange for the shiny new Rangefinder. As soon as I had the new camera in my hands, I felt a rush of excitement. Better equipment made for better photos. *Prize-winning* photos. I looked up to find the woman and Frankel staring at me with distaste.

"Once I sign your orders," she continued, her voice firm, "you will embark on the British Merchant Navy ship *Surveyor* harbored at the undamaged area of the Docks."

"What's that again?" I looked from Frankel to the woman who, I realized, had not told me her name. This must be an outpost of British intelligence. Echoes of Francine began to tickle the edges of my subconscious. This had the markings of my wife's machinations.

"It's your big chance, Tusley." The familiar voice belonged to someone standing behind me. I swung around to find Tom Young, fresh as a daisy, holding up one bandaged hand. "I had orders to accompany Churchill to his next conference. Not possible now." He laughed, but no one else did.

Did he just mention Churchill?

"Think of it, Tusley. Churchill. *Churchill.* I daresay you're perfect for it."

The old lady interrupted, wrinkling her nose at Tom Young. "The ship leaves in precisely seventy-two hours. You will be on it, Mr. Tusley. There's too much danger to go directly to Canada. The German U-boats are in Canadian waters. You'll go to New York."

"Correction: there are U-boats in *all* the waters, Martha—" Tom said, but she fixed him with a watery stare, then turned back to me.

"My understanding is you have family there. In northernmost New York."

"Children," Frankel piped in, frowning.

This was more than unusual. I was being sent home.

But… Churchill. They couldn't be lying about that, could they?

"The conference in Quebec City will be public knowledge by the time you arrive," the woman named Martha continued. "You'll have special access." She slid a sealed letter into my jacket pocket.

"Get on with you, then!" Frankel said. They rushed me out the door, slamming it shut as I picked my way back down the crumbling steps.

"Ah, my Francine, you weave a tangled web," I muttered, pulling the new Zeiss over my head, eager to get a good look at it.

Churchill was in my future, and I held up my new baby to get a better look. I released the flawless German camera from its case, giddy with anticipation.

This camera was at least three years newer than the one I'd handed over. The back was marked with the model name and number: Super Ikonita 532/16. This meant it had a better lens, and a markedly better shutter speed. A superfast model that could capture almost anything. I wouldn't have to use a flash very often now, and that could save my life, not to mention the photo opportunity. No Kodak I'd ever handled had the elegance of this amazing contraption, even back when Mr. Eastman's booming voice still echoed off the concrete walls of his basement labs in Rochester.

It was obvious that the next place for me was Quebec City. By way of Rochester. Cameron Plumb seemed to know too much about me. And what about that strange assignment to go to Plumb's mother's house in Solihull? Why hadn't anyone else mentioned it?

Cameron Plumb had talked about his mother, back in the Resistance tent, where I'd left him behind. A mother, I suspected, who had raised a son to tell lies, pretend fairytales were real, idealize war. His reedy, overly dramatic voice was still ringing in my ears.

Greatest actress there is. What exactly had he meant by that?

The ship bound for New York wasn't leaving London Docks for seventy-two hours, according to old Martha. Just enough time to solve the puzzle of Cameron Plumb. And what better place to start than his mother's house, someplace near the city of Birmingham? A little town called Solihull. The place he'd called home.

I didn't even feel like I had such a place.

I dashed out to the busy thoroughfare, leaving St. James's behind me. Victoria Station was dead ahead. I stopped when I heard the rush of steam and a short one-note train whistle. If I ran, I could catch a northbound line up to Birmingham city—it was only two hours north of London central—and get to Solihull from there.

SEVENTEEN

Solihull

AUGUST 1943

Terry

I arrived in Solihull just as evening approached. Without much effort, I found the address Plumb had given me. Not quite sure what I would say, I knocked just once on the red-painted door.

A beautiful woman, dusted head to toe with white flour, answered the door with a look of happy surprise. I was immediately arrested by her looks: large green eyes framed by a million lashes. Long, luxurious auburn hair. Older, with sensuous lips, an hourglass figure; she was quite beautiful despite her flour camouflage. Cameron had her narrow chin, her high cheekbones.

"Mrs. Plumb," I said, not sure how to begin, how to explain why I was here, when I, myself, wasn't even sure. "I recently met your son."

Her green eyes got wide. "Who are you?"

"My name is Terrance Tusley—" I said.

Without hesitation she proceeded to drag me into the cottage. "Oh, call me Annie!" She plunked me down on a couch loaded with pillows. "Terrance Tusley! Finally!"

She stared at me with those green eyes, her beautiful face a hodgepodge of emotions: surprise, delight, and rank curiosity. I stared right back at her, wondering vaguely what she meant by *finally*, before she jumped up and rushed through a small archway to the back of the house.

"I'm making roast beef, 'ang on, don't want to burn it!"

I heard a loud bang of an oven door closing, and she reemerged, wiping her hands on her apron, all traces of white flour gone. She looked lovely, like a woman in a magazine photo.

"I want to hear everything! You'll stay for dinner, of course!" She short-stopped at a decanter and poured two hefty drinks into matching blue pottery mugs and the comforting smell of brandy hit my nostrils. As I took one from her, I could not get over how photogenic this woman was, in the dim light of her English cottage. I wondered where Mr. Plumb, her husband, must be. Cameron hadn't mentioned him. She looked to be around forty, but that was impossible if Cameron was her son.

"I know what you think." She smiled at me. "People are always quite surprised by Cameron and me—everyone we meet thinks we're brother and sister!" She laughed and fluffed her magnificent hair.

My fingers twitched to pull the Zeiss to my eye, but I resisted the urge and placed the camera on the small table next to me. The bone structure of her face, the proportions of her figure, and her coloring—they would all pull perfectly in a black-and-white photo.

"Cameron's dad died in the Great War." She leaned toward

me confidentially, as if I were a new friend—and not a total stranger who'd just knocked on her door in the dark of evening. "I was eighteen and still carrying the baby. I delivered Cameron in hospital two months after his dad was killed." She drifted over to a framed tintype hanging on the wall behind the lamp, caressing it with her fingertips. The image of a dour man with a mustache stared out from the old tintype, his features obscured in the dim light of the parlor.

"I had my career and a baby all alone. I was determined to continue to trod the planks, as they say. Cameron's kept me whole, he has! He saved me from boredom, and ruin! That he did."

Annie Plumb plopped herself onto the sofa next to me.

"Trod the planks?" was all I could think to say, completely disarmed by her.

"Oh my, Terrance, haven't you heard of me?" she asked, her green eyes imploring. "*H.M.S. Pinafore*, *Pirates of Penzance*, and so on, don't you know!"

"Well, you do look like you could be in the movies," I started to say, but she interrupted me with a merry laugh.

"You sound like Cameron!" She nodded toward the side table, where the cup of brandy she'd poured me was sitting untouched. "Drink up! I want to hear all about Cameron and you! Yes, yes, just drink up!"

She downed her brandy in one go. She fixed me with those green eyes until I picked up the mug and took a small sip, which seemed to satisfy her. She let out a peal of laughter and then sighed. I don't think I'd ever seen anyone switch between moods so easily, and I found myself falling under her spell, Cameron Plumb be damned.

"Cam's dad played Dick Deadeye and I was Josephine," she said. "Oh, such lovely times, but then he had to leave me. Called to war—an untimely end in the trenches, like far too many—"

A knock at the front door sent her sailing off the couch. In a moment she was back, with three companions behind her. One was a man of small stature, almost child-size, with copious hair on his arms and face. Two hefty women were behind him, talking a mile a minute, one a dyed blonde, the other a brunette. Both women were heavily made-up and loaded with costume jewelry.

"Come one, come all!" Annie's voice rang out. "Terrance, this is the troupe!"

I was about to question what she meant, but instead I looked more closely at their faces, their wide, expectant smiles.

Stage makeup. Theater people. Naturally.

"Pleasure to meet you all," I said. The motley crew acknowledged my greeting in a noisy clamor and headed for the table. I settled into the only remaining chair. Annie stood next to me and placed a hand on my shoulder.

"A—friend—of—Cameron's," she intoned with great seriousness.

The troupe lit up like bulbs on a Christmas tree.

"Really now!"

"'Bless us! Is 'e still traipsing around Europe?"

"Always the ladies' man!"

"Ya got 'im fixed up right with that *fer-tography* gig, yeah?"

Annie Plumb silenced them all, her hand held high. "I did nothin' I'm ashamed of! 'e's a great talent, I just gave 'im a little push."

As we ate the elaborate supper Annie had prepared, she asked me all kinds of questions, wanting to hear about me and my encounters with her son. Her guests seemed equally interested, interrupting with even more questions about Cameron. What we were doing in France, how we'd met, etcetera. I tried to answer them best I could, but it wasn't easy—I'd lost count of how many brandies I'd had. At well past midnight, Annie Plumb's guests said their goodbyes and left as they had come in, talking nonstop. I helped Annie clean up. We stood side-by-side, dish towels in our hands, as if we'd known each other forever.

"I will always be grateful for my boy! I'm so proud of 'im!" she said, wiping a tear from her eye. Annie Plumb then set down her dish towel and guided me back to the couch. "Don't go anywhere, right, m'love?"

The clock on Annie's side table chimed 1 a.m. and, at that moment, I had a change of heart about Cameron Plumb. People who were close to him loved him. He was accomplished and capable. He was still my rival for the Pulitzer, but he was an honorable competitor I now felt I could somehow trust.

Cameron had a home base. And a cheering section, to boot.

Who was I to question that?

As suddenly as she'd disappeared, Annie Plumb materialized next to me. "Dear Terrance, please take these and return them to your brilliant wife Francine." She slipped something into my hand and smiled, delighted at the look of surprise on my face.

I stared down at a pair of large, glittering earrings, twisted gold wire adorned with pearls and rubies. Before I could say anything, she placed a warm hand on my arm.

"Tell her I love her," Annie said. "I will never forget what she did for me in Paris so very long ago."

So, this was the package I was sent here for. Not a message, wrapped in paper. Not a sealed, encoded letter. A personal thing. And I recognized these particular baubles. Francine was wearing these very earrings on the night we met. This final surprise hit me like the shock wave on the London Docks.

Annie Plumb was another spy. Of course. And she was guiding her son Cameron. But did he know? Maybe not, and frankly I didn't care. I sized up my beautiful hostess, trying to picture her in the early days, when Francine would have met her. Those two must have been quite the duo.

"Of course, Mrs. Plumb. I'd be happy to."

I slid the earrings into my top jacket pocket and buttoned it shut.

"I must go now," I said, and she smiled.

Outside Annie Plumb's ruby-red door, rain drifted down into the fog. Before I could walk away, my thoughts still a jumble from the whole evening, she stopped me, turning me back around to face her.

"Does 'e still have the Zephyr coat? It was from 'is dad's costume in *Pinafore*..."

"Yes," I said, looking directly into those green eyes. "He most certainly does have it."

She nodded and closed the door without another word, and I turned back toward the train station.

It was late—far past the last train out of town. But I'd still make my ship if I caught the first morning train back to London. The station was empty, no one in the ticket booth. Not even an English bobby anywhere in sight.

As I stretched out across an empty bench at the station, I imagined myself walking through my own front door, the Rochester summer warm and bright.

Home. Would Francine be there to greet me? A message from Pall Mall would have reached her already, and she would be expecting me. We'd head up to Quebec together, leaving the children behind, making up some story to keep them at bay. I fell asleep thinking about the earrings from Annie Plumb in my pocket. This would be the first of my many questions for my wife, once we were alone. I'd ask Francine to tell me the real story behind these colorful echoes from her past, about the old days in Paris before she met me. And I slept until the first train whistle woke me in the dawn of a morning rain.

EIGHTEEN

Rochester

NOVEMBER 1983

Katie

I pick up a photograph that Troy left behind in the attic. It's of less interest to him because it's not of a war zone. In fact, this particular photo depicts where peace talks took place. And Harry was also, for a moment in time there, at peace with himself. Until he wasn't.

I sit down on the attic stairs, the pills finally taking effect, and let the scene play itself out like yet another movie in my bottomless repertoire.

Our old house in Rochester. Sometime around the last week of August, 1943.

Dad came through the door, the bright August morning sun like a halo all around him.

"Welcome home!" I screamed, jumping up and clapping

my hands. He stopped and looked me over, his little girl all grown up.

"Katy-did, I need a coffee," he said, pulling his camara from around his neck and setting it down carefully on the hallway table.

"Coming right up, mister." I said, alarmed at how tired he sounded. "Lucky you, there's some left from breakfast."

He settled into the La-Z-Boy recliner and I ran to the kitchen. The percolator was still plugged in, and I brought him the hot coffee as fast as I could, proudly poured into the clay cup Harry had just made in art class.

He took the coffee, but didn't seem to notice the special mug. "Where is everyone?" Dad asked, looking around the empty living room.

"Oh, Joe stayed out with friends last night, you know him, he's the town's social butterfly," I said, careful to keep the jealousy out of my voice. "Mother was going to go alone, but at the last minute, she took Harry with her to Quebec."

Dad's eyebrows rose.

"President Roosevelt will be there next week," I continued. "Mother thought it would be nice for Harry to see him, you know, after what happened."

"What do you mean, 'after what happened'?"

His reporter's brain was already at work, seeking out the facts.

Didn't he remember my letter?

"Mother said no—" The screen door banged before I could finish, and Joe walked in, looking bedraggled, wearing yesterday's clothes. He started to head upstairs.

"Wait a minute, son," Dad called out.

Joe slouched back over to the living room and flung himself into the corner chair.

"Dad," I quickly asked, filling the sudden silence. "Why are you home?" I was sitting on the edge of my seat.

Joe stayed quiet, watching Dad.

"Well, I'm not supposed to spill the beans, but what the hell, the news is out—I've been asked to go to Quebec City and photograph Churchill!" Dad sat back, smiling.

I jumped up out of my chair. "Churchill—and Roosevelt, too? Oh, Dad, please take us with you," I squealed. "Joe, let's all go! I'll phone Mother in Quebec, she'll be so excited, won't she?"

I detected a noncommittal nod from my brother.

"I promise I'll get all of us back here in time. School doesn't start for a few days. That includes you, Mr. High School Junior!"

"Junior? That went fast," Dad said, scratching his head. "And Harry…?"

"Fourth grade, Dad." Joe's voice was barely audible.

"Fourth grade already?" Dad drummed his fingers on the clay mug. "How much time is your mother spending in Quebec these days?"

The room took on an icy feeling. Joe and I shrugged.

"It's fine," we said in unison.

Then Joe cleared his throat. "It's you she'll want to see."

Dad looked at Joe, then me, the misshapen coffee cup balanced on his knees.

"It's you she'll want to see," I echoed, bowing my head to avoid his eyes.

NINETEEN

Quebec

AUGUST 1943

Terry

Invisibility was key. That, and timing. These words I repeated to myself over and over on the train journey to Quebec City with Katie and Joe, trying to prepare myself for what could be the most important photo opportunity of my life. As the train jerked from station to station, my mind was filled with every photo I'd ever seen of the two great men—Churchill and Roosevelt. We'd bought any newspaper we could find in the Rochester train station before we boarded, and they were strewn across the seat now in a jumbled pile, digested and done.

I sat back, satisfied. First, the photo shoot. And then a quick visit with Francine, get her to answer a few questions about that cast of characters who seemed to already know me in London.

Tomorrow, I'd be on my way back to Paris.

The train swayed along Lake Ontario out of Rochester, then to Utica. We climbed the mountains past Lake Placid and Saranac, arriving at lovely Lake Champlain, where we changed trains in Plattsburgh. Katie and I stood together enjoying the refreshing lake air while Joe popped into the station, emerging with a guilty look, a bottle of Coke, and a fistful of Hershey bars, which he handed out to us, keeping two for himself. Katie gave him a look.

"One's for Harry!" he protested. She shook her head at him, and I had the feeling that all was right in my household.

We hopped onto the connecting train, and I thought about my game plan. Presidents and prime ministers had their security men, unscrupulous fellows who thought nothing of ripping your film from your camera and banishing you to the hinterlands, where no lens could see.

This would be different. I had orders in my pocket from British intelligence. I would get a front-row seat.

We had lunch in the dining car on the second leg of the journey. Katie talked nonstop about life at home. It was good to hear her voice and see the young woman she was turning into. She wasn't a beauty like her mother—she looked more like me, poor kid. Francine had told me the boys were calling on her, though. She was tall and slender, funny and upbeat. Joe avoided eye contact with me for the whole trip. I'd corner him later to get the scoop on his damn life.

Once in Quebec City, we split up. Leaving Katie and Joe at the train station with cab fare to go and fetch Francine and Harry, I promised to meet them in the stands at 5 p.m. sharp.

A white van with a red-and-white medallion in the back window was idling on the road in front of the station. A cardboard sign below the medallion said PRESS ONLY. I jumped in.

At the conference site, I was directed to the Chateau Frontenac, Quebec's top hotel, situated high above the city, where dinner would be served and a photography event would be carried out under the watchful eye of US and Canadian intelligence, not to mention British agents. I checked in and showed the event organizers my orders from Tom Young. They said they would take care of me.

Initially, the Canadian government had revealed that only Churchill was visiting Canada's Prime Minister Mackenzie King, and the newspapers had been bloated with stories of fishing expeditions, late nights and whiskey, cigars and serious talk. But everyone in Quebec City knew that Roosevelt was in town, up from summering in Hyde Park, and the stories speculated about who was calling the shots—old Mackenzie King was probably just the empty-headed host. Everything the newspapers said was conjecture; no interviews had been given. The most truthful portrayal of the conference would be found in the photographs. Churchill had been captured leaning out of his train car on the way up, cigar in mouth, two fingers held up in his famous Victory sign. Wish it had been me who'd taken that damn photo.

Bleachers had been set up on the hotel grounds for one short viewing of Mr. Roosevelt, Mr. Churchill, and Mr. King. I'd been given a special red press pass printed with the British Union Jack on the back. It would be good to find a place where I could view the proceedings straight on, my Zeiss at a zero-degree angle from my intended line of sight, without having to crane my neck left or right.

I milled around the hotel grounds, nodding to other photographers, making small talk, rechecking my camera. A white stage figured prominently in the center of the grounds, with chairs lined up across the middle. The stands for guests were set up way back behind the photography corps. At exactly four o'clock, a mass of men surrounded the stage. Photographers swarmed, picking their spots and guarding them like dogs around meat.

At least two dozen impatient men milled around me, with their bulky Speed Graphic cameras, setting up tripods for the big picture. A collection of Rolleiflexes hung from a few guys' necks as they jockeyed for closer positions. I saw one or two Kodak Medalists, this being not so far from Rochester.

"You're standing in my spot!" Some slick-haired kid was barking at me, his equipment hanging all over him, his clothes a disheveled mess.

"Shut up—you're late," an old fellow said to him calmly. "Ground is precious. You should have planned better."

The boy swore at us and shuffled toward the back. The press corps got busy, knees bent into the grass, everyone paying attention to his equipment. I kept my eyes up front, where four men wearing long coats and fedoras detached from the protective group of black suits next to the stage.

They nestled close to something low to the ground, bulky and slow-moving.

I realized with a start that it was President Roosevelt. He was surrounded, being moved toward the stage almost imperceptibly behind the men in the coats. The low sunlight glinted for a split second on the metallic spokes of the wheels of his great wicker wheelchair. I clicked the shutter, only for my personal collection. Editors would not publish any evidence of the great man's infirmity.

With a series of quiet grunts, the men hoisted Mr. Roosevelt onto the white stage at the back corner and, in one swift movement, had transferred him to a regular chair at the end of the line of chairs. None of the other photographers were watching all this activity on the stage. And I could see why. The guys on the stage were doing a great job concealing the president.

The men moved away, and Mr. Roosevelt was revealed to the world, big as life. He sat alone, legs crossed, cigarette holder at that famous angle, hatless, grinning. It was like he emitted sunlight. The crowd burst into applause, shouting his name, and the president threw his head back, receiving the waves of adoration with unbridled joy. I thought I caught it, my shutter flying a split second before a dozen others clicked around me.

I turned to scan the stands. Francine, Katie, Joe, and Harry must be back there somewhere, on their feet with everyone else.

A new hush fell on the crowd, and I pivoted to face the stage. Mr. Churchill had arrived, fat cigar and all.

The crowd broke into applause again. He sat down next to the president, leaned his elbow on one knee, and glared out at all of us from beneath a porkpie hat. Even among the mass of front-row photographers, his penetrating gaze found me. Holding eye contact with him, I moved forward from the dense middle of the crowd, assured of my special status.

I strode up to the stage and sighted Churchill in my viewfinder as he sat back, placed a hand on Roosevelt's arm, and said something in a low voice, causing Roosevelt to tilt his patrician head toward him.

The lighting was right, and I took the shot.

The sound of flashbulbs popping and cameras clicking and whirring around me was like an orchestra hurtling through the final movement of a symphony. Obviously, at least twenty of us had secured the exact same photo.

And just like that, the photoshoot was over. The leaders of the free world were leaving, and the grand music of cameras had stopped. Mr. Roosevelt was again surrounded by black-coated men, moving discreetly behind the scraping distraction of white chairs being put away.

Something in my gut told me there was another shot, a better shot, but I couldn't put my finger on what it could be. Some of the photographers around me began to pack up and go, leaving their flotsam behind. Trampled grass and a few lost lens covers. Crushed yellow Kodak film boxes and Lucky Strike wrappers. The stage was empty now, except for a boy sweeping up.

"Dammit," I muttered to myself. I scanned the green lawn, making sure I had all my equipment, when something caught everyone's attention.

About forty yards out, a tall woman in a tight-fitting dress strolled across the grass in the setting sun—graceful, lovely, and turning heads.

Francine.

She seemed to glide toward me, slender arms swinging with every step, her dress floating around her willowy frame. She stopped in the cooling grass, bent down, and removed her sandals, gracefully draping them across one shoulder by their straps, barely breaking her stride.

One of the photographers wolf-whistled, and a chorus started up among the others around me, then fell silent as Francine drew closer. The men generated an electric anticipation. Eyes eager, mouths open, they pulled their cameras back out of their pouches and stopped to photograph her as she strolled toward us. But I knew that none could ever really capture Francine. I caught her eye amid the sea of flaring flashbulbs in the growing darkness, and her taut face melted into the smile only I could create. She never quickened her pace, but changed her direction ever so slowly so that her trajectory would intersect with my standing point—her only objective.

As Francine reached for me, the early, transparent moon cleared a blue cloud above Chateau Frontenac, lighting up her hair.

"Lucky you," some guy behind me said.

"Beat it, all of you," I growled. They dispersed, some leering at my wife's figure with a sigh before picking up their things.

"Welcome home, *mon chéri*," Francine whispered, laying her head on my chest.

"This is not our home, my dear," I said, caressing her cheek.

"Well, I got you back here, enjoy it, *non*? Did you have a nice few weeks in Paris?"

"Just barely worth it," I said, holding her close to whisper in her perfect ear. "I almost didn't get out of France in one piece. That was a tricky setup."

"I have no idea what you're talking about, of course." She nuzzled my neck. "More important, Mama's having one of her parties tonight. It's very possible that Mackenzie King and his wife could stop by..." She paused, smiling. "You can leave me tomorrow, but tonight you are mine. We'll celebrate our anniversary early, *non*?" She looped her arm around my waist. "Tonight you come to Mama's house, bring your camera... and we find someplace..." Her lips grazed my cheek.

"You go ahead," I said, pulling her in close. "Gather the children, and I'll meet you at your mother's house."

Francine sighed. "My mother never tires of these political windbags who come to her house. Will you be a long while?"

"I'll be there when the party is in full swing. Right now, I have to find Churchill."

Francine smiled in the shadows, the evening light catching her red lipstick that matched her toenails.

"I know where to find him," she purred.

She took my hand and guided me across the empty expanse of lawn. There, a few yards away, about a dozen sedans were parked side-by-side in a long line. At the end of the row sat an open-air, yellow Rolls-Royce, luminous in the blue-black evening.

And then I heard Churchill's famous voice. Gravelly, properly English. I could not see the man in the shadows, but the voice was definitely his.

I spied an empty wheelchair beneath an enormous, leafy tree.

FDR's wheelchair.

Francine pointed to the Rolls. As my eyes adjusted to the darkness, I could make out the two men in the front bench seat. Churchill and Roosevelt. Shoulder to shoulder, speaking in serious tones. Roosevelt was propped up, ramrod straight. There were no photographers around, no glint of camera equipment, no smell of flash. I wrapped my fingers around the press badge hanging from my neck and took a step toward the car.

Francine put a hand on my arm.

"*Le moment, mon chéri*, is when they aren't talking. And when you are done here, it will be my turn in front of the camera. It's been far too long."

She melted away in the darkness.

I nodded and pressed on, holding my breath. The opportunity would be brief. I didn't want them to see me. I silently circled to the front of the yellow sedan to a spot less than ten feet from them. There was a perfect light source, just behind and above the sedan: a lamppost near the trees. I dropped to one knee, and in the moment when they'd turned their faces away from each other, each man thinking his own thoughts, I gently clicked my shutter, capturing these two very photogenic leaders, the lamplight forming a sort of halo around the shot.

This had to be the one—the picture that would make the cover.

About twenty feet away, I noticed two figures, barely visible, under the lamppost. In a flash of recognition, I realized they were my children. I moved closer, staying quiet. Katie was on her knees, her figure bent toward Harry, who stood next to her. She was saying something quietly to him, and he dropped his small head to his chest, nodding as she spoke. Beside them was Roosevelt's wicker wheelchair, illuminated from above. Katie's left hand rested on the top edge of the wheelchair, her right hand on Harry's arm. I was no more than a few feet away, ready to crouch to one knee as I slowly moved the Zeiss to my eye.

In an instant, a flashbulb triggered just behind me. Katie and Harry cried out. Their hands flickered like white flags, covering their faces from the intrusive flash of light. I spun around to see who had taken the picture. That young, untidy kid photographer—the very one who'd been rude to me earlier—stood up from the grass, brushing off his trousers.

Just then, Churchill's voice rang out in the darkness. "Not authorized!" He pulled the wet cigar from his mouth. "Bloody hell, not authorized!"

Security men were on the kid photographer in an instant, hustling him off.

"C'mon, Harry, Mother will be looking for us!" Katie said, taking off.

"Harry," I said softly, stepping toward him.

He bolted after Katie without even looking in my direction.

TWENTY

Rochester

NOVEMBER 1983

Katie

The phone is ringing downstairs. How long in God's name have I been hanging out in this stupid attic? Slowed by those damn pills, I pull myself up to my feet, unsteady.

The phone is insistent. Who would be calling right now?

Troy. I stumble down the stairs and reach the kitchen, desperately pulling the receiver off the hook.

"Hello!" I yell.

"Mom!" Troy's voice crackles over the line, and I mentally applaud my mother's intuition.

At least something's working right in my head.

"Honey, this is so unexpected!" My words come out thick and disjointed. "And, and—delightful!"

He goes on talking, not noticing. I smooth my hair, feeling better immediately, just from the sound of his wonderful, man-boy voice, but it's hard to make out everything he's trying to tell me. I pace by the kitchen table, back and forth, as far as the coiled phone cord will take me, nodding like an idiot, as if he could see me.

"Troy, I hear something in the background, it's noisy!"

"Helicopters! There's only one phone at the post, Mom, and it's outside!"

"I'm so glad to hear from you, honey," I say, but then the cold realization fills my lungs like thin air.

My son, my only child, is speaking from a place where bullets fly.

"Please come home," I plead.

"That's funny, Mom. Gotta go. There's a line of guys behind me. They need to use the pay phone. I'll call again when I can."

The dial tone blares in my ear for a few moments before I hang up, glad right now to have the little red pills inside me. I pull out the bottle from my bathrobe pocket. It says on the label it calms you down. The green one, though, peps me up uncomfortably, and the pink one's purpose is somewhat unclear. Dr. Pine's office isn't open yet to discuss these pills.

I can't cut through the fog in my head, and suddenly I hear a voice, low and manly, coming from the upstairs hallway, near the attic stairs I've left down in my rush to grab the phone.

I walk up the hallway and reach down to fold the stairs, to close the attic door.

"Ma'am?"

A pair of shoes appears on the topmost step. They are gray at first, then strengthen to a strong black color, the sunlight from the attic slanting down to create a blindingly bright shine on the spit-clean leather.

The shoes descend the stairway. Left foot first, then right.

I back up and cower against the hallway wall.

A tall man in a blue officer's uniform with ribbons and badges and a hat jammed down on his head now stands on the first step, looking at me. I blink. He removes his hat, revealing an ugly open gash across the top of his head, blood congealed around it.

"Is this the hospital? I need a hospital," he says.

"This is my house," I say. I'm going to vomit.

"I saw the pictures up there," he says, gesturing with his thumb up the stairs. "They were flying into the windows of our Huey! It was so hot, we knocked out all the windows. It was kind of neat."

I am unable to do or say anything.

"I've never seen pictures like this," he says, holding something out to me.

It is the photograph of Dad sitting cross-legged on a hot tarmac in Bien Hoa. Shirtless.

"Why is he smiling?" he asks.

I fight back the sick feeling and answer him, trying to control my shaking. "He enjoys what he does," I say. I take a step toward the officer. The cloth of his uniform wavers in the sunlight, and I can make out the intricate pattern of spiderwebs woven in the dusty fabric. I cannot grab the fabric.

"You are in my imagination. I am not afraid of you," I say.

"Well, ma'am, that's good," he begins, but the distinctive *tuk-tuk-tuk* sound of helicopter rotors cuts across the hallway from somewhere overhead, possibly on my roof. A strong, hot gust of tropical wind kicks up, coming straight down the stairs from the attic, and I grab the banister before I get knocked off my feet.

"You want to know about that photo?" I say, desperately hanging onto the banister.

"Ma'am, please keep your head down, those rotors can slice your head right off," he says, his uniform beginning to ripple in the wind.

"I'm telling you, just listen, okay?" I'm shouting over the helicopter blades now. "When Troy was eight, *just eight*, you know? Dad brought Trombone to my Washington DC home for dinner! Ten years ago! 1973!"

"Ma'am, I need..."

"Wait, wait! You haven't heard it all! They were meeting up to talk about the good old days in Vietnam!"

I can hear my own voice bouncing down the hallway.

"Well, that's really somethin', ma'am! Who is Trombone?" The officer touches the top of his head with bloody fingers.

"Trombone was Dad's helicopter pilot! For years!"

The officer takes a step back up the attic stairs, as if he's changed his mind about coming here. I try to touch him again, but my hand goes right through him.

"Ma'am?" the officer says, good military form, calm and collected. "Can't you see I'm injured? I need a hospital."

"You asked me about the photograph, I'm telling you about the photograph."

I take a deep breath, refusing to be denied this chance to explain how I see things, how things were—and always will be—for me and anyone who strays into my father's path.

"Trombone brought that photograph with him," I say, pointing to the picture flapping in the wind tunnel where the officer stands. "My son Troy couldn't *believe* that was his *grandpa* in the photograph. Dad and I showed Troy *all* the pictures then, *all of them*. Hanging in frames all over my house, we talked about them all through dinner. Trombone egged him on, like always. Your grandpa is a *hero*, Troy, *your* grandpa. And Dad, sitting there at my dining room table, smiling and smiling. He still thought he had a shot at the Pulitzer then."

"You need to call a doctor," the man says.

I realize with complete clarity that he's right, and I race back down the soft, carpeted hallway to the kitchen.

"What are you doing now, Katie?" Old Aunt is there, in her corner kitchen chair. Her shaky voice sends shivers up my spine. She stands up, stronger than I thought, no longer needing the umbrella to lean on, and she's taller, too. She takes a step toward me.

"Let's go and visit the shed out back," she says, pointing to the shiny sliding glass door. "And watch your father develop some lovely photos of the war."

If I run, I can get away from her. The pain of my body slamming into the glass radiates across my face, my collarbone, my chest. I'm flat-out on the kitchen floor, and the room is spinning, and she's hovering over me, dabbing the blood off my face before she flutters out of sight.

TWENTY-ONE

Quebec

AUGUST 1943

Terry

Dominique's party ended at three in the morning. Luckily, the children had been escorted to bed at a reasonable hour, although I had a sneaking feeling Joe had found an escape route from his grandmother's house down to Old Quebec to sample the nightlife.

The conference was already being hailed as a success, but as the weekend wound down and late summer bled into fall, I knew I would return to Europe as planned. The action would not be abated by talk alone, even with such great men at the helm.

But first… Francine.

And now, finally, my wife stood before the mirror. I reached out and slowly undid the buttons that ran down the back of her shimmering evening gown.

"Some party," I said. Our eyes met in the reflection. "The Canadian Prime Minister seems to be on pretty friendly terms with you. Or was it Churchill who was flirting?"

"Too old!" She laughed, turning to face me. She reached out, and her fingers caressed my face, lingering on my lips.

"None too old, none too young," I said, pulling her closer, her gown falling like water from her lithe body.

"But none of them are truly you," she breathed into my ear.

I gave her the earrings from Annie, and she put them on. They looked spectacular on her, the only adornment she now wore.

I picked up the Zeiss from the bureau. Our photo shoot could begin.

She moved to the window, and the moonlight cascaded across her body. I took the first of many pictures of her, the earrings glinting against her neck. My wife, the famous Francine D'Or, friend of the Cheese Man and who knows who else, was once again mine. Time apart evaporated, as it always did. I kissed her full, and she let her supple body melt into me. The first kiss, whenever we were back together, held us like liquid fire. We fell onto the borrowed bed in this room at the top of Dominique's house—this sprawling salon, with its patrons and its patriots, its newspapers delivered every morning, only to be scattered in passionate anger at night. The well of shadows between her breasts was like the curve of a winding Parisian alley, hidden away but known to some, a secret place deliciously shared, a destination earned and honored. We surrendered to each other and to all we stood for, together or apart. Forever.

Morning light spilled in from the tall windows. She was already getting dressed, admiring herself in the mirror, the earrings completing her ensemble.

"Where does Annie Plumb fit in?" I asked, taking one last photo. A morning portrait of her, in profile, her reflection captured in the mirror.

"I helped Annie Plumb out of a jam a long time ago. The Russians had taken a liking to her. That red hair …" Francine's voice trailed off.

"And her son, Cameron?"

"He was a child—around Harry's age. A young boy. *Doué*. Clever. Bright."

"He's *that* young?"

"*Non*, he is only a few years younger than you. And many years younger than *moi*!"

Vanity. I'd forgotten for a moment how important these little things were to my wife. She didn't have anything to worry about. No one would ever guess she was older than me by half a decade. She was, as the French say, *éternelle*. But I needed more information. What was it about Cameron Plumb that endeared him to so many?

"So, you haven't seen him since he was a little boy?" I prodded.

"It sounds like he's doing well?"

"You're not answering my question."

"*Quelle question*?" Francine said, batting her lashes.

I said nothing, waiting.

She sighed just then and looked me straight in the eye. "Okay, *mon chéri*. Just this once I will tell you. It was before I met you." I watched as Francine carefully fingered the earrings from Annie, lost in thought. "She was in danger. Because of her young son."

"And …?" I prompted.

"And … I got her out of it."

"And how did *you* stay safe?" I asked.

"*Krasota.* That's what the Russians called me. The German spies called me *wunderschön*." The word rolled off her tongue. "Beauty was revered in those days."

"Still is, judging by the reaction you get, Francine."

"But I don't care about them. I have a mission, *chéri.* I am here for you. I am, as they say, all yours!"

We both paused, and then we broke out laughing. I knew that was the most I was going to get out of Francine about Annie and Cameron Plumb. I stayed where I was, sprawled across the bed, watching her. She was already back at the mirror, standing tall, her hair done up for the day, her makeup perfect.

The model spy.

"Put the film in a safe place, please, Francine?"

"*Eh bien*, I will take the film with me to Rochester. I do go home occasionally, you know, despite what Katie may tell you. I am a good *courrier* too, perhaps not as good as you. It is our agreement, *non*?"

"That's not what we said, Francine, and you know it."

"Ah, yes. There was a *seconde partie*. What is the *Life* cover worth to you?"

The question hung in the air.

"You could give up what you do, you know," I said.

"And play at being a housewife and mother? I think not, *chéri*."

"Yes, you're too finely tuned for that, and Katie is doing a marvelous job, isn't she?"

Francine bristled. "You knew what you were getting into, the night we met in *Par-ee*."

"As did you." I said, remembering with fondness my old Kodak with the billows. The cabaret, the noise, and the laughter.

We savored the moment, *la repartie*, as we always have. Luxuriating in each other's company, unable to extract ourselves. Even the children knew they couldn't enter our hidden world. It came into being that night in the French cabaret, more than twenty years ago. Our love was exclusive, exhaustive, incomprehensible. Separate and apart. Like us.

"I was the only prize—*le beau prix*—back then," my wife said, pouting. "And, what prize, *exactement,* do you seek now?"

"It's the new Pulitzer. The biggest prize there is, for photography."

"Ah, you should consider what price you are willing to pay for such a prize. Not that I would ever understand. Anyway, I am happy that Annie Plumb remembered me after all these years."

"Young Cameron's all grown up now," I said, still trying to detect a flicker of recognition.

"Of course! I imagine he is quite a..."

I could see she was trying to find the right words as I gripped the satin bedspread in anticipation, hoping she would pronounce him a dunce that I needn't worry about.

"*Tour de force.*" She laughed as she said it, pleased with herself. "Like his mama, Annie."

I sat up, suddenly irritated. "Yes, I get it. I need to go. It's getting late."

"*Oui.* Until we meet *encore.*" She blew me a kiss before prancing out of the room.

As soon as she was gone, I bounded off the bed and rushed to dress and pack my things.

As I turned to leave the room, I caught myself smiling in the mirror.

Cameron Plumb. Whoever he was, he sure as hell wasn't any goddamn *tour de force* that was better than me. He could eat my dust. I knew where I needed to go.

Paris was where the Pulitzer would be.

TWENTY-TWO

Rochester

NOVEMBER 1983

Katie

I sit up, dazed. There's blood all over my blouse. The glass door is cracked from top to bottom. Head swimming, I lay back down on the floor, dark red swirling into little creeks and streams against the yellow-and-white checkerboard linoleum. Eyes wide open, I turn my head and see little Harry over at my kitchen table, poking at his dinner. I'd slaved over that stew. He nibbles at the bread, quiet as always, his head bowed. I try to reach out to him, and now I am suddenly standing beside him, and his thin shoulders shudder at my touch.

"We're like two thieves living in a stolen house, aren't we?" I hear myself say, trying to sound lighthearted.

He looks up at me. "Will Mother and Dad come home and kick us out?"

"I honestly don't know." I laugh, somewhat inappropriately. He is only nine, after all.

Someone is knocking, knocking incessantly at the front door. I float across the kitchen to go answer it, leaving Harry alone in the kitchen.

Inky Matthews, Dad's buddy at the *Rochester Observer-Herald*, appears in our hallway. He's let himself in and hurries up to me before I can protest.

"Yer Dad's photos from Quebec made the front page, Katie!" Inky is waving the newspaper in my face. The paper rustles loudly in my ears. "Whaddaya think of the printing job?"

My father had captured Mr. Roosevelt and Mr. Churchill together on the white stage, each looking in a different direction, away from each other, but their upper arms touching, leaving no gap between them, like a two-headed dragon.

"Looks great, Inky," I say, not wanting to hurt his feelings.

Mr. Roosevelt's cigarette holder, long and slender like a magician's wand, hovers upward from his mouth at that familiar angle. That part is good, I think.

"These newsprint pictures take a lot away from the subject," Inky says, jabbing a blackened finger at the photograph. "I seen them in person once! Mr. Roosevelt on a campaign stop in Albany, Mr. Churchill at a train station in Buffalo."

He says this with pride, as if these happenstance occurrences lend him authority, which, in a way, they do.

And now, I am sitting at the kitchen table with Inky, vaguely aware that I'm having a hallucination *inside* a hallucination. Harry silently watches us. Inky's hands are spread across the kitchen tablecloth, smudging the fabric with printer's ink. I try not to stare at it, knowing Inky has no idea he's just ruined it.

"Harry was very glad to finally see the president in person," I say.

No comment from Harry. I try to distract myself from the tablecloth, knowing the blemish would have to be removed before Mother comes home. Whenever that would be.

We run out of things to say. Inky clears his throat, uncomfortable.

"Time to get back to work. Nice seeing you, Katie. You too, Harry." He gets up from the kitchen table, but I put my hand on his arm.

"Inky, have any other pictures come across Sam's desk related to the Quebec story? I think Harry and I accidentally got into a shot."

He tilts his head thoughtfully, touching his stained fingers to his chin as he backs away toward the door. "Ya know, that sounds fantastic, Katie. I'll look for it."

"No, please don't publish that one!" I say, alarmed, but he's already left. The screen door bangs behind him, and I watch him meander down the driveway, hands in pockets, whistling.

The screen door continues to bang. Louder and louder until it is earsplitting. I am back on the kitchen floor, flat on my back, holding my hands over my ears, squeezing my eyes shut.

"Ma'am? Are you all right?"

The mailman is banging on my sliding glass door. I register his blue uniform, his matching cap, his tanned face awash in concern. I scramble to my feet and slide the door open, careful to avoid the jagged shards of broken glass at my feet.

"Watch it there, ma'am, that door is broken! I thought a deer ran at it, happens all the time around here, I heard a crash when I was out front! *Jee-zuz-pete* I'm glad I came around back to check it out! You're covered in—"

"I'm fine," I say. "Thank you. I just slipped on the new floor.

You are so sweet. Thank you. Please, you can go, and thank you again!"

I laugh, my head pounding.

"Well, if you need an ambulance ..." he says, noticing the blood.

"We're tough up here. We're 'upstaters,' right? I'll just go get a dishcloth and clean it up, thanks again. You can get back to your route. Thanks."

He finally leaves, looking back at me doubtfully as he winds his way down the driveway back to his route. I wave to him from inside the door, smiling brightly. When I am sure he is gone, I drag myself upstairs to the bathroom. As I dab the blood from my cheek and wind the gauze around my left hand, I feel Harry's presence again. I am back downstairs and—yes—he is still at the kitchen table. Dinner is done, the dishes cleaned and put away, although I have no recollection of doing them. The soiled tablecloth still shows the pitch-black blemish.

Harry makes no mention of it. But what young boy cares about such things?

"Where is Joe?" Harry asks me. "Where does he go every night?"

"I'll ask him when I see him, Harry." I am trying to remain calm, but panic is rising in my chest.

Harry seems to sense it, and his blue-eyed gaze steadies me. He is a calming force, this little brother of mine.

"Yeah," he yawns. "You ask him, Katie. Ask him."

He picks up the toy rifle leaning against the stove in the corner.

I call to him as he climbs the stairs to his bedroom, the gun's slender barrel visible above his blond head.

"You never really leave that rifle behind, do you, little buddy?"

He doesn't turn around. I look down and see I'm gripping the sides of the bathroom sink, and I violently shake myself loose from the memory. Sighing, I finish bandaging up my hand, avoiding my face in the bathroom mirror. I don't need to see even more damage done.

TWENTY-THREE

Quebec

SEPTEMBER 1943

Terry

I caught the last train from Quebec to New York that morning. At Penn Station, I stopped for a bottle of whiskey and a carton of cigarettes, knowing I'd need them to persuade anyone to let me board. The *Edmund B. Alexander* was taking on journalists with a valid press pass—if they came bearing gifts.

I barely made it to the dilapidated *Alexander* before they pulled in the gangway. The captain's ensign had eagerly accepted my bribe and allowed me to board. The voyage would be a full five days long—utter tedium—crammed in with some five thousand nervous enlisted men. I stood at the railing and watched the troops wave goodbye to their loved ones, but I kept my camera hidden away so as not to become a pariah among these brave soldiers, many of whom would never return. Chasing scant sleep in whatever empty nook I could find, I woke on the fifth morning to a cloudy dawn, the creaking ship finally docked in

Liverpool. The train ride down to London passed through bombed-out Birmingham and quiet villages. I dozed off.

I never expected to see Cameron Plumb the minute I stepped off the platform at Euston Station.

He emerged from a cloud of steam, waving to me, his Speed Graphic tucked under one arm, a duffle slung over his shoulders. I squinted through the morning fog to see that he also had a Kodak Retina slung across his chest and a folded newspaper under his arm. The man was like a walking storage cabinet.

"Finally! I've been waiting here forever!" Cameron shoved himself next to me on the bustling platform and unfolded the newspaper, holding it out for me to see. "Look—you're on the cover, old bastard. Congratulations."

I stood there, speechless, gazing at the front page featuring my photo of Roosevelt and Churchill on the white stage at Frontenac.

"Tusley," Cameron said, snatching the paper away and hurtling us forward through the crowd. "How in God's name did you get to Canada, of all places?"

"Tom Young sent me to Quebec on special assignment."

He stopped dead in his tracks, his big coat flapping around him. "Tom Young is the chief propagandist for the British media. And my boss! Canada? Bloody hell, Terry. You must have really impressed the bloke."

"Well, actually, I might have saved his life on the London Docks."

"All while I'm cooling my heels in the outer reaches of Vichy France. What the hell, Tusley!"

"Well, I guess my work speaks for itself. Why didn't you tell me that's who Tom Young is?"

"I thought you knew. You acted like you knew everything back in that tent."

We both noticed several soldiers loitering nearby, listening in. Cameron grabbed my elbow and hustled us along.

"He'll want something from you, bloke," he said, his voice low. "Now that your photo is on page one—that's the game he plays—at some point, you'll have to give it to him."

"I don't work for Tom Young," I said flatly.

"Fine with me. I used to believe that lie, too. We'll go after Vivienne, then. We can easily travel to Salerno. We've taken the south. *Viva Italiana*!"

"She is one of thousands of refugees, Cameron. She will disappear."

"Not Vivienne. Not the disappearing type. She is likely to be in Lyon, looking for her brother, but if we miss her there, she'll be back in Paris. That's the real story."

"And an opportunity to see who can take the prize," I said, finishing the thought for him.

Cameron smiled that annoying smile. "Check in with the press desk and meet me in the canteen. We'll walk to the pub from there and I'll enlighten you about my plan."

And with that, he sauntered away down the dock toward the barracks buildings, the figure of him set against the white-gray London sky. His massive coat, caught by the sea breeze, swept outward from his frame.

I had no choice. He was *that* photogenic. I pulled my Zeiss forward and leaned into the shot. At exactly the distance of thirty-five feet, where I could capture him in full, where the wood planks beneath his feet would create the diminishing line, I pressed the shutter, just once, and slid the Zeiss back into its leather case.

Perfection.

Maybe Cameron Plumb had a viable plan. He'd been right so far, goddammit. And now I knew that Annie Plumb, his beloved mum—and my wife's old friend—was directing his every move.

And he had no idea.

"Lyon. And then Paris?" I called out to him. Getting back to Paris had to be the ultimate goal, or I was going to shake him off, for good this time.

He turned, the Zephyr coat draping him like philosopher's robes.

"I knew you'd come 'round." He grinned.

TWENTY-FOUR

London

SEPTEMBER 1943

Terry

Vivienne. Cameron was clearly obsessed.

If Vivienne Last Name Unknown was my ticket to the front page, if the story of her search for her brother was what would get me closer to the Pulitzer, then I would follow Cameron Plumb to get there, get some of the kind of fact-based shots I knew Cameron was not interested in, and then part ways to head to Paris.

In the metal shelter that served as the base pub, over a dish of something that looked like meat pie, we devised a plan. The next night, armed with press passes, we hopped onto one of the many Royal Navy ships bound for Italy from the London Docks by way of the tip of Gibraltar, which was now controlled by the British. Then onward to Salerno, safely secured by the Allies only a few weeks before.

I was running out of time. The war could be over by the

new year. This wild goose chase after Vivienne had better be worth it.

We arrived in Salerno during unseasonably warm autumn weather and tried, without success, to flag down an Allied mobile unit with enough room to carry both of us and Cameron's bulky equipment. So, we simply started walking down a dirt road out of the port of Salerno.

We rounded a curve and stumbled into a man in clean shirtsleeves, holding a battered bullhorn.

"What the hell," the man shouted, elbowing Cameron hard in the chest. "You're on the set! Get out of the way, you morons!"

I blinked.

To our right, director's chairs were lined up along the grass. More shirt-sleeved men scurried around us, their faces frozen in scowls.

"Didn't you hear him? Get off the set," one of them yelled at us.

A half-track lurched toward us with a mechanical roar, an immense black movie camera mounted on top. A tall, white-haired fellow in a beret and white scarf was positioned majestically behind the camera. He stood out like Moses directing traffic. At least two dozen men in various states of disarray loitered on the ground around the half-track.

John Huston, the famous movie director, or at least somebody who looked exactly like him, yelled into a megaphone.

"*Moan!* Start *moaning*, you idiots! Don't look at the camera!"

Cameron dragged me off the road. He put his finger to his lips and pointed down. A corked glass bottle was lying in the dirt. I squatted down and rolled it over. It was half-full of some sinister-looking dark red liquid. There was a label pasted on the front of the bottle. Scrawled across it were the words Fake Blood.

I looked up at Cameron in surprise.

"C'mon, Tusley," he said. "We can take the long way around, so we don't disturb them."

"What the hell are they doing?"

"Did you think we were the only ones recording history?"

"But Salerno is already won!"

Cameron smiled. "Not if no one was there to record it." He was already moving on, unruffled, picking his way across the edges of the set.

Now I've seen everything, I thought. Storytelling. That was all that mattered here.

"Okay," I said, catching up to him. "About Vivienne. Tell me the story you're concocting."

"Not concocting. It's all true." I could see the windup as clearly as if he were a pitcher on the mound. "She was raised on the streets of Paris. She told me her grandparents were prominent Parisian Jews before the First World War. They were taken from their storefront in the middle of the day. That was in 1940." He spoke as if he were reciting a fable to a small child.

It couldn't hurt to play along. "And her mother, her father?"

"No father that she ever knew. Her mother was a drug addict with two bastard children, Vivienne and her older brother, Max." He paused. "They ended up living on the streets of Paris. Vivienne's mother abandoned them. Vivienne said she'd avoided prostitution with her charming mix of smarts and speed."

I glanced at him sideways. Annie's red hair came through in

his day-old beard. He was her son, no doubt about it. A love for the dramatic. Cocked-up sets. Captured on film.

"So, you picked her up in a Parisian cabaret."

Cameron stopped walking and turned to look me full in the face.

"Tusley, I don't know what all these questions are about."

"You can't possibly believe that story. Think about it, Cameron! She's as polished as a diamond. She is known to the *maquis*. She must have had training. She's no street urchin."

"Tusley, most people in France, especially those being targeted by the Nazis, don't divulge every detail of their past. They are happy to be alive. She's lost her brother and wants to find him. What else do you need to know?"

"Just the truth, Plumb. In fact, that's what we both should be chasing after. Why did she allow you to photograph her? She must have known you were shooting for the cover."

"At the time, she felt that perhaps Max would see it, and know she was alive."

"Don't you think she'd figure that *other* people would then see that she's alive? Maybe people who would want her dead? For someone on the run, she seems to seek out a lot of exposure."

Cameron thought about that for a minute. "She is taunting them, perhaps."

"That's one possibility," I said. "She's definitely transmitting *some* kind of message, to *somebody*."

Hitler was tracking down every Jew and so-called undesirable in France. Vivienne, from the little I'd seen of her, was something special. She'd be quite the prize for the Nazis. The perfect person to help them set a trap for the Resistance. I felt my heart pound with dread, just thinking of what they would do to her once they were done with her. But she was smart. She would know, and act accordingly. She would never put her *amis* in danger. And she would find a way out, to avoid capture.

"Terry!" Cameron's face was flushed. "You think she's playing some sort of cat-and-mouse game!"

I could see Cameron was serious now, no longer relating falsehoods he'd been fed, lies Vivienne likely had to tell him, to protect him, as well as herself.

"I think it's possible," I said, feeling the pull of the Pulitzer.

"A diplomat named Varian Fry is being allowed to operate out of Marseille," Cameron said breathlessly, "to aid Jewish persons 'of exceptional merit' to emigrate legally to the US."

I'd read about this man. A recent *Life* picture showed him leaning out a train window in Lyon, proffering visas like candy. The outstretched hands of the crowd had obscured his face in the photo. So, she could be headed there, thinking she could find her brother. But the Nazis would be hot on the trail, especially if they knew her. Vivienne's face had just been plastered across *Life* magazine, proving to them she was alive.

Cameron practically sprinted forward. "She's worth the trip, old boy—we need to save her."

"That's the plan, *old boy*," I replied, grabbing the loose flaps of his coat. "I'm right behind you."

TWENTY-FIVE

Rochester

NOVEMBER 1983

Katie

Little bits of paper are scattered across my kitchen table. My next task is to consolidate them into a workable list with addresses. My wounds all nice and bandaged, I am ready to start. The newness of the house ebbs around me like a lake while I sit in my rocky little boat of sanity, fifteen minutes away from my next pill.

My parents' diamond anniversary. Quite an accomplishment. Sixty years of marriage, in a manner of speaking. Barely any of it together. How much damage could they do? A shocking amount, as it turns out. And I will have my say. I will speak for the dead, and for those who put themselves in harm's way. Egged on by the famous Terrance Tusley and the absent Francine Tusley. A duo as powerful as the gunpowder inside a bullet casing. All we need is a spark to make it explode.

Happy to oblige.

I root around Troy's empty bedroom for a notebook. I find a tattered spiral one under his bed. I flip through pages of teenage doodles. Hot girls on roller skates. Elaborate drawings of guns. I fold back the notebook at its spine to a blank sheet, worried I might rip something precious, something belonging to Soldier Troy. Sitting at his boyhood desk, I copy down the list of names and addresses for the big anniversary party. French-Canadian upper-echelon names from Mother mingle uncomfortably with the macho-bullshit names that Dad supplied: Jacko, Freebee, Mac, Cam, Tom.

I touch Trombone's name, dead center on Dad's list. I picture his long fingers on the helicopter controls, ferrying Dad in and out of Saigon, to the Mekong Delta, high over the hot jungle and the screaming children in the bombed-out huts. Trombone, towering over me on the floor with a needle and a smile.

Manny would have a cow if he knew Trombone was anywhere on this list. Have to keep that one to myself. I can handle Manny. That's what marriage is about, isn't it? Knowing each other's soft spots.

After everything we've been through, Manny thinks he knows all of mine.

I tap my finger on the notebook page. These are the people my parents stayed with, the ones they each spent years with, everyone on these bits of paper better known than the husband or the wife would ever be to each other. The list is getting long. I'll do a final check before I have the invitations printed. Mother can be contacted, once you get past her personal secretary—assuming she hasn't fired her latest one again.

Dad grudgingly agreed to the party, but he had a list of demands, one of which was a party tour of the mighty Kodak

Tower downtown. It's a busy place. I'm not sure they could accommodate this many people, even if the host is a vaguely famous photographer and a former boy-wonder who ditched Kodak—twice—for a life of glamour, hopscotching around the world's war zones.

Maybe Joe can arrange it; he's more embedded at Kodak than anyone. His boss must be somebody important, overseeing a bunch of snotty PhDs like Joe. Problem is, my brother is even harder to get a hold of than Dad.

I'll see what I can do, but I'm pretty sure Kodak's not interested in Dad anymore. Terrance Tusley's photographs are now the subject of academia. There's even a college class based on Dad offered, not by one, but *two* Manhattan schools. The students analyze him, and the classes include a tour of the exhibitions of Dad's photography. It's still a matter of debate, and the topic of a senior thesis or two, I'm sure, as to whether his photographs, those hideous things he created, are actually art. And, if not, what are they? Twisted tributes to my brother?

My father, when he's had a few too many, tells me what it's like in New York, masquerading as a guest lecturer in the film and photography department at one or another brand-name school. I take in the timbre of his voice across the telephone line, the pauses to sip from his highball glass. He describes in great detail how the students trail behind him down the busy Manhattan streets, carrying their syllabus papers and notebooks, marching like troops in formation, winding in and out of the little Soho galleries that dot the streets of downtown New York City.

Without any effort, I can picture all of it. My father pulling the gallery's heavy plate glass door open, and stepping inside. The students following him in. The gallery owner bowing his head in recognition, his attention immediately drawn to the crowd of young people, making sure they don't damage anything.

Dad would stop, hands clasped behind his back. Gaze up at his work, his photography installed in fancy frames like some sort of *art*, leaving the students to decipher them on their own.

These pieces—these photographs of war and pain—they are his weapons now. They speak for him, don't they? Especially on one particularly painful topic. I know he'll never get over it. He'll never come home, sit for awhile with me, talk to me.

When he sees me, he thinks of Harry.

TWENTY-SIX

Occupied France

SEPTEMBER 1943

Terry

It was true—the Italians had surrendered. Allied convoys were openly snaking northeast, all night long, toward southern France, and Cameron and I hauled ourselves onto one of their trucks in exchange for the sardines and crackers I'd so craftily pilfered from the *Edmund B. Alexander*. I assumed the Germans were everywhere, cut off from supplies, and the fear now, at least for me, would be to find a posse of them hiding in somebody's barn, wounded and ready to use up the last of their ammunition on any English-speaking idiot who wandered in.

When the boys on our truck dropped us off, assuring us we were close to the border, we found ourselves miles from anyplace, where wide plains rose into a mountain range. The air was colder. Autumn was settling in. We walked about three miles in the early dawn and came upon an unmanned wooden gate next to an empty tollhouse. We kept going, exhaustion creeping upon us, and finally we found an abandoned railway station. All the signage was in French. We had crossed the border into France. Collapsing onto hard wooden benches that felt like feather mattresses to us, we fell into a deep sleep, out of the elements. When we awoke, Cameron dug into his duffle.

"Bully and biscuits," he muttered, breaking open two tins. I didn't relish the flavor, but it was better than starving. I shared the chocolate bar I'd saved from Plattsburgh, amazed it was still in one piece in my jacket pocket. Cameron laughed at the sight of it.

"You are just one surprise after another, old bloke!"

"Shut up, someone will hear us," I grumbled, wondering just how difficult this trip was going to get. Having enough chocolate was the least of our worries.

We'd agreed on our story: two journalists looking to get a ride to Hitler's Paris. No one needed to know about any side trips to search out a missing Jew and her brother. They would have laughed, in any case, at the futility of the journey. I went outside to pee and noticed with surprise that, overnight, snow had fallen in the foothills. A horse-drawn covered wagon was moving slowly along the frosty road. A single man sat at the reins.

Before I could alert Cameron, he'd already exited the train station and was waving his arms around to flag down the man with the wagon, his duffle swinging wildly from his shoulders in the swirling snow. The driver finally noticed us and turned his horse in our direction. He looked like a typical French farmer, wearing overalls and a straw hat, reminding me of the Cheese Man.

The driver stepped down—grabbing a shovel from the wagon

first—and looked at us warily. He was easily twice my weight, taller than either Cameron or me. I walked over to meet him. *Au secours*—help. War correspondents. We needed a ride north. My broken French was the only thing that stood between us and starvation. We took our cameras out and, with great seriousness, showed the farmer what we do. He nodded and waited, arms crossed on his massive chest, still holding onto that big shovel, impervious to the cold.

Cameron, shivering, seemed to understand first. With an authoritative nod, he proceeded to gesture to the farmer to lean one massive shoulder against his faded red-and-blue painted wagon. I watched with amazement as Cameron wordlessly created the shot. I stood to one side as Cameron expertly framed the farmer in his viewfinder: pale blue overalls, a scowl across his bearded, ruddy face. Cameron knelt in the snow and held his Speed Graphic. He turned to me.

"Join me, old boy, if you want a ride out of this place!"

Not a photo I cared about for myself. This was Cameron's setup, not my type of subject. When he was done, he tucked the Speed Graphic into his duffle, a look of satisfaction on his face. The farmer noticed Cameron's other camera—the Retina—slung across his chest and maintained his pose. I found this comical but stayed quiet.

"Je suis René," the farmer coughed out.

"*Fini*," I said.

Farmer René, relaxed and smiling now, didn't kill us with the shovel—which he easily could have done, and buried us with it too—but rather took two large, fresh baguettes from his rucksack, and gave us one while he bit off a large mouthful of the other one.

Watching us from beneath bushy eyebrows, he swept his arms out, his dirt-encrusted hands pointing dramatically across the fields that fanned out for miles on every side, rimmed by mountains to the south and a silvery river in the valley below. Between bites of baguette, he spoke quickly in a mix of French and English. He told us about the little bands of Nazi soldiers—*coullions*, assholes!—men too drunk from their pilfered French wine—*voleurs*, thieves!—wandering his countryside, firing their pistols, wreaking havoc in the hamlets, looking for Jews, talking about deportation, asking where the closest operating rail stations were. Weren't the Germans and the French *les cousins?* René spat out the word. He said the Nazis wanted to know where to find the old stone homes of the Jews, the stately synagogues where their elders gathered, and, despicably, the Jewish children's schoolhouses.

So, now we knew who was on the trains. The rumors were true. I looked over at Cameron. In the air was the question about Vivienne—was she on one of them?

"Can you give us a ride to Lyon?" Cameron asked René, apparently forgetting our agreement not to reveal too much. The farmer nodded, and the deal was done. We scrambled inside René's ancient covered wagon, our legs dangling out the open back, second thoughts be damned, nestled against stacks of hay.

For several quiet hours we rode that way, facing backwards, silently admiring the rolling scenery we were leaving behind. Cameron and I sat shoulder to shoulder, jostling in time with the horse's gait.

As we rounded a curve in the road, both of us heard it, then saw it.

A heavy locomotive crawled across the valley to our right,

spewing smoke, pulling a line of railcars with slatted sides in the cold. The train came nearer as the tracks converged with our little dirt road. Sooty, black smoke intermingled with the drifting snow, the locomotive's warning whistle like an animal's howl. It was moving at a glacial pace. As we traveled along in René's wagon, the train was suddenly right beside us, and then we'd be separated again by a turn in the lane or the tracks. When it came close, we could see that the railcars were jam-packed with people, fully exposed to the wind and the snow. Eyes found us, or stared straight ahead, unseeing. I glimpsed the fringe of a white-and-blue prayer shawl on one man. The slow roar of the locomotive engine pierced the quiet.

We counted twenty, maybe thirty, railcars. They traveled north, like us, but the tracks veered northeast. A voice barked out in German from the middle car, and René quickly guided his creaky wagon off the road and took a sharp left, away from the tracks. It got quiet, and I looked over at Cameron. He pulled out a cigarette pack from his coat pocket, hands shaking. René's wagon drifted back onto the dirt road, the huffing train within earshot, getting closer. Cameron had a fearful look on his face, and I felt the absurd need to comfort him.

"Cameron, you don't even know if anything Vivienne told you is true."

"Perhaps *everything* she told me is true," he said. "Besides, I have nothing else to believe."

"Let's see if we can get to Lyon in one piece, and then you can figure out what you believe."

Silence settled over us. I slid my Zeiss from its leather case.

"What are you doing?" Cameron asked, a note of worry in his voice.

"I'm taking a picture of that train. You have your Retina out and ready, you can do it too if you want. The bureau will just pick the best ones to publish. And they'll be mine."

"What if the Nazi guards on the train see you?"

"If they shoot me dead, you can take a picture of that, and get another cover."

"You know we can't take pictures of dead people, Terry." He nodded toward the train. "And those people…they are doomed."

I tossed the camera strap over my head and leaned out the back of the moving wagon, planting my feet on the rotted floorboard. We were coming up to a twist in the icy road. The wagon slid a bit, and Cameron caught my arm to keep me from falling out. I brought the Zeiss up to my eye. Peering through the viewfinder, I focused on the slow-moving train, winding along about forty yards away. I snapped the shutter, advanced the film, and took picture after picture. The people. Children, too. All crammed together in those railcars, going to who knows where.

"You'll use up all your film," Cameron said, resignation in his voice.

I sat back, the train disappearing beyond my focal length. "That's why I'm here," I said.

"Apparently," Cameron tucked the Retina away into one of the extra-large pockets of his coat. And with that, he leaned back against the piles of hay and passed out asleep, his brow furrowed. He looked older, exhausted.

I laid my head back as well, the warm hay poking through my jacket, my mind a swarm of sickening thoughts. Something like sleep began to slip over me.

I awoke, startled, to gunfire and bolted upright before I was shoved back down, smacking my head against the floor of René's wagon. Cameron's face hovered over mine, his eyes wide.

"Nazis. *Imbéciles!*" René's voice reached us from the front of the wagon.

"Tusley, someone's firing at the wagon! Keep your head down!" Cameron whispered.

The shots came to a sudden stop. So did the wagon.

"*Das ist verboten*!" a deep voice yelled out.

Cameron was taking deep, shallow breaths. He leveled his gaze out the back of the wagon, suddenly grabbed his heavy duffle, and leaped out into the snow. I tried to catch the tail of his coat, but he hooked left, the duffle banging against his back. I jumped out after him, but stayed hidden behind the back of the wagon, able to see enough to assess the situation.

A giant black Mercedes had pulled up beside us, Nazi flags fluttering in the cold breeze on either side of the windscreen. It must have been approaching the wagon from the north, and René didn't see them until it was too late. Two men in full officer dress surrounded poor René, standing in the snow, looking like a cornered bulldog, hands on his head.

Cameron sauntered up to them. I squelched the urge to call out to him and stayed where I was. No one had noticed me. Yet.

And then Cameron Plumb broke out in the best German I'd ever heard.

"*Vielen Dank, Monsieur René. Guten Tag, meine Herren. Wäre es möglich, dass Sie uns nach Paris mitnehmen könnten*?"

You had to hand it to him, all three of them jumped. I had no idea what he'd said, but I did detect the word *Paris.*

"*Halt, nicht bewegen*!" the fat one said, reaching for his pistol.

"*Ich bin Fotograf*," Cameron replied smoothly. "*Ihr Oberkommando weiss schon, dass wir hier sind.*"

My German was more than rusty—practically nonexistent—but I could reasonably make out what Cameron was saying: he was a photographer. Not a soldier. But to claim he was here at the order of German High Command was like taking the Nazi's Luger and pointing it at his own head.

I had an overwhelming urge to run, but Cameron's performances were mesmerizing, as I already knew. I stayed put.

Without taking his eyes off them, he crouched low, opened the flap of his duffle, and pulled out a tripod. As slowly as I've ever seen anyone move, he extracted the big Speed Graphic, and like a magician in a top hat, he pulled out his film cartridges with great ceremony. The Nazis stood, transfixed, pistols still pointed at him. René was frozen in place, his eyes searching around the wagon for me. He saw me and didn't even flinch.

Good man, Farmer René.

Cameron lofted the bulky camera high over his head. With his free hand, he fanned the film cartridges like playing cards, creating a dazzling display of his wares. The Nazi officers were silent, mouths agape.

"*Ich bin Fotograf*," Cameron repeated. "*Die Schönheit. Ich bin auf der Suche nach Schönheit.*"

I knew this word: *Schönheit*. It meant beauty. My Francine was one of these: *wunderschön*.

It was working. The two officers began to nod in agreement, following Cameron's lead.

It was now or never.

I stepped out of the shadows of the wagon. "*Nous sommes en route pour Paris, le grand Paris, le bijou du Fuerer!*" I fiercely hoped, walking up to them, so exposed, that these stinking Nazis were buying my strangulated French, and understood that I was complimenting them on Hitler's jewel: Paris. "*La cité éternelle*," I continued, striding up to stand beside Cameron.

"*Bleiben Sie stehen*," the big one said, his tone deadly.

"*Meine Herren, wir sind nur Künstler auf der Suche nach Schönheit*," Cameron said again, silky and assured.

We waited in silence for the Nazis to shoot us in the snow. And then . . . they laughed. Two crazy photographers—one of them their own, one your friendly neighborhood French collaborator. The stunt had worked. The fat one re-holstered his pistol. Cameron laughed along with them, gesturing to me to do the same. Only René kept frowning, his hands still clasped behind his head, but he soon joined in, to save his life if nothing else. Cameron was nodding madly, like a marionette tangled on the end of its string. We went quiet, each man with his own thoughts.

Schönheit. Beauty. Everyone wants that.

"*Gehen Sie mal*," the skinny Nazi said. It didn't seem like a question. Let's go.

Behind Cameron, another train rounded the tracks, about five or six miles away, its smokestack belching smoke. If the Nazis saw us bear witness to these trains, we'd be shot dead.

"*Oui*!" I shouted, sprinting toward the Mercedes. Cameron picked up his things and followed me. The Nazis opened the trunk and handed us two fur coats. They indicated we should wrap ourselves in them.

"*Est ist kalt*," the fat one said, apparently concerned about our comfort, and I couldn't help but wonder who the previous owners of these furs were. Cameron crammed his Zephyr coat into his duffle, carefully folding it around the Retina hidden in its cavernous pockets. We reluctantly slipped on the furs. They had a light smell, like smoke. Cameron slung his duffle over his shoulders. The fat Nazi smiled at him, reached into the open trunk, and produced a bottle of wine. He blew on it, sending an ashy dust across the snow at our feet. With a flourish, he presented it to René.

"*Merci, merci*," René said, taking the bottle and bowing stiffly. He looked at the two of us like we were already dead men and then clambered back into his wagon, yelling at the horse to hurry up.

"*Steigen Sie ein*," the skinny Nazi said, sweeping his pistol in the air.

We slid into the back seat of the Mercedes, and they climbed into the front, the fat one behind the wheel. From the back of the sedan, racing away to Paris, Cameron and I could just barely hear the long, low whistle of the death train behind us.

TWENTY-SEVEN

Occupied France

SEPTEMBER 1943

Terry

An hour passed, then another. The men up front talked occasionally, but mostly they were unnervingly silent. I guessed we were still traveling north. We'd descended into another valley. No more snow.

I could not forget the trains. We veered onto another road and were no longer following their tracks. I pulled back the sleeve of the heavy fur coat and glanced at my watch. It was now two in the afternoon. We'd know our fate by nightfall. Cameron had fallen dead asleep beside me. I decided sleeping was how he dealt with stress.

I sat rigid, alert. When the Nazi officers chatted in front, their conversation was too muffled by engine noise to make out any real words—they sounded like the atonal rise and fall of something inhuman, like the hissing and sputtering of those damned locomotives.

Rumors about the death camps had surfaced as early as January 1940. I was like Matthew Brady, drawn to the killing fields of the Civil War. I wanted my shoes to chew on shards of glass, my bended knees to get bloody in the war in Europe. The terrible desire had awakened me from my sleep, in the cold, familiar Rochester night, Francine sometimes beside me, sometimes not. It took weeks of midnight scheming to figure out how to get a gig as a field photographer and to convince Francine that our savings would be best used to fund me, one-way, to Paris. I'd be her courier. Once we landed on a solution that worked for both of us—and the children, of course—nothing could stop me.

That December, I had let my editor at the *Rochester Observer-Herald* know I was going to try my hand as a war photographer, going freelance to Paris. Sam had looked at me over the top of his horn-rimmed glasses, holding my resignation in his veiny hands.

"You sure?" He'd shouted over the clatter of typewriters. "You got a family! Ain't you a little old for this?"

His face was lined from the years of early deadlines, late catastrophes. The life of an editor grinds men into a stupor. He'd fared better than most of his peers, who'd usually died of a heart attack by his age. They mostly wrote their own obits, stashed in a drawer beneath the cigarettes and the whiskey bottle.

"Tell Inky Matthews to keep an eye on things at the house. Francine isn't around a lot."

"Well, none of my business anyway. That Katie of yours seems pretty self-sufficient—for a teenager," he'd said, eyes narrowed.

"They'll be fine," I'd said, sprinting out the newsroom door before he could protest any further.

The Nazi on the passenger side twisted his arm over the top of the front seat. I froze, expecting the muzzle of a pistol.

"*Hier*!" He tossed something into my lap. I looked down at a block of cheese wrapped in oilcloth. It was branded with a large red splotch of French lettering that had been cut off on one side. *Fromage Comté*. Very high-end. Francine had schooled me well. These guys must have raided a mansion.

I spotted a road sign outside my window. Lyon.

"*Merci, nous pouvons marcher à partir d'ici*," I said in my calmest voice, reaching under the fur coat to tuck the cheese away in my jacket pocket.

"*Was zum Teufel willst du*?" The Nazi spun in his seat.

I had his full attention. Either he was going to let us out here, or we were going to be shot. It was fifty-fifty at best. I cleared my throat.

"*Tant de possibilités*!" I elbowed Cameron awake.

To my surprise, the officer nodded to the driver, and they stopped in the middle of the road. Both of them got out of the sedan. Their doors banged shut, fully rousing Cameron now. Without even asking me, he clambered out of the car with his heavy bag. I jumped out after him.

We were at the edge of a village, surrounded by yellow buildings, twenty or thirty yards away. Behind the Nazis, heads popped out of open windows and then disappeared. The fat Nazi was staring up at the tall white sign: *Bienvenue à Lyon. Marseille—320km. Paris—470km.*

The Nazi then pointed at me with his gun, apparently unaware that people were quietly watching from the windows of the buildings behind him. "*Vous restez ici*," he spat out, his accent terrible.

Stay here? I'd be happy to. I felt my shoulders drop with relief.

He gestured to Cameron with his other hand. "*Magier, Zauberkünstler*," he said, smiling. "*Mal sehen, wie schön Paris heute abend ist!*"

Magier. Magician. I didn't have to know any more German to understand. They were taking him, alone, to their beautiful Paris. Not to kill him. To take pictures.

"Eh… *Donne-moi …ton film*," the fat one said to me, looking pleased with himself as he holstered his pistol in his waistband below his protruding belly. He stepped forward and stuck out his hand.

"*Mon film*?" I asked, a sick feeling rising in my throat.

"*Schnell!*" The skinny one still had his pistol out, and he had it trained to the center of my forehead.

"*Non, nein*," I said, backing away. I bumped into Cameron, who was like a rock behind me.

"Give it to them, Tusley. It's that or your life," Cameron whispered, his eyes locked onto the barrel of the skinny Nazi's gun.

I broke open the Zeiss and ripped out the film, tossing it to the ground at Cameron's feet. I flung off the smelly coat as well, and threw it into the dirt. The skinny one picked up the coat and the film and shoved them into Cameron's arms, who was wagging his head at me, muttering *Künstler* in perfect German loud enough for us all to hear.

Künstler. Artist. The Nazis both guffawed and then they all three got back into the black sedan with its tiny Nazi flags and sped off, heading north.

I stood stone-still in the road, the dust from the car blowing past me, shocked by what had just happened to my film. As soon as the car disappeared from sight, leaving only a cloud of dust visible in the distance, a swarm of villagers spilled out of the buildings. A woman at the head of the crowd was running directly toward me.

I blinked at her approaching figure, at her gleaming brown hair, the abalone clasp glinting in the sun. Her eyes were filled with tears.

Vivienne.

"He was right! You are here!" I stammered.

"They will kill Cameron," she said, her voice shaking.

"No, Vivienne. The curtain is not yet down."

And then the French villagers surged forward, swarming Vivienne and me. There must have been fifty, sixty of them—old men, women in yellow scarves and blue aprons, children in caps shouting *bonjour, bonjour* at me. They turned as one force in the direction of the departed Nazis' car, even the children shaking their fists and spewing the vilest profanities.

"*Fils de pute*!"

"*Va te faire foutre*!"

Vivienne was laughing and crying at the same time. My fear and my anger ebbed, overwhelmed by this display of resistance.

These were my wife's family, her bloodline. That same ferocity, that same passion. Francine's methods may be different, but she was as present as if she were standing next to me. She was a part of this painting, the strong layer beneath, like the resin that acts on canvas, to keep the oil from seeping in.

TWENTY-EIGHT

Occupied France

SEPTEMBER 1943

Terry

Vivienne pulled me away from the crowd, leading me through an archway into a wide open-air courtyard. Potted plants and marble benches with thick legs decorated the perimeter.

"What is this place?" I asked, my shoulders warmed by the late afternoon sunlight, golden and filtered, that cut across the tiled floor. The stink of the Nazis' fur coat drifted away.

"I found it *quand je suis arrivée*, just a few days ago." She swept out her arms and walked to the center of the antechamber.

The circular courtyard surrounded her like a movie set, enhancing her skin and playing off her flowered dress, a too-thin garment worn beneath a gray cardigan that fell to her ankles. The light caught the knit of the sweater, making it look like a shimmering fog around her. A tattered kerchief was knotted around her neck, iridescent silk, once light blue.

"Perhaps this was a happy place. Now it is empty," she said.

"Everyone who could have left town must have vamoosed out of here, before things got bad," I said.

"*Oui,* they took everything they could carry. Only a few remain here." She glanced around, petite in the vaulted enclosure. "Of course, I am always traveling *toward* those things, when others run away!" She laughed ruefully. "Tell me what happened, Terry. Where are they taking *mon ami* Cameron?"

"He impressed the Krauts with his showmanship," I said. "I don't think he's in danger, the lucky bastard."

She cocked her head to one side, eyebrows raised, not understanding.

I thought for a moment. "*Illusionniste,* Vivienne. *Magicien,*" I said.

"*Allons*! *C'est difficile à croire*!"

"Well, believe it. That's what happened."

"Those men… they are *facilement en colère*!"

"Quick to anger? No, the Nazis are cold. They want someone to document their triumph in Paris, Hitler strutting his colors, a spectacle not to be missed. After that, who knows what they will do with him?" I felt uncomfortable just thinking about it and pushed the thought away. "In any case, I need to get to Paris, not waste my time here in dusty Lyon."

I made my way over to a bench and started to unwrap a fresh roll of film. "Given up searching for your brother?" I asked, loading my Zeiss.

A moment passed.

"He is dead," she said quietly. "I heard they dragged him onto one of those trains."

She stared at me, her face inscrutable. The sunlight had shifted, cutting a path across the stone floor.

I felt terrible for her.

"What will you do now?" I asked, knowing she had very few choices. I thought I saw a flicker of defiance in her eyes, reminding me, again, of Francine.

"Terry, I have lost everything, and I did not have much to begin with." With that, she crumpled to the floor, then laid down, her dark hair obscuring her face. "I heard about Wanda, I will follow Wanda," she choked out.

"Who is Wanda?" I asked, puzzled.

"A musician, *une belle* Jewish musician, escaped from France." She grabbed at my hand, suddenly frantic, pulling me down. "Terry, *écoute-moi*! Listen closely! She went to New York, she found a piano down in *le* New York metro, she played until the symphony found her, the New York symphony! They found her and now she lives *la belle vie*."

There, on the cool stone floor, our eyes met, and I could see the intensity of her feelings. But this was not my business, and I could not have cared less about someone named Wanda.

"I hope you find her, Vivienne. But I can't help you do that. You understand, right?" I released my hand from her grasp and stood. "I have to stay in France. There's something I came here to do."

Vivienne lifted herself gracefully from the floor and stepped away from me, smoothing her dress, regaining her composure. She regarded me from the shadows now, her face serious. "You are something different from Cameron."

"I have different goals," I said quietly.

Her eyes sparkled in the dim light. "And yet, I think in the bones you are brothers."

Her phrase rang a bell inside my head. Cameron had once

referred to us as brothers-in-arms, or something like that. Was it back in the abbey setup?

"That's impossible, in any case," I replied. "Cameron Plumb and I are as different as—"

"You doubt me, *eh*?"

I regarded her for a moment. "Actually, Vivienne, I think anyone who doubts you would be a first-class fool."

She smiled at me, the entertainer in her basking in the compliment. I saw a change—her beauty casting its own light, glowing like a golden lantern in the final rays of daylight. The indirect light in the courtyard no longer just surrounded her, but rather emanated from within her.

An idea for a photo suddenly formed, unbidden, in my mind.

"You see that far wall, Vivienne? You would look beautiful posed against it. Think of the exact opposite of how you just felt. Think..." I struggled for the right word in French. "Um... *à l'envers*. Upside down."

Without hesitation, Vivienne kicked off her chunky shoes and slid out of the long gray sweater. She dropped to the floor with the grace of a dancer and swung her body in one artful movement. In a flash, she'd created the perfect pose: lying on her back on the stone floor, her legs up in the air, crossed at the ankles, her feet gently resting against the stone wall—her whole body long and lean. I gasped as the flowered dress fell away from her, revealing a corset underneath, tattered black netting and threadbare magenta velvet that glowed in the perfect light that seeped in from the open archway behind us.

From her toes in the air, her whole body flowed down, cascading into a pool of her hair.

I sensed a creative chemistry between us, two artistic souls working together. She was the muse, inspiring my ideas to create timeless images of beauty.

What had Cameron called me? A *künstler.* An artist.

Without another word, she moved from one pose to another as I changed angles and camera settings, catching light as it cascaded across her face and body.

Each pose played out to become an expression of the different emotions only a trained actress could express. Even Francine with her natural beauty and poise could not match Vivienne's devastatingly beautiful execution.

She locked eyes with me through the camera lens and the golden hour passed.

I finished the roll and held it out to her.

These photos were not the truth I wanted to express in my war photography to get the Pulitzer. They were another kind of truth, from another place inside of me.

A place that Vivienne now inhabited. Let her have them.

She jumped up and swiped the film out of my hand. "I want to go with you to Paris, to say *au revoir* to Cam," she said, twisting the kerchief back around her throat. "There is nothing more for me here in Lyon."

"Then we have to figure out a way to get to Paris," I said, taking a step toward her in the dark. "And then you need to go find… what was her name? Wanda."

"I *will* find her, Terry," Vivienne said. "And I will find a train to Lisbon, and I will find a ship to New York. But, first, I will say *au revoir* to Cameron. He has been a friend to the French for many months."

The hands on hips, the set jaw. Like my darling wife Francine, only pure and unadulterated. I didn't want to tell her that we would likely never see Cameron again.

"We'll need to hitch a ride to Paris to try to find Cameron," I said softly.

"We don't need transport. I have a car. And petrol."

She laughed at the look of surprise on my face, and she kissed me, and the room began to spin.

Again, I thought of my wife. It was cocktail hour in Quebec. I pictured the men in my mother-in-law Dominique's salon, Francine throwing her head back, laughing, choosing one of the powerful—or soon-to-be-powerful—to be her companion for the night.

The night was young. The mood was right. I reached out to Vivienne.

"So, what are you going to do with that film?" I asked, pulling her close.

"Ah, wouldn't you like to know!"

"Tell me again why the French aren't winning the war?" I started to kiss her.

She laughed again, her shoulders relaxing in my embrace.

"Oh, but we are, *Monsieur* Tusley. We are."

TWENTY-NINE

Occupied France

SEPTEMBER 1943

Terry

Vivienne and I set off together after midnight in her rickety borrowed car. We ditched it about three-quarters of a kilometer out of Paris city limits and walked the rest of the way in the dark, entering at rue de Crimée after midnight. We arrived at the old cobblestone avenue I remembered, in the middle of the 19th Arrondissement. But the cafés on the corners were empty. The people, missing. The lights, extinguished. Everything was closed, and it was eerily quiet.

I stopped, stunned at the stark absence of the very essence of the Paris nightlife I knew, even under the Occupation. I'd only been gone a few weeks. I fingered the strap of the leather case holding my Zeiss.

"Where is everybody?" I asked.

"Dead or hiding," Vivienne said flatly.

The trains had seemed like enough of a nightmare. Paris was not only occupied, it had been knocked unconscious.

"The AP bureau should be right here," I said, dismayed.

"Nothing is the same. I had rooms up there, rue de Limone," Vivienne whispered. "I will return for good, after the Nazis are gone."

"I'll remember to come find you there."

"*Oui.* You will come here to find me, Terry Tusley," she said firmly. "*Mais maintenant*, let us locate *mon ami* Cameron. *Suis-moi*!" And with that, she sprinted forward in the dark. After a few quick lefts and rights, she headed down an alleyway, and I stayed close to her.

"Where the hell are we going?" I asked, breathless.

"*Là*," she said, pointing.

A woman emerged from the darkness of a *boulangerie*. Her dress hung from her like curtains.

"*Nous recherchons un photographe Britannique*," Vivienne said to her.

"*Bonsoir*, Vivienne, *bonsoir, vite, vite, par ici…*" the woman whispered, her voice raspy in the night.

"She knows your name," I said in surprise.

"Of course," Vivienne replied. With a faint nod, the woman guided us into her shop, then out the back and along the street, where another matron met us, and then yet another.

"Vivienne!" Someone gestured from a doorway. We dashed toward it and threw ourselves through the open door.

Three women stood just inside. Upon seeing Vivienne, they covered her with kisses on each cheek. Vivienne stepped back and introduced me.

"Terrance Tusley, *un photographe international*," she said, bowing her head.

"*Ah, un photographe*," one said admiringly, and they all echoed her, nodding.

Without further ceremony, they pushed us out the back. Vivienne ran a few steps ahead and scurried through an open cellar door that protruded from the cobblestone alleyway. I followed her down a set of ancient stairs that led underground. As we descended the stone staircase to a dimly lit hallway, I detected a faint rattling sound, muffled behind the thick walls that surrounded us.

Teletype machines.

Vivienne and I looked at each other.

"I think we've finally found the AP bureau," I said.

Before she could respond, a door opened a few feet away, flooding the hall with light. Two men emerged, their faces obscured in the shadows. I grabbed Vivienne and pulled her behind me.

"Who the hell are you?" I growled, trying to sound more menacing than I felt.

One of them looked at his watch. "Late as always, Tusley. Good thing I'm a patient man."

I would recognize Tom Young's haughty voice anywhere. He stood before us dressed in a Nazi uniform.

"What the…" I said.

"I'm not patient, however," the man behind him said. "And we need to get going."

"Cameron!" Vivienne squealed. "*Quelle surprise*!"

She ran to him, nearly knocking him over. As my eyes adjusted to the wavering light, I noticed Cameron Plumb had more equipment strapped to his body than I'd ever seen one man carry. Two duffle bags hung from him now, one with the tip of a tripod sticking out.

"Good to see you alive," I grunted, peering at Cameron over the top of Vivienne's head.

The next thing I knew, two German officers appeared next to Tom.

"Don't worry, they're with me. I'll explain on the train," Tom said, inviting no argument.

Tom and the two other men hustled me, Cameron, and Vivienne through a labyrinth of tunnels to the Jourdain Metro station where we stepped onto a waiting train, which, like the station, was empty.

Just before I made it to my seat, I noted a Nazi outside my window, standing over a cowering man near the tracks, a gun pointed at the poor man's head. I sat down and watched them, presuming the Nazi hadn't seen us get onto the train. Cameron sat across from me, and Vivienne sat beside him. Tom and the two men settled at the back of the train car. Everyone was looking out the window. The Nazi was screaming something unintelligible at the man, and I knew this scene would not turn out well. I thought about pulling out my Zeiss, but after a glance at Cameron, I hesitated. He was shaking his head.

"All right, children," Tom said, placing one hand on Cameron's shoulder. "All you need to know right now is that you're part of a very important mission. No talking, until my Cameron says it's alright."

And with that, Tom spun around and sprinted to the back of the compartment, dropped into an empty seat between his two men, and promptly fell asleep.

We three looked at each other but said nothing. Cameron turned his face to the window. As the train pulled out and sped past dozens of stations in the dark—Longueau, Amiens, Etaples, Boulogne Sur Mer—the hours stretched on. We were silently racing northwest, toward the coast of France, but I had no idea why. Night slowly turned to day.

Finally, I couldn't take the suspense any longer. Tom wouldn't tell us anything until his precious Cameron said it was okay. I nudged Cameron's knee with mine, trying to avoid awaking Tom or his men.

"Cameron. *Cameron*!" I hissed. "Where is Tom Young taking us?"

Cameron struggled to take his attention off the window. "Did I ever tell you about the night of July 27, 1942?" he asked, pulling the straps of his heavy bags over his head.

Apparently, he thought it was safe to talk now. I glanced back at Tom. Dead asleep. Vivienne and I exchanged glances.

"There was a production of *A Midsummer Night's Dream*," Cameron continued, in a sleepy voice, as if recounting a dream. "Behind Place Pigalle."

Vivienne watched him, a rapt expression on her face. "*Dites-nous…*" she said. "Tell us."

Cameron finally also glanced back at Tom and his men. All three were snoring now, and I spied the top of a flask protruding from Tom's pocket. Cameron cleared his throat dramatically, leaned forward on his elbows, and fixed me and Vivienne with a mischievous look.

Here we go again, I thought. The guy was a born storyteller.

"In the center of Paris," Cameron began, "…arranged by Madame Lily Pastré, a one-night only, open-air performance was planned. The orchestra was comprised of two dozen Jewish musicians. It was the most beautiful, the most daring act of defiance, to keep the flame of culture alive in Paris. All costumes and scenery were burned afterward. The Germans never found anyone associated with the play. They knew about it, of course, but they could never capture anyone or do anything about it." He sat back with a sigh. "I wish I had been there."

Annoyed with the digression, I turned to Vivienne. "Where exactly do you think we're headed?"

She smiled. "We are going to be asked to be in a play, *comme les acteurs* that Cam loves so well."

Cameron nodded.

"What's in the bags, Cameron?" I asked, impatience clear in my voice.

"All-weather gear, Terry."

At that moment, Tom stood straight up, eyes red and angry. "Listen up, you three. I'm not the enemy, so relax, will you? I work for the British press, and the government. Both. As Cameron here well knows. There's a name for me, I don't much like it…" he paused, sitting back down.

His henchmen continued to snore away.

"Propagandist," said Cameron. He wasn't smiling, and I glanced at Tom to see how he'd take this.

"Yes. That's right!" Tom said with warmth. "I know how to get around, and I provide what's needed. Encoded messages, secret lodgings, false papers, all that. We have been given a job."

He paused, letting us absorb.

"Why are you telling us this?" I asked.

"Because you need to know, when we get to Calais, to just do what I tell you to do."

I kept my mouth shut, mulling this over.

Cameron piped up. "See? I told you, back at the London Docks, that once Tom helped you—once he gave you an opportunity, like the photo shoot with *Churchill*..." The Prime Minister's name practically dripped from Cameron's lips.

"What? That I'd owe him something in return?" I asked, incredulous.

"Oh, Cameron," Tom chided in a tut-tut tone. "Can't you just forget it? I had to give him *something*."

THIRTY

Occupied France

SEPTEMBER 1943

Terry

I sat forward, all ears now.

"Here's what you need to know, people," Tom continued. "When we get to the station stop, we'll be near the coastal village. A local car mechanic will arrive to move us in his lorry to a house close to the sea, and from there, once we hear the all-clear on the wireless, he'll lead us down the cliff—a cliff so steep I'm hoping the Germans won't see us—to the sea."

"Okay, Cameron, why are you playing along?" I asked.

"I'm just building my portfolio, as you are."

I sank back in my seat. Tom cleared his throat, impatient.

"*As I was saying*, our whole party will then wait in the caves for the dinghies to ferry us out to a ship hiding offshore." He was lacing and unlacing his fingers nervously.

"For what purpose?" I asked.

"To photograph the most extensive deception ever planned in the history of war. Well, modern war. We'll be part of—"

Before Tom could finish, a roar filled the railcar. The train came to a screeching halt, throwing Tom forward onto the floor. Smoke filled the railcar. Tom's men—suddenly and unpleasantly awakened by the roar—shoved us through the gaping hole at the front of the car, but not before Cameron flung his camera bags and all his equipment across his shoulders. Shouting and running, the salty mist filled our lungs as the ground quickly churned to wet sand in a pouring rainstorm.

A second bomb exploded on the tracks behind us. The ground bumped up beneath me. Tom raced past me, his soaking wet form perfect, like an Olympic racer, followed by Vivienne, who bolted past me and was quickly several yards in front of me, keeping her head down in the torrent.

I saw bright flashes of artillery fire from the ridge high above us. A house loomed ahead, and a man stood outside in the rain, frantically waving us in. It had to be the lorry driver. I no longer could find Cameron or Vivienne in the chaos. The house loomed up, a safe shelter, close now. I bypassed the front door and ran around to the far side of the stone building and leaned against the cold, wet outer wall, breathless. Suddenly, Cameron slammed against me. We were both soaked to the skin. The whine of airplanes, low at first, rose to a crescendo over our heads. We looked up simultaneously. The planes had British markings. They were strafing the coastline, trying to protect the men on the beach and the small group of landing craft that were starting to move ashore.

"Get out your camera, Terry!" Cameron shouted to me over the deafening thunder of the airplanes.

"What about Vivienne?" I shouted back.

"Don't worry about her, Terry! She's got more lives than a blinkin' cat!"

Cameron threw his duffle bags onto the ground. I watched with amazement as he assembled a set of cameras on tripods in the downpour.

He punched my arm. "Get—out—your—camera!"

"Right!" I pulled the Zeiss from its rain-soaked case.

"Let's get back there!" Cameron snapped, grabbing his entire setup in two arms like gawky children he was carrying to a playground.

He dashed about twenty yards back to where we'd run from and sheltered himself behind an outcropping of rocks. I ran after him. Rain lashed us sideways. Planes screeched overhead. Cameron quickly set up one camera on its tripod, adjusted his other camera on the second tripod, and pointed them both toward the sky. He then covered both cameras with canvas blankets he must have procured from Tom Young to protect them from the rain. He moved back and forth between the two setups, pressing the shutter on one, then the other, sometimes first looking up with his naked eye, photographing again and yet again the airplanes flying overhead, changing out those bulky film cartridges. He repositioned the second camera to focus on the cliffs where the German antiaircraft gun emplacements were being blown to bits.

I pulled my Zeiss up and pointed it at the sky, standing shoulder to shoulder with him in the bedlam. Spitfire. Mosquito. I tried to position myself, my feet slipping in the wet sand. The rain splattered my lens. I couldn't get a clear shot. The planes were deafening. I swung my head down, keeping the viewfinder glued to my face and out of the rain. Through the lens I caught view of a few dozen men running onto the beach from the landing craft.

"Get a shot of the planes! I'm running out of film!" Cameron yelled over the din, his bag of spent film cartridges weighing him down in the mud.

I turned my attention to some new action on the beach. I could make out the uniform markings of a small band of Canadian special forces trying to land.

Sunlight broke through the storm clouds. The scene was magnificent – of the men charging onto the beach, of the waves crashing around them. I took the first shot, a Pulitzer Prize winner for sure. But in a moment, things changed. The landing craft was hit with German artillery fire from the ridge and exploded into a brilliant blast of broken pieces, helmets and body parts flying everywhere, mocking the heroic planes screeching above our heads.

I clicked the shutter again, taking one photo after another. I trained the camera on one man's face, as he desperately jumped from the landing craft to the beach, capturing the anguish in his features as machine-gun fire from the ridge tore him apart, a gruesome image, but I could not help but be intrigued by the light and shadows of the scene, the white, black, and red colors of the shapes, spectacularly beautiful at the same time. I could hear someone shouting my name in the chaos. I turned and saw Tom Young running toward me, waving his arms wildly.

I knew this is not the heroic story Tom Young wanted to tell about this operation.

It was not the direction he gave to his stooge, Cameron Plumb.

But it was the truth I wanted to expose about the war. I changed film, pocketing the first roll, reloading, and repositioning myself in the chaos. Something struck my shoulder, hard. I pulled my camera from my face to find Tom Young at my side, his face contorted in anger.

"You moron, Tusley! No dead bodies!"

"It's my duty as a journalist, Tom!"

"You are a first-class fool, Terrance Tusley! I'm dispatching you back to where you bloody well came from! Do you see that dinghy over there, about twenty yards away? Run there! You and Cameron, run there now!"

He shoved me forward and practically dragged me to the waiting dinghy that bobbed silently in the water, hidden beyond the beachfront. From a distance, I could see Vivienne was already there, crouched down at the back of the boat with her arms covering her head in the storm. Cameron was standing over her protectively.

When had he left the beach?

Tom and I reached the dinghy, breathless, and then he spun me around like a child.

"Enjoy the ride, asshole. It'll be your last one with me," Tom said, his wet face twisted into a sneer.

He stomped away. Cameron left Vivienne's side and followed Tom like the loyal dog he was, leaving me speechless on the rain-splashed deck of the dinghy.

We rode the dingy in silence to a small, bullet-riddled ship just out of sight from the beach. I boarded the ship, noting how the skipper stood grimacing, holding onto the ship's wheel in a white-knuckled grip. Without another word, the ship raced at breakneck speed across the English Channel. I stood alone at the railing, wind-whipped, watching the gray skies slowly give way to weak sunlight, scanning the waters for a German U-boat. We were all in a state of shock, but a collective sigh of relief emanated from the crew and company when we docked at Dover and lined up to disembark, wet and tired and some of the men bloodied. The minute I stepped onto the planks, Tom was once again by my side, his fist clutching at my jacket.

"Give me your film, Tusley. We can't use any of those shots. National security, all that..." He reached across me for my camera. "At least Plumb had the common sense to photograph the planes overhead."

"What the hell, Tom!" I wrenched myself out of his grasp.

He put his mouth so close to my ear I could feel the heat of his breath. "Can't let it get out about an unsuccessful landing attempt in France, mate, even if it was a deception."

The men filed around us. They looked shaken and weary. I turned and saw Cameron in his seaweed coat, a mess, his equipment hanging all over him. He met my eyes and said nothing. Vivienne hid herself behind him, shivering, her arms wrapped around her body. They swept past me without a word.

At that moment, I hated them both.

"No," I said to Tom. "I'm not giving you my film."

But he seemed not to have heard. He was still attached to me, looking straight ahead now as he muscled me toward the line of metal huts at the far end of the dock.

"What were you thinking, Tusley?" Tom's voice was louder now. "Those brave men gave their lives today on that beach and they are going to be remembered for their heroic effort, not for the disaster you photographed. We're trying to show we are winning the war against the Germans, not losing it!"

"I'm taking photos of the war and the reality of what we're getting into—" I snarled back, but he stopped in his tracks.

"Too dangerous!" He was openly yelling now.

The rest of the men moved around us, glancing back at us. They'd seen arguments before, and they gave us wide berth.

"Too dangerous to what?" I kept my voice low. "Your propaganda campaign? Not the story you want to tell?"

"To the war effort, you idiot!" Tom's blue eyes were bulging. "Millions of lives are at stake, that's why we were risking ours on that beach today!"

"I'm taking photos that reveal the truth about what's really happening! My photographs—*not* Cameron Plumb's—will be in demand by every news outlet in the world!"

"You're a dangerous fool, Tusley. If the public could handle the truth, believe me I'd be the first to tell it to them."

I laughed ruefully at this, but he just stood there, glaring at me.

"Your photos are never going to be published anywhere, Terry Tusley," Tom said quietly. "Never. I will make sure of that. You're too dangerous to the war effort to be out on the loose taking those types of photos."

Before I could even register my shock at what he'd just said about censuring my photographs—forever—he topped it off with a smirk.

"I'm sending you back to Rochester."

"You have no authority over me!" I gasped. "I'm an independent photojournalist!"

"You could be a *dead* independent photojournalist from that stunt on the beach today. You're just lucky your wife has enough influence to keep you alive."

I felt a red-hot anger rise up the back of my neck at his thinly veiled threat, and his casual reference to Francine made me instantly realize just how deeply involved she was in every single move I made in Europe.

In the next moment, Tom Young shouted to two MPs, instructing them to escort me directly to the nearest train station, explaining in great detail that they should stay with me until I was on a ship headed directly back to New York.

In my last defiant move, I ripped the film from the camera, exposing the long ribbon of raw, precious film, and threw it to the ground, grinding it into the dirt with the heel of my boot.

"Now all you have left, Tom, is your fairytale story from your day at the beach."

Tom stared at my ruined film, brown and curled like a dead snake at his feet and took a step backward as if it might yet come alive and bite him. He then quietly pulled out a cigarette and lit it while the two MPs pulled up closer. With a cold look, Tom blew the smoke in my face.

"Have it your way, Tusley. You're not my goddamn problem anymore. I have bigger goals than dealing with fools like you."

He didn't know about the roll of film hidden in my jacket pocket.

"Have it *your* way," I said with a smirk. "The film is destroyed forever."

“Terry!” Vivienne’s voice reached me from the far end of the dock. She started forward, as if to join me, but Cameron held her back. He then nodded at me, his face serious, and adjusted his heavy photo equipment across his lean frame, the bag of spent film cartridges like an albatross around his neck.

I thought back to our conversation in the Resistance tent.

He’d won the duel, hadn’t he? But the war wasn’t over yet.

THIRTY-ONE

Rochester

SEPTEMBER 1943

Terry

Francine was waiting for me when I arrived at the Rochester train station after I'd been banished from Calais by Tom Young.

She was leaning on our Chrysler, smoking a cigarette, dressed in a tight, tailored dress, her curves mirroring the curves of the car.

My prize wife.

"Welcome home, *mon chéri*," she said, letting out a breath of smoke.

I regarded her a moment more, my jaw unclenching for the first time in ages.

"You're good for the eyes, Francine. Where are the children?"

"I left a note for Katie and the boys saying I would be back for a few days. They do not know you are here." Francine smiled. "You and I are going to take a short holiday at our favorite cabin in the woods."

"Perfect."

"Dinner?"

"Not hungry," I said, placing my arm around her waist, aware of the stares of the other passengers disembarking from the train.

"Of course you are, *mon chéri*." She turned and reached inside the open car window. As she leaned into the car, I could see the curves of her statuesque body from the back, from her high heels to her calves, up her long legs to her perfect ass.

And I wasn't the only one noticing.

She turned and handed me a Coke bottle and a sandwich from my favorite deli.

"Get in, darling," she said. "I'll drive."

Nothing more was said until we arrived at the cabin, just as twilight was turning into darkness. The place was old but perfect in every way. Nestled at the end of an abandoned road, it had been our hideaway for nearly twenty years. Anytime Francine needed to drop out of sight, only I knew this was where she was. The lake sparkled outside the cabin windows like a Van Gogh painting in the warm summer night, set in tones of cobalt, blue, and black.

I opened the door to the cabin. It was already lit and a fire glowed in the fireplace. The warm bearskin rug that welcomed us into the living room—its snarl as fierce as its fur was soft—was truly the best part of our home away from home.

Katie had been conceived here, as had Joe.

The well-stocked bar was wide open, the bottle of Crown Royal at the ready. I made myself a Manhattan and then a martini for Francine.

"How did you know I was on that train?" I handed over her drink and she took a sip.

"I received a telegram from England, they travel faster than slow ships."

"From Tom Young?"

She was silent a moment. "I burned it. However, *mon chéri*, it gave me plenty of time to contemplate our situation and plan for your arrival."

Without another word, we finished our drinks. I reached for her, and she buried her face in my neck.

"There is no one but you," I whispered into her hair.

"There is no need to lie to me," she laughed softly. "But we save the best for each other, *non*?"

Lying naked next to me on the old bearskin rug, her body and eyes glowing from the firelight, she looked more comfortable, more at home, than most women in their finest evening gowns. A flicker of memory brought back Vivienne in her too-thin dress, in the old stone courtyard in Lyon, but it disappeared with the scent of my wife's perfume, and the touch of her hand.

"I know everything that happened with Tom Young," Francine whispered.

I stretched my body over hers until there was nothing between us but an errant flicker of firelight.

"And?" I asked, stroking her hair from her face.

"You will have to decide what you will do next." She paused, her eyes dark and liquid. "My darling Terry, what prize will you now pursue?"

I'd had a long time to think on the arduous journey home, dodging mines and U-boats in the Atlantic, watching the faces of the sailors around me, their relief and delight in the welcoming arms of their wives when we reached the docks in New York. On the long train ride up to Rochester, thousands of miles from a war that raged not just to the west of us, but also in the faraway east, I had already decided what prize I was going to pursue.

But it had all depended on the reception I would receive from my wife.

"The lake must be cool and refreshing," I said, pulling her up, her body like reflected marble in the soft light. "Let's run down to the beach."

With a laugh she grabbed an old beach blanket off the sofa and ran buck-naked out into the warm summer air. I followed her, breathless. The sand was cool on our bare feet, and a single cloud loitered in front of the bright new moon. We made love in the water, and as we lingered side-by-side on the beach in the dawning light, I let the dry, sugary beach sand sift through my fingertips and thought of my film, lying dead in the sand at Dover, with Tom's military police ready to strong-arm me out of existence. He'd made it clear I would no longer be able to get my work published. Kodak was the only answer. Back to the basement lab where my passion had been born. To wait it out, until Tom and others like him were no longer a concern. And I wouldn't be able to resume my old side gig with Sam at the *Rochester Observer-Herald*, either.

"Do you understand what happened in Calais, Francine?"

"That is in the past," she whispered. "You did not answer my question, *mon chéri*. What prize will you now pursue?"

I pulled her closer.

"You are the prize, Francine. *Je n'aime que toi.* I love only you."

She threw back her head and laughed.

"We are quite a pair of liars, *non*?"

I searched her eyes, for I knew the truth was there.

"You don't believe that, do you?" I asked.

She reached up and stroked my cheek. "We have been to this place so many times. Not just the cabin. Not just this beautiful lake, swimming in the moonlight together. We have been here as one—together, always together. In any situation, any circumstance. *Comme deux roses...*"

She smiled at me as if the rest of the world simply didn't exist.

"Two roses. Yes." I said, returning her smile. "No thorns. I think I will have to be here for a long while. You don't have to stay in Rochester. Katie and I will manage the house."

"*Oui,*" she said, acknowledging our newest situation in a single breath. "And now we go back to our mortal lives."

"We'll just tell Katie I'm back for good. She doesn't need to know more than that. And..."

"Yes, my love?"

"She could be useful someday. What do you think?"

Francine again threw her head back and laughed, full-throated this time. I tried to keep the surprise off my face.

"Our Katie is not the same—er—*matériel* as you and I." She was serious now.

"I don't think you give Katie enough credit." I stood and pulled Francine up from the sand and wrapped my arms around her, warming her shivering body with mine. "I need to get into Hawk-Eye Works, at Kodak. And we need to keep it quiet."

Francine searched my face, then nodded. "We can do that, I think. But we will need some extra coverage for you, *mon chéri.* I'll ask Ed to call the house, give you one or two assignments. Let Katie pick up the phone."

"Ed, from Blue Star?"

"*Oui*. Then she will think you are doing nearly nothing at Hawk-Eye Works. But still, I must ask... What *will* you be doing there?"

"I'm going to help make film no one can force you to rip out of your camera."

"And how in the world, Terry, do you plan to do that?"

"The film will be in an airplane, flying high above anyone's censoring grasp."

We both looked up to the dome of stars twinkling above us. The night was beginning to wane into the blue hour, with dawn creeping like a thief just beyond Pinnacle Hill.

"Ah. Aerial photography." Francine said in the semi-darkness. "And how long do we have? That project will take years, not months, *mon chéri*."

"We've got a long way to go to catch up to our enemies. I won't be going back to Europe. But I have a favor to ask. I have a roll of film from Calais..."

Francine looked into my eyes and nodded, then she silently pulled the beach blanket off the sand and wrapped herself in it from head to toe, her face hidden briefly in its soft folds.

And in the glow of the blue hour, I was reminded of Cameron Plumb, standing before me that morning in the Resistance tent—his face hidden in the folds of his damned tattered blanket, his big camera and his heavy duffle on the ground at our feet—and I felt the pull to leave her, to go back and finish the duel, knowing that Francine and I were never truly apart, no matter the distance between us.

But Cameron Plumb—and the Pulitzer—would have to wait.

For now.

PART TWO

The Effect

"As photographers, we bridge the chasm between imagination and reality. We are, in a word, essential."

—Cameron Plumb

THIRTY-TWO

Rochester

NOVEMBER 1983

Katie

I remember Dad arriving unexpectedly on the doorstep in the fall of 1943, nabbing a job at Kodak and staying with us—if you could call it that—for almost eight years, between the end of one war and the start of another. I was the best, most practical daughter. I packed his lunch every day and made dinner every night for him and the boys. Time tended to get away from him in the lab, but I had everything at home under control. Mother dropped in occasionally. Frankly, I was happier when she wasn't there.

And then, the first of many calls came.

His name was Ed Mahoney. The photo agency was Blue Star. From their lofty offices in New York City, they'd come across my father's photos from Paris. They needed a stringer. I didn't mention anything to my mother, who seemed to think Dad was at home a lot more than he actually was.

Without any hesitation—or explanation—Dad placed his German-made Zeiss on the mantelpiece, nabbed a brand-new Kodak Retina from a cabinet at work, and threw himself into the assignments. They were small gigs. A couple of trips down to the city, a few train rides to DC to photograph congressmen. It seemed like nothing, and it went on for years. Apparently, his Kodak boss didn't care.

But Harry sure did.

Dad brought back a new issue of *Life* from every jaunt. The magazine had become even more famous for its photography, and we'd recently entered a *police action*, in South Korea, which the magazine was covering in depth. None of my father's city photos ever seemed to make it into the vaunted magazine, and he seemed just fine with that. This surprised me a little, but it was a relief to know he'd stopped chasing the dragon.

Harry, just turned seventeen, followed Dad around the house like his shadow. This was early September 1951, and Harry, by then, had developed an ominous fixation on those big photographs splashed across every page of *Life* magazine.

"How did they get that shot, Dad?" Harry pointed to the latest issue, spread open on the kitchen table after dinner.

"Oh, the photographer can position himself between his subject and the light," Dad said in his typical offhand manner.

"Nice," Harry said, and Dad nodded, whether at Harry or the damn photograph, it was impossible to tell.

A well-lit photo of a Seoul storefront, the frame wide enough to catch the American rifle leaning in the doorway on pages five and six, laid out across the gutter in the middle. An evening shot of children running in the rice fields, so stunning, taken from a safe distance as they ran to the combat unit for shelter, their arms and legs impossibly slender against the backdrop of bamboo.

One day, right around this time, when Dad was away in New York on some crazy assignment he didn't bother to explain to me properly, Harry took a detour after school, down Morris Street to the Rochester army recruiting office.

"Why did you do that, Harry?" Joe asked that evening, sprawled across the living room carpet, chewing on a pencil, college books thrown open. "If I'm not going to Korea, you sure don't have to, little buddy!"

Harry had stood, tall and smiling—smug even—in this, his first adult decision. I was speechless with surprise. Dad's Zeiss stared down at us from its perch on the fireplace mantel. It was like the three of us were looking at Harry, his blond hair, his fair skin, how he glowed with pride. He didn't need to say anything. He didn't even pretend to explain.

As the sun dipped down behind the Adirondack Mountains that surrounded the house, the gathering darkness touched everything but him.

Shoulders back, chin up. He was already a soldier.

Harry, Harry! You were gone to war not two weeks after that fateful decision. What called to you from the photographs? Was it the iridescent black Han River, full-bore on the cover of the *Life* magazines that Dad kept bringing home, Korean junk boats and fishermen, warships silhouetted behind them in the sunset?

Days later, Ed from Blue Star called yet again. Then Dad finally got the courage to tell me what the hell was going on.

"You're going *where*?" I was standing in the kitchen, dish towel in hand.

"Blue Star wants me to photograph the hometown boys landed in Inchon," Dad had replied, trying to sound casual. "Ed said I was perfect for the job."

Fear gathered in my throat.

"What about your very important work at Kodak?" I could hear the pleading tone in my own voice. "Aren't you indispensable or something?"

He smiled at this compliment, but I could see it wouldn't deter him.

He knew he didn't need my permission. And, as they say, when opportunity knocks… besides, they don't give Pulitzers for photographs that show up behind the ads for vacuum cleaners. Even I knew that was his goal. He couldn't hide it, watching year after year as other men won the biggest prize there is.

This was a Page One opportunity for Dad. Both of us knew it. And we had a hometown boy there ourselves, didn't we?

"Ed practically swooned when I mentioned that," Dad smiled brightly.

"Harry being in Korea is bad enough." I frowned. "Having you both in harm's way is what worries me. And I'll be alone here, with Joe off at college."

"I'll be home soon enough," he replied, still smiling. "This isn't a big deal. Just Truman's way of protecting us."

I looked at him skeptically.

"Katie." I could hear the imploring tone in his voice. "Truman fired MacArthur almost five months ago. It's a big deal to dismiss your commanding officer in wartime. Truman needs some good press."

"Yeah, right. That's why you're going. You have a soft spot for Truman."

"No, I want to see Harry," he reassured me. "Nothing'll happen. I guarantee it."

A moment passed.

"Sure, you do," I said, wiping my hands on my dishcloth.

Without any further warning or notice, Dad was on a plane out of LaGuardia and made his way somehow onto a cargo ship departing from the Navy port in San Diego, ecstatic to be back in the action again.

And, of course, happy at the prospect of seeing Harry.

At least, that's what I believed at the time.

THIRTY-THREE

Near Seoul, South Korea

SEPTEMBER 1951

Terry

Harry'd been assigned to the Comms unit as a specialist. It wasn't hard to track him down. In a few days, we were standing side-by-side, Harry and me, next to a humming teletype machine, sweating our asses off inside a converted rice silo in the jungle surrounding Inchon. He showed me the side of his canteen. It was plastered with newspaper clippings of my old shots from Paris. The few that made it into print.

"How did you ever find those?" I asked, humbled and proud.

"Oh, I can track things down when I want to," Harry said, his arms crossed neatly over his chest, his uniform somehow crisp in the humid air.

I smiled in wonder at my boy's ingenuity.

"You were there!" he exulted. "You photographed the heat of battle!"

"Well, I did my best..."

The teletype machine rattled to life.

"Those photographs helped save the world from the Nazis!" Harry's youthful exuberance rose above the clatter. "And now we have to do the same with the Chinese, the red commies!"

"Harry, you shouldn't believe everything you're told," I started to say, but he cut me off.

"What if this were Rochester, Dad? Wouldn't you want me to help if it was our home?"

"But it's *not* our home, Harry. It's just scenery." I felt like this was a teaching moment, to make him understand what was real and be able to separate it from some cockamamie story.

He looked at me, uncomprehending.

"Remember, Harry… they fired MacArthur," I whispered, leaning in so no one could hear. "What kind of war are they running when they fire the commanding officer?"

His face took on an unsettling blankness. "Dad, you know better than anyone that the facts can be twisted up to say anything."

I stared at him, his stern expression, marveling at how well he'd been trained. And in short order, too.

A tiny ribbon of worry infiltrated my brain, but he elbowed me gently.

"Hey Dad, don't stress about it, okay? You did your part. It's my turn now, right?"

He reached over and pulled a thin paper sheet off the teletype.

"Word must be getting out that we're here," Harry said, scanning the paper. "*You* found me with no problem." He gestured to the men standing a few feet away. "They're not happy right now."

"Well, it's my job to find you," I started to say, but again he cut me off.

"Yeah, I guess that's why they call it the free press." He

frowned. "Hey! Come to think of it, somebody came by yesterday, looking for you." Harry poked his finger into my shoulder.

"Me?" I asked, startled.

I just got here. Who would be asking for me?

Harry got a faraway look, then he snapped his fingers. "A Mister Cameron Plumb! That's it. He wanted to know if you were around. He said he was going to Wonsan Harbor. I wish I could see those big Navy ships!"

Before I could register this news, Harry clapped me on the back. "We're definitely pulling out today, Dad, so you're lucky you caught me. Want to come along? It'll be way more exciting than this old rice silo!"

"No, I'll just take the photo they sent me for, with the other hometown boys, and then be on my way," I said absently, my mind still focused on Cameron Plumb. He was here in Korea, goddammit.

"Is anyone else here from Rochester?" I asked Harry, trying to distract myself.

"Inky's cousin is in our unit, I'll go grab him," Harry said, just as an imposing figure appeared outside the silo's screen door.

"Tusley—now!" the man barked at Harry.

Harry gave me a quick nod and joined a group of young fellows standing outside with the staff sergeant. I followed him out, the flimsy screen door slamming shut behind me, and I pulled my camera to my eye. They were assembled in a semicircle just outside the door in the narrow courtyard. I tried to find the shot, maneuvering around the group. The sergeant was old—appropriately grizzled for the photo.

"Fellas, raise your hand," he said, looking at the boys from under bushy eyebrows. "... if any of you has combat experience."

None of them, Harry included, raised a hand. The sergeant glanced sideways at me for just a moment, and my heart skipped a beat. Harry stood at attention, his blond hair just catching the sunlight, his pale hands clasped together, almost in prayer. Then I took the shot.

"Are you that Cameron Plumb fella?" The sergeant growled at me, his face red. "I heard they sent some damn photographer around here yesterday! I thought he was told to bugger off!"

"No! I'm not Plumb!" I said, highly insulted at the mix-up. "I'm here to photograph the hometown boys! And one of those boys is my son, right here—"

"That's *all* we need," the sergeant sighed. "You're done here, mister. Fall in, boys!"

Without another look at me, Harry followed the rest out of courtyard, marching away, shoulder to shoulder. A light rain started to fall. I quickly snapped one or two more photos.

Harry would be fine. This wasn't a real war, anyway. I would drop my film off at the nearest AP bureau.

And turn my attention to Cameron Plumb.

I'd seen Cameron's name on a photo credit when I was in Grand Central Station, standing at a newsstand. The *New York Times*. Front page. The MacArthur Special Investigation. The senators had to be positioned just right to make them look like they were hard at work, something Cameron was expert at, damn him.

In the *Times* photo, the one with Cameron's credit in extra-large type displayed across the bottom, books were piled on a vast mahogany table. Important-looking papers were spread out everywhere.

Cameron's photo had Senator Cain from the great state of

Washington, mouth open, pointing to something just out of frame. The Senate chambers loomed behind him, the perfect backdrop. Pure Cameron Plumb. They'd probably spent the morning deciding where to sit to get just the right light, taken the shot, and started drinking at some DC saloon at noon.

And here I was, wasting time in the Comms office.

Wonsan Harbor was dangerous. Not a place I'd expect to see Cameron Plumb, actor and director extraordinaire, his Zephyr coat a costume from a play. Master of the setup.

It had been years since I'd seen him. While I'd labored away in Kodak's basement, Cameron had managed to get himself where the pictures were.

I was a long way from Wonsan Harbor, but transports were leaving every hour from Inchon. All that firepower. The junk boats, providing perspective to emphasize the sheer size of the US warships. I could hitch a ride if I hurried.

From a distance, I saw Harry turn around and gesture for me to come along with them. I pointed to my camera, shook my head, and waved him away. I had more important things to do. I'd come back and find him later.

THIRTY-FOUR

Near Seoul, South Korea

SEPTEMBER 1951

Terry

The Pirate and *the Pledge*. The boys on my transport out of Inchon could not stop talking about the loss of those two minesweepers in Wonsan Harbor, only days before, that had killed a dozen men.

We were steaming forward to the harbor to join the blockade under cover of night on a ship that had seen better days. The paint was peeling and the rigging looked ancient, evidence that they were pulling every ship out of mothballs for this blockade. I found myself in the company of a dozen other newsmen standing in a line on the upper decks, leaning over the railing, cameras hanging, press badges flying in the stiff breeze. We could get blown up, die any minute, the cameras and the film lying at the bottom of the harbor. The exhilaration of it all filled my lungs.

Cameron must be on shore, grabbing all the photo opportunities he could. Or, more accurately, creating them.

When the hell would I get off this heap?

The ship finally slid up to the dock just as dawn broke on the horizon. The captain's mate shepherded us down the gangway. I stepped onto the docks, birds cawing over my head, when I noticed an officer in full dress uniform standing at attention about twenty yards away, his white-gloved hand shielding his eyes from the breaching sunlight, scanning us as we disembarked. A man leaned out from behind the officer, his coat billowing around him like a sail, pointing directly at me. The officer straightened his hat and marched in my direction, pulling a letter from his breast pocket. A white scarf fluttered in the breeze, draped across his arm. The sun was full on him, making him glow.

He stepped up in front of me.

"Mr. Tusley, I regret to inform you..."

My knees buckled and I dropped to the slimy dock.

Cameron Plumb was suddenly beside me. "Tusley, my God, I'm so sorry, old boy."

"No! I just saw him, I just talked to him!" I was gasping for air.

The photographers from the ship started running down the dock, gathering around us, the whir of advancing knobs filling the air, the men like seagulls on meat. I covered my head with my hands.

Cameron's voice cut through the fog.

"Give him some room, will you?"

"Sir, are you all right? I can arrange to send you home with your son's body, there's a freight leaving tomorrow—"

"No!" I shouted. "Anywhere but home! I cannot go home!"

Cameron crouched down to me.

"Move aside, you idiots!" he yelled up to the suffocating crowd. "Can't you see he's—"

I grabbed at his coat. "Where will I go? Tell me! Where?"

Cameron held me in his gaze. I couldn't break the connection.

Annie's eyes.

"You'll go to Vivienne," Cameron said. "To Paris, old man. I'll make the arrangements." He put his arms around me, his face close to my ear. "Me mum told me a story about you and your Francine, I spoke with her after you were in Solihull. How your wife saved us long ago. You'll disappear, if that's what you want, old boy."

I nodded. All words had left me.

The officer was looking down at us, his face pale white. The photographers had reached us. They jostled for space around Cameron, cameras up, shutters clicking in the wind. I felt the world around me swim out of view, blackness taking over.

"But—" I heard the officer sputter.

"We're brothers, you see," Cameron said to him, draping his voluminous coat around me.

THIRTY-FIVE

Paris

JULY 1953

Terry

Harry's body was flown to Arlington National Cemetery. That was home for him now.

Cameron had cabled Vivienne the day it happened and pulled some significant strings to get me to Paris. He got me listed me as MIA—my last known official contact with Harry's platoon was at the Comms hut.

Gone without a trace, like the son I'd effectively led into battle.

In my saner moments, which were few at the beginning of my exile, I'd realized that Cameron had to have paid off that officer at Wonson Harbor. Maybe he'd taken a photo or two of the guy in full uniform for his sweetheart back home. Photographs that made people happy were Cameron's currency. But I had to put it aside now. I was grateful to him and would find a way to pay him back.

Cameron's next magic trick was even more impressive. He'd

used his connections to issue me temporary travel papers and a French-made field jacket with a *tricolore* patch on the arm. He'd somehow booked me onto a French cargo plane, with no one asking questions.

Everyone back home assumed the real me had gotten killed with Harry in the mountains of South Korea. In a way, they were right. The man I was…well, he existed no longer. No one was looking for me. Even Francine would be unable to track me down.

I'd arrived at Vivienne's doorstep in Paris, broken and alone. The shock of Harry's death and ensuing guilt took forever to process. She had been through it all, losing her brother and family to the Nazis, and she took care of me in that apartment on rue de Limone, the one she swore she'd return to after the Nazis were gone.

Vivienne stayed with me all day—dozing next to me on her bed, our legs tangled in soft cotton sheets. Seasons cycled outside from fall to winter to summer, then back again to fall, but I could not leave the apartment. I knew, somewhere deep inside, that more than a year had passed. After supper, she would dose me with Cointreau until I fell asleep in my chair. In my stupor, I could hear her slip out, and I couldn't blame her.

But I started to wonder where she was going.

One night, I glimpsed a sparkling dress beneath her coat as she turned to leave the apartment. It was nearly eleven—far too late for anything respectable in the city of Paris.

"Viv, where do you go every night?" I put down the glass of Cointreau, untouched for once. Her lovely eyes traveled from the glass to my face, and she smiled.

"Ah, *mon chéri*. I have been waiting for you to ask."

She walked over to a white curio cabinet that sat in the corner of her sitting room and opened the top drawer. I followed her, standing behind her, stroking her hair. She pulled out a picture postcard with great ceremony. She showed me the back first, with its blank space for the message, the address, and the stamp.

Then she slowly turned it over, but her smile faded when I wrenched the postcard from her hand. There, on the front of the card was the Vivienne I knew ten years ago—from our improvised photo shoot in Lyon. A photochrome print, no white border, the color printed out to the edges of the cardboard stock.

Vivienne, upside down. The light so golden across her half-naked figure.

She'd barely aged since the shot was taken.

Imprinted across the bottom were the words: *Mettez Votre Monde à L'envers!*

Turn Your World Upside Down.

"Does this make you forget your sorrow, *mon chéri*?" she asked.

I was speechless.

"It is the title of my show, at *Chez Claudia*," she giggled. "I am a singer."

I could sense her searching my face for a response, but I couldn't take my eyes off the postcard.

"We can add your photo credit to the next batch we print, *non*?" I could hear the doubt creeping into her voice.

"Not the type of work I want to be particularly famous for, Viv." I handed it back to her, frowning.

"I thought you'd be honored." She was pouting now. "It is a beautiful image. Many people have asked me who took the photograph. It is like art."

She again held it out to me, and in the dim light of her apartment it looked like a painting.

"It is *life*, Terry. It is survival. How you say—"

I interrupted her, suddenly seeing it clearly. "It is more than survival, isn't it, Viv? It is triumph."

"*Oui*." Her voice was small. "I am the only one left of my family. A family forced to wear those hated yellow stars, until they were made to disappear forever. But *I* am now a star. I must make music, like *Madame* Wanda Landowska! I must sing. I must be seen. And you have helped me to do that. With this photograph."

"I'm happy for you, Viv." I sighed. "You got what you wanted. You and your heroine… what's her name? Wanda."

"But there was something you wanted too, Terry! You wanted a prize. I remember this clearly. I am not your prize, but this postcard shows me you will someday have what you desire."

She moved closer. Together, we silently gazed at the card in her hands, both of us suddenly full of the memories that came rushing forward—of the happy times before war, the bewildering times during war, and the things we loved and thought we'd kept, and the things we'd unexpectedly lost.

I looked at her in amazement, the postcard like a signpost before us.

Women like Vivienne could not be conquered, would not be vanquished.

Vivienne, and Francine—perhaps Annie Plumb—all the women they represented would fight for their place in this world, no matter the cost. And any of us who stood beside them would be better for it.

"We haven't just survived, have we, Viv?" I smiled, the new feeling of hope so unfamiliar that I felt like my face was cracked in half.

"No Terry," she said, turning to me. "We *lived*."

Without another word exchanged between us, we both knew. It was time for me to come back from the dead.

I arrived by ship at the Port of Quebec a week later, showing up unannounced at my mother-in-law Dominique's house early in the morning. The shock of seeing me was too much. Her face went ashen, and she dropped her cup of tea, the fine bone china shattering at my feet.

"*Non*. It cannot be. You are dead," she gasped.

Over her shoulder, down the hallway, I saw my wife approach us. Regal and magnificent, the light behind her, surrounding her. A young man walked next to her, looking at me with an insolent expression. Francine, five years older than me, could still ensnare any lover she wanted. She was past fifty, but she looked as beautiful as ever.

Les Filles du Roi, I thought with an inward smile.

"Terry, *mon chéri*, I wondered when you would finally appear," Francine said, her dark red lipstick vivid against her white skin. No trace of tears for Harry. Just a mask of peace. She hadn't believed the MIA story, not for a minute. But she was here for me now. That was who we were.

"Neither of us ever knows, *n'est-ce pas*, Francine?" I dropped my bag and pushed past Dominique.

"*Pas de roses sans épines*, Terry," my wife said. She nudged her man aside and out of her way. "There are no roses without thorns."

Dominique slinked off, muttering under her breath.

That night, in our bed in Dominique's house, Francine and I made love wordlessly, but the emotion had never been so strong. She did not question my absence, trusting that, somehow, I would come back to her. Whether she suspected the reason for my long absence was the secret Kodak work, or something else, I did not know or care. And I was equally unconcerned with her young men, for I knew who she was and had accepted it long ago.

We sensed the morning light coming for us like a hunter, ready as always to shatter our solitude. But the hunter had a companion this reunion night.

Harry. His ghost waited for us in the corner of the ornate bedroom.

The moon shone into the tall window, casting its white beam across Francine's body. The St. Lawrence River flowed past Dominique's vast lawn as dawn stealthily approached, the barges gently slipping downstream.

Finally, my wife spoke.

"I must tell you about Katie," Francine whispered, surprising me so much I sat up.

"Something's happened to Katie?" I asked, suddenly regretful for being so completely out of touch with my wife. With the rest of my children.

"*Non*," Francine said quickly, brushing her hand across my face in the moonlit room. "But there is something I must show you." She stood and wrapped herself in a satin robe. "*Two* things," she said, correcting herself.

I got dressed while Francine rummaged through the antique desk near the window, my mind filled with mixed-up thoughts about Harry and Katie and Joe.

She turned and handed me two cards, and for one foolish moment I expected to see Vivienne's upside-down photograph splashed across them.

But, no.

One was Harry's funeral announcement, the Army insignia engraved in full color at the top, and my heart caught in my throat. Tears swarmed my eyes, and I could not look at it. I glanced up at Francine, but her expression was inscrutable.

The second card had pink flowers on it.

We Are Pleased to Announce
The Wedding Vows of Katherine Tusley and Manuel Price
St. Augustine's Church
Two O'Clock P.M. on June 7, 1953

"Katie got *married* last month…?" I said in disbelief. "Who the hell is Manuel Price?"

Francine sat me back down on the bed, her hand gently resting on my shoulder.

"There was no real wedding, just a few neighbors. Katie was devastated, losing you and Harry," Francine began. "The funeral was terrible for her. She assumed you'd been taken prisoner, as well. She was nearly catatonic."

I felt a rage build inside—at my lack of courage, my escape to Paris. Francine must never know the specifics.

And Katie would never forgive me.

"Come back, Terry," Francine nudged me. "You are very far away. I know this is hard, but we are strong together, *non*?"

"Yes," I said, hoping she couldn't read my distress in the dimness of the room.

"Harry's funeral was a solemn occasion at Mount Arlington

cemetery, but I created a… diversion." Francine took my face in her hands, her eyes wide with sympathy for me.

"We lost a son!" My voice was a choke, and I thought I heard someone outside the bedroom door.

"Shhh!" Francine held steady, but she glanced quickly at the door. "*Maman*! Go away!"

A soft shuffling out in the hall, then silence. Francine turned her attention back to me.

"Of course, this is terrible, *mon chéri*. But from the rose petals we scatter, we must find new life."

I thought of Vivienne's words, so similar, and could barely breathe. Francine stared into my eyes.

"I met Manny Price at the Pentagon. He is a new recruit, what Americans call up-and-coming. He is all business. I like him, Terry. I've worked with him. He was perfect for Katie. I invited him to the funeral, and he understood my ask."

"What do you mean?" I asked, alarmed at what Francine was implying. Had she reached into our own daughter's heart, and planted a spy there?

Francine dropped her hands from my face. "She was mostly alone in that house for weeks before I introduced her to Manny. It was dangerous, Terry. I cannot say why, but *Maman* and I worried about her, day and night."

"Why didn't you bring Katie and Joe up here?"

Francine laughed. "Joe is in the PhD program at the university in Rochester. He is already being groomed by Kodak. And you know that Katie is not *matériel* for this work. We needed to find a safe place for her. And that place is with Manny, in Washington DC. He works there, for Lockheed."

"Stop," I said. "Enough."

The sun had risen fully now. I looked around the room. My camera bag sat on the floor. It felt like the only normal thing, the only thing I could relate to, in the room.

"Where should I go now, Francine?" My voice was barely above a whisper. "What should we tell—" I choked again. "—the children?"

"People never talk of what happens in a war zone, Terry. And our … remaining children… they are both adults now. I would not allow anyone to declare you…"

I watched as she momentarily lost her composure with the enormity of it all. I placed my hand on hers, and she gathered the strength to continue.

"The children will accept this," she said. "Joe is still living in the house. I will inform him. And I will telephone Katie and Manny as well. As far as they are all concerned, you have returned from your ordeal, and they are not to ask any questions. I will also let Kodak know, of course."

Francine then floated to the vanity and sat down in front of the mirror. She began to pin up her hair. "Of course, in my mind, *mon chéri*, you should go home, to our house in Rochester." Her tone was decisive. The old Francine.

"And do what?" I asked bleakly.

But I knew her.

Our deal, our arrangement.

"Should I assume you will be calling Ed at Blue Star, too, Francine?"

She smiled at me in the mirror, and I had no doubt.

This conversation was over.

THIRTY-SIX

Rochester

JULY 1953

Terry

A few days after I left Francine in Quebec, I woke up covered in a cold sweat, the living room spinning around me. It was the middle of the night, and I'd fallen dead asleep in my old La-Z-Boy. The TV was still on, blaring discordant organ music in the empty room. Its black-and-white screen flickered in the dark. I squinted at it, my head pounding, eyes bleary from one Manhattan too many.

Some woman was banging away at a huge piano, the keyboards set in a double-decker, her hands flying so fast they blurred. She finished with a grand flourish, triumphant.

Wavy letters crawled across the bottom of the screen: Wanda Landowska ... Famous... Polish... Harpsichordist.

The clock struck midnight, and the station went off the air. After a minute of staring blankly at a test pattern, I finally realized I knew that name.

La belle Wanda, Vivienne's heroine. Live and on the air.

She'd made it out, just like Vivienne had said, and she'd made it big time.

I got up and flicked off the goddamn TV. The silence surrounded me, deep and impenetrable.

And where the hell was Joe? Didn't he—supposedly—still live here? I'd been home for days, no sign of him.

An empty bottle of Crown Royal rested on its side by my chair, a parting gift from my wife before she told me to pull myself together and essentially kicked me out of Dominique's house. I looked dejectedly at the potato chips on the carpet, remembering how well Katie kept house before I'd left for Korea. I dropped to all fours to pick them up. I needed to make at least a passing attempt to impress Katie's new husband. They were coming all the way up from Washington, DC on Saturday.

Francine had painted a glowing picture of Manny. He sounded like a stable guy. Solid. She said Joe would be here to get dinner set up and corral his new girlfriend to help. Francine hadn't met Joe's girlfriend yet but she already didn't like her.

Femme frivole, she'd sniffed.

Typical Francine.

Joe would have to find time between grad school and his new job at Kodak to help me welcome the newlyweds home for a small party, to make up for the lack of a wedding.

It was the least we could do.

I dug out a bent matchbook from under the chair. *Bagg's Bar and Grill.* I sat back on my haunches, examining it like it was some sort of clue.

So, that's where you must be, Joe. The old Kodak hangout. Every engineer I knew rolled into that dump at one time or another. They were probably throwing darts in the back room reserved just for the Kodak guys. Late night, drinking, dropping darts on purpose so Joe's girlfriend would have to bend over to pick them up, Joe laughing, and they'd all be laughing too.

Just a great time out on the town.

My old buddies were likely slapping Joe on the back, saying how the apple didn't fall far from the tree. How glad they were I'd been found. A bunch of crap, all of it.

Did Joe ever think about Harry? How Harry would never get a chance to do anything fun?

I'd lost the best thing I had. Something real, made of flesh, my flesh. Someone who cried real tears for the infirmity of a president.

I glanced at the fireplace mantel, my bones heavy from lack of sleep. Harry's official military-issue photograph had been put in a frame with care, probably by Katie. Harry's young face, stern and white, stared out at me. Next to it, my Zeiss, ten years since I'd last touched it, gleaming chrome against black, its one eye staring at me, as well. With an effort, I lifted it off the mantelpiece.

The camera felt heavy and outdated, filmless and useless, but I threw the strap over my head and wound the advancing knob until it hit the stop. The severe mechanical sound instantly filled the living room with dreams and ghosts, and I had to rub my bloodshot eyes to get them to stop.

Then I reached up and pulled Harry's picture frame from the mantel.

I cradled Harry's photograph like a baby, searching for any imperfections. There were none. His collar with its various pins and medals fit tight against his throat. A wisp of his blond hair swept out from the military cap. He had Francine's aquiline nose, her cheekbones. He was the spitting image of her, but his eyes were different—less liquid, less inviting. He had the cold eyes of a soldier. Vacant eyes.

I'd tried to photograph those same faces in Calais.

But they were another son's eyes, another father's grief.

I trudged back to the La-Z-Boy, the Zeiss around my neck, still holding onto Harry's photograph. I yanked the lever on the side and the chair bounced flat like a soldier's cot.

This was as good as I deserved. Blotto. Like old paper, soaked with ink. The house felt like an abandoned shelter. Isolated. Disconnected things left behind. Full of silent stories. Stories that ended before they could truly begin.

I reached up and turned off the lamp, remembering how my father would leave me in the darkness without saying goodbye, to go and chase his goddamn muse.

I would make it up to Harry. Somehow.

THIRTY-SEVEN

Rochester

JULY 1953

Terry

The thumping of feet echoed from the porch stairs in the early morning light, and I was jolted awake. I kicked the empty bottle of Crown Royal under the sofa and replaced Harry's picture on the mantel just as Joe rushed through the front door. He didn't see me. I stood in the shadows of the living room, watching him for a moment.

He was bigger than I remembered.

He bolted up the stairs, and I suddenly noticed I was still wearing my Zeiss around my neck like a complete idiot. I quickly placed it back on the fireplace mantel and, in a New York minute, he was back down in a fresh change of clothes. He started down the hallway to the kitchen, then paused. He'd noticed my duffle resting on the floor, next to the telephone table. His head was tilted at an angle, his back to me. I could almost see the quizzical expression on his face.

"Hey, Joe," I said.

He didn't move or turn around. "What."

"Hey, son, let's catch up after you get done with classes today, maybe dinner at Bagg's?"

"Catch up? Yeah, that's realistic." He turned toward me now and pulled his car keys from his jeans pocket. But then he seemed to change his mind. "Let's go sit down, Dad," he said with a small smile.

I detected a tone, but it was probably my imagination. It had been two years since I'd seen him, and I was delighted that he would stay and talk a bit. He'd grown into a full-fledged man. It would be good to have a heart-to-heart. I plopped down onto the La-Z-Boy. He sat facing me, rigid in the opposing chair, teetering on the edge of his seat.

"So—" I began. "How's school going? What are your plans after you finish?"

"Well, Dad, you of all people should know. I plan to be a researcher at Kodak."

He was staring at me intently, with eyes just like Harry's. "Unless—in your wisdom—you'd recommend a different path. Logic would dictate you've had a lot of time to think about life over the past two years, being MIA and all."

I gasped, but he continued, the icy stare unyielding. "And *my* future, if not Harry's. Theoretically, you were *with* Harry, or somewhere nearby, when he died. So, Katie and I—*our* well-being, *our* welfare—should have been all you were thinking about. Correct?"

I felt like I'd been slapped. He leaned forward, glancing up at the Zeiss on the mantel behind me. "I kind of wondered, when Mom told me you were coming home, where exactly you'd been, as an MIA. But it doesn't matter now." He waved his hand in the air dismissively. "You're all in one piece, and you're back!" he laughed. "Too bad Katie missed it. She never stopped thinking about you—not for one second."

I felt anger rise in my chest at the lack of respect from my only living son.

"Glad to hear it!" I shouted. "At least she did think about me! And Harry! While you prance around with your college deferment, busy college man! No Korea for you! You wear that damned draft deferment like a loose sweater, something you happened to throw across your shoulder instead of a gun!"

Without another word, he got up and walked out of the house, slamming the screen door behind him. I followed him out, watching from the doorway as his Plymouth Valiant kicked up gravel down the driveway. The blue-and-gold University of Rochester sticker reflected the morning sunlight across his back windshield. The yellow-and-black Kodak parking decal shone from his rear bumper.

I stumbled into the kitchen, my eyes filling with tears.

Stop it, Tusley. You couldn't have changed anything—shouldn't have expected anything else.

It was the homecoming I deserved.

Coffee. I needed some goddamn coffee.

I filled the metal basket with ground-up beans and fitted the lid onto the old enamel coffee pot. The percolator sound echoed across the quiet house like faraway gunfire. I dug around until I found a cup in the pantry. It was uneven, made of clay. I pulled it into the sunlight. It said *Harry* across the front in thick, bright yellow clay letters.

I stood there, stupefied, when the phone rang down the hallway. It had to be Joe, calling from a roadside pay phone to apologize. Still clenching Harry's empty mug, I raced to catch it.

"Tusley?" The familiar gravelly voice burst into my ear, and my heart sank. "Hello? Ya there, buddy?"

"Yes, Ed. I'm here." I placed Harry's mug on the hallway table.

"Great timing, right? Am I right?"

"You were always fucking right, Ed. Until you weren't."

He ignored my remark. "Word's out at Blue Star that you're ready to get the hell out of upstate New York! I heard you were in Paris, buddy. Or was it Canada?"

I could practically see him lean into his phone at his desk in Manhattan, pulling out his umpteenth cigarette from a pack of Lucky's.

No, Tusley. You're done with this. Forever. Not even down to the city. It's over.

"Anyways," he continued. "I don't need to know. Means your passport's good."

"Passport? Wait a minute, Ed..."

"I want you to go back to Korea. I want you to go to Kaesong to photograph the signing of the armistice agreement."

"How the hell can you ask me that, Ed?"

"Because it's what you do," he said before succumbing to a fit of coughing.

The letters on Harry's mug were crooked. One of them was ready to come off. I brushed my index finger across it, fitting it back into place.

"I need to call you back," I said, and hung up.

I rolled the cup around in my palm. I turned it over. Across the bottom, etched in the clay, I recognized Harry's handwriting. *For Dad.*

I stared at the crooked letters, the misshapen cup. The house was as quiet as a cemetery.

I'd done everything I was told to do. Followed every instruction I was given, years of blind devotion, trying to make everyone happy. Joe, Katie, Harry—the entire goal was to do this for them. The plan was that I'd win the prize, and then I'd be done and go right home.

But you didn't go right home, did you, Dad? I imagined Harry addressing me with a mix of humor and gravity. My heart leaped into my mouth, and the Canadian whiskey from last night tasted hideous, as it should.

I looked around at the old house, empty and silent. Like a dead end, or—worse—a road that never ends at all.

Barely thinking, I dialed that old familiar number.

He picked up on the first ring.

"Blue Star Agency, Ed Mahoney speaking."

"I'd need a camera, Ed. I don't know where the Retina is."

I did know. It was buried in the cemetery across the road from Vivienne's apartment. I couldn't stand to look through the viewfinder. Harry was the last image that camera would ever see. And my old Zeiss was officially retired. I would never pick it up again.

"Don't worry about a camera, old man," Ed laughed. "You live in Kodak-land, don't you?"

My mind started clicking—almost involuntarily, I assessed the facts at hand. Ed was right. Kodak was swimming in Signets. It wouldn't take much to go in and take one from a storage cabinet. I knew where they kept extra cameras, the ones people ditched for some cockamamie reason or another. Perfectly good equipment in there, going to waste.

"I'll set up your account again," Ed said hurriedly, sensing my willingness, my weakness. "Now get the next train to New York, and I'll fly you out partway on TWA. I already got you a ticket."

I could feel myself melting into the old me, and it didn't feel wrong.

I cleared my throat. "What are the chances they'll sign?"

"About fifty-fifty," Ed said, the noise of clacking typewriters rising behind his words.

Things were happening again. I could be part of it again.

The prize.

"Fifty-fifty?" I quizzed him. "That's not so great, is it?"

"Life's a crap game, Tusley. What else is new?" He coughed and then he choked out those magic words. "You in?"

I let his words hang in the air a moment.

"Yeah," I said.

Without missing a beat, he shot out the rest of his instructions.

"You'll jump onto a gunnery ship in San Diego. It leaves for Pusan in two days. When you get to Korea, find the other Blue Star guys. They're camped out at the Chosun Hotel. You'll get to Kaesong with a troop convoy. The UN Command is already at the site. The Chinese and the North Koreans are on their way, according to our people on the ground. I already told you too much. I can't say any more."

He hung up and the line went dead.

I placed the receiver back into the cradle, suddenly remembering Katie and Manny. The newlyweds were heading up here this weekend.

I'd figure out some way to explain. I always did.

THIRTY-EIGHT

Rochester

NOVEMBER 1983

Katie

I hang up the phone with the caterer and drum my fingers on the kitchen table. The party is set for December third, the weekend after Thanksgiving. Almost exactly their real wedding date, although that's always been unclear, as Mother could never locate the marriage certificate.

I pour my last cup of cold coffee and work through the calendar in my mind. Troy could be back from Grenada by then. They don't have a long-range plan for keeping the boys out there, according to Manny, who always seems to know these things. It's like he has Reagan's office bugged. Well, Lockheed has its people on the inside. For all I know, Manny's one of them.

I glance down at the notes I've scrawled across the page in Troy's old notebook. The menu, the names, the addresses. All I have to do now is stay lucid enough to keep moving forward. No red pill this morning, Katie. Not today. Sixty years will be marked. I'm making sure of that. Mother and Dad can't wiggle out of this now. The grand Diamond Anniversary Party for Terrance and Francine Tusley *will* take place.

And I will finally have my say.

Standing with some authority over the clerk at the Rochester post office, I'd even succeeded at getting them to stamp the envelopes with the new Queen Elizabeth 30th Anniversary Coronation postmark, something my French-Canadian mother will hate. No one else will probably notice. Maybe Manny. No, he's too busy. Best husband in the world, but his mind is never far from work.

Lockheed has all their guys on the worksite in Washington this week to kick off next year's budget, finish up the proposal, and get the next big project started down in the massive Lockheed test facility. Guns and butter. The only two things that matter in Manny's life. He's probably boozing it up with the old lieutenant commanders and the rock-star pilots at The Jefferson on 16th Street, only a block from the White House. Or maybe he's at the Tabard on Dupont.

All my old haunts. People think Washington is crawling with politicians. It's actually awash in ammunition. And photo ops.

The box of letters sits at my elbow, waiting. Harry's death notification letter lies at the bottom where I'd buried it.

But something sepia-toned peeks out from the middle of the pile. I reach in for it.

It is an old postcard, with a posed, almost-nude photograph of a girl across it, her bare feet in the air. She is familiar, as if I'd heard about her… one of my father's drunken, rambling New York stories, told from a pay phone in a bar… and I struggle to recall… Is she in a bomb shelter? Or some stone courtyard?

I turn it over. The postmark is from Paris. August 1951. A few French words are scrawled across the small space, but they leap out at me like tigers escaping a circus cage.

Mon chéri Terry ~

Toujours,
V.

Laying the postcard flat on the kitchen table, I dig out Harry's letter, and place the two objects side-by-side. I stare at them both, my heart beating wildly.

Love and loss. Far and near. V and Harry. What did they share?

Dad, apparently.

Holy shit.

And with no effort whatsoever, I imagine the bottle of red pills upstairs, leaning its little cap against the back of the medicine cabinet door, exasperated and impatient, holding out the promise of sweet, dead-away sleep.

C'mon Katie, it hisses.

It's been dayssss. I'm in heeeere. Let me out!

THIRTY-NINE

Seoul

JULY 1953

Terry

The banquet table at the center of the cavernous ballroom at the Chosun Hotel, downtown Seoul overflowed with cameras—new Kodak Signets like mine, old Ikons, and even older Rolleiflexes. A couple of Japanese Nikkors.

Every single part of my body ached. I'd covered six thousand miles in five days, arriving in the dead of night as a party was fully in progress, and I wasted no time joining in. The guys with the typewriters stumbled away, saying their goodbyes, stories due in the morning, and now it was just me and the photo boys, tipped back in our chairs at the table piled high with photographic equipment. I glanced around, bleary-eyed. Spent matchbooks were scattered everywhere, deep red cardboard set off by tiny gold dragons embossed above Korean lettering and, in French, *L'Hôtel Chosun*. Cigarette butts littered the floor. Men of all types were sprawled around me. Well, except one was a girl.

A girl who was glaring at me over the heap of cameras.

I'd committed the crime of paying a bit more attention to her, asking her name. The other photographers had watched her bristle, apparently amused by her and her reaction to me. She stood up and walked over to me. Her helmet strap was rigged into a necklace across her collarbone, the helmet resting between her shoulder blades.

"You World War guys don't have a clue," she said. "*What's your name?* Jesus, is that all you got?"

I was at least five whiskey shots ahead of her. I couldn't get up from my chair. She loomed over me, her silhouette spinning against the paper lantern lights strung across the ceiling. She certainly had my attention.

"Well, sorry if I've offended you," I said, trying to sound sincere, despite my compromised state. "I'm Terrance Tusley." I held out my hand.

A flicker of something—recognition?—registered on her face, and she sat down in the empty chair next to me, arms crossed. I had a pretty long string of minor credits, maybe she was from New York, she damn sure had the attitude. I registered long brown hair pulled back off her face. Brown eyes. She might be someone's secretary, but then what would she be doing, waltzing around Seoul in a man's shirt, flak jacket, and pants?

"I'm sorry about your son," she said, surprising me more than if she'd offered me her bed. "I heard about it from the guys. They said you were missing for over a year, too."

"Really. You heard." I said, my throat tightening. "They all confide in you, is that it?"

"Well, at this point, nobody has to," she said. "But this is different, isn't it? You feel responsible, right? You want to talk about it?"

Miss No-Name drew out a notepad from her jacket pocket. I sensed a lioness coming in for the kill.

"Why would *you* want to know?" I snapped.

"Well, you're kind of famous," she said, inching closer.

"Have you seen my work?" A flame of pride made it hard to keep my voice low so the other photographers couldn't hear.

"Oh, yes. Terrance Tusley. You tried to publish shots of dead guys ten years ago. My uncle was in the Paris bureau. He kept everything. My cousin's house is full of rejected photographs." She quickly backpedaled. "I mean, the ones that weren't selected."

The photographers who weren't passed out chuckled in our direction. I glared at them with bloodshot eyes. They looked young—unshaven, their hair touching their collars.

"Nice. Thank you," I said. Even after all the anesthesia I'd had to drink, it hurt.

She stared at me. Her eyes weren't both brown. One was blue.

"I think you were onto something," she said. "Why did you come back to Korea? You know, after losing your son and all."

Who *was* she? Her boots were army-issue. They were muddy, with little blades of grass stuck to the soles. I tried to get up from my chair. My legs wouldn't support my weight, and I sank back, defeated. She was right. What made me think I could come back to Korea?

"I'm on a quest for the Pulitzer." My voice sounded thick, even to me. "I leave for Kaesong in the morning to photograph the armistice. That's my special assignment."

She leaned in closer and put her hand on my shoulder. "You're kidding about the Pulitzer, right?"

"Not really," I said, distracted by the silver chain that hung around her neck, visible beneath the open collar, glinting against her tanned skin.

"Well, it's delayed," she said in a low voice.

"*What's* delayed?"

"The United Nations guys got stuck on the banks of a bombed-out stream. They had to call in the Army Corps to build them a makeshift bridge, so they can get to Kaesong for the signing. The armistice ceremony is moved to Monday."

"Jesus," I said, "what the hell am I going to do in the meantime?"

"There are lots of other things to photograph here. I just got back from three days traveling with the Eighth Army. My name is Daniel. Daniel Ivers."

It was beyond me how this girl could fool anyone into thinking she was a boy, much less that there was anything worth photographing in this hellhole that took my son. "Stop kidding, okay?" I said, "I'm exhausted."

"I'm not kidding. There's places as beautiful as a postcard here."

I thought about the postcard of Vivienne as I looked into this woman's strange brown-and-blue eyes. She was nothing like Vivienne. Nowhere near Francine. And yet, a comrade in this wasted place. Confident. Cocky, even. I shifted forward in my chair.

"Okay, I'm game, Daniel Ivers. What is there to photograph here?"

"Korea's a land of mountains, trees and rivers. The scenery is amazing," she said, brushing a wisp of hair away from her face.

"Scenery," I repeated, recalling how I'd flippantly used that word in my final conversation with Harry in the rice silo, just before he left me forever.

"What else would you call it?" She held me in her warm gaze.

"That's for the copywriting guys to worry about, isn't it?" I said.

She shrugged and jammed on the helmet. Black lettering across the front said IVERS. She pushed a few cameras aside on the banquet table and drew one out from the pile, sliding it into a case before I could see what it was, then swinging the case out of the way.

In a moment she'd transformed into one of the boys. The helmet cast dark shadows across her cheekbones.

I reached out and touched her arm.

"What's your real name?" I asked.

"I go by Daniel Ivers," she said in a tone that didn't invite any debate.

"Fine. Everyone needs an angle. I haven't been on the battle-front for a while, Daniel Ivers. I must seem a little rusty."

"Well, then, you have to come out and see it all again, through those old, experienced eyes of yours. Go get some sleep. You've got time you didn't expect to have, right? Meet me at sunset tomorrow. Eighteen hundred hours, right here, Terrance Tusley. I want to go when that mountain casts the longest shadows."

Evening. She wanted photographs that looked dreamy and beautiful. Another Cameron Plumb. Well, what would be the harm in going along with her? I had an extra day. "Eighteen hundred, Roger," I said. "What kind of camera are you using?"

"You'll see," she said, smiling.

She sauntered across the ballroom to the stairway that led up to the rooms, her army boots smacking the marble floor with every step.

Was there any hope of the Pulitzer anymore, against this young crew? Harry had loved my work, worshipped me for it. A pang hit my gut at the thought of him. I took a long look around the garish lobby. What was I doing here? War photographers, whiskey, and surprises. The lingering smell of gunpowder and sweat. The unexpected sweetness of a female.

This was where I belonged, if only to prove to Harry he wasn't wrong.

I settled back in the chair, the Chosun Hotel ballroom finally quiet. The front desk was abandoned for the night, so I had no room to sleep in until someone got here to check me in. I'd spent a hundred nights sleeping on benches in Central Park, fresh off a press shoot downtown. I was used to it.

As I started to doze off, Cameron Plumb's face swam into my memory, lit up from within, as he displayed his film cartridges to two puzzled and amused Nazi henchmen. How he hovered over me, just off the gangway in Wonsan Harbor, my broken spirit swaddled in his Zephyr coat.

My heartbeat quickened at these memories, no matter my exhaustion.

I lived for these moments. Harry would have heartily agreed.

Joe and Katie would never understand.

I pulled my Kodak Signet off the table, held it in my arms, and rocked myself to sleep, wondering whether this Daniel person was a real threat. Whether she, too, was in pursuit of the Pulitzer.

Or whether she was only another kid on an all-expenses-paid jaunt, courtesy of her uncle in San Diego, touring Korea in the hopes of making some lovely, goddamn picture postcards.

FORTY

Seoul

JULY 1953

Terry

The Seoul that spread out all around me was barely recognizable from what I'd seen two years ago, when I'd come looking for the hometown boys and Harry. It had seemed civilized back then. I'd just met Daniel yesterday, yet here I was—as commanded—following her out of the hotel at sunset. We'd just left the immediate area surrounding the hotel when a warning siren rose up around us, hard to tell from where. The city had been taken and retaken at least four times since I was here last. Low voices murmured all around us, hidden in the shadows. Korean, mixed with some French.

Daniel got ahead of me, and I looked up and down the block, hoping to see American GIs or at least the UN forces patrolling the street. There were none. I touched a crumbling wall. Recoiling, I noticed wet blood splattered across it at eye level.

The sun dipped behind an old building and the empty alley

became blue-black. Daniel was about thirty feet in front of me now, a city block away. I broke into a crouched run and caught up to her, breathless.

She slipped into a garbage-filled doorway, and I grabbed her sleeve before she could dart any farther ahead. I had no idea what she was after.

"Where are we going?" I spat out.

"To a village called Gongya, on the edge of the city. First, I want to show you my camera."

"*Here?*" I whispered fiercely, the memory of the blood on the wall fresh in my mind.

"We have all the time in the world," she said, reaching into the camera bag cinched around her waist. She slid a small item from the pack and held it out to me with a triumphant look.

"A movie camera? You're traveling around Korea with a movie camera?" I turned it over in my hands. It was small and shiny. The housing gleamed light green, reflecting the lamps above the alley.

Instinct taking over, I checked the settings. She was ready to go.

"That's a Bell & Howell 200." She smiled. "The absolute best. My uncle gave it to me last year, along with a pile of 16mm film reels. I'm the only person here with one. I've kept it hidden from the guys. They think I'm using this." She pulled another camera from the folds of her flak jacket. Its strap was covered with dried mud.

"That's an old Bantam," I said, surprised. "You carry a Kodak, like me."

"Worthless piece of shit. It's just a decoy. I don't even keep it loaded."

"How do you get your movie film processed?"

"I hand it off to some kid in the hotel. He gets it back to my uncle in San Diego. That's all I know. We saw some of the footage in a newsreel a couple weeks ago. The film was from last winter, but it made it home!" She sat down on a slimy stone step, a satisfied smile on her face.

I closed my palms around Daniel's movie camera. It was compact, but there was no way it had the same tuning, the same responsiveness to light and shadow as my Signet. The Bell & Howell's performance would be shaky at best. Without the proper lighting it would require, this was little more than a distraction. I handed it back to Daniel, assured that she was no competition for me.

Plus, there was nothing here to photograph.

"I think we should head back to the hotel. There's a convoy taking me up to Kaesong for the armistice talks tomorrow, they could come for me tonight," I said.

"Shit that!" Daniel said. "You have a camera, don't you? You wanted to see something, didn't you? Let's go get some shots. I've been in Seoul awhile. I can speak enough Korean to keep us out of trouble."

With that, she sprang to her feet and started to run down the alley. As I crouched there, trying to decide whether to keep going or get back to the hotel, a light rain started to fall. Steam rose from the ancient cobblestones around my feet. The air was infused with a fragrance I couldn't exactly identify. Some sort of incense. Flowery. A scent to cover the stench of the garbage.

I took out my Signet and adjusted the focus ring. I aimed the camera at the rising mist. A bit of light reflected off the droplets as they danced in my viewfinder. Looking through the lens, I noticed something else. I panned across the alleyway, the camera still glued to my eye. A body, crumpled and wet, was splayed across the narrow opening of a back door. I hit the shutter, but it missed somehow—no mechanical click. I pulled the camera out to arm's length. All looked fine. I'd worked long enough at Kodak to know every camera had its little personality. As I brought it back up to my eye, the shutter advanced on its own. Goddammit. This was why sometimes it's not a great idea to take a discarded camera from a Kodak storage cabinet. I thought about my lovely old Zeiss, resting on the fireplace mantel back in Rochester, thousands of miles away. It was probably a loose fitting somewhere, shaken free by all this goddamn running. I'd just—

"Tusley!"

I looked down the alley and saw Daniel waving in the diffused blackness. I slid the Signet into its case and ran down the cobblestones toward her.

We turned a corner. A stone stairway rose up into the fog. We could see only the bottom in the gathering mist.

"This is quite beautiful," I said in wonder.

Daniel raised one hand and formed a pinhole between her fingers, squinting up the stairway. "Namsan," she sighed.

Namsan. A mystical, fog-encircled ruin. I'd read about it: a great red gondola hovering high above Seoul, its ruddy lacquered surface set with inlaid mother-of-pearl.

"I completely forgot about Namsan," I whispered. Harry's death had erased anything beautiful I'd learned about Korea.

"It's not there anymore, Tusley. Isn't that amazing? It's gone."

"What are you talking about? It can't be gone, it stood here for a hundred years!"

"If you crouch right there, you get an incredible shot," Daniel said, pointing about halfway up the rock-strewn steps, where the fog swirled in the evening breeze, revealing the sanctuary site at the top of the stairway.

It had been reduced to a pile of red rubble.

"I don't see a shot," I said.

"Well, Tusley, that's the problem, isn't it? I see shots everywhere. Victims of war. Of the drama of war."

"It's gone. It's completely gone."

"It's just changed. War changes things. What the hell are we doing here if we expect everything to stay the same?"

I stood there, barely able to see Daniel now, even though she stood so close I could have touched her.

"There's nothing to photograph here, Daniel. There's less than nothing," I said. "Give me a reason to be here tonight, goddammit! We could get ourselves killed. There's no armory, no unit presence here. We're like sitting ducks, or, worse yet, target practice."

Daniel looked at me in surprise. "Sure, Tusley. Sure thing." She pulled out the Bell & Howell and held it level in front of her chest. She led me around the side of the ruined staircase, down a side pathway, slowing her pace now. I stayed by her side, wondering at her definition of beauty, what had brought her here to Korea, and what she was looking for. What I was looking for.

"Are you filming right now?" I snapped, seeing nothing around us except burnt trees and scattered trash.

"Keep walking," she said, raising the camera up to her chin.

We turned another corner. A large tent had been erected in the desolate scene, its canvas sides rippling in the night breeze. Daniel marched confidently up to the tent, camera held high, as if we were crossing a river. Without hesitation, she pulled aside the tent flap with her free hand and walked in. I followed her.

"*Hwanyeong.*" A girl's voice reached us from the back of the tent. "Welcome."

The girl came forward. She was no more than ten or twelve years old, wearing a white dress. She bowed to us, her face a somber mask. She looked at me with curiosity.

Daniel bowed in response. "Thank you. We are here to see your father—your *abeoji*—work."

The girl nodded, keeping her eyes on me, and parted a beaded curtain behind her. Daniel stepped forward, continuing to hold the Bell & Howell at her chest, pointing it in front of her. The girl didn't seem to notice or care about Daniel's camera. I pulled the Signet from its case.

Once inside, a thunderclap shook the tent. A sudden cloudburst hammered the cloth roof of the tent, booming yet tranquil at the same time, a storm we could hear but not feel. Daniel didn't flinch.

About four feet in front of us, a man sat at a long wood table, smiling at us, wearing a white tunic. He beckoned us to come in. Up close, he seemed no older than me, weathered to the same degree. The girl evaporated into the dimness behind her father like a ghost in a play. A sheet of glowing white paper covered his tabletop. Wood-handled brushes and black sticks of dried ink lined the table edge neatly to his right. I thought of the printing press at the *Rochester Observer-Herald.* The rolls of paper, the smell of ink. The cast of chemicals in the Kodak film lab, the scent of work being done.

Without a word, the man emptied water into a small bowl,

the sound mixing with the rain outside. A tendril of smoke from an incense burner filled the tent, floral and mysterious, making me lightheaded. He picked up an ink stick and ground it into a rectangular stone that had a well carved into it.

The man selected a brush.

He held his hand high, the brush hovering above the paper. He looked at Daniel, or, rather, at Daniel's camera. He waited. *For what?*

"The brush is made from weasel hair—*jogjebi*," said Daniel. Her voice was sure and low. The man nodded. He lowered the brush into the ink.

He must think Daniel's movie camera recorded sound.

I didn't say anything.

The girl stepped toward us now, head lowered, respectful. I peered at her face in the flickering candlelight. I didn't think there was enough light to capture her. Her father gripped the brush in his blackened hand. I didn't know what to photograph next. His hand floated across the paper, his brush upright at a perfect angle like a thin sail.

"What is he writing?" I whispered to Daniel.

"I see the Chinese character—the *hanja*—for village," Daniel said, sounding very knowledgeable to me.

Daniel stood on her tiptoes, straining to see over the man's bowed head.

"The *hanja* for fire," Daniel said.

The old man nodded, kept writing, the calligraphy beautiful, slow. The rain stopped as suddenly as it had begun, and the tent was silent except for the sound of the old man's brush across the parchment and the whirr of Daniel's camera. He looked up at Daniel, his lined face lit by the candle, his expression expectant.

"The *hanja* for fire, again," Daniel said. "The *hanja* for boy. Son. Dead."

The calligrapher stole a glance at me, and Daniel looked my way, her eyes glowing. A giant wave of sorrow overtook me, a hurricane blasting away a wall of stone. The Signet pulled me down with its weight, too heavy now on its strap around my neck. A sob crushed my throat, then another, and another.

"Son," I choked out, and tears rolled down my face. The daughter materialized in front of me, touching her face, her fingers wet with tears, her mouth set in a frown, her thin chest heaving. Her white dress was stained with dirt at the hem.

Something rustled next to me, and I turned, barely able to see through my tears. Daniel was holding the Bell & Howell up high, the lens pointed directly at me.

At me, not the old man.

"What are you *doing*?" I shouted. "I'm not one of your fucking victim stories!" I threw a wild punch at the camera.

She ducked, and I stomped out, the damp air like a slap on my face. I stumbled down the pathway, the mud giving way to cobblestones beneath my feet.

Daniel caught up to me, grabbing my arm.

I wrenched away from her. "You set me up!" I said, standing up to her in the stinking Korean street.

"Every loss is a story, Terry."

"So, that's what you take pictures of? Loss? Grief? Desolated cities?"

"Well, I thought *you'd* understand, of all people," she said. "You were one of my inspirations."

Her uncle must have had the whole cache of my photos that

weren't destroyed. The boy in the truck at the abbey. The faces in the mud at Calais.

"I'm not looking for sympathy, or for anyone to inspire." The last word caught in my throat. I thought of Harry and his canteen, plastered with my photos.

Daniel slid the Bell & Howell back into its case. "So, what are you doing here, Tusley, if not to inspire anybody with your photographs?"

"It's time for me to get to Kaesong," I said. "I'm heading back to the hotel to meet the UN convoy. I have real photos to take. That's what they pay me for."

"And just what do you consider *real*?"

How would I put it into words? Some called it the moment of truth. Or being in the right place at the right time, at the intersection of history and destiny. If I could have been there when the red gondola blew up, right when it happened, then I would have had a prizeworthy photo. Real moments of truth are so bizarre, they can never be imagined or set up; they just happen, and you have to be ready to capture them.

I was at a loss as to how to explain this to Daniel. She was so wrong, making moments out of nothing, forcing them to occur.

"You're photographing things after they happened," I finally said, spreading my arms out wide to indicate the devastated cityscape all around us. "And that's important, but it's not the point of photography. You have to want to be there and let it unfold all around you. That's what people are looking for in a photo… the unfolding itself. So they can *feel* it."

Her eyes glistened in the dark and she took my arm. "The night is still perfect, Tusley. Let's go back to Namsan and take pictures from the top. You can see the whole burned city from there! The silhouettes are amazing. Starving people are lighting fires all around the ruins to cook their food."

"Daniel, you don't—"

At that moment, the screech of tires filled my ears, and I spun around, ready to duck and cover.

A soldier waved vigorously at me from a covered half-track about twenty feet away. The UN patch on his arm caught the light of the street lanterns swinging overhead.

"Are you Terrance Tusley with Blue Star?"

"Oh my God, yes! I'm Terry Tusley!" I yelled, shoving Daniel out of my way.

"We're heading up to the armistice, sir. Are you ready?"

"I'm damn ready!" I held my camera close to my chest and jumped inside, knocking into a group of helmeted boys sitting on the benches.

The sergeant barked at me from the end of the bench. "You! Photographer! We have to make a few stops to get the rest of the unit, they're spread out all over the goddamn place. We won't get to Kaesong 'til dawn!"

"Sure thing, sir," I said, hanging onto a strap for dear life as the half-track careened down the rutted road. A young boy looked up at me from under his helmet. He couldn't have been more than twenty years old.

"You want my seat, mister?"

"No, thank you," I said, feeling a pang of self-annoyance that I was old enough to inspire such deference.

He looked squarely at me, and I relented. The other fellows shifted over politely.

And with that, we set off into the night.

"Would ya mind lettin' me look at your fancy camera? My father taught me how to use one when I was back home, in Chicago..." The young boy's eyes were fixed on my Signet.

I smiled and pulled the camera strap over my head.

"This is neat!" His young face was pressed against the viewfinder. "Someday I'm gonna have one of these babies!"

"If you live long enough, Peterson." It was one of the other men, his face puckered with scars. I felt the urge to slug him, but I just looked around the half-track. Everyone was watching the two men.

"Oh yeah, I'll live," Peterson said cheerfully, never taking the camera from his face. "You just gotta be good at dodgin'."

The sergeant stood up in the swaying vehicle, glaring at me.

"That'll be enough, y'all," he said. "Chatter is what fucks us up. Keep it to yourselves."

In an instant, the image of Daniel, and of all that just happened, was extinguished from my mind, and I felt clean and purposeful again, riding in this truck of heroes to the armistice.

We were part of the unfolding. Those moments just before the event itself.

Daniel could go to hell.

FORTY-ONE

Seoul

JULY 1953

Terry

The grim sergeant sat at the open back of the half-track, eyes scanning, ever vigilant for something unexpected. The conversation ticked up, low and sparse, but the sergeant didn't chide anyone; he was too distracted now. Cigarettes were shared. These boys were just like Harry. By the time we drove up the wide dirt road to Kaesong—adding more soldiers all along the way—it was well after midnight. Another Army truck sped past us, but our transport crawled along at a snail's pace. I felt like we were a moving target, but the ceasefire had been agreed to.

Hopefully, nothing would happen. But, if something did, I was ready.

Hours passed. We dozed fitfully. The beginnings of dawn broke across the horizon. The truck must have been stuck in second gear, but the rise and fall of the boys' voices acted like a nourishing cocoon, refreshing my mind, helping me forget about the Bell & Howell and the wet blood on the stone walls of Seoul.

We were on our way to the armistice. There would be pictures there.

We all sensed the truck slowing down even more, then stopping. The boys around me readied their rifles and adjusted their helmets. A nervous silence filled the air, sweaty and ripe. I squatted to see out the filthy windshield. A figure was walking alone on the dirt road. A massive coat billowed out around him. He was tilted to one side, weighed down. Metal reflected the breaking sun.

It could be no one else.

"Tell the driver I know him," I said to the sergeant.

"Who the hell is he?" he barked.

"He's a photojournalist. He's with the British Press Corps," I replied.

"No shit. And *you* know him," the sergeant said. "Y'all like a *club* out here, yeah?"

The sergeant jumped out the back of the truck and I dropped to the ground behind him. We scooted around front. The driver turned off his headlights, the road coffee-brown under the rose-tinted sky. The figure turned at the sight of us. He carried at least four cameras, a duffle bag, plus a canvas pack. He recognized me even this far away and gave a whoop. He hurried up to us, his equipment banging like pots on a rack.

"Terry? You came back!" Cameron Plumb shouted. "You finally came back!"

"Where you headed, sir?" The sergeant's eyes skimmed the mountain range that encircled us.

"Kaesong, of course!" he said, clapping me on the shoulder. He jumped into the half-track as if he were carrying nothing at all. The boys moved over for us to sit.

"Vivienne was just what you needed," Cameron said quietly. "You haven't aged a day."

"Bullshit," I snorted.

"Well," he laughed. "Vivienne plus a bit of time at… where did you say is home? The wilds of north New York?"

"Yes, Cameron," I said, noting the boys around us were hanging onto every word.

"I guess it makes sense, finding you here." Cameron rearranged his cameras on their straps, like they were children who needed tending. "Back to find the truth, old boy. Always looking for that elusive thing, am I right?"

"I'm here to photograph the armistice, just like you." I said. "Although it's beyond me why you'd come all the way out here now. I've seen your byline, it's everywhere."

"Give it a rest, Terry. I have a million people calling me for jobs now, it's true. I get my pick, and I wanted this last one in a war zone. Of course, my secretary accepts my assignments for me now."

"Your sec—"

But he interrupted me, a faraway look in his eyes. "I'll be done with you Yanks after this. When I reestablish myself in London, I could be knighted. Wouldn't *that* be grand! Then it's back to Parliament for me. Those wigs photograph so beautifully, don't you think?"

"Cameron, who sent you—"

"Pipe down now, Terry. I need forty winks, but I'll take ten." He leaned his head back against the canvas, and promptly went to sleep, his expression tranquil. I remembered the nap in the back of the Nazis' car.

This guy could sleep through anything.

"The napping knight," I muttered, shaking my head, evoking a ripple of low laughter from the troops.

We wound our way up the road to Kaesong, the jagged mountain range barely visible through the open back of the truck. I glanced at the faces of the young boys beside me. Any jocularity was now gone. They looked tough and scared at the same time. Each one looked like Harry, no matter the color of his skin or the set of his jaw. All far too young. In stark contrast to Cameron, who was by now lightly snoring, they all sat forward, pensive.

No doubt some were thinking of home.

What did Harry think about in his final moments? Did he, too, wish he were home at the moment of attack? Did he look for me behind him, hoping I'd be there to protect him? I hid my face behind my hands as the truck ate up the road. They never found the canteen covered with my pictures, but he'd had it with him. It never left his side. Lost somewhere in the firefight, it was probably buried in the muddy field where he fell. A Korean civilian would find it someday and wonder why on earth anyone would splash pictures of another war across a drinking vessel.

I hunched forward and stared at the muddy path that stretched back to Seoul. Pebbles from the road wedged themselves into the half-track's tires, like an endless circle of ground-up bones. Riding here with a pack of boys who put their lives on the line every minute, I thought with disquiet about the price of the Pulitzer, and what it meant, in real terms, to be the highest bidder. Despite all this, despite Harry, it still called out to me, as it had in those early days. Before, whenever I'd thought about it, it had been as light as air. But now, here on the road to photograph the Korean War armistice, jostling against *Sir Cameron*, I could almost taste the prize, sense its weight. Its pursuit had become a cross and a burden. An albatross. When would it be mine to carry?

The truck rumbled to a stop. We were at the site, and I could feel my heart quickening. I jabbed Cameron awake. The half-track backed up to a line of enormous tents that had been set up side-by-side. We waited for the orders to go in. From the back of the truck, we could make out three North Korean soldiers who stood at attention in front of one of the tents. As the sun crested over a faraway mountain range, I noticed that the North Koreans' bayonets looked rusty, and the soldiers did not look threatening, only exhausted.

A gray-haired US commander emerged from the tent and waved us over with a brisk inflection of his hand. Another man stepped out of the tent and stood next to him. His golden hair shone in the morning sunlight. He spoke to the commander and laughed, his teeth so white that they flashed behind his lips. The officer nodded solemnly, spun on his heel, and they went back into the tent.

"Tom Young." Cameron sighed.

"What the hell!" I exclaimed.

"All out!" The sergeant shouted to his men.

We swarmed out of the truck.

Cameron had an intense look, his eyes darting from tent to tent.

The promise of getting the shot that would catapult me over people like Cameron Plumb, or even Daniel Ivers, seemed to flit away in the bright Korean mountain air. Considering the head of British propaganda was here, and he'd summoned the great Cameron Plumb to come, the likelihood of my getting any good pictures just dropped like a bowling ball off a cliff.

I was up for it, though. Let the duel begin.

FORTY-TWO

Seoul

JULY 1953

Terry

"Get behind me, Tusley!" Cameron strong-armed me, trying to hold me back.

"Forget it!" I pushed back at him. "You'd still be hitchhiking if we hadn't stopped to pick you up back there."

"Yes, you're right, old boy." Cameron smiled. "We should go in together. Linked arms, shall we say, into Tom Young's circus tent!"

We both ran to the tent, but he stopped short and took a wide step away from me, turning in a graceful movement, his Zephyr coat flying out in the breeze.

"Terry, wait a minute," he said solemnly. "Your son gave his life for this moment. You need a good vantage point today. The best one, in fact! I'm going to find it for you, eh?"

Another setup.

"No," I said, but he was tilting his head to one side, staring at the Signet hanging from my neck.

"What in God's name is that camera?" he asked. "Bloody hell, Tusley! Here, take one of mine." He thrust a camera into my hands and rushed into the tent.

"Bastard," I said. "So much for linked arms!"

I looked down. He'd given me a new Graflex Pacemaker, made in Rochester by Kodak's competitor. Never a dull day with this guy. Nice camera, though. I slid the Signet away into my waist pack and threw the Pacemaker's strap over my head before following him into the armistice tent. He'd halted just inside the entrance. The tent was about fifty feet wide, pitched high in the center. It felt as big as the main concourse of Grand Central Station, but nearly empty of people.

"Front and center, Cameron Plumb!"

That hated voice.

"Front and center!"

Young sauntered toward us. It had been ten years, but he was impossibly youthful, blond and tan. Cameron hesitated, then hunched his shoulders and marched to him. The gray-haired commander stood at attention next to me, just inside the tent flaps. He was in full-dress uniform. Several rows of many-colored bars were on display across his top left breast pocket, and I pulled the Pacemaker up to my eye, but he placed his big hand over my lens and frowned at me.

"Hasn't started yet," he said in a deep voice.

Tom waved impatiently and the commander stomped over to him. I followed.

The four of us stood now at the far corner of the tent. But something seemed off. There was almost nobody here. Just a few scattered soldiers loitering around the edges of the tent. The boys in the truck seemed to have disappeared. I looked at my watch. Seven hundred hours. The place should be in full swing by now. Up in front of us, a low, broad stage and a long table had been set up. The commander stood next to Tom, silent and frowning. Cameron pulled his Speed Graphic forward.

And Tom, goddamn him, finally noticed me, standing next to Cameron.

"Tusley." Tom raised his eyebrows, then recovered himself, deftly pulling out a new cigarette pack from his pocket and ripping it open.

I stepped closer to Tom, ready to tell him what I thought of him for sending me home that goddamn long-ago day. I clenched my fist into a ball.

"So sorry to hear about your son," Tom said suddenly.

Cameron glanced up.

I felt a rush of blood flood my face. Two soldiers patrolling near us slowed down, curious.

Cameron cleared his throat. "Ready whenever you gentlemen are," he said.

This was not the time to take a swing at Tom, however much I wanted to. We watched in silence as a soldier neatly laid out papers on the signing table. There was a disturbance at the back of the tent, and we turned to see a platoon of ten or fifteen men muster and stand at attention. I searched their faces. None of the boys from the truck. More began to join them, filling the tent.

Again, I brought the Pacemaker up to my eyes and adjusted the focus.

"Oh, no, Mr. Tusley," Tom said, placing his hand on my arm. He pointed to the back of the tent. "The action is coming in just about … now!"

We all swung around to see where Tom was pointing. A line

of about twenty Korean men wearing wide bamboo hats was being paraded up the center of the armistice tent, led by the platoon of boys from our truck. The Koreans were ragged and thin. Tom walked over to them, welcoming them in. Their faces were nearly hidden by their wide, woven hats. Each clutched a small bundle and an official-looking white piece of paper. Tom gestured for them to sit in the wooden folding chairs on the stage. Each one bowed to Tom before sitting down.

I looked over at the commander. His brow was furrowed, his eyes locked on the Korean civilians. A million questions popped into my reporter's head, and I strained to see what was on the papers they held in their hands. As they settled themselves uncomfortably into the stiff chairs, I recalled Matthew Brady's staged photographs from the Civil War, in the theater of battle, his subjects' eyes sometimes vacant and fearful, sometimes confrontational. Even my hero Brady could stoop to drama.

There was something wrong about the scene. Where were the diplomats? I'd been gone from the battlefield for a long time, but this…?

I couldn't contain myself.

"What the hell is going on here?" I demanded.

"The first North Korean prisoners to cross the parallel, gentlemen!" Tom shouted, his arms open wide. "Finally free, released to return to their farms, their families, their freedom in their homeland of democratic South Korea!"

The platoon arrayed on either side of the prisoners stood at attention, and Tom glided back to us. Cameron's Speed Graphic was trained on the row of Korean men. He had a clear shot, and he calmly took picture after picture, the shutter clicking loudly in the quiet tent.

I watched the commander, his medals and bars flashing, his name plate rising up and down on his heaving chest. Tobin. Ronald K. Tobin. He was barely controlling his rage. I hadn't had time to study up much before getting out here, but one fact was general knowledge: there were no Korean peasants willingly lining up to be returned to their land. That had been the failing of the last try. Koreans simply don't switch sides. They'd rather kill themselves first. It had something to do with honor. I realized that Daniel would probably know; she had a good grasp of Korean culture.

But she wasn't here, was she?

"We didn't get the North Koreans to release any prisoners to the South. Am I right, Commander Tobin?" I asked quietly.

He ignored me, his attention fixed on the stage. But Tom had overheard me.

"You, Mr. Tusley, are quite mistaken," Tom said firmly. "We agreed to repatriation of prisoners. That's what their papers say."

My mind was racing. Our leader, Harrison, should be here. The leader from the other side, Nam Il. Maybe a Chinese delegate. All these men would be here by now. And there would be a lot more people in this room, if this was truly an armistice talk. But there was no one except Tom Young, Cameron Plumb, and a commander I'd never heard of.

"Where are the diplomatic delegates?" I asked, loud enough for all to hear me.

Tom simply smiled. "Get out your camera, Tusley," he said.

"I will when there's something real to photograph," I retorted. "These are local men, not prisoners of war! You *gave* them those false papers they're holding."

Cameron glanced at me, but then he bent down on one knee,

switched out his spent film cartridge, reloaded, and began to shoot another set. I peered into his open camera bag. Several new film cartridges were lined up neatly inside, ready for use.

He jabbed my leg with his elbow. "Why aren't you getting any shots? This is the best position, we can both get the picture credits, get out the Pacemaker, Terry!"

I noticed one of the Korean men pull something from the pocket of his vest. American dollars. He was looking at them curiously. I pulled the Pacemaker up and checked the film window. I could focus on the currency, I was close enough—

The film compartment was empty. God Damn Cameron Plumb.

Tobin finally stepped up to Tom, his patience spent.

"I demand that you tell me…" he barked.

"You have your orders, Commander," Tom said coolly.

"My orders didn't include a goddamn publicity stunt with fake prisoners of war," Tobin snarled.

"It only took a minute, my man here got the shot, and now the delegates will be allowed to enter the tent." Tom grinned.

Just then, a loud pack of camera-laden photographers burst in, at least thirty of them—a confused mass—spilling through the tent flap where we'd entered earlier.

"Come in! Come in!" Tom yelled, sweeping past us across the enormous canvas room to greet them with open arms. Tobin was still frowning, but Cameron rose from the dirt floor, next to me, flushed and grinning.

"That should do it!" he said, packing up the Speed Graphic. "Nobody will get those shots! Nobody!"

Cameron Plumb could go to hell. After so long, he was still someone's lad. He would never stand on his own. He would forever follow his master of ceremonies. I looked down at the useless Pacemaker hanging from my neck. I couldn't call this a miss. I would wait. The delegates would come in as soon as this stupid prisoner stunt was out of the way. That was the real news. And I had the Signet. I was sure it was fine.

The light was ideal now. I rotated my stance, mechanically, as if I'd been born for this moment. I moved away from Commander Tobin to a position about six feet away. The commander was perfectly framed against the line of Koreans, right in front of me, the daylight coming from behind me through the open flaps, bathing him in broad daylight. The Pulitzer. It was going to happen here. I could get my shot of the grand commander right now. I drew the Signet from my waist pack and pulled the camera to eye level. Tobin filled the frame. From somewhere on my right, a breathless soldier sprinted across the room, passing me fast enough to stir a breeze I felt through my jacket. I kept the viewfinder glued to my eye as he handed a slip of yellow paper to Tobin, then ran away, beyond my line of sight. I kept the camera on the commander as he slowly unfolded the paper and read the message. I thought briefly about Harry, delicately lifting the thin sheet of paper from the teletype machine in the rice silo, the very last time I saw him.

Commander Tobin's face turned dark. I held the Signet steady to my eye. Tobin glared over at Tom, busy with the new pack of photographers. Squinting through my viewfinder, I saw the commander's jaw open as wide as a whale's mouth.

I pressed the shutter, heard its satisfying click.

"Tom Young!" Tobin's voice bellowed across the tent like a cannon, and I swung around to the soldiers lined up at the far side of the tent, their images rounded a bit by the curvature of my lens. They snapped to attention at the sound of Tobin's voice.

Keeping the camera pressed to my face, I rotated my body until Tom came into focus.

He turned at the sound of his name. I was completely sure: this moment had not been orchestrated, or rehearsed, or planned for. Again, I pressed the shutter.

I pivoted back to Tobin and centered him in my lens. I kept the camera on him as he scanned the room, his chin jutting out, waiting until the place was deathly quiet and he had everyone's attention.

"I have my orders!" Tobin shouted, holding up the yellow paper.

Click. The decorative rainbow of battle pins disappeared into the folds of cloth, then reappeared when he lowered his arm.

Click. In the sudden morning sunlight, they gleamed from his chest, shining into my viewfinder.

"No signing today. We are surrounded," Tobin announced solemnly.

In the dead quiet, Tom's voice, shaky and unnaturally high-pitched, floated across the room. "Bloody hell..."

I felt a stirring from the row of chairs where the Koreans sat, but I kept my eye on Tobin, pivoting to where I had both the commander and the Koreans in my line of sight.

In the moment between focus and finger, in the split-second between hammer and shutter, I distinctly heard the Signet delay, failing me as it had in the alley with Daniel. There was no way to know if I'd caught the exact time that the bullet, fired from somewhere outside the back of tent, hit Tobin in the chest, or the second shot that hit the Korean civilian's forehead, dead-on.

I could only watch with horror through my lens as they both pitched backward, their garments splattered in a mathematical formula of gravity, air and blood. I heard Cameron's heavy camera clatter to the ground beside me, and everyone around us hit the dirt as a stream of sniper shots splintered the room.

"Shit! Shit! Shit! Shit!" Cameron's reedy voice pitched high over my head, and then I saw him go down.

"I'm here, Harry! I'm right here!" I cried, jumping on top of him. Stomping boots of panicked men surrounded us, his Speed Graphic tripping some of them up as they furiously attempted to get out of the line of fire. The sniper shots continued, coming from God knows where. I pulled him closer beneath me, grabbing at his coat with my fists, its slippery fabric almost yanked out of my hands by the men who climbed and rolled around us, desperate to get out of the way.

"Stay down, Harry, it'll be okay, stay down," I yelled, and we huddled on the dirt floor together, me sprawled over him, seeking shelter from the storm of bullets and scrambling men who slammed like thunder above us. I held the two of us as close to the floor as I could, and in a blaze of recognition I saw Cameron's face, not Harry's, white and sweaty, buried in my arms.

From somewhere outside the tent, the gunfire escalated in pitch, a sound that ripped through the air, and the roar of a single helicopter cut through everything, clear and methodical, a symphony of gears and rotors. I picked up my head long enough to see a man race into the tent, in full combat gear. He was shouting something—two syllables, I couldn't make it out, and then his voice reached me over the din.

"Tom Young! Tom Young!" he yelled above the commotion of the men.

Cameron wrenched me back down. The Signet and the Pacemaker were wedged between us. I slung them back and out of the way.

"Oh my God, cover your head!" Cameron howled.

I strained to see what was happening across the room while Cameron kept trying to pull me down. Tom's blond head appeared amid the confused, panicked crowd. The soldier who'd been calling out his name ran at him and locked him in a protective bear hug. I watched with amazement as the soldier half-carried, half-dragged a panicked Tom Young out of the tent to the broad sunlight. Only Tom Young. The soldier didn't try to save anybody else. A minute later, one helicopter took off.

The place was suddenly silent. Not even a groan from the fallen men. I thought about Tobin, who'd got it first. No one to run in and save *him*.

Cameron, spread flat-out on the ground, arms around me in a bear hug, stared up at me, eyes wild.

"We're stranded here," he said in a whisper, his hands shaking and his face glistening with sweat.

I wrapped my arms around him. He was freezing cold. "No, Cam, that's not going to happen. It's just not. Tobin had to know—the moment that he read his orders—he was going to get it, and that Tom's stunt before the real talks had sealed his fate. But we're safe, for the moment."

Cameron looked somewhat lucid now, but he wasn't moving, and his arms were still around me. He wasn't letting go anytime soon.

"Someone had enough time," he whispered.

"To disrupt and destroy," I finished. "But they're gone. The damage is done. They're running for the hills now."

From far off, we heard the thundering sound of a second helicopter. In less than a minute, it landed outside the tent. I hauled Cameron to his feet.

"The Speed Graphic! I can't leave it!" He grabbed the shattered camera from the spot where it'd gotten thrown, pulling the strap over his head before I could stop him. He gathered his equipment and his duffle together and strapped them to his body before he collapsed against me.

More UN troops swarmed in from the back, as if they'd been dropped from heaven. I dragged Cameron through the opening where we'd come in. The sunlight was blinding. From across a grassy field, a stout man was running toward us, waving his arms.

"Are you Terry Tusley?" he shouted beneath the spinning rotors.

"Hell, yes, I am!" I said, still hanging onto Cameron, who was like dead weight in my arms.

"Daniel sent me! Get in, you two!" he shouted.

The man was strong enough to pull Cameron off me. We ducked beneath the whirling rotors and jumped into the helicopter, throwing ourselves across the metal floor. Cameron crumpled into a heap, wedged behind the pilot's seat. I crawled over to the window to look out, just as the pilot was taking off. The helicopter made its swift ascent, climbing higher and higher above the scrubby trees that snaked along the hillside on this improbably bright and sunny morning, swaying to avoid random gunfire that tried to take us down. My ears popped, and the sound of the rotors filled the compartment.

I sat on my haunches and brought the Signet up as the helicopter lifted us above the armistice tent, Tom's circus tent, the failed and battered tent of peace dwindling ever smaller below.

"What about everybody else?" I asked, my voice faint against the rotors beating above our heads.

"We came just for you, but somebody'll get 'em all out. More birds are comin' in," the pilot shouted. As soon as we cleared the tree line that fell away beneath our skids, he slid on a pair of aviator sunglasses, and glanced at the co-pilot.

"Hey, Trombone, you buckled up?" he said to the man who'd dragged us in.

"Ain't yet, Roy," the co-pilot responded.

I was shaking, but I recognized the Louisiana Creole. French but Southern. I squinted at him in the strong sunlight. A cigar stub was jammed into the side of his mouth. "Thank you," I managed to say.

"You're just lucky we're here," he said, popping open his side window and tossing out the soggy remains of his cigar. "They got the *gris-gris*, the voodoo curse on it, right, Roy?

"The *what*?" I shouted.

"The North Koreans rejected the treaty, called it off at the last minute and surrounded your location." He sat straight in his seat and fastened the safety straps across his ample body. "They had time on their side. Ain't nothin' like time, man. Can't buy it for no money!"

"How do you know that?" I asked, getting up into a squat so I could hear them over the noise of the rotors.

"It's over, man," the pilot said, his eyes straight ahead. "They're gonna move the talks south, and fucking get it over with, but at another location."

"The commanding officer was shot dead in there," I said to the man called Trombone, clutching my Signet, unable to let it go, to put it away or even look at the film window to know what exposure I was at anymore.

"Well, they made their point, didn't they?" Trombone hollered, pulling a bottle of whiskey from somewhere under his seat, and unscrewing the top. "They didn't like *something* that was going on in there, did they? No, sir! They wanted to make *one more goddamn point* before it was over!" He took a long swig before stretching out his big arm and offering the bottle to me.

I waved away the bottle. That was the last thing I needed. He shrugged, turned forward in his seat, tilted back his head, and guzzled the whiskey like it was water.

Tobin. The commander's name echoed over and over in my head as we vaulted upward, his booming voice pounding inside my temples. He was killed for nothing. Commander Tobin, all bedecked with his hero's ribbons, gone like a thundercloud after the rain. And those poor peasants. And those boys. For a propaganda stunt that didn't need to happen at all.

"All you goddamn journalists wanna be famous," Roy the pilot said. "Here's a hero shot for you!" He pushed forward on the stick and the helicopter pitched down so that all I saw were trees through the windows. Trombone laughed and whooped drunkenly, clutching the whiskey bottle tight to his chest.

I gripped the compartment's aluminum edging to keep from sliding across the metal floor. Sunlight washed over us through the windows. I felt the warmth move across my body. I grabbed onto a tattered loop attached to the wall, straining to get my face as close as possible to the window in the swaying cabin hold. The sky all around us was a vivid, unsettling blue. I was bathed in the sun and the sky of Korea, suspended by nothing more than a set of flimsy rotors whirring above majestic, jagged peaks that were topped with the remnants of snow. We glided over them, and the silhouette of the helicopter traversed the hillside, the shadow of its rotors vibrating black against the snow.

It *was* beautiful, as Daniel had said. It was the place my son fell on his journey to find the world I'd created out of thin air. I slid the Signet back into its case. There was no way to capture what I was seeing.

Trombone turned and shouted to me, his voice thicker than before. "You're a little old for this, ain't you? Y'all should be home with your—"

"*This* is home," I said, my eyes on the dappled landscape, white, green, and brown, passing by below us. The endless blue sky all around us.

I glanced over at Cameron. He was propped up against the back of the pilot's seat, staring straight ahead at nothing, his coat like a shroud, the shattered Speed Graphic clutched in his shaking hands.

FORTY-THREE

Rochester

NOVEMBER 1983

Katie

I wake up weeping, flopped across the kitchen table in the dark, the postcard at my elbow, its ghostly image like a piece of silent film cut from a reel.

The phone on the kitchen wall is ringing. I fight through the fog to answer it, too stupefied to even say hello.

"Katie? Are you there?" Manny's familiar voice floats across the miles from Washington, DC. "I'd almost hung up!"

"S-sorry, honey," I say, wiping my face with the back of my hand. "I was just napping. What time is it?" I glance at the kitchen clock, trying to clear the cobwebs from my head.

"It's seven. I'm still at the office. Just thought I'd check in before we go down to the bar."

I hear him pull up the metal window blind behind his desk. It makes a zipping sound in my ear. "Geezus-Cr…!" he exclaims. "Is it dark outside already?"

He's fifteen stories up, in the corporate headquarters, a stone's throw from the Pentagon. I can picture the lit-up façade, the streetlights, the people out and about.

"How's everything going in DC?" I say, trying to sound cheerful.

"These guys would go out every night if they could, especially the test pilots! Have you heard from Troy? Lockheed is already pulling our guys back home. They're assembling at Granada airport."

"Oh, honey, I'm so worried," I start to say, but he interrupts.

"Worried? No, we shouldn't be worried!" He is almost shouting, and part of me knows he's not shouting at me, exactly, but it still feels like shit.

"Manny, when are you coming home?" It's not lost on me that I seem to ask that question over and over. The letters to Dad, unanswered, brimmed with this question. Silence was the only response, so I jump a little when Manny actually answers.

"Katie, I'll be home on Friday. I love you, baby. I'm sorry you're up there alone. We didn't plan on Troy enlisting right after high school. I guess Reagan's ads were too much for the boy to resist!"

"Right," I say, doubtful that the ads were the only thing influencing my son.

"What else is going on?" Manny asks.

I hesitate, knowing what will happen.

"I've sent out the invitations for Mother and Dad's anniversary party."

Silence on the other end of the phone.

"Manny, did you hear me?"

"Yes, baby. It's nice of you. Gives you something to do. And Francine will get a chance to doll up."

"That's no way to talk about my eighty-three-year-old mother," I say, although his remark about keeping me busy doesn't sit too well either.

"Who's bringing her to Rochester from Quebec?" Manny asks.

"Joe. He's bringing Mother and someone named Tricia."

"Newest girlfriend?" Manny sounds skeptical.

"I guess so. I haven't met her. I think she's one of his PhD friends. Doctor of something. If they get married, they'll be Doctor and Doctor, instead of Mr. and Mrs. I always think that's funny." I'm trying to lighten the mood, keep him on the line just a little bit longer, while I come to myself in this big, empty house.

"Okay." He hesitates. "What about your dad?"

"Well, for someone I haven't seen in ten years, he sounds pretty chipper about the idea."

I'm on a roll now, like a real person planning a real party.

"They both gave me loads of people to invite," I continue. "Mother is excited, you're right. I've only talked to Dad over pay phones. Goddammit, he'd better come."

I'm getting a little angrier than intended. Manny has to focus on work, after all. He doesn't need this shit.

"Do *you* know anyone on the list?" Manny asks, his voice tentative.

He sounds like a young man again. I can sense the tension in his throat. That's what thirty years of marriage will do for you. It's nice, actually. Hard to believe Mother and Dad have been married exactly twice that.

“Remind me how I found you,” I say, trying to ignore his last question.

“Is Trombone on the list, Katie?”

“After all these years, you think it matters?” I respond, feeling heat rise across the back of my neck.

“You’re delicate, baby. Don’t invite him.”

“Don’t worry. I’m sure he’s clean now. Else he’d be dead.”

As soon as the word leaves my lips, I regret it. I sink into the kitchen chair, suddenly dizzy.

“How can you even—wait a minute, baby, hang on,” Manny says.

From far away, I hear Manny’s beeper go off, the one he wears 24/7 clipped to his belt. A minute passes. I can hear him talking on another line. Then he’s back.

“I gotta go. General Pierce agreed to have a drink with us. They’re all heading downstairs. This could mean the contract is ours. Sorry, baby, where were we?”

“My parents’ anniversary party. Remember when we ran away and got married, Manny?”

“Yes, baby,” he says, but he sounds rushed.

“We came back up to Rochester for a belated wedding dinner,” I say, but again I regret where this is going. Manny cuts me off.

“You mean when we drove seven hours to your old house, and your father wasn’t even there?”

We both pause.

“*Rien de génial n’est fait sans passion*,” I whisper.

“Nothing great is done without passion,” he says, translating without hesitation.

“Your French is getting good, Manny. Mother would be proud.”

"The intelligence is in French. It's the designated international language."

I hear him tapping his finger on the receiver, impatient. I am determined to keep him on the line.

"I found something when I went through a few moving boxes today," I say.

Manny doesn't need to know that this particular box didn't move from DC with us, that it was here in Rochester for the past forty-odd years, gathering dust behind the counter at the Rochester post office.

"Katie, I have to run."

I can sense his impatience, and how everything about him is tied up in his job, and the men waiting in the lobby.

"I found a postcard, from France," I continue. "Only it's not a regular postcard. There's a girl on it. I think I found Dad's—"

"Well, I guess twenty years in Vietnam can mess up anyone's mind, baby," he says briskly. "I want you to un-invite, or *désinviter*, that clown Trombone. You fix it, Katie. You fix it before they all descend on that nice, new house you're in, up there in Rochester!"

He hangs up.

I love my husband. He's pulled me out of the blackness of night, the torture of withdrawal, and given me a son. A son so perfect, so complete in every way.

I can't fix it, Manny. I won't fix it.

Troy's senior photograph lies on the table down the hallway, in a school-issued envelope. It arrived after he'd already left for Grenada. I don't need to pull the picture out to know how exquisite he is. Neither the heroin I shot up nor the cocaine I smoked ever found their way to him or scuffed his photogenic goodness. Trombone only gave me the best, the most premier top-shelf junk direct from Vietnam.

And here at my elbow, printed on vintage cardboard somewhere in wartime Paris, is a woman so lovely that you don't need to see her face to know her beauty. She is French, and this was probably taken during the Nazi occupation. I examine it more closely. Dad would have been in the thick of war, a long time away from the old Rochester house by then. Mother was always in Quebec for one reason or another. Leaving behind me and Joe and Harry—making dinner, doing homework. Living. The letters to my missing father pouring out of me like water from a fountain, swirling into elegant shapes that climb high in the air, draining down, ultimately, into a bottomless nothing.

Who is this woman in the photograph? My fingers caress the image of her long legs, and I feel a warmth for her, she is so petite and perfect. Dad didn't need to come home for anything, did he?

But wait.

He did always go back to Quebec, to Mother. She spoke of him with irritation but also something else. He would make his way back to her over the years, no matter what. What was it about them that endured?

"*Rien de génial n'est fait sans passion*," I whisper to the empty house.

"Nothing great is done without passion," it whispers back.

But, truth be told, I couldn't see what was so great about my perennially-absent parents.

FORTY-FOUR

Seoul

JULY 1953

Terry

Wonsan Harbor glimmered into sight beneath us. Our helicopter flew over the UN fleet standing guard in the port. The fleet was impressive, stretching out as far as the eye could see. The Signet felt heavy in my pack, like I was carrying the body of Commander Tobin with me. We swung over the peninsula and soft-landed in the courtyard next to the Chosun Hotel, a few hundred feet from the building. Trombone yelled at us to stay inside the helicopter until the rotors stopped spinning.

It was roasting hot by the time Cameron and I stumbled out onto the grass, and then Roy and Trombone and their miraculous machine took off. In a matter of moments, it was just a speck in the brilliant blue sky.

Cameron still had two cameras strapped to his body and was gripping the remains of the Speed Graphic. The Zephyr coat was plastered to his body, soaked through with sweat. His expression was unreadable. From across the courtyard, a man strutted out to greet us. Tom Young. He was in shirtsleeves, clean-shaven, and it boggled my mind to think how he'd smoothed his way out of that armistice tent without a scratch.

"Bastard..." I muttered.

"He has known me for a long time, but this is unforgivable," Cameron said, taking in a deep, shaky breath and letting it out slowly.

"Because you weren't in on it?" I asked, irritated.

Cameron continued to glare at the head of British Propaganda, who looked like he'd just stepped out of a magazine ad for Van Heusen.

"No, because I almost died this time," Cameron said. "And that was never part of the deal."

"And *you* dying, that's more important than anything, right?" I grumbled. "Let's find a place to develop this film, okay? Tom Young isn't worth our time." I tugged on his sleeve.

Cameron threw the ruined Speed Graphic to the ground at Tom's feet.

"I left the Queen's Coronation to photograph that half-assed setup," Cameron said to him. "You escaped alone without a scratch, leaving everyone to die back there, including me!"

"You'll come to Panmunjom, then? That's the next try. These photos will be worthless, anyway." Tom responded, unruffled. "I see you both got out alright, although I wouldn't have laid good odds on Tusley..."

"A commanding officer died, and an innocent man!" I shouted.

"Yes, well, it could have gone better," Tom replied. "And you'll give me your film, Tusley. Seems to be a recurring theme with you."

Before I could even spit out a reply, Cameron kicked the broken Speed Graphic into the bushes, and dove at Tom, knocking him to the ground, fists flying in a heated frenzy. Neither one was a good fighter; they looked like a couple of wrestling schoolboys.

"Okay, cut it out!" I yelled, stepping between them.

At that moment Tom Young startled me with a light-handed punch to my face, reminding me of the first rule of any fistfight: never get between two idiots in a brawl. I threw a harder punch back at Tom, knocking him to the ground, his mouth bleeding, and pulled Cameron away from him.

"You might need a medic, old boy," Tom said, popping up like a toy puppet and glaring at me, nose to nose.

"Yeah? I don't think you'll be flashing that million-dollar smile anytime soon!"

He poked a finger in his mouth. He'd lost a tooth in the fight. "I'll call the dentist over. They have one here just for me."

"Bollocks to you, Tom," Cameron said, still lying in the dirt, sweaty and spent, his two remaining cameras still strapped haphazardly to his body.

"Suit yourself, Plumb. You'll get no help from me anymore," Tom said, brushing the dirt off his pants and tucking in his shirttails. "Not giving up the film, eh, Tusley? Must truly stink, then."

I took another step toward him. Coward that he was, he backed away.

"You'll regret it," he said. "I kept your byline out of any worldwide press for ten years. I can manage ten more."

"Like hell you can," I replied, knowing it was an empty threat.

The propaganda setup had killed the negotiation. And someone would take the blame. Tom Young was far from untouchable, but he obviously didn't think so. He smirked, then turned and disappeared into the Chosun Hotel, leaving us in the courtyard alone.

"He didn't care if I'd died for that shot," Cameron said.

"Part of the job you took. You knew it would be dangerous." I wondered for a moment if Annie Plumb knew the danger she was putting her son in, even if her direction was discreetly conducted behind the scenes.

Probably not, I decided.

"You saved me, Tusley. You saved my life back at the armistice," Cameron said, making no move to get up from the grass.

"Nonsense. It would have taken a lucky shot to get you. We'd already hit the dirt. They only wanted Tobin." I remembered the truck that sped past us on the road to Kaesong. "They had time because of all the confusion with those goddamn prisoners of war who weren't prisoners at all, but recruited from Seoul and paid to go up there."

"When I got the call in London to come…"

"Tom didn't care who he put in danger. He'll never care. And," I said, pulling him to his feet. "Believe me when I say this: Tom Young would find some other poor slob to pull your camera off your dead neck, and get those pictures developed if he wanted them enough."

"Kind of makes you wonder about what you see in the papers, eh?" Cameron said, like it was the first time he'd ever had that thought.

"Yes. And I wish to God that someone had told my son Harry that."

"I suppose *you* would have had to be the one to do that, eh,

Tusley? Kind of a fatherly thing. I wouldn't know, of course. I never got to meet me Dad. But I suppose he would have told me those types of things." He paused. "When I was young."

"Sometimes those are the hardest things to say to a son," I said, ruefully. "And you're not as old as I am, Cameron."

He laughed. "You'd be surprised at how old I actually am. A theater reviewer once wrote that I had a mutable face. Never quite understood that one, I'm sure! But, you, my dear Terrance..." Cameron rubbed his scraped chin. "You may indeed be the youngest man I've ever met."

I looked at him. "What the hell does *that* mean?"

"You have the energy of a man half your age! You will never stop in your pursuit of the prize in these war zones, will you? Let's consider the duel a draw for now. I'm done with these." He held out his two remaining cameras to me.

"You're *done*?" I said, glancing around for the Speed Graphic.

"I've been chasing a place to set a play, but the actors never follow my direction, and the lighting never works," Cameron said, despondent. "I'm done with these types of propaganda set-ups. I should've stayed with the Queen. I'm going back to England."

He then dropped his cameras to the ground, where they landed with two soft thuds in the patchy grass.

"Stop being so dramatic, if that's even possible for you," I said, shaking my head in disbelief.

"I wish I'd met Harry, Terry."

"Why?" I wasn't sure I liked where this was going.

"I'd have told him that wars aren't glamorous, or beautiful. It's just dying, and people who make up stories to sell."

I watched in amazement as he waded into a bed of trumpet-shaped flowers and proceeded to stamp on his Speed Graphic, smashing it to pieces. He bent down and picked up the flash assembly, still intact, and turned it around in his hands so that the bulb faced him.

"That's not always the case, and you know it, Cameron."

"I'm going home. Maybe you're done, too?"

The question hung in the air. I knew that home was not the same for me as it was for Cameron.

For me, it was an empty place.

"I'm staying," I said.

"Even though it's clear you may be chasing after lies?" he asked, incredulous.

"I think I can figure out what's real and what's not."

"You're assuming you can tell an honest man from a liar," he said. "Even without looking through a lens, that's difficult to do."

"*To thine own self be true*," I said. "Shakespeare. Your own countryman."

"You Yanks don't know enough of the Bard to be useful to yourselves," Cameron replied dryly.

He angled his body just so, his chin held high. He placed one foot in front of the other, the flashbulb held out in front of him.

He cleared his throat and addressed the flash. "*There's no trust, no faith, no honesty in men; all perjured. All forsworn, all naught, all dissemblers. These griefs, these woes, these sorrows make me old.*"

He then turned and sprinted out of the courtyard like Peter Pan—lightweight, nearly flying, free of the camera equipment that had always weighed him down. Still holding the broken flash assembly, he stopped short in the alley that ran alongside the Chosun courtyard.

"Take my other cameras, Tusley!" he called to me. "Put them to good use."

He dropped the flash assembly onto the pavement in the alley and stomped on it. His flashbulb exploded with an almost elegant sound into the asphalt under his heel. He wiped his hands on his coat, sauntered out into the broad boulevard that ran past the hotel, and was gone.

The remaining two of Cam's perfectly good cameras lay where he'd left them, abandoned on the grass at my feet. I bent down and retrieved the first one. An Argus C3 Brick. Brand-new. I picked up the second one. A Kardon, practically a relic from WWII, when we couldn't get any German Leicas.

I lifted them both over my head by their straps.

And so, the duel ends, I thought. For now, anyway.

I knew what I had to do.

I had the photo of Commander Tobin in my camera. With Cameron essentially out of the game, I was the only one with any photos of the failed propaganda stunt, and this one—unlike Calais—wouldn't get buried. I wanted to expose Tom Young's botched setup to the world. I needed the right person to publish my work, and that person was one Ed Mahoney, Blue Star Agency. I just needed to see the photo for myself first.

I needed a darkroom.

FORTY-FIVE

Seoul

JULY 1953

Terry

Daniel was propped up in an old velvet chair off to the side of the empty hotel lobby, head hung down, snoring. The sun had begun its descent, casting golden light across the enormous room. Her helmet was on the floor beside her. I tiptoed past, knowing I would have to thank her later for sending that helicopter to get me out of Kaesong, whatever her motives. Right now, I had film burning in my camera and I needed to get it to Ed in New York. But I wanted to see it for myself first.

She stirred a bit and I stopped, barely breathing. I didn't need any of her tricks, any of her unplanned trips down dark alleyways.

A soldier materialized at my elbow. "Can I help you, sir?" He looked to be about eighteen. He glanced around the quiet lobby, nervous.

"I need the New York photo bureau, here's my press badge,"

I said, suddenly feeling a light breeze. I turned to find the front lobby window had been shattered, the discarded matchbooks scattered like dead leaves across the marble floor.

"What happened here?" I asked, surprised.

The soldier frowned at me.

"Look, mister, we're all waiting for the armistice to get restarted. Most of my unit was up at Kaesong today. They're bringing bodies back, got it?"

"I'm sorry, Private. I need a darkroom."

"Did you *hear* me, sir?" He looked at me with disdain.

I switched to my most fatherly tone.

"I'm just back from Kaesong myself. I need to develop this film. It can't wait."

"My understanding is there's a film courier who comes around here every evening, can't you—"

"No. I'm not handing over my film without developing it first. It's too important. As you can see, soldier, the situation is changing, and fast."

"Understood," he said, nodding. "It sure is. *The Baltimore Sun* still has a mobile lab here. Out the front doors, take a right down the first alley." He looked me up and down. "We're making them bug out as soon as the new treaty is signed. We all are." He paused. "What's left of us."

I thanked him and walked out the front of the hotel. *What alley?* I stopped, unsure of which way to go.

"Hey, Terry, welcome back to beautiful Seoul!" Daniel said, bounding up beside me, her helmet clamped down onto her head.

"Daniel!" I turned in surprise.

"What did you get?"

I considered her a moment. She was blocking my way now, hands on hips. I felt gratitude, mixed with my usual suspicion. I decided to put the suspicion away for the moment.

"Thank you for sending Trombone. Can you take me to *The Baltimore Sun* darkroom?"

She nodded. There was no denying it; Daniel knew everything there was to know about Seoul.

"I'm not sure they have enough photo paper for all the shots you might have, Terry," Daniel said, eyebrows arched.

"We're running out of time, standing here chatting about it!"

"Sure. Right this way, Grandpa."

I let the comment pass and followed her. The main avenue was deserted, like the lobby. I looked up and down the boulevard. Cameron Plumb, and any remnant of him, had disappeared like a rabbit in a magic trick.

I kept up with her, never letting her out of my sight, following her down yet another alleyway that jutted at a forty-five-degree angle off the main boulevard.

"There," she said, pointing.

All I saw was a ramshackle shed built out of discarded wood, sitting alone next to a pile of rubble, at the end of a dead-end alley. A hand-painted sign hung next to the crooked door. We walked up to it. '*The Baltimore Sun—Far East Bureau*' was scrawled across it.

"Grandiose, isn't it?" I scowled at the sign.

"Most of us just send the film back to the States. They obviously can't develop anything from my Bell & Howell here. But if you want to see your shots, this is the place," she said, her tone more serious than before. "And I, for one, can't *wait* to see what you took in Kaesong."

"I'm not going to show you anything, Daniel."

"Sheesh. Okay. I thought we were friends now," she retorted, knocking on the dilapidated front door.

A face appeared from the inside, looking through a tiny viewing window fitted with a piece of irregularly shaped glass that had been cut into the door. A pair of eyeglasses was all I could make out through the warped glass. As soon as the person inside saw Daniel waving beside me, he opened the door and yanked us into a tiny vestibule. He slammed the door behind us, turned and opened a second door, pushed us inside, and stood with his arms crossed in the red light that filled a space no bigger than my hall closet back in Rochester. Coming in from the alleyway, I couldn't see him at first. One bulb lit the room, screwed into a wood block strung up with wiring that dangled across the single long table. A neat pile of military-issue interoffice envelopes rested on the table edge. Three metal pans full of liquid sat side-by-side on the table. A few 8x10s hung at an angle, dripping wet, from a clothesline that ran across the room just above our heads. A working darkroom. My smile must have been glowing in the semi-darkness.

"What do you need?" The man's voice was squeaky in the dark. "Jesus, you got a lot of equipment! And, by the way, *The Baltimore Sun* will own the rights to anything you develop in here."

"Terry Tusley," I said, sticking out my hand. "I thought Southerners were known for their hospitality."

"Well, Maryland's not that far south," he said.

"Apparently," Daniel said, laughing. "Terry, this is Frank Jaspers. He runs the Korea bureau for *The Baltimore Sun* and sometimes *The Washington Post*."

"Did run. We're outta here in two days. We have a guy on his way to Panmunjom, and he'll leave Korea directly from there. We're ready to pack up shop. Whattaya got, Terry Tusley?"

I drew the cameras over my head and set them on the far end of the table. I hesitated to pull the Signet out of my waist pack. *The Baltimore Sun* wasn't going to own anything I had. I looked at Daniel and, without another word, she put her arms around Frank's shoulders, and stuck her face in front of his. He visibly melted.

"I think we have to go back to the Chosun," she said. "Together."

"Promises, promises. You're full of shit as always, Daniel," Frank said with a sigh. He looked across her at me, enjoying the moment.

"Don't set anything on fire," he said.

"I think this is a water-related process," I replied, as Daniel dragged him out the two little doors.

Finally, I was alone.

The tiny room felt as familiar as an old friend. My whole body knew that I had something, I really had something, in the Signet. I pulled my camera from my waist pack and set it on the table. I didn't trust the ratty old red lightbulb. I spied a black darkroom bag draped across a tattered chair in the corner. I pulled it over the camera and popped open the housing. The roll of film fell easily into the bag.

I inspected the baths and tested the solutions, pulling three alkaloid strips from the small pile on the table. I reached into the bag and placed the film into position. I bathed it with the three solutions, one after the other, like the film was a baby that I loved even before it was born. I agitated it first with the developing bath, then switched over and swished it in the fixer. By the time I had the film hanging to dry on the clothesline, my hands were shaking.

The old chair made a loud scraping noise across the wood floor as I pulled it closer to the hanging film strips and collapsed into it. And then the tears fell, alone in this tiny darkroom, because all I could think about was when Francine gave Harry his first bath, how he'd cried and yowled so loud that all of Rochester must have thought we were drowning him. But we knew that it was a cry of life that came out of him back then.

The film would need an hour or two to dry. I sat straight in the chair and took a few deep breaths. The smell of the chemicals reminded me of my shed back home, and of my years at Hawk-Eye Works—an overly glitzy name for the basement lab at Kodak—working behind blacked-out windows, and how Ed from Blue Star had reached out to me like an angel from heaven...

And now I was here.

It would take a long time to figure out how to make it all up to Harry, how to pull him close to me, when before I couldn't, but that now I thought maybe I could.

I glanced up at the negative. I jumped to my feet, knocking over the chair behind me. I grabbed a loupe, pulling the negative on its clothespin down to my eye. I peered through the loupe. Even in this light, even with an image so small, the negative revealed Commander Tobin's face registering the shock just as the bullet got him, and the Korean peasant was a complete and unobstructed figure, his angular hat knocked back off his head, taking a simultaneous hit. Tobin's bars and ribbons were distinct, and I could even see a flash of sunlight reflect off the pins fastened to his collar. It was an action shot, like the second the bat hits the ball out of the park. It didn't even need a caption—it was blatant; it explained the price of war, but also the price of trying for peace, and that violence was never going to end, no matter how many treaties we signed, no matter how many platitudes we said or printed.

Introducing those poor Korean peasants into the proceedings without proper vetting caused a cataclysmic failure. The propaganda had ruined any chances for success. And it was clearly all Tom Young's fault. I hoped Ed would agree. I hoped some goddamn editor would agree. It was time to stop the bullshit, and let us do our work, which was, pure and simple, to show up and record it all, and not change things by being in the mix with setups and drama that didn't need to happen at all.

I took the negative down and pulled three pieces of contact paper from the box at the end of the table. The enlarger was a damn old thing, but when I turned it on, the lamp worked just fine. The unshielded heat from the enlarger lamp made the hair on my arms curl up as I laid the negative in. The image held to the photo paper like a child to its mother. In a matter of an hour, I had three photographic paper copies of my picture hanging by clothespins over my head, drying in the acrid darkroom.

There was no place else in Korea that I needed to go. This was it. Panmunjom was already scheduled, and I didn't even want to be there. It would be swarming with photographers, and then they'd be kicking us all out. Tom wouldn't dare pull another one of his stunts.

As I regarded my 8x10s dangling from the clothesline, something made me look closer at the image on the wet paper. There, in the upper corner, part of a face had made it into the frame. Blond hair. Just an edge of a mouth.

"Harry," I whispered. "Harry, you're here."

I was near him. I could feel it just as surely as if he were standing beside me. Harry, reflected across the inside my camera, projected together with the image onto my film.

A moment of silence, just me and Harry.

And then, the loudest bang exploded right outside the lab.

"Goddammit! Harry!"

I yanked the photo paper off the clothespins and swiped my negatives off the tabletop. I grabbed an envelope from the pile at the table's edge, slid the developed pictures and the negatives into it, and tucked it under my jacket. I slipped the Signet back into my waist pack, picked up Cameron's cameras and flung them across my shoulders. The Signet, the new Argus, the old Kardon. Check, check, check.

Another explosion shook the shed, the floor vibrating violently beneath me. It couldn't be more than fifty yards away. Steady, Tusley. You're almost there.

I threw open first the inner door, then the outer door, and hurtled myself into the alleyway. Another mortar blast blew up behind me, knocking me off my feet, and *The Baltimore Sun* photo lab was no more.

I stood up, shaky, then I ran through a swarm of screaming children, back to the Chosun Hotel, clutching the envelope of photos and negatives to my chest.

FORTY-SIX

Rochester

NOVEMBER 1983

Katie

The postcard reflects the waning light from the window. I bring it up to my nose, trying to detect any hint of perfume that could still surround the elegant woman posed across it, top to bottom.

Stop being ridiculous, Katie. It's just cardboard.

It's weathered the time well, though. I don't care right now if Manny doesn't want to know the truth about this lovely thing.

I do.

In my distraction I knock Harry's notification letter off the kitchen table. It falls to the floor in slow motion, gliding side to side like a discarded feather falling from a nest. I pick it up and hold it next to the postcard. I scan the two objects, analyzing. They are both yellowed, taken on the color of warm sunlight. Although they are made of different types of paper, although one is heavy cardstock and one is onionskin, they are equally arresting, equally important.

They begin to talk to one another.

Harry letter: *Who are you, "V"?*

V postcard: *I am your father's French lover. Et vous?*

Harry: *His forgotten son. Dead, too.*

V: *Ah. Tant pis. Too bad for you.*

A sharp knock reaches me from upstairs. I know who it is. Unsteady, I rise, the resilient postcard clenched in my left hand, the delicate letter dangling from the fingertips of my right.

The bathroom, where the noise is coming from, is the very last door at the end of the hall. I pass Troy's bedroom. His laundry is folded on the bed where I'd left it months ago, after he'd picked through it and decided on the absolute minimum he should bring to boot camp. Then the master bedroom, with its big maple tree outside, swaying in the breeze on this cold November night. I wonder if the moon is out. I wonder if I can remember how to open a window to see the moon, and whether I would fit through that window, and whether two stories is high enough up to jump and be done with all of this.

I finally reach the bathroom. The knocking is coming from inside the medicine cabinet.

I hold the postcard and Harry's letter flat onto the mirrored cabinet door, throwing my entire weight against them, making sure the cabinet door can't swing open on its own. The silver mirror sparkles around the edges of the postcard and the letter, reflecting the dim light that seeps into the bathroom from the living room downstairs.

The knocking sound is louder, louder, louder.

"You fucking cut it out, okay?" I say to the medicine cabinet, as if the bottle of pills is a child of mine, one who could be disciplined with a strong tone and some follow-through.

The knocking stops.

"Something beautiful, a gift from Paris for my birthday," I sigh, gazing at the postcard pinned beneath my open palm.

Harry's letter shines translucent, the typewriter keystrokes sunk deep into the thin paper, the ink from each letter bleeding ever so slightly from the strike of the typewriter key.

"We regret to inform you..." I say out loud, my voice high and clear in the empty house.

The searing words are no less painful now, thirty-two years later. An arc of time beneath which I've walked, hesitated, crawled, and hidden, finally emerging out to daylight, and to Manny, and to Troy.

But neither of my fine men is here with me now, in the dark. Neither has the time for me.

I pull back, and the postcard and letter flutter down into the bathroom sink. Something moves behind me, a reflection in the mirror. Another ghost. He is glowing, indistinct. But it is him.

"Back again, Trombone?"

"Hey, I just wanted to meet Terry Tusley's little girl. Your daddy said he had a little girl back home," Trombone says, his voice gravelly and rich, his Southern Creole rounding out every syllable.

I can feel the excitement of seeing Trombone rise in my throat. But his eyes aren't on me right now. He's staring into the bathroom sink.

"Dad lost track," I say. "I was already a grown woman when he left for Korea."

"Why are you leaving them important papers where they could get ruined, Katie?"

"They fell down," I say.

"You look like you need a break. You want some stuff? I got some really good stuff from Saigon."

He rummages around in his Army-issue duffle bag for the needles and the stash of shit.

"What stuff do you have today, Trombone? That last batch was really—"

"*Laissez les bons temps rouler*, Katie," he says, just like he always did and always will.

Let the good times roll.

I squint into the hallway, trying to make out his silhouette in the dark. Maybe I can ask him a new question this time. After all, ghosts have all the answers, don't they?

"Trombone, do you think cameras know what they're doing?"

"You ask *me* about cameras? Your daddy, he's swimmin' in cameras, your brother he's some bigwig at Kodak ain't he? And your own mama—" Trombone stops, his face more guilty-looking than usual.

"My mother? What about my mother?" I ask, and we are back in the Washington townhouse, me squatting on the hardwood floor with him, the spent needles scattered, empty, and Troy coming home from Miss Shaw's third-grade classroom any minute, the school bus turning the corner of Pennsylvania Avenue, on its way to Foggy Bottom, just rounding the corner off H Street.

"I gotta run, okay?" Trombone says. He tosses his duffle across his back.

"Can you just answer the question?" I say, dropping to the cold floor of the bathroom.

"So many questions you got. Take it easy, girl. You don't need anything, just this nice place here in Washington, with all the pictures on the walls. See that one?" he says, pointing somewhere over my head. "That's a picture your daddy took of me and my slick right there! I loved that bird. She got shot out from under me in the Mekong. But I didn't worry. I had friends everywhere. They came and got me," he says, then pauses. "After a little while."

Georgetown sunlight spills across my Rochester hallway, even though it's eight o'clock at night, and I can finally see him in all his glory, backing down the beige carpet, almost too big for the space. Trombone is my height, but powerfully built, and he has a way that makes people join him in convivial friendship wherever he goes. I know this, because I can see it from the abyss where I live my life.

He pauses, scratching his chin in thought.

"The camera's intent is to see something *forever*," Trombone says. His eyes are shining. They are liquid, like two cups of coffee set on the broad, dusky cloth of his fine face.

"See what, Trombone, my love?" I say, wanting my question answered before he evaporates into the darkness of the hallway. "What is the camera really supposed to see?"

He hesitates for only a second.

"You, honey," he says, and then he is gone.

Me. The one who would play messenger for my father, personally finding a way to get his pictures into print, brainwashing my son Troy along the way. The way Dad brainwashed my brother Harry.

I can never forgive my father for the way he talked to Harry, letting him think something ugly was beautiful.

I look down at the postcard in the bathroom sink. My mother was beautiful, and even she wasn't enough.

A small knock comes from inside the medicine cabinet, tentative and gentle.

I cannot ignore it this time.

FORTY-SEVEN

Seoul

JULY 1953

Terry

I stepped around broken glass to find a working pay phone at the back of the lobby in the Chosun Hotel. I finally reached Ed through a series of garbled connections with various invisible men and women intoning "One minute, please."

As I waited the interminable minute, I pictured Ed's face swathed in a cloud of his own cigarette smoke. How he'd be tipped far back in his comfortable office chair, secure in a modern skyscraper jutting into the blue midtown Manhattan sky.

I gripped the phone receiver as Ed puzzled over my explanation. I heard his chair squeak, and I imagined him bent forward, elbows on his desk, head in his hands.

His usual posture of skepticism, born and bred in the canyons of New York City.

"So, you have only one picture to send me," he said, his voice heavy with disappointment.

My shirt was soaked, and the camera strap cut into my shoulders and back.

"It's Harry," I said, again. "It's my son, Harry."

"There's too much noise on the line, you couldn't have said what I thought you said."

A picture of a dead man. A commanding officer. It would be amazing if this was the first photograph I landed on the front page of a New York paper.

It's the picture Harry would have wanted to be a part of.

I could hear Ed wheezing. I pulled Cameron's Argus Brick up to my eye, holding it easily with one hand. The camera felt thick and solid. I gazed through the viewfinder past the blown-out front doors of the deserted hotel. The street out front—in fact, all of Sogong-Ro—was pure chaos. Rubble everywhere, orphaned children wandering in rags. Women crying. Inside the former ballroom, the table that had held all the cameras was not only empty, it was destroyed, its jagged remains scattered into a far corner. Through the shattered plate glass window, I could see open-air jeeps moving along the ripped-up pavement outside. It didn't matter. I had Harry in my camera, and I would do anything in my power to honor him.

"Tusley, if you got a good shot at the failed talks, and the next set of talks haven't started, then we could have a real problem with the editors doing anything with it, you know what I mean?"

"Did someone already tell you not to publish anything from me, Ed?"

"Well, I can't say," he exhaled into the phone.

"If anyone from the British side said not to print it, then you have to print it. Right? You know that, Ed!"

"My instructions now are to keep you out of Panmunjom!"

He was yelling into the phone. "And that's from my own boss, so screw you, Tusley, if you think I'm ready to lose my goddamn job over some highfalutin point you're trying to make over there!"

I slid down to the filthy floor, the phone cord stretched tight, the receiver heavy against my face. What was I doing here? You can't fool a New Yorker. You can't go saying you have a ghost in your film and expect him to buy it. You can't fly into the radar of the head of British Propaganda, refuse to hand over your film, and not expect him to retaliate. Just when I began to lose faith, the phone line crackled back to life.

"Okay, send the picture," Ed coughed into the receiver. "Navy air mail. Find a guy named Phillips in the comms outfit—if it hasn't been blown up—so it's sure to get here within the next forty-eight hours. It has to get here fast, or no way."

"You'll see, Ed. It's a great picture."

"Yeah, sure," he said. "So… What do you want to do now, Tusley?"

New shouting reached my ears from outside. It was insistent. French. A phrase that sounded exactly the same in English. *Se rendre*. Surrender. A shout back in Korean, unintelligible to my ears. I gripped the phone.

"Nobody's dying for nothing. Not as long as I have a camera," I said.

"You're not making a helluva lot of sense anymore, you know that, Tusley?"

"Yeah, I admit that," I said. "It's been kind of crazy."

"Maybe this wasn't the greatest idea, sending you back there, buddy. I can pave your way back home. There's a transport leaving Wonsan Harbor every five minutes."

"I want to stay in Southeast Asia," I said, surprising myself.

"You sound like a goddamn lunatic," he said. "What's happened to you over there?"

I pictured the unending pack of Lucky Strikes, the smoke suspended in the air around him. Towering windows, cascading sun. The tin-stamped ceiling high above Ed's head. A place where no enemy bullet would dare fly.

He wasn't destined to be in harm's way. He hadn't earned it, like me and Harry.

I straightened myself up against the pockmarked wall, calculating at breakneck speed. How much film did I have left, was the stockpile here already empty, did Daniel have a secret stash. Fuck Daniel. Cameron's cameras were probably bursting with unused film, whether—

Ed again coughed into the phone. The line was getting tenuous, and his voice went in and out. "Well, the French are digging into Indochina… there's this loc—tion we've dropped a few——into, to take a couple photos. You can get——by Navy boat—Wonsan, then they—new, big helicopters ferrying our people in, workhorses I think they call 'em—jump on one to . . ."

His voice sounded far away, and the word "photos" had been barely audible. But I heard it.

Ed got close to his receiver. "Here it is, I got it: Dien Bien Phu—"

"Tell us where that is, Ed," I said, then quickly corrected myself. He didn't need to think I was completely off my rocker. "Tell *me*, I mean."

"Vietnam, Terry. It's a deluxe French garrison, fifteen-thousand French soldiers, led by a colorful character, guy has about five names." He paused, the line again starting to break up.

"Yeah, says here——some French major, Christian——Marie Ferdinand——*De La* something—Christ! Well, anyway, they——everything you need: film, liquor, cigarettes.... They're looking for photographers—willing—take a risk. Can probably get you out there by next Wednesday at the earliest, can you get yourself to—"

"Ed!" I snapped, thinking there was no time to waste. Harry could get impatient. He wasn't a dawdler, that boy of mine. He'd lead me to the next great shot.

"Yeah, what *now*?" Ed shouted, probably startled at the change in his mild-mannered, upstate photojournalist.

"Is there action at this place called Vietnam?" I asked.

I heard him draw a labored breath.

"There will be," he said, exhaling with a rattle into the phone.

FORTY-EIGHT

Dien Bien Phu, Vietnam

JULY 1953

Terry

"*Pour qui te prends-tu*?"

Who the hell was I? Good question.

The tall French officer blocked my path to the gigantic canteen behind him, waiting for an answer in the blustery wind as the rotor noise from the helicopter died down. He looked annoyed, his rain-slicked face drawn into a sneer.

So, this was Dien Bien Phu, Vietnam. Another far-flung French colonial conquest. No one here yet to concoct a fake story, just the real thing, playing out for all the world to see, once I got myself situated.

Harry would be proud.

"*Je suis*..." I started to answer, pulling out my soaked press badge for him to read.

"*Et qui vous fait signe*?" He was glaring at a second helicopter that had just landed, resting a few yards behind me.

"Who's waving?" I asked, squinting up at him. I turned to see where he was looking.

How in God's name…? She was standing next to the heli, waving to me in the rain.

Daniel.

"*Une autre journaliste*," I sighed, and with that the French officer turned his back and marched into the canteen.

She'd found me a pilot with space in his skid and I thought we'd said goodbye in the courtyard of the Chosun Hotel. But she must have found another helicopter. A stocky man jumped out of the pilot's hatch, pulled off his headgear and strolled over to Daniel.

She gave him a hug before she hurried toward me.

"Your photo of Tobin made it to the *Post*!" Daniel was breathless with excitement.

"What? How could—"

She threw her duffle bag into the mud, crouched down, and started to unzip it.

"What the hell are you doing here?" I shouted in the twilight, my heart racing at the thought of the photo making the front page.

"She's welcome to go anywhere I go," said the pilot, his voice raspy and deep, a Creole drawl, and I looked up to see a familiar face.

"Trombone!" I said.

"*C'est moi*."

"Terry, you're on the map now! The *New York Post*! My uncle got the paper sent to Seoul, special delivery to Trombone!"

"Front page?" I blurted.

"Front page, yes sir! Let's get out of the rain and I'll give it to you." She dropped her voice. "This is the most amazing place, Terry. I came here two weeks ago with the supply transport. The French are trying to prove something. They think they can establish a stronghold here and keep all their territories across Indochina."

"Yeah, well, good luck with that, right?" Trombone laughed, and the smell of whiskey hit my nostrils.

"What do you mean?" I asked.

Trombone grunted. "There's a lot more of them Vietnamese right here than fucking Frenchmen!" He turned to her. "How long are you staying here, Daniel? I can come pick you up when I bring in the—" He glanced at me and didn't finish his sentence.

"Tusley's okay, Trombone. He owes you his life, right? You can talk. He's one of us. And, he lost his son in Korea."

"Shit, Daniel," I said. "You don't have to tell everyone."

"Why not?" Trombone asked.

"Because…" I started to say, but I thought better of it.

Because he's in my camera, that's why not, I thought.

Trombone cleared his throat. "Talkin' about it is the best tonic there is. See y'all later. I gotta go."

He started to walk back to his helicopter, and when he was about fifteen feet away, I felt the jungle around us close in, foreboding and black. The rain was starting to pour.

"When are you coming back?" The words left my lips before I could stop them.

Trombone walked back patiently, like I was a child who needed another word before departing.

"You will *not* believe how often I come here, Terry. I bring food. I bring ammunition. I bring guns and liquor and sometimes they have me bring a couple of gals from Saigon."

He paused. "I can bring you *anything you want,* Terry," he said pointedly, glancing at Daniel. "I also bring the mail… Which I almost forgot about!"

He dashed back to the helicopter and dumped a big mailbag under the rickety shelter at the edge of the landing pad.

"*Mon Dieu*! I gotta get out of here before I can't see a goddamn thing!" Then he ran back to his helicopter and started her up, the shiny wet rotors turning slowly at first.

In a minute he'd roared into the deepening gray sky.

"Show me the *Post*," I said, turning to Daniel.

"It's pouring. Let's get inside."

"Do you still have that movie camera?" I asked, reaching for the door of the canteen, and holding it open for her.

"Do you still keep your photos secret?" she responded, walking into the room ahead of me.

"Are you getting tired of pretending to be a man?"

"I never get tired of it," she said, plopping the wet helmet onto her head.

I stopped in my tracks when we entered the room, taken aback by the scene before me. It was alive with noise and laughter, awash with light. At least twenty uniformed Frenchmen were drinking from crystal glasses, speaking rapid French, here in the middle of the jungle in far northern Vietnam. A generator chugged from somewhere inside. On every table, a white tablecloth, a bottle of wine.

Not the scruffy outpost I'd expected.

A woman's voice wafted over the noise. "*Non, non*, I sing over there, at the front!"

She wore a flowered dress, and she was pointing to a spot with a little stage, her red fingernails glinting in the light of the overhead lamps that were strung at intervals across the high beams.

"Sister, you'll sing where I tell you to sing!" the man, clearly American, shouted back at her.

I sensed Daniel slip away from my side into the vastness of the room. The girl turned toward me.

"Terry!" she exclaimed. She sprinted across the canteen and kissed both my cheeks.

"Vivienne! What the hell are you doing here?" I asked as she led me to a table.

"*Le* Major Général Ferdinand invited me," she began, but the men around the room were watching us, and she didn't continue.

I didn't need to know anything more. We had no ties, no promises had been made. Besides, I was a married man, wasn't I?

Daniel suddenly appeared beside the table, her helmet casting a shadow across her face. "Hey, Terry, can you watch my duffle? I'm going to get a few shots outside," she said in her alto voice, covertly looking Vivienne up and down. "You seem to have friends here. I'll just be gone a minute."

Before I could stop her, Daniel dropped her bag at my feet and slipped out the canteen door.

"*Qui est-il?*" Vivienne asked, her brow furrowed.

"He is a photographer," I said curtly, a bit annoyed with Daniel. "His uncle is some big wheel in San Diego."

"You are traveling with him, now? And not *mon ami* Cameron?"

"I travel alone, mostly. You know that."

"*Non*, you do not travel alone. Someone is always with you. When you walk, you cast two shadows."

"You're a crazy Frenchwoman."

"Terrance, where is Cameron?" Vivienne repeated, serious now, as if Cameron and I were attached to each other in her mind.

"He went home, Vivienne," I said. "He left Korea after the… well, let's just say he's thrown in the towel on war photography."

"Oh." She stopped me with a stare.

"What's wrong?"

"Cameron must know something we do not!" Vivienne sat and wrung her hands, a motion so unlike her. "I do not think your *ami* should go outside at night." She stared at the canteen door.

"What are you so worried about? This place doesn't seem like—"

"I do not want harm to come to him, because he is with you," she said quickly.

Before I could think about what she just said, a little band gathered next to the bar, tuning up their instruments. Four strapping Frenchmen, complete with berets and violins, pulled their chairs into a semicircle near the bar and started tuning up. Vivienne glanced up at me. The single silver microphone awaited her. A uniformed soldier, dripping wet, walked over to us. Trombone's mailbag was slung across his shoulders. He dropped a letter onto the table.

"*Pour vous, monsieur,*" he said, then spun on his heel and stomped away.

I turned it over. It was postmarked Quebec.

My dear wife was more connected than the Paris Metro.

Along the top edge, I noticed a yellow stain. Extra glue. It had been opened and resealed.

Vivienne was trying mightily not to look at me, or the letter in my hands.

"*Vas-y,*" I said, gently pushing her away. "Go sing."

FORTY-NINE

Dien Bien Phu

JULY 1953

Terry

I ripped open the letter. Francine's perfume filled the air. The scent took me back for a moment to our borrowed bedroom in Quebec City, where the curtains billowed in the breeze off the St. Lawrence River.

"You tracked me down in record time, this time," I muttered under my breath.

Her lacy handwriting slid across the page.

Mon Chéri,

I write this in English so the French spies at D.B.P. make no attempt to read it. Their English is very poor. Well-done on your work in Rochester. I knew it was best for you to lead the project. It kept you busy for a few years, no? We are using your film solution for a new contract they won, and our new son-in-law did a fine job of getting everything in order.

I hope that you are staying safe in Vietnam. You are too far north. There is a place in Saigon where the photographers are gathering. It is called the Caravelle Hotel, maybe you should head over there. I know for certain that the French will triumph, but I do hope you have a... I do not know what to call it in English... plan de sortie?

Je t'embrasse,
Francine

Exit plan. She wanted to know if I had an exit plan. What a soothing sentiment. The rest of the note barely made any sense. She was referring to the work I did at Kodak before Korea. What did that have to do with Vietnam?

I shook the envelope. Nothing more.

"Damn her."

"Damn who? Would you like to share this very expensive Beaujolais with me?" A sweaty man plopped down next to me, holding out an open wine bottle and two glasses upside down by their stems. "We got only the best here."

"Oh, nothing," I said, shoving the letter back into its envelope. "Yeah, sure."

"Marv Perkins," he said, his voice unsteady, obviously a drink or three ahead of me. "US Military Assistance and Advisory Group."

"Really." This guy looked like he couldn't find his way out of a barn.

"Shh..." He said drunkenly, placing one finger to his lips. "We're training the people here in secret. We haven't declared war or anything. No one's supposed to know we're here." He poured the wine into the glasses, spilling it on the tablecloth.

"What the hell could *you* advise anybody on?"

"Good question. Damned if I know. Nobody in charge speaks English. There's about ten of us here, more coming in." He sat back to take a sip. "Anyways, I was just trying to be friendly, since the one and only woman here seems to be someone you know, and you're not one of those goddamn French lackeys."

He flung a field cap on the chair next to me, and turned his attention to Vivienne at the bar. I glanced at the cap. It was brand new, not a mark on it. A big pin was stuck into one side. I leaned in closer. A shield surrounded letters that ran in an arc, spelling out "First Division" in English.

A round of laughter rippled across the humid room. Vivienne was now in the company of at least five handsome French officers. Marv turned back to me, smiling.

"She's some kind of French starlet, right?" he asked.

"She's had a few brushes with fame, I guess," I said. No need to mention the goddamn postcard. "I'll take some, if you're sharing."

"Things are always nicer when they're shared," he said, spilling wine on the floor as he filled my glass.

"How many of those bottles have you nailed?" I asked.

"Lost count," he said, laughing.

Was this all that was going on at Dien Bien Phu? Fine wine, white tablecloths, and, for some reason, Vivienne? I tried to ignore the sound of her laughter wafting over the room, velvety and musical above the voices of the men. And where the hell was Daniel? Her duffle lay at my feet, calling to me to open it up and pull out the newspaper with my photo on the front page. But I had to get rid of this guy first.

I held out my empty glass.

"Another?" I smiled.

"*Bien sûr,*" he said in his best fake French, refilling my glass to the very top. "Man, it's hot here! I hail from a pretty little town on the edge of the Everglades, in ole Florida. You'd think I wouldn't mind the heat here, but I do! And you?"

"Rochester, home of Kodak," I blurted out. I'd had two glasses of wine in quick succession. I hadn't eaten anything since yesterday, and the advisor, or whatever the hell he was, was starting to look a little blurry.

He tipped back in his chair. "Kodak cameras, American success story, right? Do you work for Kodak?"

"In the basement," I said, knocking back a third refill. The humidity and laughter all started to swirl into a droning white noise.

"Kinda old for the mailroom, aren't you?"

My empty glass felt slippery in the humidity. "I was a chemist at Kodak."

The wine had a stupefying effect. Maybe it was the heat. The lights. Or Vivienne's voice floating across the room. If she was sleeping with the top commander, General What's His Face, I'd…

"You don't say? And here I thought you were a press guy, with all those fancy cameras. What did you concoct back there in Rochester?" He leaned forward and looked at me with bloodshot eyes.

"Really, really, *really* big film," I said, gesturing with my hands in the air to a width of about two feet. Francine's letter fluttered to the floor.

"Well, you are some lucky fellow!" He slumped over the table.

"I'm also a war photographer," I offered, but he was out cold.

Another man, dressed identically to my drinking buddy, suddenly appeared next to Marv and pulled him to his feet.

"Excuse me, mister. C'mon, Marv. You need to get to bed," he said, dragging him away.

I pulled the bottle over and poured the last few drops into my glass, remembering the wine in the trunk of the Nazis' sedan, dusty, stolen from somebody's wine cellar. The furs and the cheese between the fat one's teeth.

"What am I doing here?" I sighed.

I picked up Francine's letter and held it up to my nose. The paper's scent had dissipated. I peered again at it, wilting in the humidity.

I knew it was best for you to lead the project.

I thought about my desk at Kodak, the endless hours working out chemical formulas for infrared, large-format film that would resist extreme cold while also retaining the ability to repel intense heat. We were discouraged from asking too much about it. Anyway, I tried to get away to New York whenever Ed had an assignment for me.

And what was that reference to Manny? I squinted at Francine's loopy script.

Our new son-in-law did a fine job of getting everything in order.

I'd just missed meeting Manny before Ed sent me to shoot the armistice. I didn't know exactly what his job was down in Washington, DC. Francine said he was a Lockheed guy, airplane contracts for the government. Francine said Katie was happy, but I never got the chance to assess this for myself. I'd up and left for Korea without any notice to Katie. I could picture her coming through the screen door of the house in Rochester, this Manny guy right behind her, hauling in their luggage for a weekend stay. She would call out my name a few times, and then she would realize that the house was empty.

A little pang of guilt stabbed my stomach. Maybe it was just the wine. I could have let her know I wouldn't be there.

I sat back, pondering Francine's note, when my foot brushed past Daniel's duffle bag.

I slid the letter back into its envelope and jammed it into my waist pack, behind the Signet. I reached down and grabbed Daniel's duffle by the handles. I had my hand on the big flap when a giant boom reverberated from outside the canteen, followed by rapid gunfire.

The door banged open, and Daniel tumbled in.

She fell to the floor, her helmet still on her head. From across the canteen, Vivienne screamed. She ran to Daniel, the men following her in confusion, pistols drawn, shouting over each other. Vivienne got down on the floor with her, and through the swarm of men I could see both of them, Daniel's army-green jacket and Vivienne's flowered dress. My first thought was of a colorful, blossoming tree that had been cut to the ground.

I pulled Cameron's Argus Brick forward and brought it to my eye.

The French officer who'd met me at the helicopter was at my elbow. "*Non*!" He swatted at the camera and turned to the room.

"*Finissez de manger*!" He gestured to their dinner plates full of food. "*C'est rien.* Is nothing."

The men stared at him, the sound of booming outside getting closer. They picked up their forks and started to eat, looking uncomfortable.

Then the officer turned to Daniel and Vivienne with a sneer. "*Debout*. Get up."

They did as instructed, Vivienne visibly shaking. I detected that familiar look of defiance on Daniel's face, hidden as it was beneath her helmet. She didn't seem to be injured. The men, several with white cloth napkins tied around their necks, said nothing.

"*Mais, monsieur...*" Vivienne sputtered, but the officer took her by the arm, ignoring Daniel.

"*Chanteuse,*" he said, turning on his heel so all the men could hear him. "Serenade us, *mademoiselle*! Zee wine eez not yet done." And with that, he firmly guided her back to the bar.

She looked over her shoulder at me as crackling gunfire resonated from just outside. Daniel sidled over.

"Tusley—" she whispered.

"Are you okay?" I said, looking for any signs of injury.

"Yes," she hissed. "But we need to get out of here! These guys are going to get slaughtered."

"No way," I scoffed. "There's a bunch of American advisors here. An outpost like this is going to attract attention from the locals, you know that! A goddamn French General, his wine and his mistress—"

"No." Daniel cut me off. "The situation here is changing, and fast. Those weren't a few snipers, Terry. I'm telling you, we have to contact Trombone and get the hell out before it's too late."

"Isn't this exactly what we came here for?"

And by we, I meant Harry and me, I thought.

Another boom from outside, closer now.

"You're a glutton for punishment now, aren't you?" Daniel asked. She squatted to retrieve her duffle. "I usually try to select my location based on life expectancy."

"Well, we can't always be that lucky, can we?" I retorted, thinking of my son.

The band picked up their instruments and continued to play at the front of the canteen. Vivienne's voice rose tentatively above the music from the bar.

Another boom from outside the canteen door.

"Get down, Tusley," Daniel said, dragging on my arm until I was under the table with her, the white tablecloth hiding us from view, but we could hear all around us the clinking of glasses, the sound of silverware on china, the strained conversation of the French soldiers, pretending nothing was happening outside.

"What did you see out there, Daniel?" I asked.

"Well, come to think of it, nothing a front-page war photographer couldn't handle." And with that, amid the sporadic gunfire from outside, Daniel opened her duffle and pulled out something wrapped in layers of burlap.

The *New York Post*, in all its glory, fell from her hands into mine. It was dry and perfect and creased in the center. I could almost smell the newsprint.

My fingers grazed the image, a full 4x5 rendering, only three inches from the headline. Commander Tobin's face was noble, full of defiance, caught in heroic shades of black and gray. He looked shocked but not beaten. I'd captured the precise moment of the hit.

"I gotta say, it's a pretty great shot, Tusley," Daniel murmured. "I can't believe they actually printed it."

I nodded, smiling. My photo credit was printed in tiny letters along one edge: Terrance Tusley, Global/UP.

I looked closer. There he was. Harry. Nearly hidden behind them.

At the moment of action, forever there, wherever the hammer fell.

And I knew, if I wanted to get my pictures published, I would have to be very careful who I sent them to. This was a one-off for Ed at Blue Star, but I needed to establish my portfolio. This was just the beginning.

Insistent gunfire outside erupted much closer than before.

"Trombone will have to get us as soon as possible, before they can't get any helicopters in or out of here," Daniel said. "He must already have heard—"

"There are fifteen thousand French soldiers quartered here, Daniel."

"They will all be dead in a few months. They will be too stupid to leave."

Another boom, and a sound like fireworks. Marv Perkins, the drunken adviser, had said there were about ten American advisors here, and more coming. They, like Vivienne, would never sign up for a suicide mission, I was sure of that.

But Francine's convoluted letter was clear on one point. The place to be was Saigon, not here.

The Caravelle Hotel.

"How long do you want to stay under this table, Daniel?"

"Let's see what they do. I figure the French have enough supplies for a few months, but the North Vietnamese can wait a lot longer than that. For now, under the table feels perfect." She pulled out her Bell & Howell and started checking the settings.

I folded the newspaper and shoved it under my jacket as another boom resonated outside the canteen. Harry would find me, no matter where I was. The thought was reassuring and frightening, like I was handling an unstable chemical.

"I think my camera is haunted," I mumbled.

"So, what else is new?" Daniel snorted.

FIFTY

Rochester

NOVEMBER 1983

Katie

Dr. Pine says the hallucinations will eventually stop. I guess that's a good thing, although, to be frank, they are the only company I have now. I retrieve the Letter of Regret and the Postcard of Beauty from the sink. That's what I'm going to call them from now on. Thankfully, the sink is dry, and they are undamaged.

I fold the letter around the postcard, feeling like they belong together. Deep in my heart, I know my father slept with this woman. I think about Trombone and the days we laid together, our arms full of puncture holes, while Troy was in his elementary school, learning his ABCs.

Who am I to point fingers?

Dad just always seems so innocent, so completely unaware of how his actions affect other people. Manny, needless to say, isn't a fan. That trip up to Rochester when we were first married set the tone, and it never changed. We'd traveled all day from Washington, DC. Seven hours, counting bathroom stops.

When we got there, the house was empty.

"Your father is a complete loser," Manny had said. "He's not here. We came all the way up, and nobody's here. I don't care if I ever meet him, now."

"Mother's coming," I'd protested. "And Joe should be home soon…"

Manny reached out and lifted my chin.

"I'm starving. Where do people eat, up here in the wilds of Rochester?"

"Bagg's," I said. "We can walk there, it's close, but—"

Manny's face lit up. "Thank you for not making me drive one more minute."

"A lovely summer stroll in upstate New York," I said, trying to make light of the situation.

"It's no nicer than Georgetown, Katie," Manny said. "Someday you'll see that."

I started to follow him back out the door when I noticed that one of my father's UP notepads was lying open on the telephone table in the hallway.

"Manny," I said, picking up the pad. "Look at this."

I recognized Joe's handwriting. Manny stood by my side and started reading it out loud.

"*Caravelle Hotel.*" He scowled and looked off into the distance, then refocused on the note. "*Saigon, All the journalists. Ed.*"

"That must be Ed from Blue Star. He was always calling my father with assignments."

"Assignments? What kind of assignments?" Manny narrowed his eyes.

The years of keeping secrets from my mother about my father taking those trips to New York when he was supposed to be at Kodak caused a trigger effect. I'd held my tongue like an expert witness. Manny glared at me a second, then his expression softened.

"Well, how would *you* know, baby?" He'd ripped the page from the UP pad, folded it up and slid it into his shirt pocket. "Let's go to dinner. Which way to Bagg's?"

As I'd guided my new husband to the old Rochester watering hole, I'd silently repeated the place names from the scribbled note in my head, so I wouldn't forget.

Caravelle Hotel. Saigon.

Dad.

FIFTY-ONE

Dien Bien Phu

AUGUST 1953

Terry

I made sure Vivienne left on the very next helicopter transport out of Dien Bien Phu, giving her enough cash to get back east, and then, I told her, onward to Paris.

"*Non,* I will stay in New York," she'd said.

"No, you will go to Paris," I replied.

"I think she's going to New York," Daniel interjected.

"Don't you have something else to do?" I'd said to Daniel.

The next day, Vivienne was gone.

Daniel and I ventured outside a few times, in daylight only. We didn't have a death wish, and we weren't completely crazy. Trombone and another pilot named Howard flew in and out, at terrible risk, bringing supplies. By the end of the first week, they could barely make one or two flights to us, and supplies were already running low. The wine cellar, which, amazingly, the French officers had built beneath the canteen, was the first to empty out.

Little by little, the food also started to run low.

Daniel kept pressing me to get out. One more photo, and I'd be ready to jump into a helicopter behind her. In the meantime, the pilots couriered our film back to Saigon when they could, and it went by God knows what route to the States.

Trombone brought us color film and mail. One fine day, a few weeks later, he produced a mailbag that contained one lone package, addressed to me. I ripped it open. It was an immaculate *Life* magazine, glossy, big, and in full color. My shot was on the cover. It showed a French gunner poised behind a small, French-made artillery cannon. Beside the cannon, incongruously, was a table with a white tablecloth, four chairs set neatly around it. The French officers had dined beside the cannon only minutes before an ambush by the North Vietnamese.

What the photo editor either didn't see, or slipped past the censors, was the dead body of a French soldier, mostly hidden behind the tall grass, about ten feet from the gun. His yellow-blond hair shone in the setting sun, the golden glow bouncing off the green metal artillery. I squirreled the *Life* magazine away with the *New York Post* containing the front-page Tobin shot, both publications wrapped in burlap for safekeeping.

Daniel and I were done here. I got the shot and told the truth. Harry would agree.

We took Trombone's next transport out to Saigon. When we finally flew out of Dien Bien Phu, we left behind thousands of stubborn French regulars. No more wine or white tablecloths; the cloth was needed for bandages.

Trombone's bird lifted us only yards above gunfire that crackled from the mossy jungle surrounding the French citadel. We landed in Saigon at dawn. A pink blush warmed the landscape as far as I could see, and the prettiness of the city struck me hard. While, right now, it felt much safer than Dien Bien Phu, I knew that soon this place would follow the fate of Seoul and return to its rightful inhabitants. I was sure of it. How would that story play out? And what photo opportunities awaited me here?

When we got to the Caravelle, Ed had already reserved me a room, anticipating I'd find my way there.

At least twenty other journalists were milling around the fancy lobby. Daniel and I steered clear of them and put together our plans for staking out the city.

Marv Perkins, the American I'd met my first night at Dien Bien Phu, was, apparently, part of a trickle that would gush into a torrent of advisors. They were everywhere in Saigon.

So, this was the secret war he'd drunkenly told me about.

Trombone told us about an underground trail that was being used to move Chinese guns into Vietnam. Daniel wanted to find it. Next, we needed to establish a courier track back to the US. Again, I felt wary: now that I was on the cover, people would be watching my work. I wouldn't let my hands be tied. I would shoot whatever I wanted. I had to keep clear of the censors somehow, those purveyors of propaganda, and anybody else who stood in the way of the truth.

The hotel clerk raised his eyebrows upon seeing my signature when I checked in.

"*Monsieur* Tusley? My name is Tran. *Il y a une lettre pour vous.*"

He was impeccably dressed in a white suit. Smiling, he pulled a small, peach-colored envelope from one of the wooden cubbies behind the desk. I turned it over with a sigh, half expecting to smell Francine's perfume. At the upper left of the envelope, small handwriting spelled out the return address.

Katie Tusley-Price. Washington, DC.

"Well, well..." I murmured.

"*Il y a autre chose*?" Tran looked at me with a pleasant expression on his face.

"Um, yes, there is something else. Where is Comms, to get a message back to the States?"

He looked at me blankly. "*Où est la—*"

A tall man strolled up to us. He had a Leica hanging from his neck. He was also wearing dog tags. Signal Corps, or just some interloper, I figured.

"I can help you, mister. The South Vietnamese Communications Bureau is down rue Catinat," he said. "Reuters, the British wire service, has an office there."

"I don't want Reuters, thanks," I said.

"Aren't you a snob! I never heard anyone turn their nose up at Reuters!"

"Well, let's just say I'm not a fan of British news outlets," I said, thinking of Tom Young and his threats.

"Who, exactly, are you trying to contact?" he said.

I looked down at the envelope in my hands.

"Forget it," I said, backing away.

I didn't need anyone at all, come to think of it.

I had Katie.

I had a direct line to someone who lived within five miles of *The Washington Post.*

FIFTY-TWO

Washington, DC

SEPTEMBER 1953

Katie

Not long after Manny and I found out that my father had left Korea for Vietnam, a strange package arrived with the morning mail at our townhouse in DC.

"Can you believe he took those pictures, Katie?" Manny threw the *New York Post* and the *Life* magazine across the hardwood floor. They slid under the sofa together like children hiding from punishment.

"Manny!" I bent down and retrieved them. They were pristine-perfect, arriving by airmail all the way from Saigon, a place I could barely locate on a map.

I sat down and laid them across the big envelope. The return address was emblazoned across the brown paper.

Caravelle Hotel. 19 Công Trường Lam Sơn, Saigon, Vietnam.

I'd found him, actually found him, and he had answered me back.

He wanted to make sure I saw his work. And it was true; I hadn't been visiting the newsstand with any regularity.

Now I would.

"He must be on top of the world," I said, so proud of myself for finding him. It had only taken a simple trip to the Georgetown University library while Manny was at work. I'd scooted over there when we got home from that disastrous trip to Rochester. I'd handed the librarian a small slip of paper with just three words on it. Caravelle. Hotel. Saigon. It was all I had, but it was enough. I'd sent a letter to my father in a hopeful frenzy. But this! I couldn't believe it. I held the envelope tight on my lap, my heart banging with excitement.

I looked up, grinning at my husband. "He's just proud to finally get on the cover," I said, grazing my fingers across the printed papers.

But Manny was frowning.

"Your father is a goddamned traitor," he said. "The press is supposed to make us look good, not like we're a goddamned bunch of idiots, allowing our commanders to get shot at the armistice table in Korea, or dining on white linen while the red commies slaughter innocent villagers in Vietnam!"

"He's a war photographer," I said in surprise. "It's all he ever wanted."

"He's a Kodak chemist! He's not some *journalist*." The word dripped like venom from his tongue. "And now he's in Saigon. We don't want him there!"

Manny's forehead has a vein that pops out when he is angry. It was popping now.

"Who's *we*?" I asked, but Manny just stalked out the front door, already late for work.

The packages from Dad often felt like they had once been wet, the jungle moisture having evaporated in transit, the words half-hidden beneath a splash of light brown mud or splattered with the faded red of dried blood.

Ah, but that was later.

The earliest letters were still clean and white; the first one was quite long, almost chatty, Dad's proud note to go along with the amazing front page photos. As time went by, they were nothing more than instructions: what to do with the film. Short and terse, it was as if he'd used the first letter to dig a trench, turning the rich soil of our alliance, each one like a packet of seeds that he intended for me to plant. He'd begin each one by naming the season. This was his way of marking time, by acknowledging the changes in the way the light slanted into his viewfinder.

Every letter started the same way. *Dear Katie-did.*

A peculiar warmth would spread over me at those words. Whatever my father asked for, I willingly provided. It was like I was a member of his club, communing in our special way, protecting the world from lies.

But what protected me from Dad?

I learned to hide the brown airmail envelopes from Manny, separating any that came in from the morning mail before he'd see them, not sure why he got so angry where my father was concerned, whether it was because Manny's job was related to the military—they were clients, after all. Well, it didn't matter. He would leave for work, and I'd pull out the latest delivery. Even after Dad made his name and become somewhat famous, the packets came. By then, he could have just sent them to his editor. But something kept him from sending the film directly to Blue Star. Did he think it would get intercepted? I didn't know. It was a huge responsibility, and I loved it all: the artful packaging that my father employed for the contents of each envelope, more and more as time went by... artifacts from the front, or the jungle, or whatever they called the ever-changing landscape of Vietnam. I'd stare at the envelopes before I'd open them: my name, hastily scrawled across the front. At top left, my father's return address. That precious thing. It was better than a birthday cake. Heady as any speedball. It didn't matter if Dad kept the letters I sent him or if he threw them away. I wondered sometimes if he was really reading them because he never quite responded to the questions I put in them. But what could I expect? The man was in a war zone.

I watched the mail like a hawk.

One day, a thick packet arrived. Out tumbled a remnant of soft red silk cloth, the letter nestled between two yellow Kodak boxes of undeveloped film, the handwriting blotchy and hurried. The note asked me to do something I had no idea how to do.

Spring 1954

Dear Katie-did,

Make sure Joe stays in his graduate program and keeps his job at Kodak, although with Harry gone—God bless his soul—I don't think they can draft Joe. Something big is coming, and I want him to stay out of it.

Give this film to someone at The Washington Post. *It's not possible for me to get it out any other way, and don't tell your mother anything.*

Gotta run—Dad.

The first time I tried to bring his film to *The Washington Post*, I was wearing my best dress from Saks, but the old security guard at the door glared at me over his tortoiseshell glasses.

"You can't just wander into the lobby of our *Wa-shing-ton Post*, little lady!" His booming voice echoed off the vaunted marble walls.

"My father is a photojournalist in French Indochina. He asked me to give this to the editor," I said, keeping my voice down.

The couple at the other end of the lobby glanced at us.

I reached over and pressed his wrinkly arm, feeling like I could win this man over.

"I'll give you ten dollars to get it upstairs," I said.

"Don't you come back here, missy," he said, taking the money and the bulky envelope.

But I did come back, again and again. The security guard's name was Milton. He divulged to me one day that he had a son in the diplomatic corps in Vietnam. I could tell that Milton would take film from me for as long as I asked him to, because he was worried about his son.

A few weeks after I brought that first roll of film to Milton, and after I'd delivered two more packages to him, I opened the exalted *Washington Post* to find a photo on page two with my father's credit across the bottom. The print showed an American advisor in a jaunty beret and rolled-up sleeves. He was wearing aviators and flashing a bright smile. He was instructing a group of South Vietnamese soldiers in a round of target practice. The Vietnamese men held American guns and wore crisp uniforms. I didn't show it to Manny. Over time, my father's envelopes contained ever-bulkier contents. More and more rolls of film.

I started a secret scrapbook, hiding it in the back of the hall closet. I thought about how to frame up the photographs, and where they would go on the white walls of our Georgetown brownstone.

Someday.

The demand for news photography was growing, and a man named George Asman left his job at *Life* magazine to open his own developing lab on Pennsylvania Avenue. I heard about him from Milton—security guards always seemed to have the inside scoop—and went to his shop. This was a much faster route to publication, not just for *The Washington Post*, but any news outlet.

A short gentleman with thick glasses stood behind the counter. After a while, he and I were old friends.

"Terry Tusley's daughter! What do you have today?"

"Eight rolls, Mr. Asman. Need the negatives back, as well as the finished photos."

"Call me Mickey, honey. How fast do you need 'em?"

I usually had two hours between drop-off, photo developing, and hailing a taxicab to some coffee shop on K Street or N

Street, only a few blocks away from the White House, where a man—somebody variously named John or Frank or Steve—would meet me, smiling as he slid the bulging envelope under his sports jacket. Dad's photo credit was my reward, and now I knew what I was carrying around, and how valuable it was.

Film and photos, film and photos. All while Manny was away at work.

FIFTY-THREE

Washington, DC

DECEMBER 1963

Katie

"What's that?" Manny said when he came home unexpectedly early one winter day, complaining of a sore throat. It was the start of a bitter cold winter in DC, and Manny was outdoors a lot, testing a new project on the tarmac out at Andrews Air Force Base.

When I'd opened the latest package from my father that morning, I'd pulled out something that looked like clothing, the ragged remnants of a child's outfit. Puzzled, I'd nudged the package apart, feeling sick once I recognized the contents: small, torn shorts, child-size. What was going on over there? A little button top caked in dried mud and blood, a soiled baby blanket. The clothes and blanket were wrapped around four yellow boxes of Kodak film and a green cardboard box that looked different from the others.

Bell & Howell. Your Best Studio Quality Movie Film.

I was peering at it when Manny walked through our front door, his eyes like bloodshot question marks.

"Oh, something I found in the neighbor's trash," I said, quickly re-bundling the rags, hiding the film within, and dropping them onto the floor. "Someone must be throwing out old baby clothes, I'll wash them out and see if anyone at the shelter downtown wants them."

"Ah, thinking about a baby, right?" Manny said, trying to embrace me around the waist.

"I don't want your cold germs, big fella. Get upstairs and I'll make you some chicken soup," I said, backing away from him.

"Thank you, that would be nice." He coughed, loosening his tie. "The generals approved our design package. I can finally grab some sleep."

"A new spy plane?" The words escaped me before I could stop them.

Manny paused.

"Where did you hear about that?" He locked me in a stare, and I wracked my brain to avoid telling him I'd been reading *The Washington Post*, which, by then, was questioning our military involvement in Southeast Asia.

"Just a lucky guess?" I smiled charmingly.

He wagged his finger at me.

"Nice try, Dick Tracy," he said. "Don't get all women's lib on me, okay? Stick to the vacuuming. Let the men do their work." He trudged up the stairs to the bedroom, and his hoarse voice wafted down the hallway. "The place looks good, Katie. Need some pictures on the walls, maybe get a decorator?"

I heard him hit the bed and then I scooped up the filthy baby clothes and the fresh film.

"Okay, although, you know, we could frame up Dad's published photos," I shouted up to him. "That would be keen, wouldn't it?"

No answer. In a second, I heard snoring.

"Sure it would, Katie-did," I whispered, looking down at the awful bundle in my arms.

FIFTY-FOUR

Saigon

APRIL 1954

Terry

In the spring of 1954, only weeks after Daniel and I got out, courtesy of Trombone, Dien Bien Phu fell.

The Caravelle in Saigon was my new home.

The hotel was a downtown destination of choice for the rich. People with time on their hands. A serene place, where high-end, well-dressed Vietnamese men quietly nodded at me as they came and went. A far cry from the situation at Dien Bien Phu, and I found it puzzling. There was press presence here, though, and the faint sense that the place was about to change. A bunch of rooms had also been taken by a scrappy young crowd of photographers. Although they had a different point of view on what was going on here, they'd seen my work. At shared dinners they affectionately called me "Terry" or "Tusley," or even "old man."

Things between me and Francine remained quiet. French-Canadians like my wife were neither supporting nor opposing the decisions made around French Indochina while the French nationals who'd built their beautiful homes here tried to go about their lives in this jungle colony they called home, thinking this would all blow over. Some were leaving, most were undecided.

Spring melted into autumn, and a new year arrived.

I went on walks, my camera dangling from my shoulder. French architecture pervaded every avenue, and I heard French spoken every day, although the Vietnamese, like the Koreans, clung to their ancient ways, quietly resisting erasure. They had their own internal problems, the Buddhists becoming more vocal about their opposition to the new American-backed president, Ngo Dinh Diem.

It was easy to see the underlying tension if you looked closely. One clear Saturday morning, two overconfident American journalists from Los Angeles rented a set of rusty motorbikes and took off into the jungle A week went by, then another. No one heard from them again.

I resolved to keep to myself then, my eye focused on the rising numbers of incoming American advisors at the Caravelle. No D-Day landing, no blasting from town to town, like in Europe. Instead, our government was sending men wearing soft hats, not helmets, carrying nothing more than a clipboard and revolver. They towered over the Vietnamese with their crewcuts, their cocky attitudes and their trim, muscular builds. The advisors shied away from pictures as a rule, although I got a few shots when they weren't looking. I started sending them off to Katie, along with my new credentials—the cover shot of Commander Tobin that Daniel gave me, and the photo that nabbed a *Life* cover from Dien Bien Phu just before we left—lovingly wrapped in burlap, just in case she'd missed seeing them on the newsstands herself.

There was something sinister about the advisors. They were my countrymen, but they separated themselves from the correspondence gang at the Caravelle Hotel. If I were going to find Harry, it would be near where they operated, just beyond my focal length, hidden somewhere inside the photographs I took surreptitiously of their handsome faces.

The goal of the advisors was unclear. The slow transfer of military knowledge from the Americans to the South Vietnamese was well underway, but we wouldn't do what the French had done; the US wasn't interested in colonizing Southeast Asia, just in keeping out the commies. At least, that was the official line. I had other ideas, but I kept them to myself.

And, as much as I trusted Daniel, there was one other person who I knew would help me find the truth in the deceptively beautiful and lush city of Saigon. Someone who spoke French with the most charming lilt. Who knew her way around back alleys and who could build a network to rival Francine's.

I pulled out my wallet and extracted a folded bit of worn paper. Vivienne's Paris address was scrawled across the front.

"Would you like to join me in paradise, Vivienne?" I said to the slip of paper.

I was startled out of my reverie by a familiar voice over my shoulder.

"Tusley," Daniel said. "Wake up, dude."

"What do you want, Daniel? And I'm not asleep." I folded the bit of paper so Daniel couldn't read it.

"You could've fooled me. You realize that both the North and the South are starting to kick out the French, don't you?" She was pointing her brand-new Leica at me. The edge of her frown was visible around the camera body that covered most of her face. The Bell & Howell was secured to her waist in its small brown case.

"That may or may not be true," I said, swatting her Leica out of the way.

"I saw that piece of paper," she said. "Planning to invite your French girlfriend back to Vietnam?"

Ignoring Daniel's remark, I waved over to Tran, who was stationed at the front desk, calmly watching us. He nodded to me.

"Sir?"

"Has the mail gone out yet today?" I asked him.

"In precisely one hour," he replied.

Daniel was insistent. "Do you even know where Vivienne is?"

"I told her to go home to Paris from Dien Bien Phu, remember?"

"I don't think she was planning to follow any orders from *you*, Terry," Daniel said. "Anyway, my uncle has a million contacts in New York. Vivienne the French Singer would be pretty easy to pick out from the crowd. I'll find out for you. It could take a while. By that, I mean months. New York is big, you know? But you don't care about time, do you, old man?"

"You'll never find her in New York; like I said, she's in Paris. But… you'd do that for me?"

"I'd do almost anything for you. But there's no reason for her to come here. The French are done."

Just then, the gang of young reporters swept into the lobby from the street.

"Hey, Tusley, Ivers!" Jacko called from across the lobby.

"Come with us to the Presidential Palace! Diem is hosting a press conference!" Mac and Fred stumbled in behind him. The three *Times* reporters were soaked with sweat from the humid city street. Not one of them was older than Joe.

I looked at Daniel. "Coming?" I said, standing up.

"Nope," she said, walking away. "Not interested in any puppet presidents. I'm going to find the *real* action."

FIFTY-FIVE

Saigon

JANUARY 1956

Terry

Vivienne, resplendent in a pink suit and tiny matching hat, stepped off the plane at Saigon Airport followed by a porter trying to balance several hat boxes and a steamer trunk. Two boys ran up the steps to escort her down to the tarmac, but she waved them away with her gloved hand in the bright winter sun.

Daniel was right, yet again. It took the better part of a year to find her.

As she trotted across the tarmac in her high-heeled shoes, an earsplitting boom reverberated across the airport. She found me in the crowd, broke into a sprint and wrapped herself around me, burying her face in my shoulder. Everyone else looked up at the jewel-blue sky. I was nearly blinded by a shaft of sunlight reflecting off a silver airplane with its long, elegant wings, flying so low I could feel the heat from the engines as it blasted over us. In a second, the plane had rocketed out of sight, the silver disappearing into the blue, and all was quiet.

Three guys in short-sleeved white shirts and ties ran out from the airport building. They were heading right for me. "Are you Terrance Tusley?" one of them shouted, breathless.

"Who the hell are you?" I tried to pull away from Vivienne, but she stayed glued to my neck.

"Kodak, Aerial Film division… please come with us now, sir!"

"Shit," I responded. My lovely wife had finally reemerged from radio silence, if not directly, then through her old network at Kodak. I felt the marionette strings pulling.

I looked down at lovely Vivienne, clinging to my neck.

Perfect timing, I thought with a sigh.

"Vivienne, you must be exhausted, flying all the way here from Paris. Go straight over to the Caravelle Hotel. Here's some dough for a taxi," I said, gently pulling her off me.

"What? *Trop bruyant*! Too loud," she pouted, pointing up to the now-empty sky. "But I am fine, I am, how they say, tough!" Her voice was so lilting, every man nearby stopped to look at her. She straightened her hat and took a good look at me.

"You got tan, *mon chéri,*" she said, smiling.

"Sir, we must insist," the guy in the tie said, continuing to tug on me.

"*C'est si bon,* do not worry, Terry. I can get to *l'hôtel*. I don't need money. I am…" She placed a finger under her perfect chin. "All set. Such a long journey from New York! *Je suis épuisée*!"

"New York?" I shouted, before the two Kodak guys dragged me away.

The boys from Kodak ensnared me in the final few weeks of the aerial film project I'd left behind in Rochester, and introduced me to a new project, which, I had to admit, I couldn't resist. I'd never seen a camera as large and complex as the Type II, bolted into an airplane so mechanically advanced. I was intrigued enough to travel up to Bien Hoa airfield to design how the large-format film I'd developed in Rochester would operate inside this unique camera that I'd never seen before. It was clear we were ramping up for something big and I could tell this was going to be a long-term assignment. I was happy to help. No need to check in with Francine directly. We were aligned, as always.

And she didn't need to know everything I was doing in Vietnam, did she?

I'd plant a kiss on Vivienne's cheek, slip out the back of the Caravelle through a forgotten doorway, and wait for the Jeep to pick me up in the morning to take me to Bien Hoa, twenty miles northeast of Saigon.

The seasons passed more quickly than I ever imagined they could. Never mind the rain or the heat: Saigon was the closest I'd ever felt to being home. At Bien Hoa, they even gave me my own desk with a nameplate on it. Vivienne slept in every morning, and just before I'd return in the afternoon, she would gussy up for whatever cocktail party she'd gotten herself invited to. She was soon a card-carrying member of the Jupiter Club in downtown Saigon, where she often performed, though I never caught her act myself. We'd share a few romantic hours before she left, then off I'd go with Daniel into the golden evening light to follow rumors with our cameras, one young Turk or another trailing along, learning the ropes of war photography.

But was it war photography if no war had been declared? Daniel and I debated a lot about that one.

One afternoon in May of 1959, the famous Dr. Edwin Land—founder of Polaroid and a man both revered and feared at Kodak—visited me at Bien Hoa. When he appeared out of nowhere and beamed at me, I lost my ability to speak. It had been rumored he was working with Kodak and the government on secret projects. Now I knew it was true. Two American soldiers flanked him.

"You're nearly done, you know. Thank you." He held out his hand to shake mine.

My film formula, housed inside that camera, bolted to the floor of a modern spy plane, was finally ready for some mission.

You're nearly done, you know.

I didn't feel like I was done. I kept sending film to Katie, and Daniel contributed once or twice when she saw I was getting some photos into the newspapers. The idea of a secret war was one that almost nobody wanted to touch, but evidence was mounting, and after a while it couldn't be ignored. On a TV set somebody had rigged up in the airfield canteen, we'd occasionally see old Cronkite—gray and blurry, the screen loaded with static—telling us there were activities of a concerning nature happening in French Indochina. I was eating a sandwich when I was startled to see one of Daniel's films played out as part of the broadcast news. She'd snuck outside Saigon, chasing a story about a supply route the North Vietnamese were rumored to be building underground. It supposedly wound its way through Laos and Cambodia, and the Chinese were transporting enough materiel to fuel an all-out war. They'd dubbed it Ho Chi Minh

Trail, after the Communist leader of the north. Trombone had mentioned it, but no one had seen it except Daniel, and even she had only been able to film some old ladies on bicycles near what looked like a muddy ditch. I wasn't sure what to think.

What was the truth? Vivienne had gotten nothing from her humid cocktail party conversations with French nationals trying to hang onto their routines—shopping in the Central Market, holding dinners with the resident officers and their wives. The advisors stonewalled even my lovely Viv.

The day after Edwin Land made his proclamation about my *doneness*, Viv and I packed up a picnic basket with food, carefully placing the Argus Brick at the bottom, and headed out to Cap Saint-Jacques, a little beach the French colonists had renamed and taken as their own, about an hour outside the city. We relaxed on a blanket and admired the sunlight reflecting off the blue-green South China Sea.

It was hot as hell. I refilled Vivienne's glass of wine.

"So, how are you enjoying Saigon?" I asked. She knew what I meant: Had she heard anything I should know?

"Ah." She sat back, swirling the wine. "There are still many French families left in the city. They pin their hopes on President Diem."

"Fools."

"*Oui*."

"What else?"

She batted her eyes playfully. "Is that the only reason I am here? To spy on the French? I see your Americans in every café, drinking the wine, taking the photographs, while you 'ave disappeared."

"I'm waiting."

"Ah," she said again.

A moment passed.

"Did you ever wonder, *mon chéri* Terry, whatever 'appened to Wanda Landowska?"

"Who? No," I said, scratching my head. "Why?"

"Oh… she had some interesting ideas for your work."

"Is that what you were doing in New York, Viv? Hawking that postcard?"

I felt bad as soon as I said it. Vivienne frowned at me.

"*Non*," she said, sipping her wine. "I think, now, you will find *le moment* that we spoke of, in the abbey, so very long ago…"

Vivienne emptied the rest of the bottle into my glass, her eyes glowing in the Vietnam sun. Her sky-blue bathing suit hugged her curves to perfection, her dark hair piled high under the kerchief knotted neatly under her chin.

A wisp of hair had escaped the kerchief, and I was, for a moment, painfully reminded of the photograph of Harry that sat on the fireplace mantel back home—his blond hair and his straight cap. Waiting for me to do something. Anything.

"So, what did your *amie* Wanda have to say about me?" I asked, turning now to face Vivienne. "You have my full attention."

A cagey smile crossed her face.

It was in New York where she'd finally caught up with her hero, Wanda Landowska, the Polish pianist. Viv found out the great Landowska was performing at Carnegie Hall, so she'd waited outside the stage door until Wanda emerged. According to Vivienne, they chatted so long they decided to continue the conversation at a coffee shop on the upper East Side. Two European refugees with a lot in common, and they stayed in close contact after that.

They'd meet at Grand Central on Saturday evenings, then walk together, stopping at this or that random café that stayed open all night, and the two women talked about art and beauty and war and survival until the morning crowd showed up for eggs and coffee.

"One night, Wanda brought me to a gallery in Chelsea, and, *oui*, I thought about the postcard. But I thought about *all* your photographs, Terry!"

I looked at Vivienne, puzzled. "What do you mean, exactly?"

"You alone understand beauty," she sighed.

"That's not what I—"

She interrupted me. "Wanda found a route to Lisbon in 1943, when nobody was getting out, then to New York."

"A lot of people got out, Viv.'"

"*Non*. Six million did not get out. My brother did not get out. My grandparents did not get out. My…" she paused, her head down, but I could tell she was determined to continue. "And what did you want to photograph, *mon chéri*? Something ugly, and you were not allowed to do that."

"I did it anyway," I said, thinking of Harry, and what I owed him.

"*Oui*. It was necessary. We know that now."

"And what did Wanda, the Carnegie Hall pianist, think of my photographs?"

"Art." Viv paused. "She thought you make art."

"That's not right. I photograph the truth."

"Perhaps. *Je ne sais pas*. I do not know. How can anyone know, these days? Perhaps, *mon ami* Cameron knows."

I felt the skin on the back of my neck tingle.

"Cameron Plumb? No," I said, remembering the crushed Speed Graphic, the stalking off that day in Seoul. The cameras he left behind, still in my care. "He's done with photography. I assume he's back to acting on the stage somewhere in Solihull or *Something-shire* by now."

I closed my eyes, imagining Cameron as he was when I knew him. London. Occupied France. Salerno. Korea. Creating photographs for propaganda, but also making sure he was in the right place at the right time. He'd given it all up that day in Seoul, hadn't he?

I realized, startled, that I'd been in Vietnam for six years, most of the time cooling my heels. Was I done here? Even Edwin Land had said so. And no word from Francine. What was I doing anymore to honor Harry's memory? A few photographs to Katie, the inkling that something more was going on than we really knew. I was alone, even with Daniel ready anytime to go out, even with the young Turks at my heels. But I was doing nothing.

The sun felt hot on my face.

"Ah, *non*. I have seen Cam's photographs," Vivienne said, interrupting my thoughts. "He is in London, taking pictures for *Le Telegraph. La reconstruction. Monsieur* Churchill. Do you not read any newspapers, Terry darling?"

"Old man Churchill," I muttered, glaring at my own naked toes, covered with sand. "I guess that's good for goddamn Cameron Plumb."

Vivienne regarded me for a moment.

"*N'oublie jamais*, Terry. Never forget. He is your friend."

She laid back down on the blanket and I stared out at the water.

Was Cameron Plumb my friend? And, what about Daniel? What about them all?

Was Wanda now my friend?

Trombone had saved my life. Where was he now? The sky was absent the thrumming sound of Trombone's helicopter, yet I knew he was here, somewhere. And the work for Kodak was, as Viv would say, *fini.*

I closed my eyes again, wondering if there was, indeed, any reason to be here. For myself, or for Harry. The need to find the truth, the feeling that gnawed at me day and night, for years on end… would it ever be satisfied? Advisors made for pretty pictures, but what else was Vietnam trying to tell me?

"*Qu'est-ce que c'est*?" Viv suddenly said, shielding her eyes in the sun. "What is that?" She was sitting up on one elbow, her manicured hand with its red nails pointing at something above us.

I stood and squinted to where she was pointing. Far away, at a dizzyingly high altitude, I saw the pinprick of a plane, sleek and silver, nearly invisible.

It was headed to Bien Hoa airbase.

And then, the not-so-faraway pounding of artillery.

"It's time," I said, reaching into the picnic basket for my camera. I felt Francine's presence beside me, propelling me into action, her delicate hand as surely in the basket as my own, ready to find the truth through my lens.

"We should go," Vivienne said, her brow wrinkled in worry. "*Allons-y.*"

"On the contrary, my dear." I stood, my camera now around my neck, and pulled her up from the blanket. "Now there is even more reason to stay."

She brushed the sand off her swimsuit. “To make more art?”

The question hung in the air between us.

“It’s not about art. It’s about the Pulitzer. It has found me. It has finally found me in Vietnam.”

Viv’s eyes locked onto mine as the unmistakable hiss of the spy plane echoed across the sky, with its large-format camera and my heat-resistant film spinning in a tight duet, a mere mile above our sun-kissed heads, signaling a new level of tension.

The sound dissipated as quickly as it had come.

“You mean, it’s about ’arry. Your son. Your lost little one.” She was gritting her teeth, the sun glinting off her tight jaw, her makeup perfect as always. Like iron wrapped in satin.

Like Francine.

“Yes, of course,” I said briskly. “It’s always about Harry.” I picked up our things and shoved them into Viv’s picnic basket. “Tell me: does Cameron know you are here?” I tried to make the question sound casual.

“You mean,” she said, regarding me soberly with her hands on her hips. “Does he know *you* are here.”

FIFTY-SIX

Washington, DC

JULY 1964

Katie

I met Reggie the first time outside the Midway Diner at 36th and N Street, on a hot, bright, cloudless afternoon in downtown Washington, DC.

It was 4:30 p.m. Midweek. Summer of '64. About a year before Troy was born.

The city was alive with sound—cars, buses, honking horns. I'd just dropped off a packet of Dad's film to a nervous summer intern sent by *The Washington Post* to meet me at the diner and was ready to hop a bus home. I remember thinking I needed to defrost something for dinner.

Although I didn't know it yet, Reggie has been waiting for me.

I walked up to the bus shelter. There was only one man sitting on the bench. A long gray ponytail spilled down his back. His frayed jeans ended at bare feet, which were crossed over lanky legs.

"Hey, hey, sister," he said, keeping his eyes trained on the street.

"Do I know you?" I asked, alarmed.

"Reginald Foster the Third. There will be no fourth." He stood to address me.

Speechless, I registered a string of brown beads around his neck, a mangy beard. The hair was parted down the middle, and he was wearing wire-rimmed glasses. Behind the glasses, piercing brown eyes. He made a little bow, and I remember thinking this was a seriously deranged person, about to ask for money. I looked up and down the block. No one was approaching the bus stop.

"*Doctor* Reginald Foster," he said, holding out his hand now, daring me to shake it. His wrist was wrapped with macramé bracelets made of twine.

"You are not," I managed to say.

"I am, good sister," he said, dropping his hand. "Distinguished Professor of Political Science at George Washington University. Please, call me Reggie. I don't like formality, as you can see." He laughed under his breath. "You don't have to believe me. My students will vouch for me. One of them just met you."

As the words left his mouth, the clean-cut intern burst out of the coffee shop and ran up to us, the envelope containing my father's photos wedged under his arm.

"Dr. Foster," the young man said, breathless. "Are we still meeting tonight at Ebbett's Grill? I got about fifty people to come, sir."

"Yes, Leonard. And bring as many photographs as you can. I'll need them to rally the troops. You can drop them off at *The Washington Post* afterward. I don't want to be accused of stealing—only temporarily, ah, borrowing," he said, patting the boy gently on the shoulder. "I can't afford bail on a college professor's salary."

Without another word, ignoring me completely, Leonard took off on foot. A prim older lady hobbled up to the bus stop. She stared at Reggie, a disgusted look on her powdered face.

"Let's talk tonight at Ebbett's," Reggie said, swinging the strap of a rainbow-colored bag across his chest. "Ten p.m. Back door. Just at the end of the side alleyway."

"I can't go anywhere at that hour," I protested, still stunned by the exchange.

"Oh, sure you can. You're a grown woman, aren't you?" He sauntered away on bare feet, impervious to the hot sidewalks of a Washington, DC summer.

FIFTY-SEVEN

Saigon

NOVEMBER 1964

Terry

That moment of clarity I'd had on the beach with Vivienne was the first time I felt sure I knew what we were doing in Vietnam. Not long after we watched the spy plane streak across the sky, Francine sent an intermediary to contact me—the first time in all our years together that she found she needed to do so. He said his name was Jacko Frank. Dead serious, tall, and imposing, Jacko maintained a one-way relationship with me: he provided locations that Francine wanted me to photograph, and I would follow instructions to the letter, adding my own ideas to the mix as opportunity arose.

At around the same time, hordes of reporters began to check into the Caravelle, the overflow spilling into the Intercontinental. No longer just a bunch of young Turks who would follow me around, these photographers were rude and completely unschooled in the culture and terrain of Vietnam, although one—a fellow named Larry Burrows, who had arrived in '62—was the savviest of the bunch. I wanted to trust him, but remained wary of everyone except Daniel and Trombone, and, even to these two friends, I did not divulge anything about Francine.

Katie received a packet of film from me every week, starting with the guerrilla attack on the US military quarters just outside Saigon. I would include Daniel's film. Trombone helped us occasionally relating various conversations that he'd picked up, piloting the advisors back and forth between locations in-country. He was also a good source of information about troop movements, none of which was being communicated through official channels that the press corps could access. The enlisted boys coming into Saigon got younger and younger, until nearly every one of them looked and sounded to me like some rendition of Harry: slender, smiling optimists who had no idea what was coming.

Artillery thumped just within earshot, day after day, but Viv continued to attend garden parties with the officers' wives, their iced tea glasses beading with sweat as they talked delicately about the future. She brought back whatever information she could obtain to both me and Daniel. Summer turned to autumn, then winter, then back again. Rain pounded us, the summer sun steamed us like vegetables. I started adding physical artifacts to the packets I sent to Katie, as evidence of war operations.

While it was true that I was in the thick of everything I knew I was destined for, and my photos were making it into *The Washington Post* and other major newspapers—thanks to Katie—an uneasy feeling began to gnaw at me.

Something was missing here.

No, not Francine.

I started to miss Cameron Plumb.

He was like a ghost. Daniel and I kept hearing about him—some Brit in the jungle with a camera. Other photographers told tales of catching a glimpse of a tall, pale man in a long trench coat, all alone, cameras strapped across his back and dangling from his neck. Trombone brought us *Life* magazines, and Cameron's shots would be in there, his name credit like a smack in the face beneath each photo. And this was one thing Daniel and I agreed on: they were beautiful photographs. Soldiers with knives in their teeth, cutting through the terrain. People fleeing huts engulfed in flames. Perfectly timed, perfectly rendered. Mine were more truthful: a grotesquely wounded soldier in a hospital bed tended by a young nurse, or a photo of the ever-present advisors showing a group of nervous South Vietnamese how to load their US-issued guns. These moments were full of story too, and they weren't staged.

Back and forth the rivalry went. I'd get the front page of the *New York Post*, Cameron would get the cover of *Life*. I knew I was taking more chances because of it.

I recalled that moment in the French Resistance tent, more than twenty years ago, Cameron's sing-song voice wafting into the back of my mind.

Well, it's almost like a duel *you're challenging me to, isn't it? With our cameras! There is the new Pulitzer, you know.*

I smiled to myself. To be honest, there wasn't any winner in this thing—this competition for the Pulitzer—since Cameron Plumb was like a bogeyman in a bad movie.

No winner. Just the promise of the prize.

And I needed him to come out from wherever the hell he

was, to join me on this quest, the Lancelot to my King Arthur. My only friend. And my greatest rival.

Jacko appeared at my elbow at breakfast, nearly knocking over my coffee.

"Happy holidays, Tusley." The way he said it, it sounded like an order. He took a seat at my table, a cigar jammed between his teeth. "Pack up. You're going to Bien Hoa airbase today."

I looked at him skeptically, thinking this was a grand time for Francine and the Kodak Aerial Photography outfit at Bien Hoa to raise their hoary heads and take me out of the action.

Wasn't I *done*, anyway?

"No," I replied firmly. "They can get somebody else this time."

"She said that's what you'd say. It's not Kodak. The airbase has become a target."

"Yeah, so what?" I growled back at Jacko. "Are they trying to secure the place for a visit by LBJ or something?"

"Better," Jacko said, taking the cigar out of his mouth. "But you can't tell nobody."

"Of course," I said, feeling those tender puppet strings being pulled by my wife from her lair in Quebec City.

Jacko leaned down to whisper in my ear. "Bob Hope. For Christmas."

I sat up, surprised. Bob Hope's wartime shows were legendary. Yet he hadn't been to Vietnam. This would blow the top off the secret war. Bien Hoa was our largest, most modern airbase; it would make an impressive backdrop. They had less than a month to get ready. The stakes were high; the security prep would be off the charts.

In an instant, I knew this was perfect. And not just for me.

If there was anything that could lure my old friend Cameron Plumb in from the jungle, it would be a celebrity sighting. Staged, rehearsed, and ready to go. Just his cup of tea. He'd find out about it; he still had his network. I was sure of that.

And then we'd find out, once and for all, who deserved the elusive Pulitzer more. No photos from the Vietnam theater had—as yet—been selected. The prize was ripe for the taking.

"When do I leave?" I asked, jumping from my seat. My camera bag was up in my room. My duffle was always prepacked.

"Trombone's bird is waiting for you," Jacko said. "But he said you gotta bring Daniel."

"Why?" The last thing I needed was a distraction. Daniel wouldn't even want to go. Too stagy. Not real enough for her taste.

Jacko cleared his throat. "Trombone wants Daniel to take a reel of that starlet who travels with Mr. Hope. Ann-Margret."

I raised my eyebrows.

"… dancing," said Jacko flatly. Then he turned and stalked away.

FIFTY-EIGHT

Washington, DC

JULY 1964

Katie

I came home from the disconcerting meeting with Reggie to find a note from Manny on the hall table. The work guys had to meet up with a client for dinner, and he wouldn't be home until midnight at the earliest. This was the drinking crowd, he noted, with a tiny drawing of a martini. Manny was sorry but he couldn't reach me and assumed I had Friday evening plans with some of the other ladies on the block.

I had to stifle a laugh when I thought about Dr. Reginald Foster the Third. He looked like a lady, actually—that long hair, those beads. I was sure that Manny would *not* approve.

I stood there for a long while, trying to figure out what to do. By 8 p.m. I couldn't take it anymore. Curiosity took over, and I needed at least something to prove that I wasn't completely crazy, that this man wasn't a figment of my imagination. I picked up the phone and called a neighbor down the street whose daughter, I knew, was a student at George Washington University.

"Rita? It's Katie Price. Sorry to bother you. Do you have a second?"

"Katie! So nice to hear from you. How's that husband of yours? Mine is driving me crazy. I'm trying not to burn my house down grilling these steaks for the ambassador from Uruguay. Jesus, I hope he eats meat, I have no idea—"

The clattering of pans, and a low, muffled *Shit.*

"Okay, I'm back, sweetie. What's up?"

I lied to her, pretending I was interested in a political science class at GW, but I'd misplaced the brochure somehow. I asked if she could look up Dr. Reginald Foster in the school course catalog; I realized this wasn't a convenient time but the deadline to sign up was midnight. She put down the phone, ran to her daughter's room. After noisily thumbing through the booklet, she located his name.

"Yep, here he is, he's listed as one of the department chairs. They have his picture, too."

"Great, you're a peach," I said, relieved that, at least, *that* part was true. "What does he look like?"

She laughed into the phone.

"Sweetie, if that's why you're taking the class, I'd look elsewhere. He's a little..." Another pan clanged. "Have to beg off, darling! Frank will be home in twenty minutes, and I just burned the potatoes! Buh-bye!"

I hung up the phone and, like a person under a magical spell, I glided upstairs and zipped myself into a little black dress. How did this Reginald person know me? Had he talked to Milton, the security guard at the *Post*? Was someone following me around Washington?

Just to be safe, I jotted a reply on Manny's note: *Gone to Ebbett's. See you later.* And I drew a little heart under his martini glass.

I threw a light sweater over my shoulders, stepped out my front door into the busy, noisy night, and hailed a taxi.

Before I could change my mind, one screeched to a stop, and I got in.

"Fourteenth and F Street," I said to the cabbie.

"You got it," he replied, looking at me admiringly in his rear-view mirror.

I got there right at ten, but I was not about to blindly follow Professor Foster's somewhat sketchy instructions and walk down a dark alley to find a back door. It was still sweltering, and a lot of people were hanging out on the sidewalk. I caught the strong smell of shellfish. I nudged my way through the crowd huddled around the front door of Ebbett's Grill and I looked up. The historic building was magnificent in nighttime, its triple-arch entryway illuminated by sconces, tall windows reflecting the headlights from passing cars. I went in. I pushed past a young man smoking a cigar. The long mahogany bar was full to the brim with laughing, talking people. A big-bellied gent was immediately by my side.

"Looking for somebody, honey?" His eyes traveled down the front of my dress.

"I'm looking for Professor Foster," I said, stepping back.

"Don't know him. Professors don't mean *dick* in this town. Now, a senator, like me, that's something to tell your girlfriends about," he drawled, sliding his hand under my elbow.

He reeked of cigars and oysters and whiskey. I leaned away from him, thinking this must be one of the worst ideas I'd ever had, when Dr. Reggie Foster appeared from the back of the restaurant and strode purposefully over to me. His ponytail was tucked discreetly into the collar of his shirt. This shirt actually looked clean, and he was smiling with delight. Too much delight. Practically everybody here was lit up. I wondered if he'd been drinking too.

"Katie! You came."

To my great relief, Reggie outmaneuvered the fat Senator and escorted me past the crowd to the back of the bar. He smelled like smoke, only… not tobacco. My internal alarms went off again. What was that scent? He opened a door, and I saw a flight of dark stairs. I relaxed when I heard young, happy voices coming from below. We descended to a basement with whitewashed walls and a dirt floor, directly beneath the dining room proper upstairs.

As my eyes adjusted, I saw thick wooden beams crisscrossing the low ceiling. Ebbett's dated from the 1800s and the charm extended even down here. Smoke hovered just above our heads. I was getting a little dizzy. I could make out thirty, forty college kids, boys and girls, excitedly talking. I felt like I was dressed all wrong in my tight sleeveless dress and matching sweater. I heard *fucking Westmoreland* and *goddamn LBJ*. A student in a beret stood against a side wall and strummed a guitar. I saw him pause and lick a piece of paper, then place it back on the chipped barstool next to him. I stood behind Reggie, squinting at it. It looked like a comic book page, with tiny colorful pictures arranged in rows.

"Everyone! Shut up for a minute!" Reggie shouted, raising his arms above his head.

The students quieted down. All eyes were on Reggie. I slid away from him, unnoticed, to a dark corner. "Thank you for coming. I hope you didn't tell your parents where you are," he said in a joking tone.

The students laughed lightly. They were in his thrall. I watched with amazement. Reggie's lopsided smile reminded me of my father. His eyes took in the room the way my dad's would, searching for the right light, the correct angle, the place to set his sights.

"There is a war, people." Reggie's voice was low, and he nodded at this one or that one.

A girl near me giggled. I noticed someone give her a home-rolled cigarette, the smoke wafting up to the low-slung beams. She took an enormous drag from it, the little red tip glowing in the dim room, and passed it to the person next to her.

"There is a WAR, people!" Reggie shouted, and he raised his arms, eyes wide, eyebrows high, expectant.

The girl giggled again, then cried out a little when the boy next to her poked her in the side with his elbow. An expectant silence undulated across the basement.

"Now, I don't know where you are UN-LEARNING what I've TAUGHT you," Reggie continued. "But shake it off, children! What do you say back to Professor Reggie?"

"*What* war, Professor?" A blond boy in a black turtleneck stepped forward, turned in place, and nodded to the crowd. He stood next to Reggie, holding something behind his back.

"The *secret* war against the good people of Vietnam, that's what," responded Reggie, his voice just a bit louder. "*This* war!"

The boy in the turtleneck handed him a glossy 8x10 photograph, and Reggie brandished it in the air, holding it high, turning his body back and forth in a small arc so that everyone could get a good look. I strained to make it out in the semi-darkness. It was a black-and-white photograph of an American advisor. Smiling. White teeth. He was wearing sunglasses, the gold of his watch offset by his tan skin. The man next to him was a diminutive Vietnamese soldier who peered through the scope of a rifle, aiming it into the distance.

With a start, I recognized it as one of my father's photographs, from a batch I'd picked up at Mr. Asman's photo lab, in the stack I'd given to that young *Washington Post* intern at the Midway Diner, just this afternoon.

What the hell... was this what Reggie meant when he said he was just "borrowing" my father's photographs?

"That war is illegal, man!" The young man was shouting now, pumping one fist in the air, his guitar flung behind his back, tied to him by a strap woven into a rainbow pattern. The young people around me started to hoot and stomp their feet on the dirt floor.

My father's photographs can do this...?

The boy in the turtleneck waved my father's photograph around, getting the crowd even more stirred up. Someone passed me a lit cigarette—the same hand-rolled one, with spit on it. As I took the little cigarette—pride for my father building in my chest—I remember thinking: *Yes.*

I pulled a tentative drag and held the smoke in my mouth. It was sweet, like tea. I took a second hit and passed it on to the boy standing to my left. The sheet of repeating comic book characters was thrust into my hands. I saw Donald Duck, Minnie Mouse.

"You lick it," the girl next to me said. "It's good."

As I bent my head over the sheet, the students all around began a chant.

That war is illegal, man! That war is illegal, man!

Another homemade cigarette was passed my way. This time, I took the hugest drag on it, deep into my lungs, and held my breath, fighting the embarrassing urge to cough. The chanting continued as the smoke encircled my head and got into my eyes. I felt like I was floating. The girl next to me grinned and put her arm around me. Reggie caught my eye. He was staring directly at me, wearing the broadest smile I'd ever, ever seen.

"Doesn't the professor look like the Cheshire Cat?" I asked my new best girlfriend.

She laughed and told her neighbor what I'd just said. She had to repeat herself in all the commotion, cupping her free right hand around her mouth, yelling.

"Holy shit, man!" The boy next to her shouted. "Did she say that? That is *cool*, man!"

He passed my comment on to the fellow next to him, and soon everyone in the room was meowing and catcalling and laughing uproariously, and Reggie pointed at me, and all eyes looked my way, at my little black dress, my matching cardigan sweater, my hair-sprayed hair.

"The photographer's daughter, Katie Tusley!" Reggie bowed as if to royalty, and the entire basement erupted in applause.

I didn't know what to say, so I just grinned and grinned. These were my brothers and sisters. The ceiling swirled to life and strings of colorful lights moved and danced like animals, and the animals had stripes and dots.

Out of the corner of my eye, I saw my husband Manny, and he was not swirling and dancing like everything else. He was angry and the only one in a tie, and people were howling at him as he elbowed his way over to me.

"You are done, Katie. Done!"

To catcalls and jeers, Manny linked his arm in mine, and dragged me up the stairs to the warm, humid air of regular, normal Washington, DC. My new friends tried to stop him, to no avail.

"Bye, Professor Foster," I said when we got to the sidewalk.

"You're a mess, Katie. Wait 'til your mother hears about this!" Manny said, clucking his tongue at me.

"Sorry, Manny," was all I could think to say, giggling. "How were drinks with the guys?"

A cop started walking toward us from down the block.

"Everything okay here?" The cop looked us up and down, his hand on his nightstick.

"She got lost," Manny said, his arm still linked with mine. "You may want to break it up down there in that basement."

The cop pulled his radio out, held it to his mouth, and sauntered into Ebbett's.

Manny's frown couldn't have been deeper.

"You have a vein that pops in your forehead," I said, laughing, and the taxicabs on 14th Street looked exactly like my father's yellow-brown envelopes full of film, and there were tons and tons of taxis, everywhere, full to bursting, beeping their horns in the night. One stopped next to us, and we got in, although I didn't see how there would be room. There was too much film filling up the back seat.

"Wait, there could be instructions from my father in here somewhere," I said, trying to crawl on the taxicab floor, picking through wadded-up Wrigley's gum wrappers and a half pack of Salem cigarettes.

"What in God's name... Katie!" Manny cried, yanking me up by my sweater.

"There's a lot of envelopes here, Manny," I said, dead serious now, squished beside him on the big back bench in the cab. "And there is absolutely nothing you can do to stop them."

Manny looked at me, the city streetlights streaking by outside the taxi window behind his head. The taxi driver's eyes reflected accusingly in his rearview mirror.

Manny carefully explained to me, on the long ride back to our Georgetown brownstone—the taxi driver nodding in agreement all the way home—that my father was using me, and how he wouldn't stop until he had his prize.

"What prize?" I asked thickly, the drugs radiating around me like cheap perfume.

"Katie, I hope you can figure that out," Manny said, scratching at his close-cropped hair. "Because I have no idea."

FIFTY-NINE

Bien Hoa Airbase, Vietnam

NOVEMBER 1964

Terry

"I can't believe you and Trombone dragged me here," Daniel said, jumping out of the helicopter with a frown. She no longer wore the helmet that hid her face, and her long brown hair swung in a ponytail. We hurried from Trombone's helicopter, across the airstrip and down the central dirt pathway that led through the Air Force side of Bien Hoa airbase, our duffles heavy on our backs.

Dozens of enlisted men, officers, and nurses hurried past us, many taking note of the brand-new Nikon F that hung from my neck, a surprising gift from Trombone. I fingered the strap as we walked in the muddy dirt, my Kodak Medalist tucked away in my duffle.

"Maybe you'll get lucky, and we'll get attacked," I said, sarcasm dripping with every word.

"Well, that's why I agreed," Daniel retorted.

I shook my head in dismay as we walked to the hooch that housed visitors and press. Daniel and I had worked side-by-side for over ten years and we were like an old married couple now, bickering.

"Just be ready with that movie camera, Daniel, because—" But before I could finish, Daniel swung out her arm and stopped me dead, pointing to her feet.

"I don't think my little movie camera is going to matter much here," she spat out.

A tangle of thick electrical cables lay on the ground. Together, our eyes traveled to their source. I recognized the bulky TV broadcast cameras sitting high on metal swivels that glinted in the sun. There were three of them, all pointing to a makeshift stage at the end of an alleyway that ran perpendicular from our path. Beyond the stage, we could see a dirt field, about fifty yards long. A hammering sound emanated from the back, near a batch of half-constructed wooden bleachers. A large, fake white Christmas tree, covered in silver tinsel, lay on its side on a wood pallet in the mud about ten yards away.

"Well," I said. "That's show business."

Daniel snorted and we kept walking.

"I think you should take my Kodak, Daniel. Plus, I have a ton of extra Kodachrome film. You should shoot in color and forget that Bell & Howell," I said.

"Give me the camera and the film *now*," Daniel said, her tone serious. I obliged, and she threw the strap of my Medalist over her head, stuffing several rolls of Kodak film in the chest pocket of her shirt.

"You seem ready," I smiled, screwing the lens cap off my shiny Nikon F to examine the lens more closely as we walked.

"There's only one other person I know who needed so much equipment."

"Yeah," she replied. "And if that's who I think it is, your bogeyman just materialized." She nodded toward a far figure on the field standing next to the bleachers, his back to us, draped in a garment that reached to his ankles.

As if on cue, he turned—the Zephyr coat flapping around his legs in the humid air—and started running toward us, his many cameras bouncing.

I tried to smile, but it actually hurt to see him. I'd wanted him to be here, and I knew the rivalry had to play itself out, here in this remote place. I was fifty-four years old. An old man. I was on my third "combat tour"—chasing the light. He didn't run as fast as he used to, either, and when he reached us, he was soaked with sweat, even though it was late November. When I attempted to shake his hand, he embraced me in a bear hug instead, then stepped back, laughing.

"Old boy!" His words were laced with warmth, and I finally had to laugh.

Daniel was shocked into silence for a moment, face-to-face with the ghost she'd heard so much about back in Saigon, and I took the opportunity to look him over.

"London not treating you well, Cameron?" I smiled. "Tom Young no longer calling you for dinner dates?"

"Nah, that's been over for a while. But I see you've made a name for yourself in *The Washington Post*! And how is dear Vivienne? Still quite useful?"

Ah. He knew she was here. Of course. I glanced at Daniel, whose expression shifted from baffled to knowing. She shook her head at us.

"You World War guys *still* don't have a clue," she muttered.

Cameron turned to her, smiling, his hand out. "And you are…?"

She stood silently glowering at him. These were the sparks I knew would fly if these two ever met, back when we were in Seoul. I crossed my arms over my chest, ready for a good show.

"Women aren't here for your *use*." The words dripped from her lips.

"I never said they were," Cameron protested, assessing her as if she were auditioning for a role in his play. I saw him quickly glance at her long ponytail, her unusual brown-and-blue eyes. "In fact, I believe the reality is quite the opposite. We men would be nowhere without—"

"Before you finish that asinine statement," Daniel interrupted, scowling. "Did anyone besides me hear that whistling sound?"

We paused, listening.

"Mortar!" I shouted, pulling Daniel by her camera straps. "Run for cover!"

She wrenched away from me, and in a deafening boom, a hail of dirt kicked up all around us, the metal barracks to our right rattling in the blast.

"They're attacking the airstrip!" Cameron yelled, crawling now, his head down. "Scoot down into the shadow of the barracks and set up your cameras there! And—cover your heads!"

I ducked as another mortar dropped on the airstrip, back where Trombone had landed the helicopter to drop us off less than fifteen minutes ago. I briefly wondered about Trombone's safety before I reached into the dirt-filled air for Daniel, assuming she was still right next to me. A giant boom blasted our ears, and in the rain of dirt and smoke I saw her—yards away, running toward the airstrip. She stopped, looking trapped and unsure of which way to go in the barrage.

"Daniel!" I shouted in the din, as alarms filled the air.

"Terry! Get over here where it's safe!" Cameron's reedy voice rose above the din.

"Coming!" I shouted back to him. "Set your tripod!"

I was down on all fours, the Nikon firm in my grip. I clenched the lens cover in my palm in an absurd desire not to lose it. But I couldn't find Daniel. She was lost again in the smoky air. Suddenly, the air cleared, and I caught a glimpse of yellow, only yards away. The sound of the blast reached me before the sight reached my eyes.

Daniel flew through the air like a dove. I pulled my Nikon to my eye, all sound reduced to a low roar. I watched through my viewfinder as Daniel tumbled, head over heels, the yellow rolls of Kodak film falling in slow motion from her chest pocket, her shirt floating around her like a parachute.

I dropped the camera to my chest and reached out to her as the heat from another blast blew past my right side, past my outstretched hand, melting the lens cap into my palm. I looked at it dumbstruck for a moment before I was dragged away by the collar and thrown against the barracks.

"Terry!" Cameron said breathlessly after releasing my collar. "Your hand!"

He tore the lens cap from my skin and chucked it away. He wrapped me in the Zephyr coat, and we huddled there, unspeaking, until we were surrounded by an eerie silence. In a moment, ambulance sirens began to blare. Men shouting. Running with stretchers. We were hidden in the shadow of the barracks, ignored, our cameras strapped to us like children. Medics with red crosses on their armbands stumbled over Daniel, sprawled out in the muddy path. Startled, stopping, they lifted her onto a stretcher and kept on running. Over my shoulder, Cameron's camera shutter clicked. I looked up at him, the pain in my hand starting to spread.

"She was…" I stammered. "She—she stood for truth."

"And she always will," he murmured, crouching in the dirt, his face hidden behind the camera as he reset his orientation and adjusted his focus ring.

Sitting on my haunches, I pulled my Nikon up, ignoring the pain, and wiped the lens clean of the mud that had flicked across its delicate curved surface. Silently, the two of us remained hidden, shoulder to shoulder, deep inside the darkness of the chaos.

Click, click, click.

PART THREE

The Aftermath

"For a few brief moments, in a handful of places, we had undamaged film. Working cameras. The idea was that we could steal the light. And bend it to suit our illusion."

—Cameron Plumb

SIXTY

New York City

DECEMBER 1983

Terry

Professor McMickle is always anxious to get things started. He snaps his fingers impatiently at some lanky boy from A/V, lurking in the dark corner of the lecture hall. The boy runs to the front of the room, pulls the white screen down from its roller and hooks it to the pin at the bottom—the zipping sound like the unsheathing of a weapon. The kid sprints over to the slide projector, screws around with the focus lens, glances at me, then scurries away like a rat in an abandoned compound.

I touch the advancing button of the projector. Always a few blanks at the front, then the first image snaps into view.

Everything, every goddamn thing, is predictable.

Except for that.

I look up at the image projected on the screen.

"For God's sake. For Christ's sake," I say, like I always do. Like I have for ten years.

"This one first, Professor?" I ask, my voice raspy now. McMickle nods at me in the semi-darkness.

But it doesn't matter which one is first. They are all just doorways into different nightmares.

The students lean forward as one combat unit, their lecture hall seats creaking together, synchronized, an expectant, high-pitched upsurge of sound. I walk over to the projector screen, stare at the outsized image. I turn my back to the students.

I point up to the photograph.

"The bright blue sky suddenly went dark," I say. "In an instant, the bombs were dropping all around us. We were at Bien Hoa."

I wait a beat.

"Daniel blew up before my eyes, red-and-purple-and-white bone. Black-and-blue, burned flesh."

"Go on," the professor coaxes, a collective breath drawn in the classroom.

"A yellow roll of Kodak film slipped from what had been my friend's top left pocket, fell from midair in slow motion, and the tattered shirt floated back down to earth," I say, turning to my audience, their illuminated faces rapt in the darkened classroom.

I step in front of the projector light. The gold chain around my neck catches the bulb, and the unlucky students in the front row blink in unpleasant, temporary blindness. I pull on the cuffs of my immaculate shirt, waiting.

A hand goes up, tentative. Barely visible in the light, but I see it. My eyes aren't what they used to be, but movement in the dark is still my specialty. The barest wind that moves a banana leaf would catch my attention, but I don't honor the raised hand with even a flicker of accommodation.

I turn back to the projector screen. I need to finish.

"That's what was left, see the yellow?" I point again. "Right there in the mud."

I always stop after the first slide. No matter which photo is on the slide, the image and the story snake together and strike between the eyes. I turn again to face the students, nestled in their extra-comfortable Ivy-League seating. Their eyes glisten in the darkened lecture hall.

"The plastic lens cover melted into my hand," I say, holding up my right arm for the millionth time, showing them the purple scar seared across my palm, which they now can see fairly clearly, their eyes adjusted to the dark. "See?"

A gasp before someone speaks, usually a boy, although lately the girls are braver than they used to be. But no one is brave like Daniel. Daniel, who leads me to Trombone. Trombone, who poisons Katie. Katie, who gets my pictures to *The Washington Post*. And, finally, *Life* magazine. Front cover. So many of my friends, crouched beside me, holding ground for too long, cameras cradled in our hands, enemy shells bursting all around us.

But that's another story in the carousel. I just don't know where it will present itself. Professor McMickle likes to play around with the order, shuffling the slides between lectures. He says it keeps the material fresh.

"My father showed me that photograph in a *Time/Life* book about Vietnam when I was in high school." The voice reaches me from somewhere in the back of the classroom. Young. Like Harry.

No need to respond to that one, so I wait.

Another brave soul pipes in.

"That's the picture that made me want to be a photographer."

Heads nod, including McMickle's. It's like a puppet show, and I—finally the puppet master—entangle them in my hidden strings.

"Can you show us the gallery work?" The voice is female.

"Let's move on," I say.

"Terry, we have those slides. Let's talk to them." The professor's tone is even, like we haven't had this exchange a thousand times. "This is an Art in Photography class. They want to hear your analysis."

"This is *soooo* cool." The swoon comes from the front row. Low register, male. My grandson Troy's voice, the last time we talked on the phone. Before he left for Grenada, my photographs tucked into his kit.

"We're going to talk about all eighty-one slides in the carousel," I say, striding forward toward the student in the dark. He shrinks back in his seat, a look of alarm clear in the shadows. I stop mere inches from him. I can feel the professor perking up a few feet away, ready to intervene. As if there is anything I could do to the boy.

"I'm sorry, sir," the boy starts to say, but I swiftly turn my back to him and stride back to the gigantic, looming projector screen.

"For what you're paying in tuition, son, you deserve the whole bag of shit."

The lecture hall ripples with low laughter, and now I have them, and all the ones who made it—and all the ones who didn't—can rest assured that I will bring them home.

"Jake, go get the second carousel of slides. It's back on my desk. Pronto." The professor's tone is clipped. The A/V boy runs out the side door. The red exit sign trembles with the slamming of the heavy door.

The class is content to just stare at me now, sizing me up, afraid but wanting more words from the grandmaster. No, not words. There is no need to talk. They want the photographs. Flat as the quiet surface of a lake. Little containers of time. Wordless letters from someplace else, someplace other.

A place not unlike Grenada.

I squint at my Rolex. The train to Rochester is at 4 p.m. I have less than two hours; we need to hurry it up. I think of what a far cry this fancy thing is from the cracked-face Timex I wore for years before it finally exploded, so full of blood it dripped.

Whispers rise from the student body, impatient for the A/V kid to get back with the rest of the slides. Muffled, fragmented conversation from the back row. A battalion nervously awaiting the "go" order. I stand perfectly still, a skill I perfected over the years, keeping the camera steady.

Katie's voice had a pleading tone to it on the pay phone this morning. I don't know what the hell she's expecting. A goddamn anniversary party. Stupid. Katie had been insistent, tracking me all over New York to get information over the past few months, calling everyone she knew. But Francine and I don't need other people to arrange things for us. We do just fine. I'd seen my wife about four times this year. She's kept her figure, but her face gives her away. Or maybe she just looks like that to me. Sixty years is a damn long time. She'd ranted about the invitation that Katie sent out.

I will not even open it, Terry! It arrives in my boîte aux lettres, *and what is the first thing I see? The English Queen's Jubilee stamp!* Incroyable!

Such little, petty things. That's my wife. But I didn't open it, either, when it arrived in the mail.

"Surprising, though, for Francine to agree to a party," I mutter aloud before I can catch myself.

A few students glance at me in the darkened room, then look away. McMickle takes a step toward me.

"You okay?" He sounds concerned.

"Couldn't be better," I say. "Next time let's just put the gallery slides up front."

"Oh, I don't know," he says, his voice dropping to a whisper. He leans in, touches the sleeve of my shirt, a co-conspirator, a ringmaster. "It pays to make 'em wait, eh? Adds to the show."

I nod and stroke the gold bracelet that encircles my right wrist, heavy and solid. The gallery posters brought in the most money. I don't know what Vivienne showed them. Or how Wanda Landowska, a woman I never actually met, managed to introduce herself to the most selective gallery owners, convincing them that my war photographs were art, that the packages I'd sent to Katie could be turned into shadowboxes—time capsules for sale. Even the postcard was on display in some places, doctored to show Vivienne in full glory. I sometimes tried to picture Vivienne and Wanda, refugees who found each other in New York, their conversations low, heads bent over strong coffee in Café Figaro, one of their many outposts near Bleecker Street, cajoling any gallery owner who'd accept a free pastry. Vivienne, still beautiful, and Wanda, her pianist's hands still strong, clasping and unclasping her hot mug. Viv maybe even allowing a few tears to fall into her *pain au chocolat*. Viv would have pulled out the postcard from her chic purse, the French cardboard so carefully preserved.

"*Regardez, mes amis*," she would have said, her voice a whisper in the noisy coffee shop, her fine fingers caressing the image. "*Je suis à l'envers*."

"Upside down," Wanda may have translated in a whisper to the gallery owners, the coffee shop hustling and bustling all around them. "She had a lover, a war photographer."

The scraping chairs. The laughing beatniks. Wanda would have been sitting upright, formal, her posture ramrod straight from years of keyboard fury. She was old by then, but she was connected. An accomplished musician. A survivor. She would have detected the interest piqued in the gallery owners' eyes. Beauty and war. And she would have let Vivienne, ever the *coquette*, sell them on the idea.

"Do you see the irony, *messieurs*?" Vivienne would have gazed into their moist eyes. "It was the *world* that was upside down, *pas moi*—not me."

"Do you have more?" They might have said, hearing *war photographer*, sensing an opportunity.

Jake the A/V kid is balancing the extra slide carousel in his arms. Before the classroom door can slam shut behind him, a hand reaches in, flinging it back open.

"Terry!"

He bursts into the lecture hall and careens toward me in the dim light, nearly knocking over poor Jake. The classroom jolts upright before I can react, his voice like an electric shock to the system.

The professor jumps up and scurries toward him, instantly recognizing his famous visitor. "*Cameron Plumb?* Cameron

Plumb! Students! Cameron Plumb, by gum!" He giggles at the alliteration, falling all over himself, as people tend to do around my old friend.

"Found you!" Cameron reaches me now, embraces me, laughing like an emperor in his court. "Exactly where you should be! And I'm here to take you to where you'll be going next!"

The kids leap out of their seats in recognition, clutching their notebooks and pens, and the little desks bang into their slots, deafening and sudden. Their thoughtful shyness, their tentative questions—all gone in the heat of the moment.

They run to get his autograph, tripping over each other in the melee.

How could they not? He is a Pulitzer Prize winner. People can smell a celebrity from a mile away. He's older, out of breath, but it doesn't matter. It's been twelve years since the Pulitzer ceremony. I went as a favor to Annie. She was nearly blind, in a wheelchair. But she was still beautiful, her red hair gone silver, my wife clinging to her, whispering about old times.

He's been too busy to visit his old friend Tusley since then, hasn't he? What with speaking engagements, retrospectives, honorary degrees, and so on and so forth.

I am tossed aside, the projector light still sending its beam onto the lecture hall screen behind me, Daniel's yellow Kodak film cartridge laying in the dirt like it happened only yesterday, and the students swarm Cameron Plumb, descending upon him with faces bright as the first light of bombs. He is buried in them. I can barely see him.

Cameron's arm reaches out from the mass of youth. He is waving something in my face.

I grab it.

A white card.

Please Join Us to Honor
The Diamond Anniversary of Our Parents
Terrance and Francine Tusley
A Celebration of Faithful Love

I snort.

"Read on!" Cameron shouts above the din.

December 17, 1983
Six O'Clock p.m. — Directions Enclosed
Given by their Children
Katie Tusley-Price
Joseph Tusley
and

My eye travels to the next line.

Harry Tusley (Deceased)

Goddamn it, Katie. Just had to say it. Just had to make your point. One more goddamn time.

Cameron reaches out from the mass of students and grabs my shirtsleeve.

"You're wrinkling the fabric," I protest, trying to wriggle out of his grip.

"Terry!"

"What, goddammit?"

"You tell me," he says, pulling himself free from the pack of students. "Who could resist an invitation like *that?*"

SIXTY-ONE

On the Train to Rochester

DECEMBER 1983

Terry

Cameron Plumb pulls me through the swinging doorway of Penn Station into the main concourse and expertly navigates us through the marble archways to the tracks. We scramble past the overhead signs for Buffalo, Montreal, and Toronto.

"I don't even remember getting out of there," I say under my breath.

"And yet, you did escape, old man," Cameron says, simultaneously coughing and laughing, finally letting me go. People hurry in all directions around us. He pulls a cigarette from a tarnished, mirrored case with a veiny hand and deftly lights it. "You were always good at moving on."

The Amtrak barrels into the platform behind us, drowning out my *Fuck you.*

I can still see Harry's name emblazoned across that invitation, thrust in my face by Cameron. The shiny black ink lettering, stark against the bright white cardstock. The feel of the raised type in my fingers when I'd grabbed it from him. It is buried now in the pocket of the Zephyr coat, where he'd jammed it before he wrenched us both out of the lecture hall.

He's still smiling as he steps off the platform onto the train. I want to be happy to see him, but the heartburn rises in my chest, our old rivalry as fresh as it was so many years ago. The Pulitzer stands between us like the gates of heaven. He is on the inside, while I can only stand apart and look, regretful as every other sinner.

I follow him onto the train, less eager to go to my own anniversary celebration than he is.

He sweeps toward two plush seats at the back of the train. A few young businessmen in suits step out of our way, staring. If they were going to sit there, they'd changed their minds.

Something about Cameron feels famous.

We settle in across from each other. He rests his head against the maroon velour headrest and promptly falls asleep, the lit cigarette clenched between his teeth, a well-worn tan leather camera case on the seat beside him. He's slept like this a thousand times before; it takes no effort for him. Ever the traveling photographer. I, of course, am without a camera. It's been years, and I no longer carry one. But the pull still drags at my neck. My fingers twitch, hungry for the shutter. Old habits die hard.

I scrutinize him while he sleeps, remembering the ride in Farmer René's wagon, almost exactly forty years ago. Meeting him on the road to the fake armistice in Kaesong, laden down with cameras, this very Zephyr coat hanging from his shoulders. How he lunged at Tom Young in the courtyard of the Chosun Hotel. The twenty years side-by-side in Vietnam, crawling alongside boys who all looked like Harry to me. The passing of time has been kind to Cameron's face, I think, but his body shows the strain. He is thin and nearly transparent in the seat, and he wheezes in slumber. The cigarette dangles now between thin, dry lips. The smoke comes out his nose. Thousands of air miles. Hundreds of hours at sea. Time spent with troops in every jungle and desert and bullet-pocked city. He was somewhere awful yesterday, and somewhere just as bad the day before. Still ducking and weaving. Pausing to enjoy a girl whose name is unpronounceable.

Trying so hard to stay alive, until you're actually death itself.

I am seventy-eight, a carefully preserved specimen, and no longer in that life. I own the lovely house in the south of France, and Vivienne, who claims she won't leave French soil ever again, sometimes comes by to entertain me. The yacht on the French Riviera. The sun—the only light that really matters—has warmed my skin to a tawny color. New York is strictly for lectures and gallery talks, and I usually escape by now, before this damn city winter gets inside me. I've stayed young this way, absolutely no doubt of that.

I'd tried to guess at Cam's age that long-ago day in Quebec, in bed astride my wife, my hands full of her impeccable body, my head full of Churchill and Roosevelt and Francine's stories about Annie Plumb and her young son, an actor named Cameron. I'd thought of him back then as an overgrown kid, a snotty man-child, and I'd written him off.

Big mistake. But it didn't matter now. The job had caught him up to me.

"At least you have money," he says through the cigarette, eyes still closed. "I'm glad you kept the coat."

"Yes," I say, running my fingers through my New York haircut. "It was magnanimous of you to give it to me, at the Pulitzer ceremony. In front of all those people."

"Yes," he says, his eyes still closed. "It is as if we've been together for the last twelve years, knowing you were wearing it."

A lovely photo had surfaced recently in *Vanity Fair*. It was the one I'd taken of Cameron in this coat, the WWII shot, taken from behind on the London Docks, executed in glorious Kodak Tri-X black-and-white film at 100 ASA and 200 speed. Only took four decades to make it into print. The caption included his name, but not mine. The coat billowing out like a shroud, the British sky dark behind his silhouette, soon to be full of German Messerschmitts. Or a Korean sky, pierced by Trombone's single, lifesaving helicopter. Or a Saigon sky, so full of Hueys they resembled bees swarming the nest. It didn't matter. I was done. Was it worth it? Like a pristine artifact kept under glass, I am invisible. Only the photographs speak. That is the artist's way.

But then, how would I know?

And what about Harry, a ghost I'd chased for twenty years across the landscape in Vietnam, before I finally gave in, and accepted the truth: he was a figment of my imagination, no more real than a torn baby blanket, twisted and pinned in a colorful collage, made into art.

I sink further into my seat in despair, and Cameron Plumb opens his eyes.

"I can hear you, you know," he says. He is frowning, and I see the face that was beside me in Cam Lo Valley, sixty kilometers south of the demilitarized zone.

"You cannot," I say, knowing it was me who'd let twelve years pass, the jealousy too hard to bear at the Pulitzer ceremony, where I'd been professionally obliged to applaud him as he accepted the award.

"Your eye was always good," Cameron says in a low voice. "You just didn't want to play to your audience. But they found you, in spite of yourself. The beauty of your work was recognized by fellow artists. This is your folio of work, Terry. It is all that remains. Now, where did I put those train tickets?" He rummages through his pockets, distracted by the sight of the conductor approaching us from down the aisleway.

"Is that how you see it?" I ask. "I'm a museum piece, and you're a journalist?"

"Well, if you want to put it that way…"

"Screw you, Cameron."

"Well, I don't think anyone remembers my Pulitzer. It was a decade ago."

"Decade plus two years. And everyone in that lecture hall remembered it."

"Leave it to you to remember exactly," he says. "It meant so much more to you than to me."

I think about that for a moment.

"We just both wanted something," I finally say. "What's wrong with that?"

"Absolutely nothing," Cameron says. "Unless…"

"What?"

He leans forward. "Unless we never did tell the story we were supposed to tell."

I lean forward as well, and our foreheads are nearly touching. I don't pull back.

He is my brother, after all.

"We did," I say. "Right?"

"Yes," he replies. "We did."

The overhead lights in the train car reflect in his eyes like the flash of gunfire, and we are together in Da Nang, some crazy sergeant screaming at us as we scramble to take cover in the stinking river while the unit gets strafed from every direction. Cameron had actually pulled out a tripod; it was strapped to his body and he'd managed to steady it on the muddy riverbank.

We did everything we'd wanted to do. And now it was time to go home. Francine would be dabbing makeup on her still-pretty face. Katie would be getting dressed. Joe would be complimenting his new girlfriend's outfit as they get ready to go. A few friends and a lot of alcohol.

Didn't sound that bad to me now.

"What time are we supposed to get to Katie's house?" I pull out the invitation.

"We're not going to your daughter's house," Cameron responds, taking the invitation from my hand.

"What are you talking about?" I say, starting to rise from my seat before he places a steadying hand on my knee.

"I have some amazing news for you," he says.

I sit back, suddenly realizing that I'd followed Cameron onto the platform and into the train like a sheep to slaughter. I hadn't even looked at the train's marquee before we jumped onboard.

"Just tell me we're still going to Rochester," I groan, glancing out the train window at the setting sun, remembering now what it's like to be with Cameron Plumb.

"We *are* going to Rochester, old man," he says, palms up, his hands formed into the familiar flourish I know and hate so well. "Only, to someplace grand."

I'm trying to absorb this when the conductor appears over my shoulder. Cameron calmly hands him two prepaid tickets from his camera case. The man glances at us from beneath the stiff brim of his cap as he punches the cardboard, his mouth set in a line. And we are a pair again, just like in the old days. The conductor's expression says it all.

What the hell are you two up to?

Cameron nods at him and he moves along.

"There's nowhere grand in Rochester, Cam."

"Oh, I beg to differ," he says, as he smiles and crushes his cigarette into the little ashtray in the armrest. "I've heard that Eastman Theatre is quite beautiful!"

"Eastman Theatre!" I jump out of my seat, and the train veers around a curve, nearly throwing me off my feet. Cameron pushes me back down.

"It will be quite beautiful! I've seen pictures of it, it's like Royal Albert Hall, isn't it?" Cameron continues, as the lights in the train car flicker overhead.

I can feel the panic rising in my throat.

"Wait. No." I say, confused by this sudden change. "We are just going to Katie's new house!"

"*Shhh*, this is supposed to be fun," Cameron says, his voice like honey, and we swerve into a tunnel. The lights inside the train go out completely, and all the passengers stop talking at once. It is deathly quiet, except for Cam's steady breathing, an audible hiss, his little wheeze like a light song, and I notice that his head has a tremor to it, nearly imperceptible, almost impossible to see in the shadows.

Coming out of him is a low hum, and I remember it all now. The falling asleep in the most dangerous situations. How he would slow down, survey and take stock, especially at the beginning of a shoot. The setup all in place to his satisfaction, the players in position, the propaganda machine's jaws wide open, ready to take his film and propel him onto the world stage.

Fueling the myth.

I look into his eyes in the near-darkness. I can practically see the bamboo groves that surrounded us, closing us in, sometimes protecting us, sometimes protecting the enemy.

Cameron again leans forward in his seat. "I am so happy for you!" He exclaims, just as the train exits the tunnel.

Unable to find the right words, I turn to look out the window into the early evening. We are nearly there. Upstate New York. Looming maples and oaks whoosh by our train like giant hands, grasping at us and failing, grasping and failing, as we fly on steely tracks to that most distant of places.

Home.

SIXTY-TWO

Rochester

NOVEMBER 1983

Katie

"What do you mean, come down to Eastman Theatre?" I'm yelling into the receiver at Manny, my hair in curlers, the phone cord twisted around my bare arm. "We're expecting everyone here at the house in thirty minutes!"

"Baby…" Manny's voice is muffled by the sounds of a crowd, talking and laughing behind him. "Your mother planned something special, and she changed the location. She got a hold of everyone, even *my* guys from the Pentagon! I think your father is in a state of shock. He just arrived, with that Pulitzer photographer, Cameron Plumb. They're getting mobbed. Your mother is a piece of work, let me tell you!"

I am alone, standing in my bedroom in my slip and pantyhose, clutching my new polyester Diane Von Furstenberg wrap dress in my left fist. The house is ready, almost blindingly sparkling. This is it. This is the day I've been waiting for.

What the hell is Manny talking about?

"Dad? Dad is there, too?" I can hardly get the words out. "At Eastman Theatre?"

"Yes!" Manny shouts into the phone. "He looks great, goddamn him!"

"Are you saying—"

"Hey, don't blame *me*! She hijacked your party. I had nothing to do with it."

"I thought you just went out to get some tonic water..."

"She got my beeper number!" He is really yelling now. "How could an eighty-three-year-old woman do something like that!"

I sit down on the edge of the bed, the dress scrunched up beside me.

"Please, Manny. Tell me what's going on."

"I don't know, baby," he says, his voice calmer. "That Francine, she's in fine form, bossing everyone around. She's—"

He pauses, and then I hear a woman laugh.

"Who is that?" I say, clutching the receiver.

"Welp, that's your brother's girlfriend. She's pretty good-looking, for a chemist!"

"Godammit, Manny!"

"Look, I know you're upset, but you will love this—it's a great party! *Better* than what we planned! It's a big deal, a really big deal! Literally hundreds of people are going to be here! I didn't think they knew that many people, actually."

I cannot speak. He is laughing, and then: "Katie, Trombone is here." Manny's tone is dead serious now.

I drop my head to my chest in shame.

"I just saw him—older, but definitely that son of a bitch. Godammit Katie!"

"I—"

"Just get over here. It's walking distance from the house. I can't come home to get you! Too many people are coming in."

"I can't." My voice sounds hollow.

"Katie," he says gently. "Look, it's a beautiful evening. Everything will be okay. The snow looks nice. They plowed. They put down salt. C'mon, it's three blocks, max. It'll give you a chance to clear your head, and you'll be ready to see them, and wish them a stupendous wedding anniversary… And then you can explain about Trombone, right?"

This can't be happening. Everyone is supposed to come *here.*

Eastman Theatre. What the hell. The appetizers in my fridge, the alcohol in my pantry, the caterer who will arrive in forty-five minutes with the anniversary cake. The carefully selected accusations I'd planned. Usurped once again. By *them.*

I had it all planned. But here. In my own house. In front of a handful of their closest so-called friends, who probably also have a lot to answer for.

This is different. This will be a showdown.

I'd swallowed those pills not twenty minutes ago. I didn't even stop for a glass of water, just gulped them down dry. Two red ones plus an extra yellow one for good measure.

I had no time to lose. And now, even less so.

I take out the curlers, dropping them to the floor one by one. Put on the dress, smooth it out. Step into the shoes. I pop off the cap of the bottle of red pills and empty the entire contents into my hand, the pills rolling lusciously around in my palm. Twenty or thirty. All that's left. I glide down the stairs, pull on my coat, and let the pills spill into the coat pocket. I float out the door, clutching my coat around me.

I am the likeness of a bird, flying with intention into the cold winter night.

SIXTY-THREE

Rochester

NOVEMBER 1983

Katie

I round the corner of Gibbs Street, shivering in my thin dress and coat.

I stop short, awestruck.

Eastman Theatre, majestic as a wedding cake, towers over the dark city block. Glittery golden light spills onto the snowy sidewalk from its gigantic doorway. I am close enough to see people, masses of shimmering people, filing through its lavish entrance. Cars pull up and pull away. Taxicabs. Laughter.

A woman comes out to greet people. She is easy to see in the light. A profile I know so well. Tall, slender. Her hair is white now, piled atop her head. She wears a gown that sparkles in the reflected glow. Although I am hidden in shadow, she somehow turns toward me. A sound floats on the bitter winter air, out to me.

"*Ma fille.*"

Daughter.

I shrink back, and she is waving. The people around her all turn to look, but they are blinded by the marquee lights, some shielding their eyes to squint down the dark street. I walk forward as if pulled by a string. Mother reaches out a milk-white arm and encircles my shoulders in a strong grip.

"Katherine, come in from the cold, come in! It is so good to see you *ma chérie*!"

Like the automaton I am, I kiss her on both cheeks to a sprinkling of applause. We are swept into the theater, the cheery people like a knot all around us. I cannot escape.

Manny emerges from somewhere in the lobby, his face bright with sweat, his eyes searching. He finds me, locks his sights on me, and breaks into a little trot.

"Here you are! Come, Katie, let's find a place for your coat," he says, smiling broadly, extracting me from my mother's grasp. "Give us a minute, Francine. She'll be right back!" He places a hand on the small of my back and guides me up the grand staircase. Before I can say anything, before I can yell or cry or feel anything at all, he pulls me through a narrow door at the far end of the balcony.

We are alone in what appears to be a dressing room. I glance around to see a cot with a pillow, a hat stand in the corner. Heavy brocade curtains at the window.

I turn to face him, planting my feet on the plush carpet. I will not move one step more.

"Katie," he begins, wincing under my withering glare. "Your mother asked me for the list last week. She made it difficult to say no, I didn't know what she was trying to do."

"And what *is* she doing, exactly?"

"She's arranged for *Life* to honor your father with a lifetime achievement award. He'll be on the cover in January, all his pictures in a special layout, including the gallery ones, his whole portfolio! Nice tribute, after all these years. Not that he deserves it, I think he's a helluva bastard. I don't know how she managed it. It's not the Pulitzer, but it's an incredible honor, and it's all a surprise. There's even a couple of two-star generals here! This is a great networking opportunity for me..."

I cannot speak. Did Manny even suspect what I'd planned? How I'd humiliate them, openly scoff at their sixty years of so-called togetherness? But I can't do that now. This is too big, so much bigger than me.

It always was.

I collapse onto the cot, exhausted.

"Take off your coat, baby," Manny coos, sitting down next to me.

A long sigh escapes me. The whole thing, the invitations and the lists and fighting off every goddamn hallucination so I'd see it through, finish it...

"You okay?" Manny looks directly at me, hope in his eyes.

There is a knock at the door.

Manny winks and squeezes my hand. He gets up and takes a step toward the door, then he stops and looks back down at me.

"You're still in your coat," he says, disapproving.

I sit up and start to slip it off, so used to taking orders from him. Then I remember what's in my pocket. The pills. Twenty, thirty. Enough to do some irreversible damage, goddammit.

"I'm cold," I say.

"Stand up, baby."

I stand, leaving the coat on.

"You in there, Katie?" It's my father's voice.

I can make out fierce whispering. French.

Manny opens the door.

My father stands before me, his face lined and tan, older by far than I remembered. A glint of gold shines at his throat in the brightly lit balcony hall. Behind him looms my mother, ramrod straight, and, by comparison, looking much older, the makeup caked on her face like a doll gone bad. I can sense her wanting to push him out of the way. I cannot sort through my feelings. Love. Hate. Fear.

"The ceremony cannot start without us. *Allons-y*!" My mother's voice crashes over my father's shoulders.

"Wait a second, Francine." Manny's tone is smooth. "She's almost ready. Why don't you both come in for a second?"

Manny steps back, bowing and receding away in the face of the royal pair, and my parents sweep in. My father smiles, but his photographer's eyes size me up, framing me.

"How long has it been?" Dad asks, and then his attention skips briefly around the room, and I know, as I always have, that he is instinctively looking for the best light, like an owl searches for a mouse.

"Forever," I say. "Just forever."

"*Quelle absurdité*!" My mother sniffs, looking me up and down.

"Everyone is here," my father says. "I want you here too, Katie-did."

"Why does it suddenly matter where I am?"

The words hang overhead as if on clothespins, fresh negatives dripping from a string.

Dad scowls and scratches his chin. "It *always* mattered. What are you talking about?"

His Rolex shines in the dim light of the dressing room, vainglorious and distracting. He is a stranger I've known forever but can never see clearly. He is close enough to touch.

"I can never forgive you," I blurt out, and Manny tries to reach out a restraining hand on my arm, but I shake him off. He retreats to a corner, hurt.

A laugh escapes my mother.

"Nor I, you." Her voice rings clear in the empty air.

"Now, Francine, don't make fun," Dad begins, but I interrupt him, my words flowing like a swollen river over a dam.

"What do you mean, *she* can't forgive *me*? What the hell does that mean? And *you*," I say, pointing at Dad. "Always looking at me, *through* me, that fucking *camera* glued to your face!" I sink to the cot, my head pounding.

The sound of shouting floats up from the main lobby below us.

Nothing from Dad. Absolutely nothing.

"We do not have time for this, Katherine," Mother scolds.

I look up at the two of them. Mother and Father. Real people, not hallucinations.

Which is worse?

"Katie's been sick, very sick over the years," Manny says, low and faraway. "It took a long time for her to get off the drugs. She was an… an *addict*, thanks to your friend Trombone."

My father shakes his head. "No," he says, matter of fact. "At least, *that* wasn't my fault."

"She won't come down unless *you* ask her to, Terrance," Mother says. "She only ever listened to you."

Dad pauses. I feel a sick phlegm rising in my chest.

"Katie-did," he says. "The whole thing was a surprise to me, as well."

I force myself to stand. "That's no excuse," I say. Two reds, one yellow. Hang on for the ride, little ones. "You left me all alone, never cared, never called!"

"*You* were safe, *you* were taken care of," Mother interjects, her voice calm.

"No, that's not possible! I wasn't—" I shout, but she cuts me off.

"*I* was taking care of the world," Mother says, her tone haughty. "And your *father* traveled in great danger to expose the truth to light. *You* were the one who was safe!"

"You are both insane," I say, trying to back away.

And, again, my mother lets go of a ringing laugh.

"That is the marriage," she says perfunctorily. "You may not approve. It is not your concern. It does not matter what you think. This party, it is for *you*, really. Your father's photographs are exactly what kept you safe at home."

I cannot listen to this.

"And what about Harry?" I ask, trying my best to stand up to her in the little room.

"Harry would have approved," she says calmly.

"How the hell would *you* know?" I shout again.

"Because he was a hero. But you." She sneers at me. "Pills, drugs. *Mon Dieu*."

"I lost my brother," I say, tears starting to flow. "Someone I was entrusted—no, forced—to care for."

"Forced to love your brother. *Mon Dieu*."

It's like she's punched me in the jaw. I drop back down to the cot. A man juts his head through the open doorway. Faint light from inside the dressing room illuminates his handsome face, creased and worn in all the right places.

"Showtime, everyone!" His accent is British. He is smiling.

He clasps my father on the shoulder and bows to my mother.

"I am the master of ceremonies, after all." He laughs. "Cameron Plumb waits for no one!"

Without another word to me, my parents turn and step out of the dark room, escorted by the handsome man. Manny slinks after them, not looking at me anymore.

A surge of noise erupts at the sight of my father and mother.

All hail the King and Queen.

As the ruckus from the theater lobby swells up the staircase and bleeds into the darkness of the dressing room, I reach inside the pocket of my coat, the rest of the pills obediently rolling into my waiting palm.

THE END

AUTHOR'S NOTE

The inspiration for this story began with a friendly argument at our kitchen table one evening between my husband and our son. Both are photographers who often shoot the same subjects at the same time and compare notes. The ribbing was comedic, but the intensity was real: Who got the better shot that day? Who used the light to superior advantage? Who had the more artistic angle? Whose equipment was more sophisticated?

And—most importantly—whose photograph told the whole story?

In that moment, I suddenly wondered if war photographers had the same debate, sitting in a mess hall in some far-flung war zone. And thus, the characters of Tusley and Plumb sprang into my imagination and would not leave. Not only that, they also attracted friends, lovers, and other rivals—people who were as passionate as they were about controlling the story, be it truth or fiction, or something in-between. This gang of misfits maneuvered around minefields both real and artistic: secret service agencies (as personified by Tusley's wife Francine), propaganda machines (Tom Young), and, of course, the vaunted publications and prizes of their day, namely *Life* magazine and the new Pulitzer Prize for Photography, which was established in 1942.

To keep the characters talking, I launched a new and fascinating journey to research war photographers and the roles they play, how they might interact with (and are used by) the global intelligence network, and the goals and objectives of wartime media.

I learned that Kodak played a vital role in many wartime venues with their startling innovations such as large format film and equipment for aerial photography and reconnaissance. This was Kodak's golden age, when engineers flocked to Kodak's Hawk-Eye Works, a lab with blacked-out windows in the heart of Rochester, New York. I also learned much about the history of photography from its earliest days under the leadership and vision of George Eastman and others who put cameras into the hands of storytellers around the world. I loved learning about the Zeiss Ikon so beloved by Tusley that his daughter Katie felt a sibling's jealousy about it, and the big, heavy Speed Graphic lugged around by Plumb, a camera that symbolized the journalism of that era. The handheld movie camera used by Daniel is almost the exact one my own father took home movies with, and so the use of that camera in the book is a loving tribute to my Dad as well. Both Korea and Vietnam ushered in a more realistic type of photojournalism, and I was grateful to speak with so many veterans who would readily explain how war photographers travelled with them into battle. The photographers did not always have the admiration of the soldiers: several expressed exasperation with the artists in their midst, finding them cold and unhelpful, but others were grateful for a person whose only role was to record the events, and make sure that folks back home saw—in vivid pictures—just what was going on "over there".

But can we really believe what we see in those very photographs? The women in this story play perhaps the most important roles in examining this central question. Through the female characters, we see events from multiple perspectives, from Katie's drug-fueled hallucinations to Vivienne's confident skepticism. Daniel leads Tusley down every back alley as she prods him to see the raw beauty around them, and Francine answers no question directly, forcing her beloved husband to make up his own mind about the choices they've made as a long-married pair. In writing this story, I began to view Francine as a powerful, persuasive presence: a woman who never needs to explain herself. She is that enigmatic operative who, like so many women, must be all things to all people: mother, daughter, lover, and the rock who Tusley returns to, again and again. Because, finally, at its core, Folio grapples with the idea of home, a concept many of the photojournalists I interviewed do indeed struggle with, unsure how to manage the magnetic attraction they feel to go and bear witness to the drama, tragedy—and photo-worthiness—of war.

I mentioned above that I conducted an extensive amount of research. It would be impossible to cite here all the scholarly papers, online interviews and academic research I had the honor and privilege of accessing over the years that I've been writing this book. Early on, I went to a live speaking event in which David Hume Kennerly, the famed photographer (who won the 1972 Pulitzer Prize for Feature Photography for his Vietnam War photographs) talked about his main goal: to be the only one in the room, at just the right moment, camera in hand. His zeal to be first—to be *only*—stayed with me. I visited a gallery in Portland that hosted a traveling exhibit of huge photographic reproductions from Vietnam, and spoke with the photographer who was embedded with the troops. I read with gusto the esteemed war photographer Lynsey Addario's memoir, as well as the famed Robert Capa's early autobiography of his photojournalism in World War II. I visited Blue Moon Camera in Portland so many times to handle these beautiful relics from another time, and asked a million questions of their knowledgeable staff. Eight years of research, writing and sharing have taught me that it takes more than one person to write a novel.

Many thanks to Whitney Otto for her love and care and intensive writing classes, as well as the incredible knowledge base of the Oxford Writers critique group and the University of Chicago Writer's Studio. My biggest thanks go to my editor Judy Gitenstein, who never gave up the ship no matter how much I argued with her, as well as Marco Pavia and his team for producing this beautiful edition and truly making my dream come true. Unending thanks to my husband David for reading (and correcting) every chapter too many times to count and sharing his extensive knowledge of cameras and the art and science of photography with me, as well as so many great fellow writers and friends who cheered me on and read early drafts: Joni Blecher, Lisa Ard, Abbie Raeke, and Chris Coward. Special thanks to Portland's own Willamette Writers and Eric Witchey's weekly Parallel Plays for providing the creative outlets (and accountability) I needed to *just write*. Thank you all.

BIBLIOGRAPHY

Acheson, Dean. *The Korean War*. New York: W.W. Norton & Company, 1971.

Ayed, Nahlah. *The War We Won Apart*. Canada: Penguin Random House, 2024.

Addario, Lynsey, *It's What I Do*. New York: Penguin Press, 2015.

Ang, Tom. *Photography The Definitive Visual History*. New York: DK Publishing, 2014.

Anne Sebba, *Les Parisiennes*. New York: St. Martin's Press, 2016.

Bergman, Ronen. *Rise and Kill First*. New York: Penguin Random House, 2018.

Capa, Robert. *Slightly Out of Focus*. New York: Random House, Inc., 1999.

Chapnick, Howard. *Truth Needs No Ally*. Columbia Missouri: University of Missouri Press, 1994.

Collins, Douglas. *The Story of Kodak*. New York: Harry N. Abrams Inc., 1990.

Crickmore, Paul F., *Lockheed Blackbird*. New York: Osprey Publishing, 2016.

Darman, Peter. *Deception Tactics of World War II*. New York: Metro Books, 2017.

Fischer, Julene. *The Vietnam Experience – Images of War, Combat Photographer*. Boston, Massachusetts: Boston Publishing Company, 1986.

Gustavson, Todd. *Camera*. New York: Sterling Publishing Co., Inc., 2009.

Jones, Berard E. *Encyclopedia of Photography*. New York: Arno Press, Inc., 1974.

Karnow, Stanley. *Vietnam A History*. New York: Penguin Books, 1997.

Leekley, Sheryle and John. Moments The Pulitzer Prize Photographs. New York: Crown Publishers, Inc., 1978.

Taft, Robert. *Photography and the American Scene*. New York: Dover Publications, Inc., 1938.

The Canadians at War, Volumes 1 and 2. Reader's Digest Association, 1969.

The Vietnam Wars 50 Years Ago. New York: Life Books Time Home Entertainment, 2014.

WWII. New York: Prentice Hall Press, 1989.

Ward, Geoffrey C. and Burns, Ken. *The Vietnam War*. New York: Alfred A. Knopf Penguin Random House, 2017.

BOOK CLUB DISCUSSION TOPICS:

1. Why does Tusley begin his story with a reflection on the meaning of "home"? What do you think "home" means to Tusley at the beginning of the novel? At the end?

2. Katie tells her side of Tusley's story throughout the novel. Whose point of view is Katie really expressing? What does she think of her father's life work? Does she hold her mother Francine accountable for her own addictions? Why or why not?

3. Harry is deeply affected by his father's photographs. Do you think Tusley explained his work's purpose sufficiently to his son? Did Tusley make the right choices when it came to Harry, or any of his three children?

4. What was Francine's motivation in using Terry as her courier? Do you think her first priority is the happiness of their long marriage, or is Katie correct in saying they were never together, and barely had anything to celebrate?

5. What do Cameron Plumb, Daniel Ivers, Trombone, and Vivienne have in common, if anything? Do their actions affect Tusley, or is he on a mission with no partners? Does Tusley see everyone as a rival? Do others feel that way about him, or are the friendships these characters develop truly heartfelt?

ABOUT THE AUTHOR

Bobbie Calhoun is a playwright, essayist, poet and novelist. Her work may be found online in *Talking Writing* Literary Journal, Medium and Storied Stuff, and she has published a book of poetry through Belgrave House. Her next novel, *Model Daughter, Model Spy*, will be published in 2026.

www.ingramcontent.com/pod-product-compliance
Lightning Source LLC
Chambersburg PA
CBHW020015120726
47903CB00004B/1292

* 9 7 9 8 9 9 2 7 3 7 3 0 1 *